'I believe every Australian needs to read this book. Powerfully told and deeply affecting, this book lays bare the courage, heartbreak, and resilience of the LGBTQIA+ community in a way that feels both urgent and timeless. It's equally as moving as it is suspenseful. I found myself gripped, unable to put it down, desperate to know what would happen next. Woven through with sharp, current references and an amazing sense of place, it feels entirely of this moment. For anyone who has ever questioned why Pride matters or sought to understand the journey toward visibility and acceptance, this story is essential and unforgettable.'
Mitch Brown, former West Coast Eagles AFL player

'Carpenter writes with a raw honesty and reaches deep to uncover truths that resonate. He reminds us of the power writers have to transcend and stir something profound within us all. I am hooked!'
Victoria Madden, Showrunner/Producer/Writer

'Resurrection is a real page-turner and so hard to put down. The novel skillfully evokes a period where homophobia and violence were vicious undercurrents in Australian society. J. T. Carpenter has written a thriller which peels back layer by layer to reach the novel's shocking climax. This book is a must-read!'
Diane Minnis, Sydney Mardi Gras 78er

'Having moved from regional New South Wales to Sydney at 17 in the middle of the AIDS crisis, this evocative work by J. T. Carpenter brings to mind the wild mix of emotions of the time. Only a few years after the incredible bravery of the "78ers" who proudly fronted the first Mardi Gras march and were punished for it, the memories of that time are painted with depth and potency in *Resurrection*. Apart from delivering a complex and excitingly mysterious story, it also serves as an important purpose in today's reality. The weekend "sport" for young thugs in cars going out for a night of "gay bashing" leaves deep scars. The murders of young gay men thrown to their deaths over the cliffs of beautiful beachside Sydney suburbs has been a twisted dance of horror, only revealed over decades. Resurrection is important work for these and so many more reasons! It pulls no punches and yet, uplifts and empowers!'
Paul Scott-Williams, CEO JOY Media (JOY949)

'*Resurrection* is an absolute cracker. It has it all – a gripping, tense multi-layered story, a host of finely-crafted thoroughly believable characters, and at the same time this extraordinary novel reveals what our society has learnt (and sadly, what it still needs to learn) about tolerance, acceptance and humanity.'
Dennis Coard, actor

'*Resurrection* empowers those afraid to speak, those whose voices have been silenced. I felt empowered and resilient reading this, as if I were reading some of my own stories and tragedies, yet still feeling the strength to continue the fight."
Jessenia Marquez, survivor of the Pulse Nightclub shooting (Florida, USA)

'J. T. Carpenter's *Resurrection* is a gripping and essential read that powerfully illuminates systemic injustices, expertly weaving fiction with the sobering realities of Australia's queer history. *Resurrection* acts as a pen shattering the dark, shining a necessary light on the silenced, and exposing the profound rot of authority."
Jojo Zaho, Drag Performer, Advocate & Storyteller

'*Resurrection* is Australian crime fiction with heart. Authentic, raw, and deeply relevant. A crime set in the past with devastating relevance to today, it's a bold and timely debut. His voice is one we need right now, unafraid to explore the shadows while holding onto empathy and humanity.'
Tania Doko, singer and song writer

'The authenticity and visceral world created is deadly. *Resurrection* is aptly titled, a voice for the voiceless. Journalism is the onus of truth, and this novel carries that responsibility with power and authenticity. It seeks justice for past injustices and becomes a conduit of healing for victims and communities, past and present. There is no higher religion than truth.'
Nathan Phillips, actor (Wolf Creek, Australian Rules)

'As one of the original Sydney Gay & Lesbian Mardi Gras 78ers, I was struck by how parts of this story echo real events, when hate crimes were committed, and police brutality was appallingly rampant. These were moments of our past that still have missing pieces, grieving families, and carry deep relevance today. *Resurrection* is a powerful, well-written, and compelling read.'
Johnny Whitehead, Sydney Mardi Gras 78er

'Incisive and beautifully written, Carpenter has crafted a deft and masterful story - I was riveted! Cassandra Murphy is a ripper of a character, and I'm already excited for the next installment. I absolutely loved this!

Roz Hammond, actor (Muriel's Wedding, The Librarians)

'Resurrection is sharp, descriptive, punchy, and colourful; I was completely obsessed from the moment I started reading. It's a gripping, character-filled mystery that brilliantly flashes between the past and present of Australian life, showing how much we've changed and, in some ways, how far we still have to go. The characters are vivid and fully realised, and the exploration of protest, prejudice, and identity feels both truthful and vital.

As someone whose own life was shaped by the illegal police raid on Tasty nightclub in the early '90s, an event that led to a landmark class action and ultimately inspired my creative career, I found this story profoundly moving.

Resurrection straddles art, entertainment, and social commentary with real heart. It reminds us that from loss can come passion, creation, and change.

Like Cassie Murphy, we all must learn to live in the moment - to face the past but not be defined by it. This book made me feel every emotion across the spectrum. As Molly Meldrum once said: "Do yourself a favour," and read it.'

Gerard O'Connor, former Manager of Tasty Nightclub (Melbourne)

I acknowledge the lands of the Wurundjeri, Yorta Yorta and Waveroo people, where I both set and wrote Resurrection. I pay my respects to their Elders, past, present, and emerging. For tens of thousands of years, these breathtaking lands and waterways have been cared for by First Peoples custodians with a deep, unbroken connection to Country. That connection was never lost, and sovereignty has never been ceded.

I also acknowledge Australia's diverse LGBTQIA+ communities and their allies. I pay vigil to those who were discriminated against, terrorised, and murdered, particularly throughout the 1980s and 1990s, many of whom never saw justice. To all those who have fought, and continue to fight, for equality and recognition: thank you. To those who have experienced, or are experiencing, violence because of their sexual or gender identity: I see you. I hear you. And I stand with you. You are not alone.

J. T. Carpenter is a distinctly contemporary voice in Australian noir. A writer whose work blends propulsive, screen-ready pacing with deep emotional resonance. His stories don't meander; they move. Fast, honest, and unflinchingly human.

Before turning to fiction, Carpenter spent nearly thirty years working with young people across education, mental health, and emergency disaster recovery. Standing alongside communities in their most vulnerable moments, he witnessed firsthand the fractures created by trauma, loss, and systems that can fail ordinary people. These lived experiences shape his writing, giving it authenticity, urgency, and a rare emotional clarity.

A former guest radio presenter and recipient of an Australian Commercial Radio Award (ACRA), Carpenter also founded a national foundation addressing male suicide and violence, and has long been a respected voice in conversations around masculinity, wellbeing, and cultural change. He has previously published non-fiction, but Resurrection marks his first step into crime fiction: a bold, emotionally charged debut that sits at the intersection of purpose and pulse.

Writing with the intensity and emotional intelligence of a filmmaker, J.T. Carpenter brings something fresh to the genre: crime fiction built for *now*. Cinematic, compassionate, and unafraid to expose the raw edges of modern Australia.

RESURRECTION

Not All Secrets Stay Buried

J. T. CARPENTER

JTC PUBLISHING
www.jtcauthor.com

First published 2025
Paperback ISBN: 978-1-7643154-0-1
Ebook ISBN: 978-1-7643154-1-8
RESURRECTION Not All Secrets Stay Buried

Cover design: Nick Castle Design (nickcastle@btintertnet.com)
Cover image: J. T. Carpenter

For my family.
Thank you for keeping me grounded, even when my head was off chasing ghosts. You are my reason, always.

To Val McDermid.
The Queen of Crime, who lit the spark.

And for those whose stories are yet to be told, whose truths still wait in the dark, I hope this shines a little light.

A flame burns brightest just before it dies.

—Gene Tierney

AUTHOR'S NOTE

Excerpt from a personal letter I received at seventeen...

If there's one thing I've learnt from playing a gay character, it's that they are just normal people with different feelings or attractions.

So please don't let others make you feel like a 'freak' or a 'loser.'
Stand up for yourself.
Live life to its fullest.
Look after yourself, mate.

—Heath Ledger

Before you begin, a word of warning.

Resurrection is a work of fiction, but it's built on the bones of real stories. Stories of violence. Of prejudice. Of lives lost and justice denied. The characters you'll meet are imagined, but the world they inhabit is uncomfortably close to our own.

This is a story about power, about what happens when truth is buried, and silence becomes a weapon. But it's also about guilt, remorse, and the fragile search for redemption. About the ache that lingers after the damage is done. About the people who try to live with what they did or didn't do.

Because justice isn't only about who pulled the trigger. It's about the silences that allowed it.

I didn't write this book to offer easy heroes or tidy resolutions. I wrote it because some stories demand to be told, even when they make us uncomfortable.

If you've ever struggled to understand how prejudice takes root, how ordinary people become complicit in cruelty, or how truth can be twisted or erased, then you're in the right place.

For clarity: while real institutions such as Victoria Police, the Australian Broadcasting Corporation (ABC), Channel Seven, The Herald Sun, Sky News Australia, the University of Melbourne, and others are referenced in this novel, all characters and events are entirely fictional. Although some historical events may be mentioned, any depictions of corruption, misconduct, or systemic failure are narrative devices reflecting the themes of the novel. They are not intended to represent the standards, integrity, or practices of these organisations or their staff.

While *Resurrection* is a work of fiction, it explores themes and references to real life events that may be distressing to some readers. Please take care of yourself as you read.

If you are impacted by any of these issues or themes, please refer to the support contacts at the back of this book.

J.T. Carpenter
AUTHOR

PROLOGUE

The wail of sirens cut through the cold night air.

Slumped against a rain-slicked gumtree, the lone figure gasped for breath, his lungs raw from petrol fumes and smoke. The sharp scent of eucalyptus above was oddly soothing, grounding him as his body fought for oxygen. Then, panic surged: *had he left anything behind?* Heart hammering, he ran his hands over his body, searching for cuts, blood, anything that could betray him. *Nothing.* He was clean. Relief flooded through him.

He'd chosen this night carefully. Between the fire and rain, nature itself was working in his favour, erasing every trace of his presence. And the creek trail, just steps from the house? The perfect escape route. As if it had all been meant to be.

He turned back toward the path he'd come. A faint orange glow danced against the blackened sky, flickering above the treetops like a warning.

Run.

The voice in his head was no longer a whisper; it was a scream.

Hood up. Head down. Past the abandoned drive-in. Past the sports fields and endless stretches of parkland. Keep running. Just a little further.

By the time he reached his car, hidden behind the old motorbike club, he knew he was safe. His hands trembled as he fumbled with the door. Clambering inside, he slammed it shut and reached blindly for his backpack, yanking out an old beach towel. Yellow and brown stripes. Just like the one his dad had used during those endless childhood summers. *Better times. Happier times.*

His pulse roared in his ears as he peeled off his soaked clothes, the wet fabric clinging to his skin. He banged his elbow against the window, wincing as a sudden pain shot down his right arm. Shivering, he pulled on dry sweatpants and a jumper, then slumped back against the seat, body trembling.

He ached for a hot shower. For sleep. But it would be at least another hour or so before sunrise. Only then could he pull onto the freeway, blending into the thousands of early morning commuters. Just another car. Just another face.

For now, he waited.

He had planned every detail meticulously. Tonight had been harder than last time, but he hadn't slipped. He *couldn't* slip. Not now.

He closed his eyes, knowing there would be no sleep.

By dawn, the rain had stopped. Exhausted, sore, he drove home. Hoping, above all else, that he'd gotten away with it.

Because he wasn't done.
Not even close.

ONE

Salt spray rode the gusts, sharp and bracing, stinging Cassandra Murphy's skin as her thick, copper-coloured hair lashed across her face. She drew a deep breath, filling her lungs with briny air. The heavy autumn rains had swept eastward overnight, but the sky above remained ominous. Morning winds still howled, whipping Port Phillip Bay into a restless, white-capped frenzy.

Raised in Victoria's high country, she had rarely seen the ocean as a child. Now it lay just two hundred metres from her apartment, a vast, ever-changing presence she had come to rely on. Her morning walks were ritual. A tether. A way to steady herself when the work dragged her too deep into darkness.

But this morning felt different.

The wind wasn't just a force, it was something more, something almost sentient. It rushed around her in a chaotic embrace, raw and untamed, stripping away the weight she carried. It cleansed her. Held her.

Cassie exhaled, her breath merging with the wind and for a fleeting moment, she let go.

There were mornings, lately, when it felt like she was holding herself together by habit more than intent.

Ever since her last major investigation, the one that had seen her dragged through weeks of police interviews, death threats, and a defamation claim, her nervous system had been on a hair trigger. The ocean helped. It didn't ask questions or look for answers. It just kept moving.

Melbourne had been home for six years now. Before that, she had spent nearly a decade between Glasgow and London, working herself into the ground. The UK had shaped her, toughened her. But Melbourne had a pulse she hadn't found anywhere else. The live music scene had bounced back post-pandemic. Open-air markets brimmed with international flavours. Endless shopping. All of it just a tram ride away. And nowhere on earth did coffee or Sunday brunch better.

Coffee.

The very thought snapped her out of her trance. Hunger stirred. She turned from the sea, crossing Ormond Esplanade toward Elwood Village, the craving tugging at her like an invisible thread.

The suburb was already stirring. A street sweeper rumbled past, its heavy bristles hissing across the asphalt, dragging last night's debris into neat, swirling lines. Towering London Plane trees flanked the footpaths, their sprawling limbs reaching for each other overhead like arthritic fingers. Beautiful. Messy. This time of year, their leaves blanketed everything: footpaths, gutters, steps, a golden mess of decay and nostalgia.

Cassie loved it here. Elwood was an architectural patchwork, a suburb where decades of development had collided rather than blended. Arts and Crafts cottages stood beside bland, boxy 70s brick flats. And then there were the Art Deco gems, curved corners, sash windows, ornate brickwork, still holding their own against the glass towers now creeping toward the bay. Her own apartment was in one of those Deco beauties: first floor, corner block. Solid. Full of character. A place with its own story to tell.

She passed a chalkboard outside a florist reading *Fresh proteas, new beginnings*, then paused beside a bakery window, drawn by the sight of croissants stacked in rows like golden armour. Her stomach growled, reminding her she'd skipped dinner the night before. Again.

The scent of coffee curled in the breeze as she approached Inside Out. A smile tugged at her lips.

"Hello, you," came the familiar purr, almost lost beneath the sharp hiss of the milk frother.

Jason Turner stood at the entrance: tanned, toned, perfectly groomed. His salt-and-pepper beard framed a dazzling smile; black designer glasses perched on his nose. His tight black button-up, sleeves rolled just-so, showcased a riot of colourful tattoos. Paired, as always, with fitted denim.

Cassie leaned in for the customary air kiss. "Jason."

Jason and his partner, Amir, lived upstairs with their black Cavoodle, Moira Rose, affectionately named after Catherine O'Hara's character in *Schitt's Creek*. Buying the café wasn't just a semi-retirement plan, it was about preserving its legacy. They saw themselves more as custodians than owners. Neither of them had slowed down for a second.

Jason turned. "Can I get a double-shot flat white to go, please, Evie?"

The young barista, all tattoos and piercings, blue hair shaved on one side, nodded silently, already working the machine.

Inside Out was more than a café. It was a bookshop, a performance space, a piece of queer Melbourne history. Founded in the '80s as a haven for the gay and lesbian community, it had evolved, but its soul remained. So did its coffee, still the best on the strip.

Jason fussed with his thick quiff, fingers smoothing it into place. "So, what's going on? Weren't you supposed to be visiting your folks in the mountains?"

Cassie smirked. "I'm heading up in a few days."

Jason's smile faltered, concern flickering in his eyes. Cassie wasn't ready for his next question, not this morning.

"So, how's Amir? Did he get off okay?" she asked, redirecting.

Jason huffed. "He landed in Detroit late yesterday. He's already sent me twelve texts, mostly to complain about his mum. She's moving into a new condo. Honestly, she's more of a drama queen than Amir. Which I didn't think was possible."

Cassie laughed. It felt good, briefly.

The barista slid the coffee across. Jason passed it to her.

"Today's on me."

Cassie hesitated. "Are you sure? I was…" She craned her neck, peering toward the empty glass display where the Danish pastries usually sat. Disappointment flickered across her face.

"They didn't come in," Jason said. "We have a new supplier. Well, *had* a new supplier. Long story." He waved it off, then brightened. "Hey, if you're still around Thursday, we're closing early. We're having a few of the regulars in for Easter cocktails."

Cassie smiled. "That sounds great. I'll see where I'm at."

Her phone buzzed in her pocket. Brian Cheng.

She mouthed a quick goodbye, coffee in hand, and stepped outside. "Hey, Bri. What's up?"

No pleasantries. Just Brian's breathless voice: "Cass, have you seen the news?"

"Not yet. Why? What's happened?"

Two women in Lycra jogged past, nearly clipping her. Cassie sidestepped, throwing them a glare.

"It's Hayden Foster," Brian said. "He was murdered last night."

Cassie froze. "He was *murdered*? What the fuck?"

Her voice cut through the quiet morning. An elderly woman in a velvet-purple dressing gown and fluffy slippers gave her a look of disgust as she struggled to drag a wheelie bin to the curb.

Peter Draper, her boss at the ABC, liked to call Cassie's language "agricultural." Though to his credit, he tolerated it better than any of her BBC editors ever had.

Cassie let out a sharp breath and brushed wet leaves off a low brick wall, sitting down hard.

During the pandemic, violent clashes between Victoria Police and fringe protestors had become a weekly occurrence. One face had stood out among the chaos: Hayden Foster. Short, stocky, bald head, with a body full of ink. He was a peacock. He lived for the lens. Even after lockdowns lifted, he remained at the centre of every far-right rally. None more volatile than the ones targeting trans rights advocates.

He also happened to be a central figure in her current investigation, into the Allied Patriots, a new far-right group imported from the U.S. Hayden Foster had become its poster boy.

"What are police saying? Have they made any arrests? What happened exactly?"

"Not much officially," Brian said. "His house in Preston went up in flames early this morning. It was definitely arson. There's rumours floating around that he may have been bashed before the fire but no arrests yet. Tracey's already done a live cross, but that's it so far."

"Shit..." Cassie whispered.

The moment lingered. A gust of wind lifted the hem of her coat. She thought of his face, smirking, eyes gleaming with something close to hate and felt a tangle of emotions she couldn't quite name.

"Listen, Cass," Brian continued. "Peter wants you in this morning to brief him on everything the investigations team has got on Foster. How soon can you get here?"

Cassie checked the time. "I'm heading back to my place now. Tell him I'll be there within the hour. And Bri, keep me posted on anything new that comes in."

She stood, mind buzzing. She drained the last of her coffee and tossed the empty cup into the bin outside her apartment block, then climbed the bricked staircase two at a time.

Inside, she flicked on the TV and refreshed her laptop.

The *Herald Sun* was already frothing.

"Melbourne's Next Gangland War?"

Below it, a photo of Foster's house at dawn, charred and still smoking.

Cassie rolled her eyes. "Gangland war, my arse."

Sure, Hayden had ties to organised crime figures and outlaw motorcycle clubs. But he had never been patched. Never really accepted. Not until the Patriots. Still, the media had their own narrative, and this one had ratings written all over it. She knew how this would go: headlines designed to inflame, speculation passed off as fact, and not a single question asked about the kinds of hate Foster had helped spread.

She grabbed the cleanest clothes she could find from the pile strewn across the couch and headed for the shower, her mind already assembling timelines, links, and a list of names she might need to revisit.

The story was just beginning.

TWO

The ABC Melbourne building had undergone extensive renovations in recent years. It sat on the south side of the Yarra River, nestled between the Melbourne Arts Centre, its iconic spire piercing the skyline and the sleek, modern façade of the Melbourne Recital Centre.

Cassie parked her metallic-blue Volkswagen Golf in the underground car park and took the stairs up to the expansive ground-floor foyer. Just inside the entrance, a bronze statue of a 1950s television studio camera stood guard, a tribute to the broadcaster's long history.

A towering wall of glass windows faced the city, stretching from the foyer all the way to the third-floor ceiling, flooding the space with natural light. Suspended from the rafters above, colourful banners showcased the faces of ABC radio and television personalities. Beyond the scattering of yellow, blue, and grey couches lay an open staircase and a glass elevator, reinforcing the building's open-plan design, a physical embodiment of its slogan, *Your ABC*.

Cassie took the stairs to the first floor, her footsteps echoing in the airy space. She passed the radio studios, alive with the hum of morning talk back, and made her way toward the newsroom at the far end.

"Cass!"

Brian stood from a large, shared desk and strode toward her with his usual confidence.

"Hey, Bri," Cassie smiled.

The newsroom, despite its open-plan intent, was a chaotic sprawl of desks and screens, cluttered with scripts, notes, and half-drunk coffees. Along one wall, a row of dark, windowless offices housed the technical team, while the opposite side featured bright, glassed-in offices reserved for on-air talent. Beyond a narrow corridor, the television studio sat silent now, the *News Breakfast* team had wrapped for the day, leaving behind the lingering chatter of post-show conversations.

"Let's go up to your desk," Brian suggested.

Cassie exchanged a quick wave with one of the breakfast hosts before following Brian upstairs.

He looked good today. Different. His thick black hair was tousled, none of its usual over-styled precision. He wore jeans and a fitted brown crew-neck jumper, his slim frame emphasizing lean muscle. Had he been working out? And was that a new fragrance?

"Where's the suit?" she teased.

Brian smirked. "I'm at the Supreme Court this afternoon. I'll hit up wardrobe later, plenty of time."

Cassie narrowed her eyes playfully. Definitely a new fragrance.

Upstairs, the second-floor office was noticeably quieter than the newsroom below. Cassie's desk, however, was an island of controlled chaos, piled high with papers, books, and sticky notes. Unlike the minimalist workstations around her, hers looked lived-in. Despite the ABC's push for a paperless workplace, Cassie single-handedly kept the office printer in business. She needed something tangible. Something she could underline, scribble on, feel. The same reason she still carried a leather-bound diary instead of relying on her phone.

She was convinced she was the only millennial who did.

Not that she cared.

"Any update from VicPol?" she asked, dropping her jacket and bag onto her desk before sliding into her chair.

"Not yet. But they'll be joining us for this briefing in about... five minutes," Brian said, glancing at his smartwatch. He perched on the empty desk next to hers.

"What? VicPol are coming in?" Cassie's eyebrows shot up.

Brian nodded. "Did you see *The Herald Sun* this morning?"

"I did." Cassie rolled her eyes.

"Peter has your mate doing a piece to camera for us, so long as they can review what we've got on the Patriots."

"My mate?"

"James Lawrence."

James Lawrence. Acting Deputy Commissioner of Public Safety and Security with Victoria Police. And an old friend of her father's. She had only spoken to him a few weeks earlier while digging into the Allied Patriots.

"James is doing an interview for *this*?" she asked, scanning the investigations office. With the Easter school holidays around the corner, many desks already sat empty.

Brian shrugged. "Looks that way."

"Are you doing the interview?" Cassie asked, jabbing impatiently at her spacebar, willing her sluggish computer to load.

"Nope. Tracey is. I've got the Bernaldi case to focus on today. She's already done a live cross from the site this morning, so they'll cut that in."

Cassie's gaze remained fixed on the screen, though her mind was elsewhere.

Brian leaned in. "Who do you think did it?"

"Did what?" She glanced up.

"Who killed Hayden Foster?"

Cassie let out a dry laugh. "Take your pick. The guy was an arsehole."

Brian smirked. "Do you think the papers are onto something with the gangland angle?"

Cassie scoffed. "Please."

Brian shrugged. "Some of the online chatter is intense. People are saying he was targeted by a rival far-right group, or someone in the government."

"People will say anything online. Half of them probably think he faked his death and moved to Bali."

Before Brian could respond, a booming voice rang out across the room.

"Cassandra! Brian!"

Peter Draper stood at the entrance to the office, arms crossed, his presence commanding as always. He was smiling, but the tilt of his head signalled urgency. "Bring your laptop, Cassandra."

Cassandra. No one called her that outside of work.

It had been Margaret Bowen, her old boss at the BBC, who insisted on the change. *Don't call yourself 'Cassie' if you want to be taken seriously, especially in investigations. Cassie makes you sound like a schoolgirl.*

Margaret had been a nightmare to work for, but she wasn't wrong. *Cassandra* had weight. Authority. It carried a reputation. And that was exactly how she wanted it.

Behind the name, Cassie, or rather, Cassandra, had built something formidable: a persona relentless in pursuit of the truth. A Pitbull when it came to justice and advocacy. These were all qualities she had admired in her dad. A former Senior Sergeant, a true-blue country copper, he was never one to suffer fools. Her mum, a native Glaswegian, was also a force to be reckoned with. Cassie was proud of them both and felt grateful for the values of hard work, fairness, and justice they had instilled in her and her brother.

Cassie grabbed her MacBook as she and Brian followed Peter out into the corridor.

"Morning," she greeted him.

"Thanks for coming in, Cassandra. I know you're about to go on leave," Peter said as they descended the stairs. "I've put the Acting Deputy Commissioner in the conference room. Tracey will take the lead on this one, but I want Brian in the loop in case this drags out over the next few days. Other outlets are turning this into a bloody circus. VicPol want us to cut through the noise and get some facts out there."

He pulled open the glass door to the conference room, motioning for them to step inside.

"Miss Murphy," came a deep, steady voice.

James Lawrence stood as they entered, offering a firm handshake and a knowing smile.

"Hi, James," Cassie said.

"And Brian, right?" James extended his hand.

Brian returned the handshake. "Brian Cheng. Nice to meet you."

"Likewise. It feels like we've crossed paths a hundred times but never properly met."

Cassie studied James as they took their seats. He still had that quiet authority, a presence that made people listen when he spoke. His uniform was pristine, the senior police insignia gleaming under the fluorescent lights. He hadn't changed much over the years, still physically strong, still sharp.

Reporter Tracey Longthwaite was already seated and gave Cassie a warm smile as she sat opposite. Peter took his place at the head of the table, clasping his hands together.

"Alright, let's get started. James, I'll hand it over to you. Let's get some facts on the board."

The room fell silent.

Cassie clicked open her laptop, her fingers hovering over the keyboard.

"Great, thanks, Peter," James said, shifting his attention to the others in the room. "Shortly after three a.m., Fire Rescue Victoria responded to a fully involved house fire in Preston. It was immediately apparent to crews that an accelerant had been used, and it took some time to bring the blaze under control. Only once the fire was extinguished did they discover the body of Hayden Foster in the front lounge room. Suffice to say, we're treating the property as a crime scene."

"Is it true he was assaulted beforehand?" Cassie cut in.

James exhaled sharply. "I'm afraid that's not something I can confirm at this stage. Homicide investigators are on site, and I'll update you all as soon as possible."

"What exactly do you need from us?" she asked, her tone even, controlled.

James nodded, his voice measured. "You and I have spoken recently about the Allied Patriots. I was hoping you might have further intelligence on Foster, anything that might help us track down whoever did this."

Cassie opened her laptop fully. "Most of what we have on the Patriots has come from your office. I've picked up some intel through law enforcement contacts in the U.S., but formal interviews aren't scheduled until after Easter. We know they're being funded through organised crime overseas and unlike the hate groups that came before them, these guys know exactly what they're doing. They're operating in cells, more like a terror network than some social club for racists."

"What about Foster himself?" James pressed. "Anything about his background, or anyone from his personal life beyond the Patriots, who might be relevant?"

Cassie scrolled through her notes. "Hayden Bernard Foster. Born in Melbourne in 1980, making him mid-forties. Both parents are deceased. He worked for a concreting company in the northern suburbs. Two kids, both teenagers and live with their mother. As far as we know, they haven't had anything to do with Hayden in years."

She flicked upward on her screen. "He lived alone in his late paternal grandmother's house, Norma Foster, who died a few years back. What else... a lot of historical charges: aggravated burglary, assaults, armed robbery. Yet nothing in recent years, despite all his associations. He never served any serious time either. He always seemed to walk."

She looked up, locking eyes with James. "And we know he was the guy who raped that sex worker in the early 2000s. It was a big case at the time. Again, no conviction. No jail time."

James shifted in his seat and gave a small, uncomfortable grin. "You've done your homework. That case is over two decades ago and largely forgotten these days."

"I'm pretty sure the woman he raped hasn't forgotten," Cassie said flatly.

A beat of silence. Tracey blinked. Peter cleared his throat and stepped in, his tone more diplomatic.

"James, we appreciate your time, both here and on camera. I know how busy you are. Is there something specific you're looking for? Cassandra and her team have done extensive work on the Patriots, and we're happy to pass on anything useful."

James leaned back in his chair and offered a small, closed-lip smile. "No, nothing specific. We just know how good Cassandra is at her job." He glanced at Peter. "I always told her dad that she should've been a detective. We're fairly confident we'll wrap this up quickly. If anything, it's most likely one of the Patriots themselves, muscling in for a better position."

James then looked directly at Cassie. "But if you do find anything of interest, anything or *anyone*, from Foster's past, contact me directly. Anyone at all."

There was something in his tone. The way he paused.

Cassie didn't look away.

He knows something.

"Shall we, Tracey?" James said casually, standing up. Just like that, the briefing was over.

As the others filed out, James held back, waiting until Cassie stepped closer. His smile was softer now.

"Jan and I were just talking about your parents the other day. We really should get up to see them soon." His eyes lingered. "How is he?"

Cassie sighed. "Much the same. He'd love to see you."

James nodded, his expression folding into something unreadable before he turned to follow Tracey down the hall. She was already chatting away, something about the rain.

Cassie watched them disappear before turning to Brian.

"Well?" Brian asked as they made their way back up the stairs. "What was that all about? Why was he asking all those questions about Hayden's past?"

Cassie didn't answer immediately. She was thinking. Processing. Watching the shadows shift across the walls as they climbed.

"James is a good cop," she said eventually, "but he's a terrible poker player. There's more to this than they're letting on. And I don't think it has anything to do with the Patriots."

They reached the second floor. Cassie's desk came back into view, the piles of paper waiting like unfinished conversations.

"You reckon it's personal?" Brian asked.

Cassie didn't respond right away. She reached for her keys, then paused. "You've talked about moving up. Out of daily reporting and into investigations."

Brian's eyes narrowed. "Are you serious?"

"I'm going to Foster's house. I need to see it for myself. You, meanwhile, are going to do what you do best."

Brian straightened slightly. "Okay…"

"I need you to dig. But not into the Patriots, we already know what we need to about them. I want to know everything about Foster's life. His ex. His kids. That sex worker. Every assault charge, who the victims were, how he kept walking away. Who represented him in court. I want a full picture."

Brian nodded. "What about Peter? Should I tell him I'm helping?"

"No," Cassie said quickly. "Leave Peter to me. He already knows how keen you are. He just needs the excuse. I'll talk to him when I get back."

"You really think there's more to his death?"

Cassie grabbed her jacket. "If there is, I don't want anyone else stumbling onto it first."

She turned for the stairs. Her voice called back over her shoulder.

"We know this guy. This is our story."

THREE

"Get out of the way!" Cassie grumbled, drumming her fingers on the steering wheel as the battered old Ford Ute in front of her crawled up Sydney Road. Its bumper sticker, sun-faded and peeling, read *Where the Farck is Yarck?*

It looked completely out of place. Surrounded by smart hatchbacks, silent hybrid SUVs, and gleaming delivery vans, the Ute felt like a leftover from another era, one that refused to move on. Just like the driver, she assumed.

She rolled her eyes. "Move already."

By the time they reached Brunswick, Cassie had had enough. She seized the first clear chance, threw on her indicator, and overtook the Ute in a flash of frustration. Her little Golf grumbled in agreement.

There were a lot of things she loved about Melbourne, but the traffic wasn't one of them. Peak hour wasn't even a real thing anymore. Every hour was peak hour now.

She stopped at a red light and exhaled, her hands still resting on the wheel. The city moved past her in waves: suits, tradies, tourists, students. Every nationality imaginable. All flowing past the cafés, spilling into boutiques, dodging each other in narrow laneways. Life.

An ambulance tore through the intersection, siren shrieking through the urban buzz. Everyone paused. Heads turned, eyes followed the flashing lights. And then, just as quickly, the moment passed.

The city breathed out.

The tide moved again.

Cassie's eyes drifted to a nearby traffic pole, plastered with fading stickers and graffiti. Someone had scrawled a tag in thick black marker, the last letters obscured by a torn sticker advertising open mic night at some Fitzroy pub.

She looked away, jaw tight.

This city was a long way from where she came from.

Sometimes she felt the pull of the high country: the big skies, the eucalyptus haze, the silence you could actually hear. But too many ghosts lived there now. These days, she only went back for family. For Dad.

The memory of him strapped into the radiation machine in Wangaratta, his skin grey under fluorescent light, still lived fresh behind her eyes.

At least he'd be home this weekend. And so would she. Back in Heathton Ridge. That thought brought a flicker of comfort. Even if it came with a knot of guilt.

The light turned green. Cassie hit the accelerator.

* * *

The charred skeleton of the house stood on a busy street, boxed in by police tape and a makeshift barrier of orange cones. No street parking. No drive-up press vultures.

Cassie turned down a side street and looped around to the back laneway, easing the Golf in behind a police crime scene van. A uniformed officer stood by the rear gate and nodded as she approached, recognising her immediately. No need to dig for a press pass. She gave him a small wave and cut across to the footpath.

The property was small and unremarkable, a weatherboard cottage like so many others in Preston. Norma Foster had left the house to her only grandchild, and to his credit, Hayden had kept it tidy. The lawn had been mowed. The garden, though sparse, was neat.

Cassie's gaze lingered on a lemon tree in the front yard. One half of it still bore heavy fruit. The other half, the side facing the fire, was scorched and blackened, its twisted branches reaching for something that was no longer there.

She didn't move closer.

From her spot at the edge of the footpath, she could see figures in white forensic suits combing through the wreckage. The roof had collapsed. The front wall was gone. Only the brick fireplace remained standing, like a monument to the life that had burned around it.

The wind carried the acrid smell of smoke and ash. Burned wood. Burned insulation. Burned... everything.

Hayden Foster had lived here. Right here. And now it was just another crime scene.

A man with a dachshund passed slowly, shaking his head. "Tsk, tsk," he muttered, tugging the leash.

"C'mon, Sprout."

Cassie turned her eyes across the road. Parkland stretched out in soft waves, tall gums lining a gentle creek trail, paths criss-crossing through manicured beds of lavender and mulch. A children's playground sat empty near a small car park.

There had to be CCTV. Traffic cams. Dash Cams. Something. Someone must've seen what happened.

She turned back to the house. The smell hit her again, more than smoke. Something underneath it. Something scorched and final.

"What happened here, Hayden?" she murmured.

* * *

By the time Cassie got back to the office, Brian had undergone a full costume change. He now stood by his desk in a freshly pressed blue suit, a stark contrast to the jeans and jumper he'd been wearing that morning.

"I didn't think you were heading out until later," she said, sliding into her chair.

"Yeah, uh… thought I'd get a head start. There are a few satellite hearings around the Bernaldi case that I might chase up."

She gave him a side glance. That pause. That awkward little deflection.

"What's with the hesitation?"

Brian scratched the back of his neck. "Nothing. Just… a lot on."

Cassie raised an eyebrow but let it go. "Alright."

"But hey," he added quickly, shifting the subject like a pro, "I did some digging on Foster. Not a tonne yet, but I've got a lead. The sex worker from the 2000 case, she changed her name."

He pulled a Post-it off her laptop and handed it to her.

"It was Belinda Rogers back then, but she goes by Belinda Mead now. Not a married name, a legal name change, done not long after the trial."

"The trial that never happened," Cassie muttered. "Jesus, Belinda. That's right." The name pulled at something in her gut. Old outrage. Fresh anger.

"God, I'd have changed my name too after what the media did to her. Animals. They blamed her just because she was a sex worker and the public ate it up. All that bullshit about her asking for it. People actually believed it. It was disgusting."

Her voice tightened.

Brian watched her, then gently said, "I sent you a link too. Did you see it?"

"No. Sorry, Bri. I haven't checked my phone since this morning."

He nodded at her laptop screen. "Check your inbox."

She clicked through her emails, found the link, and opened it.

Carrington Falcons Football Club. A cartoon falcon wearing a navy blue-and-white striped jersey, an AFL Sherrin football tucked under its wing, flapped across the top banner. Underneath, a messy collage of team photos. Local ads lined the side: *Mick's Meats - Proud Supporter Since 2010.*

"What is this?"

Brian stepped in, clicking through menu options like a pro. "This bit. The Under-17 Premiership Team of 1997."

He spun the laptop back toward her.

"Recognise anyone?"

Cassie squinted at the grainy photo. A bunch of boys, arms over each other's shoulders, grinning like they'd won the world.

"That one," Brian said, tapping. "Hayden Foster."

Cassie leaned in. "Bloody hell. That's him? The short one?"

"Yep."

"Wow. He has hair. No tattoos. It doesn't even look like him."

"The coach in that photo is a guy named Rodney Lindfield. He's still active with the club." Brian said, again clicking through to a different page. "This was posted a month ago, some Hall of Fame award or something."

Cassie nodded slowly. "So, we start with the people who knew him before he became... whatever the hell he became."

"It looks like Foster grew up in Carrington, in the outer east. I've reached out to Banksia City Council and the local historical society and they're digging through old school records for me now."

Cassie looked up, impressed. "You did all this while I was out in Preston?"

"Yep."

"You're wasted as a reporter."

Brian tried to laugh it off, but his cheeks flushed.

"I don't have any more than that, but we're building a picture. Piece by piece."

Cassie smiled. "It's a great start."

They'd both joined the ABC the same year, were both in their late thirties, and had naturally fallen into an easy friendship, something Cassie didn't usually allow. Work was work. Friends were separate. That line was there for a reason.

She knew Brian had once felt something more. She hadn't returned it. He was kind, smart, and dependable, but she'd learned the hard way how messy things got when feelings bled into the job. She'd already done that dance. And she wasn't doing it again.

After a quick bite in the ABC cafeteria, ham and salad on rye and a Coke Zero, Cassie got to work.

She combed through what Brian had found. Names. Dates. Faces from the past. Some pieces slotted in cleanly. Others dangled, unconnected. But something was forming.

With Foster's murder, every news outlet would be sniffing blood. The Patriots would be everywhere: headlines, hashtags, analysis pieces by people who didn't know their arse from their elbow.

Cassie wasn't about to let months of work become clickbait for someone else's podcast.

She needed a new angle. Something deeper. Something smarter.

Something that would make Peter Draper sit up in his high-backed chair and say yes.

She picked up her phone and dialled Melbourne University.

By mid-afternoon, Cassie was standing in Peter Draper's office, door swinging closed behind her.

"We need to pivot," she announced, not waiting for an invite, and dropped onto the leather couch to one side of his desk.

Peter leaned back in his chair, fingers steepled, one brow arched.

"Come in, Cassandra. By all means," he said, dry as dust.

Cassie ignored the sarcasm, she always did.

Peter Draper was a dinosaur, sure, but the good kind. A newsroom veteran, all instincts and storytelling spine. He'd been the one to coax her back to Australia, and though his wardrobe was equal parts eccentric and iconic: today's combo consisted of a red vest, yellow tie, smart slacks, and a purple pork-pie hat that now lay resting on the corner of his desk, he had a sharper nose for news than anyone she knew.

"What exactly are you thinking?" he asked.

Cassie leaned forward, elbows on knees. "Everyone's going to be on the Patriots now. If Foster wasn't killed by someone inside the group, then they'll be out for revenge. Either way, it's going to be a media frenzy. But I don't want to chase the noise, I want to tell the story behind the noise."

Peter tilted his head. "Go on."

"I want to use Foster's life to ask the bigger question, *why* someone like him ends up radicalised in the first place. What's the tipping point? What's the journey from angry teenager to nationalist mouthpiece?"

"And just to be clear, you're not suggesting a platform piece?"

"No. This isn't about the Patriots. It's about the *people* who fall down the rabbit hole. The disaffected. The lonely. The manipulated. What makes them vulnerable to conspiracy theories and hate movements? What makes someone latch onto that ideology like its oxygen?"

Peter nodded, thoughtful. "You've been stewing on this."

"I had a meeting lined up for after Easter with a radicalisation expert at Melbourne Uni. I've managed to bump it up to tomorrow morning. I want to map Foster's life as a case study. Not as a martyr. Not a scapegoat. Just… a warning."

Peter leaned back, fingers tapping the arm of his chair. "I like it. But make sure it's tight. No drift into glorification. Keep the line clear."

"Absolutely."

"And Cassie, this stays focused on *why*, not *what*. I don't want to see a swastika or manifesto quote anywhere near our screens."

Cassie stood. "No fucking chance."

Peter sighed like a man who'd long given up trying to refine her vocabulary.

"Oh, and I want Brian Cheng on this," she added casually, turning at the door.

Peter frowned. "Brian's flat out with the Bernaldi trial. That cross is his responsibility…"

"Tracey can do the cross," Cassie said. "Brian's the best crime reporter we've got, and he's already up to his neck in Foster's history. Plus, most of my team are already on leave. He's the only one who knows where the bodies are buried, and he actually gives a shit."

Peter folded his arms. "You've been angling to poach him for months."

"I've been waiting for the right story."

He didn't answer. Just held her gaze for a long beat, then waved a hand dismissively.

"Fine. You can have Brian. But I want Tracey's voice on the seven-p.m. lead."

"Done." Cassie grinned. "You're getting soft in your old age."

Peter just shook his head.

Cassie returned to her desk with a spring in her step. She fired off a quick two-word text to Brian:

You're in.

Then she grabbed her jacket and bag. No point staying in the office, she had half a dozen calls to make, and she'd be more productive at home without the distraction of newsroom chatter.

Before turning the ignition in her car, she paused. The quiet thrum of the underground carpark wrapped around her like a blanket. She opened her phone and dialled the number she'd been thinking about all day.

It rang once. Twice.

Then, that voice.

"Hello? Is that you, Cassie?"

She smiled. "Hi Dad."

FOUR

The University of Melbourne stood in timeless contrast, its sandstone spires and ivy-veiled courtyards exuding old-world prestige, even as the city evolved around it. For more than a century and a half, it had fostered some of the sharpest political and legal minds in the country, including several prime ministers.

Cassie, however, wasn't here for tradition. She bypassed the Old Quad entirely, stepping into one of the university's newest wings, a bold architectural statement of steel and glass that gleamed under the morning sun. Inside, the mood shifted. Polished timber floors, minimalist white walls, and abstract art installations lined the space. It felt more like a gallery than a university.

The corridors were hushed, emptied by mid-semester break. Her footsteps echoed as she scanned the directory and made her way up the first floor to Room 1.06. The plaque beside the door read "Dr G. Taylor – Associate Professor, Centre for Contemporary Extremism Studies."

Cassie took a steadying breath and knocked.

"Come in!"

Dr. Gillian Taylor's office wasn't what she expected. There were no overflowing bookshelves, no cluttered desk buried under papers and academic journals. It was stark, curated. A long window behind the desk offered a view of the Carlton gardens, and a soft blush armchair faced a small coffee table near the entrance.

Dr. Taylor herself was already standing. Dressed in sharp charcoal slacks, a soft grey blouse, and a fire-red blazer that matched her lipstick, she exuded clarity and precision. Her hair, silver and cut into a sculpted bob, framed her face like punctuation. She extended her hand.

"Cassandra, lovely to finally meet you."

"Likewise. Thank you for making time today."

"Please," Dr. Taylor gestured toward the armchair opposite her own. "I appreciated your call. Frankly, I find your proposed direction far more meaningful than another surface-level take on the far-right. Starting a broader conversation about extremism, how people get pulled in, why they stay, that's the real work."

Cassie nodded, settling into her seat. "That's what I'm hoping to explore. We've all seen the headlines about Hayden Foster. But I'm interested in what sits underneath someone like that. The root system. Is there a pattern? A trigger?"

"There often is," Dr. Taylor said calmly. "But it's not always the one people expect."

She removed her glasses, wiping the lenses with a small cloth she drew from her jacket pocket. "Let me take you back for a moment. Post-9/11. The invasion of Iraq. The rise of Islamic State. That period changed the entire global landscape when it came to extremism. And yet, what fascinated many of us in the field wasn't the ideology, but the psychology."

Cassie leaned forward.

"Thousands of young men joined ISIS, not just from war-torn regions, but from London, Melbourne, Toronto. Many weren't even Muslim. Some barely understood the ideology they claimed to fight for."

"So why did they do it?"

"Because they were offered something," Dr. Taylor replied. "And not just meaning. Not just purpose. They were offered kinship. Brotherhood. Identity. In a world that made them feel invisible, they were seen."

Cassie frowned. "Most people feel lost at some point. Not everyone turns into a fanatic."

"True. But some don't have the support networks. Some aren't taught how to process pain, failure, rejection. For many young men, emotion has been pathologized. Vulnerability, dismissed. They're told to harden up. Man up. So, they don't cry, they rage. They don't ask for help, they lash out. And when someone online offers them a story, 'you're not broken, the world is,' they listen."

Cassie sat back, letting the weight of that sink in.

"I call them the lost boys," Dr. Taylor said. "Every extremist movement has them. Islamic fundamentalism. White nationalism. Incels. Far-right militias. Their ideology may differ, but the pathway is remarkably similar. Alienation. Humiliation. A longing to belong. And then, someone shows up, usually online, and hands them a script."

She paused.

"And once that script takes hold? The algorithms take care of the rest."

Dr. Taylor gestured toward the window, as if the city skyline beyond it were part of the explanation.

"Before social media, extremists had to work a lot harder to find their audience. Recruitment happened in small meetings, obscure bookshops, fringe churches or mosques. Now? You can build a pipeline to radicalisation from a smartphone. And the tech companies built the pipes for them."

Cassie raised an eyebrow. "You mean the algorithms?"

"Yes." Dr. Taylor's voice was calm, clinical. "Algorithms are designed to maximise engagement. They're not inherently evil, but they are entirely indifferent to truth. They favour outrage. Polarisation. Simplicity. If you click on one video about vaccine scepticism, within hours you're being fed conspiracies about microchips, global cabals, and the deep state. If you like a few clips about male self-improvement, you're fed Andrew Tate and Jordan Peterson. Then... well, the manosphere, incels, 'alpha' rhetoric. And from there, sometimes, straight into white supremacy."

"It's a funnel," Cassie said, quietly.

"A fast one," Dr. Taylor nodded. "And unlike in previous generations, we now have kids being exposed to these ideas *before* they've developed critical thinking skills. Thirteen-year-olds watching hours of content from charismatic influencers telling them women are manipulative, the government is lying, and that strength comes from dominance."

Cassie's face darkened. "I've got a younger brother. He's a decent guy, but I see this shit creeping into the language of some of his mates. Their humour. It's like this whole twisted script of how to be a man is being downloaded into their heads."

"It is," Dr. Taylor agreed. "That's the point. Extremism has always relied on storytelling. But now, those stories are tailored. Personalised. Delivered like a drip feed, 24/7. And because they come in the form of memes or edgy jokes or TikTok's with pumping music, they don't get flagged as propaganda. They feel like culture."

"Which means they become... invisible," Cassie finished.

"Exactly."

The silence that followed was thick.

"During the pandemic, many people lost their sense of control. Connection. Livelihood. Routine. For some, that sparked empathy. Community spirit. But for others, especially those already distrustful of institutions, it amplified every grievance. Anti-lockdown protests became recruitment tools for the far-right. Public health orders were twisted into narratives of state oppression. People started believing they were freedom fighters. And for many young men, it gave them their first real sense of *identity*."

Cassie sat still, taking it all in.

"Extremism isn't about ideology first," Dr. Taylor said finally. "It's about belonging. The ideology comes later, once the emotional contract is signed."

Cassie let the silence stretch for a moment, the weight of Dr. Taylor's words still settling.

"So, what about Hayden Foster?" she asked at last. "Do you think he fits that mould? The lost boy?"

Dr. Taylor adjusted her glasses again. "I can't speculate about a man I never met, and I won't pretend to. But based on what's publicly available? It's possible. His parents died young, correct?"

Cassie nodded. "His Dad, yes. His Mum some years later."

"That's your first clue," Dr. Taylor replied. "Attachment trauma can leave deep wounds, especially in early childhood. Couple that with limited socio-economic opportunity, potential instability, poor role models... you have a young man primed for disillusionment. And if someone like that stumbles into a community, online or otherwise, that offers him identity, purpose, and control? He'll grab it with both hands."

"So, he wasn't recruited. He was rescued."

Dr. Taylor offered a faint smile. "That's one way to see it."

Cassie sat with that for a moment, the words hanging in the air like a diagnosis. Something about it felt personal. Familiar.

"It's not always so straightforward, of course. I've seen individuals from stable, loving households, radicalised under the right conditions. There are always other variables, mental health, trauma, peer pressure. But in Hayden Foster's case, I'd begin with the obvious question, who was there in those formative years? And what kind of influence did they have?"

This wasn't just about Foster anymore. It was about what he represented.

The lost boys.
The people who got left behind.

* * *

Cassie weaved through city traffic, making the short drive from the university to the Supreme Court on Lonsdale Street. As luck would have it, she snagged a parking spot almost directly out front just as a black BMW SUV pulled away.

She had hoped Dr. Taylor would hand her the golden bullet, the perfect thread to tie Hayden Foster's story into a neatly wrapped package. Instead, she left with more questions than answers, which wasn't necessarily a bad thing. Maybe her meeting later with Hayden's childhood football coach would give her something she could use.

Stepping onto the concrete concourse in front of the Melbourne courts precinct, Cassie spotted the familiar media huddle. Cameras balanced on shoulders, reporters muttering into microphones, trying to look authoritative despite the wind tangling their hair.

She scanned the crowd and spotted Brian, not with the ABC team but deep in conversation with Channel Seven's court reporter, Jessica Brady.

Cassie smirked and raised her voice. "Brian!"

Brian turned, startled, his face flushing like a schoolboy caught skipping class. "Cass!" he called, stepping toward her a little too quickly.

Cassie flicked a glance at Jessica, who now smiled with perfect poise. The woman was TV-ready: sharp-lined eyeliner, glossy pink lips, dark hair cascading over one shoulder like she was auditioning for a Pantene ad.

"I hope I'm not interrupting," Cassie said, tone teasing.

Jessica extended a manicured hand. "Cassandra Murphy. Wow. It's such a pleasure to meet you."

Cassie shook it. "Call me Cassie."

"I've followed your work for years. I'm kind of a fan."

Cassie gave her a polite smile. "Thanks."

Jessica beamed. "I've never seen you at the Logies or anything, but I've always hoped to run into you one day."

"Yeah," Cassie said dryly. "I try to avoid red carpets. It's not really my thing."

Jessica's laugh was a touch nervous. Brian cleared his throat.

"We were just chatting about the Bernaldi trial," he said, trying to steer the conversation away awkwardly.

Cassie's grin widened. "Bri, you got a sec?"

Jessica gave her a cheery wave. "Lovely to meet you, Cassie."

"You too." Cassie replied, turning away with Brian in tow.

When they were out of earshot, Cassie raised an eyebrow. "Jessica Brady?"

Brian gave a sheepish shrug. "Yeah. We've been seeing each other. It's still early days."

"Well, she's gorgeous. And friendly. Bit too shiny for my taste, but good for you."

Brian laughed. "You always know how to keep a guy humble."

"I try." Cassie grinned. "Listen, any word on Belinda Mead?"

Brian nodded. "Yeah, I think we've found her. I'm waiting on a callback."

"Great. See if she's willing to meet. Give her my number if she'd prefer to speak with me directly. I've got a meeting this afternoon with Hayden Foster's old footy coach. I might head out to Carrington early, get a feel for the place."

"He actually agreed to talk?"

Cassie smirked again. "I may have told him we were considering a TV segment on his Hall of Fame induction." She shrugged.

Brian smiled. "You want me to come?"

"Nah. This one's better solo. See if you can get those school photos from the Banksia Historical Society before the Easter break."

"On it." Brian paused. "By the way, Doctor Taylor, how was she?"

Cassie let out a long breath. "Fucking brilliant. Frighteningly smart. It gave me a whole new lens to look through. This isn't just about extremism. It's about what drives someone to want to belong to *anything* at all costs."

Brian nodded slowly. "That's powerful."

"It is. She called them the 'lost boys.'"

Brian was about to respond when a shout broke from the huddle. "Brian!"

Cassie turned. The courthouse doors had opened. Cameras swung around like sharks scenting blood.

Brian gave her a quick wave. "Talk later?"

"Pizza and beers at mine tonight."

He grinned. "Pizza and beers? Have you moved into a Uni dorm?"

Cassie laughed as she stood back and watched him disappear into the chaos. Microphones outstretched, reporters jostling for sound bites, the familiar theatre of justice playing out.

Then she turned on her heel and walked back to her car.

She had a date with Carrington. And if there was any truth to what Dr. Taylor had said, about trauma, belonging, and the messy roads people travel, then it was time she started mapping Hayden Foster's.

FIVE

Cassie arrived in Carrington slightly ahead of schedule. For her, location held just as much weight as the people she interviewed. The drizzle that had shadowed her drive down the Monash Freeway still lingered over the suburb, but she didn't mind. Carrington itself was another subject of inquiry.

33 Derby Avenue.

Hayden Foster's childhood home.

She'd looked it up on Google Street View before leaving the office, but what she found now bore no resemblance to the image on her laptop. The modest cream brick veneer was gone, replaced by a row of three newly built, two-storey townhouses stacked one behind the other.

"Damn," she muttered, as though she'd just lost a key witness.

The irony wasn't lost on her. Another of Hayden's homes, wiped from existence, as if the universe were actively scrubbing him from memory.

Carrington had been established in the 1960s and '70s, part of Australia's rapid post-war suburban sprawl. The homes built then were for working- and middle-class families, simple, practical, no-frills.

Single-storey brick veneers or weatherboards sat on rectangular quarter-acre blocks, boasting large backyards with Hills Hoist clotheslines. They were the embodiment of what was once the "Great Australian Dream." But Carrington, like much of suburban Australia, was changing fast. The sky was now interrupted by cranes and concrete. Townhouses and apartment complexes crept steadily upward. The Carrington of old would soon live on only in fading photo albums and stories half-remembered.

Cassie stepped out of the car and onto the footpath in front of the first townhouse. The ground floor was clad in mottled brown brick, with crisp white render above. The garden beds were still bare: new soil, no roots. She had hoped that standing here might reveal something. A trace. A feeling. A whisper from the past. But there was nothing. Just silence.

She brushed a damp strand of hair from her face and scanned the rest of the street, imagining what life had looked like for Hayden here in the 1980s and '90s. Weekend footy matches, backyard cricket, summer barbeques. Maybe even Sunday church. Kids racing their BMXs down the asphalt, daring each other to take corners without hands. A time long before iPads and smartphones, before kids became prisoners of screens. Where had Hayden fit among all of that?

She exhaled slowly and turned back toward the car.

A few streets away, she caught sight of a weathered street sign nailed to a wooden electricity pole: *Jennifer Rd.*

A moment later, Siri's voice cut through the silence.

"Your destination is on the right. You have arrived."

Cassie pulled up to Number 15 just as an incoming call flashed across her dash. *Unknown Number*. She considered letting it go to voicemail. Then answered.

"Cassandra Murphy speaking."

A purposeful voice replied, female. "Cassandra, my name's Belinda Mead. I spoke with your colleague…" A pause. "Brian?"

Cassie sat up straighter. She switched the car off completely and reached for her phone.

"Yes, Brian," she confirmed.

She scrambled for her notepad, flipping through pages until she found a blank one. "Belinda, thanks so much for calling," she said, uncapping her pen with her teeth and spitting the lid onto the passenger seat.

"I'm not sure if Brian explained why I was reaching out?"

Belinda sighed. "Well, I assumed it was about Hayden Foster."

"I'm sorry to open old wounds, but yes. It's about Hayden."

"Well, you would be," Belinda replied, matter-of-fact. "Opening old wounds, I mean. But I figured someone would call, after I saw the news. I just don't know what more I can tell you that I haven't already said years ago."

"I understand. And I really do appreciate this." Cassie hesitated. "Are you still in Melbourne?"

"Yes. I'm in Northcote, but I work in the city. I'm a lawyer at Beckett & Partners at the Windsor Centre on La Trobe Street."

Cassie raised an eyebrow. *Beckett & Partners?* That firm didn't deal in conveyancing and wills. It had high-end polish. A reputation.

Belinda continued, "I'm about to head into a meeting, but if you want to talk, I can meet you. Somewhere public."

"That'd be great. Whatever's easiest for you," Cassie said, holding her breath through the silence that followed.

"There's an open lounge on the ground floor of my building. It has a small café, a few shops, but it's always dead quiet until lunch. I could meet you there tomorrow, say ten a.m.?"

"Perfect," Cassie said, relieved.

"But listen," Belinda added, her voice firm now. "I'm only talking to you. No one else. And this is off the record. No interviews, no cameras. None of that."

"Absolutely. You have my word."

Cassie jotted down the details before ending the call.

She knew what this meant. The media had torn Belinda's life apart once before. That she was even willing to speak again was significant. And Cassie wasn't going to waste the opportunity.

She looked up. Rodney Lindfield's orange-brick house was one of the few originals left in the street. Out front, a weathered bottlebrush tree clung to the nature strip, its trunk twisted and lumpy from years of brutal pruning. Beyond the footpath, a neatly mowed lawn stretched across the block, bordered by tidy beds of camellias, conifers, roses, and nandinas. The windows were fitted with aluminium frames and shaded by brown-and-white striped awnings, now folded back for the colder months ahead. At the end of a cracked concrete driveway sat an open carport, sheltering a once-red Holden Commodore that had faded to something closer to rust.

A family of magpies hopped through the grass, pecking at grubs just below the surface. Cassie smiled faintly, then stepped up and pressed the doorbell. A loud chime rang from somewhere inside the house.

"G'day there, love!" a voice called from behind the tinted security screen door. The figure beyond it remained obscured. "Come in!"

The door swung open, revealing Rodney in all his beaming, weathered glory. His ruddy face, mapped with broken capillaries, shone beneath a thick, bushy moustache, like a furry caterpillar had taken up permanent residence on his upper lip. He wore oversized tracksuit pants and a faded windcheater, which only added bulk to a frame already softened by time. What remained of his washed-out brown hair clung stubbornly to the usual spots.

"Mr Lindfield, it's a pleasure to meet you," Cassie said, bending to remove her shoes.

"Oh, don't worry about that, love. And it's Rodney, please. This way!"

He flashed a leering grin, giving her a quick once-over. Cassie groaned inwardly as she stepped inside and closed the heavy wooden door shut behind her.

The interior of the house was a stark contrast to the manicured garden outside. The air was stale with trapped cigarette smoke and decades of damp. A musty heaviness clung to the walls. She followed him down a narrow corridor lined with peeling wallpaper and threadbare carpet, emerging into a cramped kitchen and dining area.

"Take a seat, love." Rodney gestured toward the cluttered table, piled high with old newspapers, books, and clothes. He swept a space clear with one arm, then grabbed the remote and muted the television just as a horse race began, the odds and runners flashing across the screen.

"I just need to keep it on, if that's okay. I'm waiting for the next race," he explained, scribbling furiously in a tattered notepad with a pencil stub.

"How long have you lived here, Rodney?" Cassie asked, placing her phone discreetly on the table.

"What's that, love?" His eyes were still darting between the screen and his notes.

"How long have you lived here? In Carrington."

"Oh, right. Well, I grew up on a cattle farm out in Gippsland. My dad and his dad were both farmers, but that life never appealed to me. I moved up here in my twenties. More women in the city, you see." He winked at her, shifting in his seat with a cheesy smile.

"I bought this place in '79. Go on, guess how much I paid for it?"

Cassie gave a polite smile. "No idea. A hundred thousand?"

"Twenty-two! Twenty-two grand! You couldn't buy a half-decent car for that now!" He chuckled to himself, shaking his head.

"You must've seen a lot of change over the years."

"Change?" His mood soured instantly. "I should've gotten out long ago. Too many bloody

47

Chinese and Indians now, for a start! Old Gilbert next door did the smart thing and moved up to Wodonga a year back. Have you seen what the Chinese have done to his house? Flattened it! Gone, just like that. Another set of dog boxes going up in its place, no doubt."

Cassie forced a neutral expression as Rodney trailed off, muttering under his breath.

"Too late for me now. I'll be here till they carry me out in a box. Oh, sorry, love. I didn't offer you a drink. Cuppa?"

Cassie declined, but he shuffled into the kitchen anyway, filling the kettle and flicking it on.

"Is there a Mrs Lindfield?" Cassie called out.

"A Mrs Lindfield?" he repeated with a laugh. "Nah, not me, love. Never been married. I dodged that bullet!" The laugh quickly turned into a hacking cough. He pulled a stained old handkerchief from his tracksuit pocket and pressed it to his mouth.

"So, you saw the story then?" he said, returning to his chair. "Hall of Fame. Not bad, eh?" He puffed his chest out. "Forty years I was at that club. Assistant Coach, Head Coach, eleven premiership flags. I still help out behind the bar down there on the occasional Sat'dy night. Keeps me busy."

"Maybe we can start with that," Cassie said, reaching for her phone. "The Hall of Fame award, I mean. Do you mind if I record this, Rodney?"

"Sure, love! Go for your life."

"Rodney, maybe you can…"

"Wait!" He scrambled for the remote, cranking up the volume. The starter gun fired. The gates flew open.

Mud and turf sprayed as the horses thundered past. Rodney roared, cursed, then cursed again as his pick dropped back in the final stretch. Grumbling, he scribbled something into his notebook and finally muted the screen.

Cassie resisted the urge to check the time. She needed to move things along, fast. She lobbed a few ego-stroking questions to help him relax, watching him puff up again. But his eyes kept flicking to her chest, and she clenched her jaw.

Enough.

"Rodney let's talk grassroots footy from the good old days," she said, leaning forward. "For example, 1997. I came across this photo earlier today."

She pulled a folded print from her bag and slid it across the table.

"Under 17 Premiers. One name stood out, Hayden Foster."

Rodney squinted. "Who?"

"Hayden Foster. Under-17s. 1997." She pointed to him in the photo.

"Oh, you mean Nugget!" His face lit up. "That's what we called him. Little fella, but damn good goal kicker. He always reminded me of a young Tony Lockett. He had a temper on him, though. Got into scraps all the time. Bit of a sad story, really. It was just him and his Mum. His dad was a truckie, died of a heart attack when Nugget was a boy. His mum was a strange one. I don't think she was right in the head. And no oil painting, either." He chuckled at his own joke.

Cassie didn't smile. "Rodney, do you watch the news?"

"Nah, love. It's all rubbish these days. Why?"

"Because Hayden Foster was murdered early yesterday morning."

Rodney's face slackened. "Murdered? Jesus *Christ*! What happened?"

"Police believe he was attacked in his home before it was deliberately set ablaze."

Rodney shook his head. "See? That's why I don't watch the news anymore. It's all these bloody immigrants, I tell ya! African gangs with machetes, roaming the streets. They chop your arm off for a set of car keys. They're bloody everywhere, and the government just keeps letting them in, the useless bastards! Poor Nugget!"

Cassie pressed on. "You said Hayden got into fights. Do you remember why? Or who he hung out with?"

"Why?" Rodney scoffed. "Because he was a teenage boy. That's just what they do. As for who he was mates with, that's a bit of a stretch I'm afraid. It's a long time ago."

He paused.

"Did you say it was a house fire?"

"That's right."

He frowned, letting out a low whistle. "Hmm…"

"Why does that matter?"

Rodney scratched his chin. "It just reminds me of Glen O'Connor's young fella. That was a house fire too. Poor kid."

Cassie's interest sharpened. "Sorry, Glen who?"

"The O'Connors. They lived over on Southcote Road. Glen was a house painter. I was a plasterer. We worked a few jobs together way back when."

"And his son?"

Rodney shrugged. "I didn't know him. I don't even remember his name. He wasn't a footy player, y'see."

"Go on."

Rodney cleared his throat. "One weekend, Glen took the missus and their young lass down to Phillip Island but left the boy at home. He was in Year 12 at St Matthew's, some of my best players came through there," he added, drifting again.

"Rodney." Cassie's tone sharpened.

He turned back to her. "The house burned to the ground. The lad was still in bed. They said it was an accident, the stove, maybe a candle? I can't remember. Either way, it broke Glen. He packed up the family and moved up to Queensland not long after. I think it was to get away from all the gossip."

"What gossip?" Cassie leaned forward.

Rodney shifted in his seat. "Look, I don't like speaking ill of the dead, and it was just gossip…"

"Rodney," she cut in. "What were people saying?"

He sighed. "Some reckoned the lad did it on purpose. Suicide."

A chill ran through her. "Why?"

Rodney stared at the muted television. Then back at her.

"Some of my lads said the kid was… a bit funny."

Cassie's gut turned. "What do you mean by 'funny'?"

51

He smirked. "A Woolly Woofter, love. You know." He flicked his wrist and pursed his lips.

"A poofter."

Cassie stiffened.

"Now don't get me wrong, I've got nothing against that sort of thing," Rodney said, waving a hand vaguely. "It's all different these days. But back then? Someone like that?" He chuckled. "He wouldn't've had it easy. Not with my lads." He shook his head, almost nostalgic. "Some of the boys used to go out looking for 'em, poofter bashing, they called it. Thought it was a laugh. But they saw it as just a bit of fun back then, y'know?"

Cassie had grown up with attitudes like this. It was one of the reasons she couldn't wait to escape life in a small country town in the first place.

"And Hayden Foster? Was he one of those lads? The ones who thought it was fun to rough him up?"

Rodney filled his mouth with air, then popped his cheeks. "Maybe. I remember Nugget particularly had it in for poofs. That would've been about the same time, I reckon."

Cassie stood abruptly, stuffing her phone back into her bag. She needed air. Between the stench of stale smoke and the rot in Rodney's worldview, she was starting to feel sick.

"I'm sorry Rodney, I've just remembered I need to be somewhere else."

"Righto. We haven't even talked about my award yet!"

"Another time."

Rodney followed her down the hallway and onto the front porch. The sharpness of the evening air was a relief.

"Alright then, love. Thanks again for coming. You'll let me know when you want to film me for the telly interview, yeah?"

Cassie nodded, face flat. She reached the driveway before she stopped.

"Rodney," she called back over her shoulder.

"Yeah, love?"

"You don't happen to remember the year of the O'Connor house fire, do you?"

He scratched at his scalp. "No. Too long ago now."

She gave a quick nod and turned to leave.

"But I do remember the time of year."

Cassie paused, turning her head over her shoulder.

"It was Easter. Easter Sunday."

SIX

Cassie had already made several calls from her car, the first to Brian, before bursting through the apartment door, kicking her shoes aside, and firing up her laptop. Rodney Lindfield had insisted the O'Connor boy's death was an accident, but the way he spoke about Hayden Foster made her stomach turn. The fact that both were connected to the same suburb, the same time period, and both dying in similar circumstances? That was enough for her to dig deeper. The timing of Easter was surely coincidental, but Cassie had long stopped believing in coincidences.

A knock at the door pulled her from her scrolling.

"Finally!" she said, yanking it open and snatching the six-pack of Asahi beer bottles from Brian's hands.

"You're welcome," he muttered. He wiped his shoes on the fraying welcome mat and neatly placed them outside, all while still balancing a steaming box of thick-crust pepperoni pizza.

Cassie reappeared from the kitchen, already drinking. "Mmm," she grunted, motioning him toward the couch. She swallowed and handed him a bottle. "Here."

Brian lifted the lid of the pizza box as they sat. "Want me to grab some plates?"

"Why? So, I have to wash them later?" Cassie smirked. "Just use the box."

Brian chuckled, shaking his head.

"Look at this." Cassie picked up a slice in one hand and tapped at her keyboard with the other before turning the laptop toward him.

"Facebook? What am I looking at?"

"I couldn't find anything online about the O'Connor house fire, but I did find a name and a year. I checked the yearbook photos on a St Matthew's alumni site. The only male student with the surname O'Connor from the late '90s was Joel O'Connor, Year 12, Class of '98." She switched windows. "Here."

Brian leaned in as she pointed to a boy in the back row of a faded, analogue-coloured year-level photo.

"See?"

He nodded.

"And there was a link to a Class of 1998 Facebook group. I managed to get in. Asking the name of the principal at the time and Carrington's postcode isn't exactly MI5-level security."

Brian waited. When Cassie didn't continue, he nudged her: "And?"

"Right. Well, there's an obituary of sorts, to students of that year level who've passed away. Three of them actually. But look here."

She scrolled. There he was, dressed in a white long-sleeve shirt, the sleeves rolled to the elbows, and a red necktie with thin gold stripes and the St Matthew's gold crest. The portrait had been taken in front of a red-brick wall, his hands clasped in front of him. He looked sixteen or seventeen, messy brown hair, dark eyes, a cheeky grin that hadn't quite grown into itself.

Underneath the photo were a dozen comments. Some mentioned a sister, Millie. One post had even tagged her: *Amelia Mason.*

"He had a sister?" Brian asked.

Cassie nodded. "I tried the link. Her profile's locked. All I could see was her profile picture, two kids in Santa hats. We'll dig deeper tomorrow."

Brian exhaled. "You really think this connects to Hayden Foster? Didn't you say the footy coach said it was an accident?"

Cassie took another mouthful of beer. "Yes, but he also said Joel O'Connor was gay, or at least that's what people thought at the time. And we know exactly how Hayden Foster felt about the gay community. Same suburb, same era. It's worth looking into."

She scrolled again. "And here's more."

Several comments mentioned someone named Laura.

I still get upset when I think about this, wrote Michele Attley in April 2009. *We missed you at the reunion last year, Laura. I remember how close you and Joel were. If you see this, I hope life's worked out well for you.*

"Laura's name hasn't been tagged," Cassie said. "Which means she's either not on Facebook or she's hard to find."

She switched back to the Class of '98 photo. "Two Lauras in the year level, Laura Towner and Laura Cassini. We need to figure out which one was Joel's friend. If they were as close as this Michele person says, she might know more about Joel than his family does."

Brian raised an eyebrow. "Why's that?"

"They were seventeen," she replied.

Of course. Brian blushed, regretting his question.

"About the fire itself... Have you tried Caroline yet?" Brian asked.

"Caroline? Caroline Perry in archives?" Cassie glanced at the clock. "It's like eight o'clock."

Brian just smirked and pulled out his phone. He tapped the screen and put it on speaker, setting it down on the table between them.

A warm, lilting voice answered almost instantly. "Well, hello, lovely Brian Cheng. To what do I owe this honour?" A hearty laugh followed.

Brian grinned. "Hello to you too, Caroline. I hope I haven't interrupted you in the middle of baking my favourite muffins?"

More laughter. Cassie looked at him, mouth slightly open.

"Oh, Brian. No, still here, working away. You know me."

"I do, Caroline. And I know you work too hard. But I'm glad I caught you. I'm here with Cassandra Murphy, we're hoping you can help us with something."

"Oh really? Hi there, Cassandra! How are you? Look at you two, working together. This is lovely!"

Cassie tilted her head, still watching Brian with quiet amusement. "Hi, Caroline. Yes, Brian's full of surprises today."

"Well, if you two are teaming up, it must be something big. What do you need?"

Caroline didn't need long. Now that most of the archived footage had been digitised, it was only a few clicks away. Before they'd even hung up, Cassie's laptop pinged with a new notification: *Email from Caroline Perry*.

Cassie raised an eyebrow. "Caroline Perry bakes you muffins?"

"Protein muffins," Brian said proudly. "Blueberry and banana. She has them ready for me when I come in after the gym in the morning. They're amazing."

Cassie just shook her head and clicked open the email. There was only a hyperlink. She tapped it.

A video player loaded. The old ABC News studio snapped into focus.

She hit play.

"Heartbreak today for a Carrington family, in Melbourne's outer east, after a house fire claimed the life of a seventeen-year-old boy overnight. More from Henry Barker at the scene."

The screen cut to shaky footage of a blackened, charred house. Yellow police tape fluttered in the wind, eerily familiar to the scene Cassie had stood in front of only a day earlier.

"The fire broke out just before midnight last night at the Southcote Road property. Fire crews made the grim discovery in a bedroom at the rear of the house. The blaze was so intense it left the structure completely gutted, fuelled in part by a large number of paint cans and other flammable chemicals stored in an adjoining garage. Police and fire investigators have been on scene since early morning. More now from District Commander Graham Golding."

Cassie's lip curled as the screen cut to a man in uniform.

"You've got to be fucking kidding me," she muttered.

Graham Golding stood solemn, his face tight, a microphone just inches from his mouth.

"We believe the deceased was asleep when the fire broke out. We've ruled out suspicious circumstances and electrical fault. At this stage, it appears to be a tragic accident."

The footage cut again, this time to a woman in a dressing gown on a suburban street, her voice thick with emotion.

"It's absolutely devastating. The sound of it woke me, loud popping noises, pop, pop, pop. I knew the family was away because their caravan was gone, but I had no idea their son was still home. He was such a friendly boy. Always said hello. They're a lovely family. It's just heartbreaking."

Back to the reporter:

"Investigators are still working to determine whether the home had functioning smoke detectors. The local CFA Chief has urged residents to check their batteries as we head into the colder months when house fires become more common. Investigators will remain on scene today, but at this stage, all indications point to a tragic accident. Back to you, Alan."

The video ended, pausing on the last frame.

Cassie let out a long, steady breath, staring at the frozen final frame.

Tragic accident.

Brian leaned back into the couch. "Poor kid," he said, catching the look in Cassie's eyes. "Weird seeing Graham Golding in it, though. He looked so young."

Cassie snorted. "He looked like a smug wanker."

Graham Golding had been Assistant Police Commissioner for Regional Victoria in the early 2000s, around the same time her dad was promoted to Senior Sergeant at Heathton Ridge. Derek Murphy had never had a good word to say about him. A city cop trying to run country policing from a desk in Melbourne, he barely set foot outside the CBD. Worse, he spent more time chasing TV cameras than doing real police work.

His ambition for the top job, Chief Commissioner, had been no secret. But when he didn't get it, he quit in protest and pivoted straight into state politics, running on a platform of division and fear. He served two terms, launched a failed bid to roll the Premier, and when that didn't pan out, moved on again. Private enterprise kept him busy for a while, but it never gave him the spotlight he craved. Now, in retirement, he hosted a weekly panel show on Sky News Australia, still peddling the same divisive crap as ever.

Cassie had even scored a mention once. *That redhead girl at the ABC with the big mouth.* Golding's sneering response after she exposed a corporate mate of his who'd been jailed for fraud and corruption.

To Cassie, he was nothing more than an opportunist with a god complex. But to many Victorians, he was a man of conviction. His arrogance mistaken for charm. His popularity hadn't waned, if anything, it had grown. Deep ties to the AFL and the Anglican Church hadn't hurt, either. Like it or not, he was still a prominent Australian.

"Do you still want to look into this? Joel O'Connor?" Brian asked. "It really does sound like it was just a tragic accident."

Cassie hesitated, then shrugged her shoulders. "No. I guess not. I just had a feeling." She reached for another slice of pizza. "Oh hey, I meant to tell you. I got a call from Belinda Mead. The former sex worker. Thanks for lining that up."

Brian shrugged. "She wasn't exactly thrilled when I first rang, but when I mentioned your name, she came around real quick. Don't underestimate your reputation, Cass. People like you a lot."

"People like that I give a shit. And I do." She wiped her fingers on a napkin.

"Investigations are very different to reporting, Bri. You'll learn that. We don't just tell the story, we uncover it. Nothing makes me happier than seeing those creeps finally get what's coming. And if that brings even a shred of peace to the victims I sit with, then it's worth it."

Brian smiled as she polished off the last of her slice.

"Before I left Doctor Taylor's office today, she gave me a contact in Sydney. There's a group up there that runs a deradicalisation program. She talked a lot about 'the lost boys,' young men who felt rejected, let down, looking for mateship and meaning in all the wrong places." Cassie met his gaze. "How do you feel about a trip to Sydney?"

He grinned. "For sure. I'd love that."

Cassie glanced down at the laptop screen, the image of the reporter still frozen in front of what was left of the O'Connor house.

"There's something in Foster's past that James Lawrence knows about, or at least suspects. He wouldn't have left us breadcrumbs if there was nothing to find."

"Do you want to meet up tomorrow after your meeting with Belinda?"

Cassie considered it.

"No. This can wait. I really want to see Dad." She paused. "In fact, fuck it. I'll still go up tomorrow as planned. Straight after I meet with Belinda."

Brian smiled, sympathetic.

"Send me the Sydney details," he said. "I'll reach out, set something up for after the break. And thanks, Cass. I really appreciate you getting me in on this. We finally get to work together."

Cassie grinned. "You sure I'm not pulling you away from *Jessica Brady*?"

Brian's hand shot back, face turning red.

"Seriously though, good for you," she smiled. "I mean, you're clearly punching above your weight, but…"

Before she could finish, Brian grabbed a cushion and whacked her arm. Cassie laughed, dodging the next swing.

He stayed a while longer, brainstorming ideas for the story, but by 11 p.m., Cassie was alone again, laptop open, TV on mute, empty beer bottles scattered on the coffee table. She'd tried to distract herself with a new Netflix series, but the feeling lingered: there was more to Hayden Foster. Something she hadn't uncovered yet.

And then there was Joel O'Connor.

If experience had taught her anything, it was to trust her gut.

She sighed, running a hand through her hair, then leaned back into the couch, watching silent images flicker across the screen. Eventually, she exhaled sharply and grabbed the remote and clicked the TV off.

Outside, the streets of Elwood were unusually quiet. Inside, her fingers tapped fast across the keyboard.

Laura.

She started with Laura Towner. Nothing. No mention in the Class of 1998 Facebook group. Google wasn't any help either. Probably married, changed her name. Cassie flagged it for tomorrow.

She tried again: *Laura Cassini.*

Dozens of hits.

The first led to a catering website. Valetta's Catering. Traditional Italian music looped in the background as a slogan stretched across the top of the homepage:

"Everything's better with Valetta!"

Cassie clicked around. A link led to a YouTube video, an old TV commercial from the 1980s. She hit play.

The footage was straight out of a dusty VHS with grainy, washed-out colours. The same music played as a young couple in matching denim pushed open the doors to a warmly lit restaurant.

A smooth-voiced narrator spoke:

"Do you love real Italian food? Buttery homemade pasta, rich tomato sauce with fresh herbs and spices. Or maybe you're just after a tasty pizza *pronto*? Melbourne's most popular Italian restaurant and pizzeria welcomes you and your family to Valetta's."

The screen filled with happy diners seated at red-and-white checkered tables, steaming plates of pasta and pizza in front of them.

Then the camera panned to a particular table. A man looked up, smiling, as text appeared:

Raymond Cassini.

"When you come to Valetta's, you know you'll be treated like family. Isn't that right, Mamma?"

The shot cut to an elderly woman, Valetta Cassini, murmuring something in Italian that made everyone around her laugh.

"Hey, Nonna!"

The camera zoomed in on a little girl with a thick black bob. She slurped up a long strand of spaghetti, Bolognese smeared across her cheeks. Then she grinned at the camera.

"*Bellissima!*"

The table erupted in laughter before they all chimed in:

"Because everything's better with Valetta!"

Final shot: *Valetta's Restaurante, Carrington Highway, Carrington (out front of Banksia Plaza).*

Cassie shook her head. So cheesy.

She clicked back to the catering homepage. A professional headshot of Laura Cassini filled the screen. *Owner, Valetta's Catering.*

That little girl in the commercial, it had to be her. The timing fit.

Now to find out if Laura Cassini was the same Laura mentioned in the Facebook comments about Joel O'Connor.

Cassie hovered over the *Contact Us* tab. Then paused and let out a long sigh.

And closed her laptop instead.

Time for bed.

SEVEN

Cassie stood and tugged the cord, the buzzer sounding overhead. The driver acknowledged her with a glance in the rearview mirror, easing the tram toward the next stop. She stepped off just past Belinda Mead's office on La Trobe Street and began the short walk back along the footpath. Above, the sun made a half-hearted attempt to break through the clouds, but the towering glass-and-steel skyscrapers swallowed it whole. A sharp wind funnelled through the city, pushing her into a brisk pace.

Beckett & Partners occupied the top floors of the Windsor Centre, one of a pair of imposing blue-glass towers, just a short walk from Melbourne's law court precinct. Outside, joining the towers, was a sprawling forecourt that stretched onto the front footpath and road. A cluster of motorbikes and scooters rested against metal parking bays, while wooden seating and raised flower beds attempted, unsuccessfully, to lure workers and commuters. This morning, they sat empty. As Cassie approached the main entrance, two suited men exited the circular automated doors mid-conversation. One pulled a vape from his inside pocket and took a long inhale. She ducked through the door, dodging the puff of sweet-smelling vapour that followed.

Belinda had been right. The small café and shops in the glass-roofed atrium between the towers were quiet, though the smell of burnt toast and coffee filled the space. A cluster of uncomfortable-looking metal chairs and tables sat in front of the café, but further along, near a window overlooking the street, two empty booths offered more privacy. Cassie took a seat there.

A quick Google search on the tram ride in had led Cassie to a recent headshot on the Beckett & Partners website, making it easy to spot Belinda the moment she stepped out of the Eastern Tower elevator. Buxom and purposeful, she wore jeans, brown-heeled boots, and a crisp white shirt beneath an open brown cardigan, carrying herself with the quiet confidence of someone accustomed to being heard.

She scanned the room, locked eyes with Cassie, and gave a small wave before heading over. Her mouse-brown hair, cut short and tucked behind her ears, framed a pair of gold teardrop earrings. Gold rings glinted on her fingers, and a sleek gold watch rested on her left wrist. Cassie guessed early fifties at a stretch.

"Cassandra." she said smiling.

"Belinda, hi. Thank you so much for meeting me." Cassie stood to greet her.

"Nice to meet you." Her voice was confident. Self-assured. No wasted words.

"I'm sorry about the choice of venue, but I knew we'd have privacy here," Belinda said.

"This is fine. I appreciate that," Cassie replied. "I normally record my conversations, but I completely respect it if…"

"I'd rather you didn't," Belinda interrupted. "I know who you are. That's why I agreed to meet. I know you're not after some trashy scoop, but I wouldn't feel comfortable being recorded."

Cassie nodded and tucked her phone back into her bag.

"Would you mind telling me a little more about what you're hoping to get from all this?" Belinda asked.

Cassie hesitated, then let go of her notepad. "Of course," she said, suddenly not wanting to make Belinda any more uncomfortable than necessary.

"I'm sorry to bring up Hayden Foster. I truly am. If anything makes you uncomfortable, just say so and we'll stop."

"Thank you," Belinda said evenly.

"I'm not here to dig into what happened back in 2000. Not directly, and certainly not to write a story about you. I'm trying to understand Hayden. Who he was and what led him down the path he took. If you have any insight into that, it would help."

Belinda studied her for a long moment, then nodded. "Sure. And again, I trust you on that. Which, after everything that happened, is something I never thought I'd say to a journalist."

"I get it. I've read the articles from back then. The way you were treated was disgusting. I'm really sorry you were put through that."

Belinda nodded, her expression unreadable. "I appreciate that. But that was the time we were living in. No one seemed to care much if a sex worker got raped. The general consensus was that a prostitute had no moral position to cry rape. As if it went with the territory. There was very little sympathy."

Cassie felt her blood pressure rise. She shifted in her seat, steadying herself. "There's no excuse for how you were treated. None. It's hard enough to come forward, let alone be treated that way."

Belinda gave another small nod of acknowledgment.

"Which is why, again, I'm so sorry to ask you about *him*," Cassie continued. "The news reports back then said he was a regular client of yours. I just thought maybe he told you things he hadn't told anyone else."

Belinda let out a short, humourless laugh. "I could've written a book on the things men told me in those moments."

She leaned back in the booth, eyes distant. "For some, it was all about that, the talking. The company. The sex was secondary. Sometimes it didn't even happen at all."

She sighed. "But not Hayden Foster."

Cassie caught a flicker of something in Belinda's expression. Not anger. Something closer to disappointment.

"You saw it all the time with some of the younger guys," she went on. "They'd come in after watching porn, full of bravado, thinking women wanted to be degraded. That we liked being called sluts. Being knocked around. That sort of thing."

"So, there was a lot of violence?" Cassie asked gently.

"No, I wouldn't say violence exactly. We had security for that. And Susan, our madam, she never tolerated it. I can tell you it's a lot worse now, though. Our firm does a lot of pro bono work supporting victim-survivors. Schools are rampant with kid-on-kid sexual assaults, and time and time again, the boys always blame it on the same thing: 'I saw it in porn and thought that's just what you did.'"

She paused. Then her eyes sharpened.

"As I said, for most of those young guys it was just about bravado." A pause. "But not Hayden. To be honest with you, I don't even know if he ever enjoyed the sex. I think what got him off was control. Controlling the situation. Controlling me."

A silence settled between them, heavy and dense. Control.

"I'll tell you this, though," Belinda continued. Her voice was steady now, but there was something steelier beneath it. "He always had an unsettling confidence. From the moment he walked in and even after..." Her voice caught, just for a second.

Then she found it again.

"After he raped me."

She said it plainly. Not without emotion, but without flinching. A fact. Something long since stripped of sting, but not of weight.

"Not cockiness, per se. It felt darker than that. Calculated. Measured. Like he knew exactly what he was doing. Like he knew he could do whatever he pleased without fear of consequence. I'd never come across that before. Not until him."

The silence pressed in again.

Cassie leaned forward. "Belinda." A pause. "Why were the charges against Hayden dropped? Was there a reason you walked away from the trial?"

Belinda shrugged, a hollow smile tugging at the corner of her mouth. "It all became too hard in the end."

"What about the police?"

Belinda let out a short, bitter laugh. "What *about* the police?"

"Surely they would've loved to have thrown the book at him?"

"Not in '99." Belinda's expression hardened. "Cassie, it was the police who encouraged me to drop the charges. They told me the chance of conviction was almost zero. That the trial would be worse for me than for him. I had a newborn to think about, and the media attention…" She exhaled sharply. "It was too much."

"It's why I became a lawyer, you know." She glanced upward toward the top floors of the building. "A senior partner upstairs reached out to me after everything died down. Paid for my degree. Mentored me. I worked hard, but I'm also incredibly grateful for the opportunity that came out of one of the worst times in my life."

Cassie hesitated. "Wait, you said '99? I thought this all happened in 2000."

Belinda's gaze drifted. "The case blew up in 2000. But the assault happened the year before."

Cassie turned away for a moment, letting the timeline settle. A subtle shift in Belinda's posture told her the conversation was winding down.

"Honestly?" Belinda sighed, her mood lifting slightly. "I try not to think about it. It was a long time ago, and my life is different now. I have my son, my house, and this great job. And now that bastard is dead…" She gave a small, wry smile. "I think, in some ways, I finally have peace. I don't know if any of that is of help, but I can't really think of anything else."

"You've been incredibly helpful," Cassie said, returning to the moment. "I really appreciate your time, and I know how hard this must be to revisit. And if it's any consolation, I'm glad the bastard's dead too."

Belinda grinned.

* * *

Inside Out was bustling now, the early lunch crowd filling every corner as Annie Lennox's *Little Bird* floated down from the speakers overhead. Cassie wove her way through the chatter and clatter, Jason spotting her instantly.

"You're still here?" he called out. "Does this mean we'll be seeing you tonight?" He grinned.

Cassie smiled. "You know I would, but I'm all packed and ready to go. I just needed one last decent coffee before it's all roadhouse swill for the next four hours."

Jason grimaced and turned to the barista. "Double shot flat white for Cassie, please, Kaia."

"So hey," he said, turning back, "I'm guessing you've been flat out with that neo-Nazi guy stuff this week?"

"Neo-Nazi guy?" Cassie raised an eyebrow.

"That white supremacist bloke. The one killed in the house fire."

"Oh, right, Hayden Foster. Yes. More than you know, actually. I'd been working on a story about the Allied Patriots, and then all that happened. It's been a wild few days."

"You know he came here once. About a year back. Causing trouble."

"Wait, what? Hayden Foster? Here?"

"Oh yeah. We were due to host Victoria Townsend, you know, the trans rights activist, for her book tour. He rocked up, full of threats."

"I remember that tour. I didn't know she spoke here though."

"Well, she didn't. It got moved to the Town Hall when it all blew up. We got the usual phone calls, Facebook rants, but that Hayden Foster bloke? He came in person. A real piece of work. He especially had it in for Amir."

"Jesus. Did you call the police?"

Jason shrugged. "And what good would that have done? He didn't lay a finger on anyone. Just wanted to throw his weight around. The next morning, the posters came down, the tour moved, and that was that. We never saw him again."

"I'm so sorry, Jason. I wish I'd known."

"It comes with the territory. We've seen worse."

The young barista slid a takeaway cup across the counter. Jason passed it to Cassie.

"Well, we'll miss you tonight. Safe travels. And enjoy your time off. Give your dad a big hug," he added with a sympathetic smile.

"Thanks, Jase." She leaned in for an air kiss and headed out.

* * *

Somewhere past Seymour, the grey skies gave way to a stretch of blue, the freeway veering northeast. Cassie cracked her window, breathing in the crisp country air. The sun was deceptive. It promised rest, but she knew better.

By Euroa, her petrol light was blinking. She'd ignored it for at least twenty kilometres before finally conceding she wouldn't make it to Heathton Ridge on fumes alone. She pulled into one of the big roadhouse chains off the freeway.

As she paid the servo attendant, her phone buzzed in her pocket. Mum.

"Hi Mum," she said, stepping back through the sliding doors. "I'm just in Euroa getting petrol."

"Hi Cassie, it's Mum." She did that thing where she announced herself, even though Cassie had just said her name. It irritated Cassie to no end. "Listen, I don't want you to panic, it's not a big deal, but your father's taken a tumble. We're at Wangaratta Hospital."

"What?" Cassie's voice sharpened as she climbed into the car and slammed the door. "What do you mean, a tumble? Is he alright?"

"Yes, yes, he's fine. He tripped up the back stairs and hurt his wrist. But he also knocked his head. They're just keeping him in for observation. Really, don't panic. I just didn't want you turning up and finding the house empty."

Behind her, a car tooted impatiently. Cassie threw up her hands in the mirror, mouthing *what?* as she glared at the driver.

"Hang on, Mum. I've got some dickhead behind me." She started the engine and pulled away from the pump, waiting for the Bluetooth to kick in. "I'll head straight to the hospital. I'm just under an hour away."

"Alright, but don't rush. Drive safe please, Cassie. I know what you're like."

"Goodbye, Mum."

Cassie's jaw was tight as she drove. If it was *just* a tumble, he'd be at Heathton Ridge Hospital. Wangaratta meant it was more serious than her mother was letting on.

More false hope, she thought grimly.

As she merged back onto the freeway, her phone rang again. A landline. She groaned. *What now?*

"Hello, Cassandra speaking."

"Oh, G'day, love. Rodney here, Rodney Lindfield."

Cassie smiled despite herself. "Mr Lindfield, hi, how are you?"

"Oh, it's just Rodney, remember?"

"Right. Of course. Hi, Rodney."

"Hi, love. Look, I was thinking after you left yesterday, I needed to call you about Nugget. You asked about the lads he used to knock around with. I've got some names for you."

"Okay, Rodney, I'm driving at the moment, just give me a sec." She reached into her bag, rummaged for a pen. "Alright, go ahead."

"Righto, love."

Cassie sat up straighter.

"First off, David Grayson, cracking little full forward. Then Brice McCrae and his mate Scott King. Actually, Scott died a while back. I think he only ever played one season. He wasn't much chop."

Cassie scrawled the names on her left forearm, her hand never leaving the wheel.

"Anyone else?"

"No, just those three. Oh, and I mentioned to the club about your story on me. They're keen to help out. They reckon you should use the clubrooms for my filmed interview."

He was definitely persistent, she'd give him that.

"Thanks, Rodney. I'm away for Easter, but I'll be in touch, alright?"

"Oh, right. No worries, love. You have a good weekend."

"You too. Thanks again."

Cassie glanced at the scribble on her arm. Three names. Reaching for her phone with her free hand, she took a quick photo. She'd promised herself this trip wasn't about work. But the laptop was already in the boot. She was now thankful she had brought it. If her dad was staying longer than expected, she'd need something to occupy her mind. Thanks to Rodney, she had her first task.

EIGHT

"NO COFFEE! Closing at 4pm."

Cassie sighed, glaring at the handwritten sign taped to the register. Thick black letters. Masking tape. Perfect. She'd just flown up the Hume at breakneck speed, pulled into Wangaratta Hospital in record time, only to be left pacing outside while a doctor fussed over her dad's injuries.

With no other choice, she trudged into the hospital cafeteria and was swallowed by the mid-afternoon crush. Nurses in blue scrubs jostled with paramedics and health workers in grey and pink polos. Face masks dangled from wrists, lanyards bounced off chests. The air was thick with the scent of reheated curry and hospital-grade disinfectant.

"You can head down and use the staff room if you want a coffee, love," the cashier said, a middle-aged woman with tired eyes and hair pinned under a black net. "It's only instant, though. We're short-staffed today."

Cassie forced a tight smile. "No, that's okay. Thanks."

Her eyes swept the room. Every table held the same sad constellation of half-empty Diet Coke bottles and foil takeaway containers. A survival economy in a place where the coffee machines had mutinied.

"Just a Diet Coke please," Cassie said.

The cashier slid a bottle from the fridge and nudged the EFTPOS terminal toward her.

"Just tap there, darlin'."

Cassie found a small table tucked in the corner near the main corridor. She slumped into the hard plastic chair, twisted off the cap, and listened to the hiss of carbonation. It felt like mockery. She took a sip, the cold, artificial sweetness doing nothing to shift the weight pressing on her chest.

Her gaze drifted to a row of dusty potted plants by the wall. It was hard to tell if they were real or plastic. The dust suggested no one cared either way.

An elderly man shuffled past on a walker, eyes fixed on the linoleum floor.

"Cassie."

She looked up. Terence Young was striding toward her, cutting through the din.

"Hey," Cassie said, trying to keep her voice level.

"Before you ask, your dad's fine," Terence said as he dropped into the seat opposite. His dark eyes were calm. Steady. Reassuring.

"Your mum's in with him now. You just missed your brother, he had to get back to the station."

Cassie's stomach began to unclench. "What happened?"

"He hit his head pretty hard. They'll likely keep him overnight for observation, just to be safe. X-rays are clear, but he's torn some ligaments in his wrist.

They've strapped it up. He'll be sore, but he'll be okay."

Cassie let out a breath she didn't realise she'd been holding. Relief curled beneath her ribs.

"Hey," Terence said gently, brushing her arm. His touch was warm. Grounding. "He's okay."

Cassie nodded, blinking back the sting in her eyes.

Terence was a physiotherapist at Wangaratta Hospital, but he spent most of his time on the road, providing outreach to smaller towns across the high country. That's how they'd met, six months ago, during a home visit for her dad. He'd walked in with that big, easy grin and dark, laughing eyes. Cassie had noticed him right away, his sharp cheekbones and warm skin, but it was how he'd spoken to her father, with genuine care and quiet patience, which stayed with her.

He'd shown interest in Cassie more than once, much to her mum's thinly veiled delight, but Cassie had always brushed him off. Too complicated. But now? She thought of Brian with Jessica Brady, and how happy he seemed. Sitting across from Terence, the quiet strength in his gaze anchoring her... maybe it didn't seem so complicated anymore.

"You can go in now," Terence said softly. "You don't have to wait out here."

Cassie didn't need telling twice.

Inside the emergency ward, Derek Murphy's face broke into a smile the moment he saw her. Pale beneath the hospital lights, but his eyes were still sharp. Still her dad.

"Hello, my darling girl," he said, voice rough with exhaustion.

"Dad." Cassie leaned in to hug him close.

"You'd think I'd know how to handle a set of stairs by now." He grinned sheepishly.

"I've got to get back," Terence said from the doorway. "I'll see you later, Mr Murphy, we've got to sort that arm out."

"Thanks, mate," Derek said.

Terence flashed a grin. "Take care."

Bernadette Murphy appeared just as he left, eyes lighting up. "Oh, you found her, Terence! Thanks, love!"

Her Mum shot Cassie a quick wink and raised her eyebrows as Terence disappeared.

Cassie groaned. "Oh my God, Mum."

"All right, all right! I won't say anything, I know how sensitive you are with that stuff."

Bernadette laughed, settling into the only chair in the cubicle.

Cassie turned back to her dad. "What exactly happened, Dad?"

"It's nothing," Derek said, brushing it off. "Just a little tumble."

"It's not nothing if you ended up here." She turned to her mum. "Why *is* he here? Why isn't he at emergency at the Ridge?"

"His medical team's all here," Bernadette cut in. "Besides, I wouldn't trust that lot back at Heathton Ridge anymore. The place has gone to the dogs since I left."

Derek rolled his eyes. "Bloody hell."

Bernadette had taken early retirement from Heathton Ridge District Hospital after Derek was first diagnosed with bowel cancer. She'd been Head Nurse: respected, feared, admired. Though Derek had been the town's Senior Sergeant, a steady, decent country copper, it was Bernadette who people found intimidating. "You can take the girl out of Glasgow, but you can't take Glasgow out of the girl," Derek would often say.

Her dad wore his police badge with quiet pride. Firm but fair. The kind of copper who made sure every victim was his highest priority, treating them with care and respect. He was beloved in the Ridge community. After the Black Saturday bushfires, he'd been awarded the Valour Medal and Medal for Excellence. He never talked about it much. But Cassie knew what it meant to him.

Still, it wasn't the accolades that defined him, it was his decency. His loyalty. His fierce love for his family.

She'd watched them both age over the last year. Her mum no longer dyed her auburn hair, the greys coming in wiry streaks. But it was her eyes, carrying a quiet weight, that had changed most. Derek's body was fading. They both knew the time left was short.

Cassie sat with him for nearly an hour, chatting quietly. He asked about her work, still invested in every detail. Bernadette read a dog-eared Woman's Weekly magazine that looked like it hadn't been touched since the pandemic.

When Cassie finally stood, Bernadette insisted on staying a while longer. "I'll see you at home Cassie, I won't be too far off," said her Mum.

"I'll see you tomorrow, Dad," Cassie said, kissing him gently on the cheek.

Out in the main foyer, Terence was waiting by the automatic sliding glass doors.

"Cassie," he said, hands in his pockets.

She slowed. "Hey."

He hesitated, lifting one hand up and rubbing the back of his neck. "Look... I know you've said no in the past, but I..."

"Yes," Cassie cut in.

"Yes? Really?"

For a long time, she'd convinced herself it was safer to keep things casual with men, sex without strings. Clean. Uncomplicated. But lately, she'd found herself wanting something more. And she liked Terence. His kindness. His steady presence. The way he connected to her dad, and to her hometown. It felt like something she could trust.

"Yes," she said again, smiling. "I'd love to have dinner with you. Anything to get me out of being alone with Mum for the night."

"Yeah?" His grin widened.

"Well, as long as you're not taking me to some fancy-shit restaurant."

Terence laughed. "No fancy shit. Got it."

"I've gotta head out to the Ridge and get settled, but I'll come back to Wang. Steak and beers at the Ploughman's? Seven o'clock?"

"Yeah, I mean... yeah! And you're really sure?"

"Not if you keep asking me that." Cassie grinned. "Yes. I'm sure. But you're buying the beers."

Terence laughed. "Deal."

Cassie climbed into her car, her head buzzing with a mess of emotion. She weaved through the Wangaratta streets like muscle memory, crossed the Hume, and settled in for the half-hour drive east. The road stretched ahead, smooth, familiar, but Cassie barely noticed the landmarks. Her hands were steady on the wheel, but her mind wasn't.

As her car swept around *that* bend, her breath caught.

It was still there.

A weathered wooden cross, leaning slightly, tucked into the scrub at the base of a giant River Gum. The flowers wrapped around it were long dead, brittle brown, greyed by time. A tattered ribbon fluttered limply in the breeze, its colour leached by years of sun and rain.

Cassie's chest tightened. She didn't need to look to know the names etched into the timber.

Kimberley Taylor. Rick Barnes. Jake Templeton. Megan Frost.

She swallowed hard, but the memory had already pulled her under.

* * *

"Cassie, please."

Kimberley's voice was already slurred, heavy with that faux confidence that came after too many UDLs.

"Just come. Rick said we'll only stay for an hour."

Cassie sat hunched over her desk, buried in English literature notes. The warm glow from her desk lamp lit up highlighted passages of *Romulus, My Father*, but the words were blurring.

"Kim, I can't," she muttered, frustrated. "I've got my lit exam on Monday."

Kim groaned. "Come on, Cass. It's Ben's 18th! Everyone's going to be there. Don't be such a..."

"Such a what?" Cassie snapped. "A loser? A snob?"

Kimberley's tone shifted. Sour. Defensive. "I didn't say that."

"You didn't have to." Cassie pushed her chair back, the legs scraping hard against the floorboards. She clutched the cordless landline phone tighter as she flopped onto her bed.

"I'm not in the mood to watch everyone get blind and listen to idiot's puke in the paddock all night. I'm not ruining my ATAR for one bloody party."

Kim's voice turned cold. "See? I knew it. You think you're better than us now, don't you?"

"Jesus, Kim. Don't start that shit again."

"Whatever, Cassie. We'll find someone else to drive us in. And what I was going to say was, don't be such a *bitch*!"

The phone clicked.

"*Me*!? You're the bitch!" Cassie hissed down the now-silent line.

"Cassie?"

Her mum's voice drifted down the hall. A moment later, Bernadette appeared, arms folded, concern softening the lines in her face.

"It's bloody Kimberley," Cassie muttered. "She's cracked the shits because I won't go to Ben's party. She only wants a lift because I've got my licence and a car, and she doesn't. Now she's pissed off because I said no."

She returned to her desk, slumping back into the chair. "I can't wait to get out of this bloody town."

Bernadette sighed. "You girls," she said gently. "Don't worry about her right now. You just focus on your exam."

Cassie nodded, though her gut twisted. She hated fighting with Kimberley. They'd been inseparable since kindergarten, through breakups, bad haircuts, teenage tantrums. But something had shifted. Cassie's eyes were on the future, while Kimberley had flung herself headfirst into parties and boys. They were drifting, and neither of them knew how to stop it.

"Stick to your course," Bernadette murmured, brushing hair from Cassie's face. "She'll come around. I'll make you a cuppa."

She picked up the phone from the bed and padded quietly down the hall.

Cassie wanted to believe her.

The hours blurred. She buried herself in notes, re-read essays, highlighted key quotes, anything to drown out the voice in her head telling her she should've gone.

She was still at her desk when the phone rang.

At first, she barely registered it, her mind tangled in Gaita's words on love and sacrifice, until she heard her mum's voice. High. Shaky. Frantic.

"Cassie!"

The panic in Bernadette's tone sent a chill down her spine. Cassie jumped up, heart hammering, and ran to the kitchen.

Her mum stood by the phone, one hand pressed to her mouth, her face ghostly pale.

"Mum?" Cassie barely got the word out.

Bernadette's eyes glistened. "That was your father," she whispered. "There's been... an accident."

Cassie's heart thudded. "What kind of accident?"

But Bernadette didn't answer. Instead, she reached for Cassie and held her tight, as if her arms could somehow shield her from what was coming.

Nothing could.

The red and blue lights tore through the darkness like sirens in the void.

Bernadette pulled off the road and onto the gravel shoulder. Cassie stumbled out of the car into the thick night air, the acrid smell of burnt rubber and fuel punching her in the chest. Her dad's cruiser was already parked near the wreck, the door flung open. But she didn't see it.

Her eyes were locked on the crumpled remains of a white Ford Falcon.

She knew it was Kimberley's mum's car. But her brain couldn't make the pieces fit. Kim's parents were away for the weekend. Kimberley must have taken it. Must have driven.

The vehicle was mangled: twisted steel and shattered glass scattered across the asphalt like confetti. One door had been ripped clean off. The roof crushed. The front end buckled and bleeding.

Cassie's stomach turned.

"Stay back," Derek's voice rasped. He looked wrecked, his uniform stained, his face drawn. "Cassie... you don't need to see this."

But she did.

Her legs moved of their own accord. Her dad stepped in front of her, but she pushed past.

Kimberley's face flashed in her mind. Laughing. Teasing. Her arm slung around Cassie's shoulders at school.

And then she saw it.

A glimpse of blonde hair through the shattered windscreen.

"Kim..." Cassie's voice broke as her knees gave way.

Her dad caught her before she hit the gravel, strong arms holding her as the sobs came in waves.

"I'm sorry, love," he murmured into her hair. "I'm so sorry."

The world tilted. The friends she'd grown up with, gone in an instant.

And Kimberley...

Cassie had stayed home.

But it hadn't saved her friend.

No mark, no score, no top-tier university offer would ever undo that.

* * *

Cassie's knuckles were white as she gripped the wheel, her eyes fixed on the road. The cross was far behind her, but the ache in her chest clung tight.

"Breathe," she whispered. But the breath caught.

It always did.

By the time she pulled into the driveway, the sun had vanished, leaving only the faint lavender glow of twilight. The house looked just as it always had, solid and familiar. The veranda light blinked to life, casting a warm halo across the path.

Inside, the scent of old wood and beeswax polish wrapped around her like a favourite jumper. The framed photos. Her dad's boots by the door. The familiar creak of floorboards.

She tossed her bag on the bed, her eyes drifting to the patchwork quilt her mum had made years ago.

"Welcome home," she whispered to no one.

Cassie showered, then changed into dark denim jeans and her favourite boots. From the wardrobe, she pulled a long-sleeved black blouse, casual but flattering. She wasn't going to overthink this.

It was just dinner. Just Terence.

She grabbed her grey wool bomber jacket and scribbled a quick note for her mum and left it on the kitchen bench, then paused at the hallway mirror. Her reflection stared back, uncertain.

"Steak and beers," she muttered. "No strings."

But even she didn't believe that.

NINE

The Ploughman's Rest was heaving. Every table in the old country pub was packed, locals in flannelette shirts and dusty work boots mingled with city-weary families, arriving in town in time for dinner and for the Easter school holiday break away. Kids darted happily between tables leaving trails of crumbs and sticky fingerprints. In the corner, a band was tuning up, the gentle hum of conversation swelling as the opening notes of a Paul Kelly classic filled the air.

"How does this compare to pubs in the big smoke?" Terence asked, a teasing glint in his dark eyes as he took a sip of his beer.

"I'll let you know after I've tried the steak," Cassie smiled. Her gaze drifted across the lively room. "I do miss this. There's just a different pace up here. It's nice to slow down once in a while."

Terence chuckled, setting down his glass. "You don't quite come across as someone who lets herself slow down too often."

She hesitated, fingers tracing the rim of her own glass of beer. "Is it that obvious?"

"Only a little."

Cassie exhaled, consciously relaxing the perpetual tension in her shoulders. She liked Terence. He was steady, unpretentious, the kind of man who felt no need to fill silences with meaningless chatter. Something about him was deeply calming, and she wasn't used to calm.

Their food arrived, and for a while they ate quietly, comfortably. The band picked up the tempo, laughter and the clink of glasses blending seamlessly with the music.

"Mum! A boy in the playroom hit me and called Milo a dickhead!" A young girl's voice sliced through the din, pulling Cassie and Terence's attention to a nearby table. A mother stood abruptly, eyes blazing, and charged off with her daughter in tow.

"Don't piss off Mama Bear," Cassie smirked.

Terence chuckled, his eyes sparkling. "Good advice."

Cassie shifted the conversation. "So, tell me something about you, something I don't already know."

Terence smiled warmly. "Alright. I used to be a pretty decent footy player once."

Cassie raised an eyebrow. "Yeah?"

"Yeah. I played for the Echuca Bombers. I thought I might go somewhere with it for a while."

"What happened?"

He shrugged, taking a mouthful of beer. "Life. Injuries forced me to rethink things. I fell into physio and realised I actually preferred helping people heal rather than running them down on a footy field."

Cassie smiled gently and took another sip of her beer. "Your parents must be proud of you."

"Mum is, for sure. Dad passed away when I was young, but I reckon he would be too."

"Oh, I'm sorry, Terence. I didn't realise." Cassie placed her cutlery down gently, her focus entirely on him.

"It's OK," Terence said softly. "It was a long time ago. I was only ten at the time. It's hard to remember much these days, except for photos and videos and stuff. I remember how he made me feel though, you know? That's what's most important."

"Do you feel comfortable telling me a little bit about him?" Cassie asked, leaning into the conversation as though everyone else in the crowded room had now suddenly faded away.

"Of course. As I said, it was a long time ago. Dad worked as a pilot, he had his own small Piper and worked as an air courier of sorts, servicing towns along the Murray and the High Country. He used to take me along sometimes. We'd land at these remote airstrips and camp overnight. Even though I could barely see out the cockpit window, he'd let me take the controls once we were airborne. Being up there, with him, it was the best feeling in the world. Just me and him." Terence's voice faded, his gaze drifting somewhere distant.

Cassie remained quiet, offering space as she always did. People trusted her with their truths. Eventually, Terence continued.

"Mob were great after Dad passed. Mum worked long shifts at the local hospital, not as a nurse like your

Mum, she ran the kitchen, she still does actually, preparing patient meals. Dad was a white fella, but all of Mum's mob are Yorta Yorta, and we always had plenty of aunties, uncles, cousins stepping in whenever we needed. They kept me in line whenever I started getting a bit full of myself," he laughed lightly.

"Is it just you and your Mum?" Cassie asked.

"Nah, I've got an older sister, Jodie. She lives just outside Port Augusta. She's a social worker for an NGO that runs programs out on a big sheep station, for mob coming out of the local prison. They help them find work, housing. Try to keep them out of trouble. Out of jail. That sort of thing."

Cassie felt her walls slowly lower with Terence, wondering why she'd resisted this connection for so long. Maybe it was exactly what she needed right now.

"Hey guys, how's it goin'? I'm so sorry to interrupt," an older waitress with teased, bleached-blonde hair, heavy makeup and a gravely smoker's voice, cut in. "Just lettin' youse know that the kitchen's closing in fifteen minutes if you want dessert."

"No worries, thanks," they both replied as she moved off to the next table.

Terence turned back to Cassie, his smile playful. "What about you, Miss Big Shot Television Journalist, tell me something about yourself."

Cassie scoffed.

"Like what?" she shrugged, returning his smile.

"Well, what kinda music are you into?"

"Music? Wow, OK." Cassie paused, thinking.

"It's a very important question. A second dinner all depends on this answer," his grin beaming.

"Oh really?" Cassie asked, leaning into his playful flirting. "I suppose I'm into a lot of local stuff. Tash Sultana, the Teskey Brothers. A bit of country. I saw Pink in Melbourne a year back, she's incredible. You know what it's like growing up in small towns, you listen to a bit of everything. Dad used to blast us with Dolly Parton when we were younger. He'd call me his little Jolene, because of the colour of my hair and eyes." Cassie laughed softly at the memory.

Terence nodded approvingly.

"Enough? Do I pass the test?" she smirked.

"For now," he said playfully. His face turned curious again. "Tell me about your time at the BBC. Your mum mentioned it, said you covered crime?"

Cassie stiffened slightly, uncomfortable memories flickering behind her eyes. "Yeah, something like that," she murmured, taking a deep sip of beer.

"You don't need to be modest around me," Terence encouraged gently.

Cassie shifted uneasily. "My Auntie Valerie, mum's sister, worked in the newsroom in Glasgow. I was based there for three years and then down in London after that. Trust me, though, it wasn't as glamorous as people imagine." She forced a smile, eager to shift the topic. "Should we get dessert?"

Sensing her discomfort, Terence dropped the topic without fuss. "Apple pie, every time," he smiled softly as Cassie looked down at the menu.

By the time the server cleared their plates, the bistro had largely emptied out. Cassie felt a real connection developing between them and she was certain Terence felt it too. There was no denying her attraction, strong, genuine, and refreshingly uncomplicated. She wasn't ready for the night to end.

Terence glanced down at his smartwatch. "Hey," he said, looking up with a hopeful smile. "There's a cover band playing over at The Royal. Not far, just a short walk, if you're up for it."

Cassie didn't hesitate. "Perfect," she said enthusiastically, warmth flushing her cheeks.

"Great," Terence grinned.

After settling their bill, they stepped out onto the street, now bathed in a passing shower. Cassie instinctively leaned closer to Terence as they dashed across the road, laughter spilling from their lips as they huddled together under awnings and street-side eaves. Tiny fairy lights strung through the trees twinkled in the drizzle, casting gentle golden halos onto the footpath. Cassie slowed her pace, quietly savouring the closeness and feeling oddly grateful for the rain.

The Royal Hotel, a grand old bluestone building, loomed ahead, music pulsing faintly through its thick walls. Terence held open the heavy door as Cassie stepped inside, instantly enveloped by the rhythm and heat of the crowded pub. As they moved into the band room, the volume grew louder, clearer. The dance floor was full, bodies swaying beneath coloured lights as people at tables shouted cheerful conversations above the music. The long bar along one wall had patrons lined up patiently, hands wrapped around glasses or phones.

"Oh, I love this song!" Cassie cried out, grinning as the familiar guitar riff reverberated around the room. Applause rippled through the crowd, and people surged towards the stage. A rich blue spotlight illuminated the lead singer, who launched powerfully into Stevie Nicks' iconic *Edge of Seventeen.*

Terence leaned close, cupping a hand to Cassie's ear. "Do you want another drink?"

Cassie turned toward him, confusion creasing her brow. "Huh?"

He mimed drinking from an invisible glass. Cassie laughed, nodding enthusiastically.

He gave her a thumbs-up, flashing a grin before weaving through the crowd toward the bar. Cassie lingered at the edge of the dancing bodies, a contented warmth flooding her chest. She couldn't remember the last time she'd felt this genuinely happy and relaxed in the moment. Nights like this had become distant memories, replaced by quiet evenings alone or low-key gatherings at Inside Out. Tonight was different. Real, vibrant, and completely removed from her usual routine.

When Terence returned, Cassie downed her drink quickly, a pleasant but all too familiar buzz humming through her veins. She closed her eyes for a moment, breathing deeply, letting the music sweep her up.

Standing here, she wasn't thinking about Hayden Foster and the threat of the Allied Patriots. Nor did Kimberley Taylor haunt her thoughts, that sad memorial cross along the road momentarily forgotten. Even the quiet dread of her dad's illness receded into shadow.

Here, in this pulsing room of music and movement, Cassie just danced, allowing herself, finally, to let go.

* * *

Tap, tap, tap.

The sound was unfamiliar but relentless. As Cassie drifted awake, her senses stirred, an odd tapping noise, a foul smell, bursts of hot air against her face. Realizing the bed wasn't hers, she froze.

A thin sliver of sunlight bled through the blinds, outlining vague shapes around her. She turned her head, coming face-to-face with wide, dark eyes, just inches away.

Her breath caught sharply. The tapping accelerated, followed by a giant, hot pink tongue slapping her face.

Cassie yelped, jerking backward. Her reaction excited the intruder further, tail thumping rhythmically against the blinds: tap, tap, tap.

"Rusty! *Rusty!*" A familiar voice called from beyond the door, footsteps hurrying. Terence appeared, exasperated. "Rusty, get out!"

The dog obeyed, bolting out instantly.

"Are you okay?" Terence asked, rubbing the back of his neck sheepishly.

Cassie stretched, smiling. "I'm fine."

"Sorry," he chuckled. "Breakfast?"

Cassie followed Terence into the bright, open living area, squinting against the flood of sunlight. Her head throbbed, a reminder of the previous night, but the savoury scent of breakfast promised relief.

Rusty reappeared, bounding toward Cassie, tail whipping furiously.

"Rusty!" Terence scolded.

"He's fine," Cassie reassured, bending to pat him. Rusty wriggled excitedly, his tan body marked with a black face, white chest and white markings on each of his four paws.

"I love Boxers," Cassie said, laughing as Rusty reared up, placing paws on her chest.

"Rusty, down!" Terence commanded, guiding him outside.

"Sorry again," Terence sighed, sliding the door shut.

Cassie laughed.

Terence's home was spotless, except for the crumpled sleeping bag on the couch. Hardwood floors stretched through to the kitchen, accented by a vintage rug. Open bookshelves lined warm off-white-coloured walls, and a faded *Echuca Bitter* sign dominated the living room.

This was the nicest bachelor pad she'd seen, Cassie thought, amused.

"I hope you're hungry," Terence said, plating poached eggs and bacon onto thickly cut buttered white toast.

"Starving," Cassie replied, sliding onto a bar stool at the kitchen bench. "This looks amazing."

"Coffee?" Terence placed a French press in front of her, retrieving milk from the fridge.

Cassie raised an impressed eyebrow. "Ah, *yes please*." She sliced into her egg, golden yolk spilling onto toast.

Terence smiled.

"I hope the bed was comfy enough and yes, I took the couch."

Cassie hesitated. "Look, about last night. I don't remember a lot. It's been a while since I drank that much…"

"Relax," Terence teased gently. "You were fine. Except maybe for when you started dancing on the tables…"

Cassie's eyes widened. "I didn't…"

"No," Terence laughed. "I'm kidding."

"Cruel." Cassie groaned playfully, shaking her head, quickly. Cassie devoured her breakfast in no time, Terence looking on impressed with her appetite. "Oh shit, is that the time?" she asked, noticing the clock on the kitchen wall. She shoved the last mouthful of yolk-soaked toast into her mouth before climbing down from the stool and looking around the room.

"It fell out of your pocket. I put it next to the bed." Terence said, knowing exactly what she was looking for.

Without hesitation, she headed back into the bedroom, grabbed her phone and sat on the bed, scrolling. "Dad's already been discharged apparently," she called out.

"Yeah, I heard," came the reply from the kitchen.

There was a missed call and a follow up text, both from Brian. "Call me when you get this," it read. Cassie hit the name on the message above and the phone started to ring. One, two, three rings. "C'mon Bri," Cassie said. "Hi, you've reached…" Cassie hung up impatiently. She tried again, but again the phone went to voicemail.

"Everything OK?" Terence asked, as he hung his head around the corner of the bedroom door. "Yeah, all good. Hey Terence, would you be able to drop me back to my car? It's our annual Murphy family Good Friday BBQ, and with Dad now home…"

"Of course. And, um…"

Cassie stilled. "Yeah?"

"I didn't mention it last night, but yesterday at the hospital, before you got there…"

"*Yeah*…"

"Your Mum kinda invited me to the BBQ as well."

Cassie rolled her eyes. "Of course she did."

"I'm sorry, I should have said something sooner, I just, I didn't even think about it to be honest. And look, I've got plenty to get on with today if…"

"No." Cassie said happily. "Dad would be happy if you were there."

"Well, as long as your *dad* is happy," Terence murmured cheekily.

"Don't push your luck," she grinned. "Can I use your shower?"

"Yeah of course, just in there," he said, gesturing. "Just wait, I'll grab you a clean towel."

Terence's shiny grey dual cab Hilux Ute sat gleaming in the driveway. The lawn was patchy, yellow in places and the garden slightly overgrown; a row of old rose bushes bordered the concrete driveway from the lawn.

The house itself was a white weatherboard, and yet despite its age and wear, there was something about this house that felt comfortable; lived in.

"The garden's a bit of a mess," Terence admitted. "That's next on the list, after painting the house."

99

Standing barefoot, holding her boots, soaking in the cozy comfort of the moment, Cassie just smiled. "I love it."

Terence smiled that big cheeky smile as he opened the car door. "Jump in."

TEN

By the time Terence pulled in behind Cassie at 27 Drysdale Street, the driveway was already blocked by Nick's black Nissan Pathfinder, and Bernadette's old Toyota Land Cruiser Prado parked beyond that. The Murphy family home, Federation styled with red brick and a burgundy tin roof, stood proudly, its veranda wrapped in ornamental grapevine now in full autumnal glory, its leaves deepening into purples and reds.

More Federation and Victorian-period houses lined the mature tree-filled streets of Heathton Ridge, imported oaks, elms, and maples standing proudly on quarter-acre blocks. The main road in and out of town was flanked by towering poplars, planted to honour local soldiers lost in past wars. Larger blocks sat on the outskirts, dotted with fibro and weatherboard homes built later, buffering the town from the surrounding farmland and vineyards.

The nearest township to the north had been built on gold money during the rush of the 1800s, grand sandstone facades and neat miners' cottages. But Heathton Ridge had grown from cattle farming, out on the flats, with the township built into the foothills of the Stanley Ranges. In recent decades, much of the grazing land had been sold to winemakers. The region's fertile ground had attracted both big-name and boutique vineyards, which brought with them a steady stream of tourists. The town's population, usually around 3,000, felt nearly double that during school holidays and long weekends. Locals welcomed the new money but remained quietly suspicious of 'out-of-towners,' as they always had.

The Murphy family Good Friday BBQ was the same every year. Derek Murphy, though descended from Irish Catholics, had only ever kept up appearances of the faith for the sake of small-town airs and graces. Religion had never been part of household life growing up, though for whatever reason, they still observed the fish-only rule for their Good Friday lunch. Derek would cook king prawns and barramundi on the BBQ, while Bernadette would roast vegetables and prepare her famous potato salad.

In recent years, Cassie's brother, Nick, had taken over the grill, working side by side with their dad, who was only too happy to pass the tongs along. The family would all meet again for a big, cooked roast lunch on Easter Sunday, but it was the Good Friday BBQs Cassie looked forward to the most.

Cassie could already smell the BBQ as she and Terence made their way up the driveway, skipping the front door and heading through the side gate into the backyard. She braced herself for the looks she knew were coming. Her younger brother, technically an adult, had never truly grown up.

Sure enough, Nick spotted them first. He turned from the BBQ, short spiky hair, tongs in one hand and a beer in the other, grinning like a ten-year-old who'd just let one rip in church.

"Oh, hello," he said, with a smirk. He set his beer down and reached out to shake Terence's hand.

"G'day Nick, how's it going mate?" Terence said, always effortlessly polite.

"They're here!" Bernadette's voice called from inside the house. Despite almost forty years in Australia, her thick Scottish accent was unmistakable, as Terence made his way up the back steps.

"G'day Mrs Murphy!" he called out.

Cassie was left standing alone with Nick, who immediately pulled a crude gesture with his tongue.

"Oh, grow up," she muttered. He just laughed harder.

Cassie then turned to follow Terence through the back door and into the house. Nick's wife, Rebecca, or Bec as she preferred, was perched on the couch, gently patting baby Olivia on the back. The little one's squished, wrinkly face peeked over her mum's shoulder, bleary-eyed and floppy with sleep.

"Hey Cassie, it's good to see you," Bec said with a smile.

"Hi Bec," Cassie replied, leaning in to kiss her on the cheek. "And hello to you, beautiful girl," she added, as Bec turned to give her a better look at Olivia.

"Here, you want to hold her for a bit? She's just had a feed, so she's a bit milk-drunk," Bec said, already lifting the baby into Cassie's arms.

"Thank you, Terence, my love!" Bernadette called out from the kitchen as Terence reappeared, balancing two full salad bowls covered in plastic cling-wrap and a roll of paper towel under one arm like a contestant in some kind of domestic relay.

"Cassie, get the door!" her mum barked.

"I'm holding Olivia!" Cassie snapped.

"It's okay, I've got it," Bec said, already on her feet. "Here, let me take one of those," she offered, grabbing one of the salad bowls and following Terence back outside.

Derek had always taken pride in the upkeep of the garden and lawns, but the inside of the Murphy house was Bernadette's domain. Unlike some of the more easy-going members of the Country Women's Association, whose homes leaned into that lived-in, farmhouse clutter, Bernadette kept a tight rein on aesthetics. Her style was country classic, not country chaos.

The polished wooden floorboards gleamed. Antique rosewood dressers sat alongside mid-century couches upholstered in floral fabric. The walls were painted a soft latte-cream, the ceilings crisp white. Ornate ceiling roses held delicate chandeliers, and picture rails displayed a careful curation of family photographs and local art. It flirted with museum-like perfection, but modern touches kept it warm, comfortable, lived in.

Cassie had butted heads with her mother over the years, usually about the state of her own bedroom or the trail of mess she left in her wake. Bernadette wasn't uptight, but she *was* proud. There was a difference.

"Where's Dad?" Cassie asked as her Mum approached, Cassie awkwardly resting Olivia on her chest. "He's resting in the bedroom. Don't disturb him just yet, he'll be out in a minute."

"How is he?"

"He's OK. Just a bit tired after yesterday. You know what hospitals are like, you never sleep well." Bernadette leant in, gently wrapping her fingers around her granddaughter's tiny hand.

"Why don't you put the telly on for her? Go on, the Good Friday Appeal should be on by now."

She moved away and grabbed the remote from the coffee table and flicked the TV on.

"Mum, she's four months old. She doesn't want to watch the Good Friday Appeal. Put *Bluey* on or something," Cassie said, eyebrows raised.

"Oh, come on, you used to *love* watching this when you were little," Bernadette called over her shoulder as she vanished back into the kitchen.

Cassie sighed and flopped back onto the couch, lifting Olivia up so their noses touched. "Your nanna's a little bit crazy kid, you'll get to learn that" she murmured in baby talk.

"I heard that!" came the reply from the kitchen.

The Royal Children's Hospital telethon had been running longer than Cassie had been alive. Every Good Friday, celebrities, community groups, real estate agents, and AFL players would crawl out of the woodwork to auction off homes, sign footy jumpers, sing novelty songs, and do live crosses to fundraising sausage sizzles across the state. Meanwhile, a room full of exhausted volunteers took donation calls from people desperate to have their call answered by one of the many television personalities on hand.

"Are you getting clucky?" Terence asked, strolling in from outside.

Cassie laughed. "Yeah, no," she said firmly. "But she *is* pretty bloody cute," she added, giving Olivia a smile as the baby beamed and kicked her legs in delight.

"Oh my God!" Cassie suddenly blurted, eyes locked on the TV. "Here, take her!" She practically launched Olivia into Terence's arms and grabbed the remote, cranking the volume.

"Get the *fuck* out!" she burst out, laughing.

"Cassie! Watch your language in front of the baby!" came an angry cry from the kitchen.

On screen, Jessica Brady was interviewing someone Cassie vaguely recognised, some soapie actor, maybe *Home & Away*? It wasn't the actor that caught her attention, though, it was the man sitting behind them in the call room, front and centre, decked out in oversized novelty sunglasses and a *blinding* yellow feather boa.

Brian Cheng.

"What is it?" Terence asked, expertly settling Olivia against his shoulder and patting her back like he'd done it a hundred times before.

"It's Brian, my colleague. *There*! With the ridiculous glasses and the feather thing! What is he doing?" Cassie said, practically doubled over. "Peter is going to *kill* him if he sees this!" The pair sat in silence as Cassie just shook her head in amusement.

"Lunch is up!" Nick called from out the back.

"Terence, can you give me a hand with the rest of this, please?" Bernadette asked, poking her head into the lounge room, bottle of tomato sauce in hand.

"Sure thing," he said, passing Olivia back in Cassie's direction.

"I've got her," said Bec, appearing again through the rear fly-screen door. "Thanks, Terence. You look *very* comfortable with her," she added, giving Cassie a cheeky grin. "I might see if she'll go down for a bit."

"There she is," came another voice, from the hallway this time.

"Dad!" Cassie said, forgetting all about Brian Cheng as she stood to meet her father's hug.

"Hello, my beautiful girl."

"How are you feeling?" she asked, stepping back.

"A bit sore today, actually, but nothing a good feed won't fix," he said, nodding toward the flow of plates, cutlery, and condiments being ferried out the back.

"C'mon," he added with a soft smile.

As they walked toward the back door, Derek whispered, "It's nice to see young Terence here too."

"Don't you start," Cassie replied, returning his grin.

The sky overhead was a patchwork of puffy clouds with just enough blue to make sitting outside under the pergola worthwhile. The recycled brick paving beneath them had been laid in a herringbone pattern, and a large timber table sat square in the centre, surrounded by weathered garden chairs. Beyond that, the freshly mowed lawn framed a lush garden of both natives and European favourites, Bernadette's Pierre de Ronsard roses curled up one of the pergola posts, their dusty-pink blooms catching the light.

"Mate, you've outdone yourself," Terence said as Nick laid down a platter of barbecued seafood in the middle of the table.

"Thanks, mate! Try one of the prawn skewers, they've been marinating overnight in lime and chilli."

"Are they King?" Bernadette asked, leaning forward for a closer look.

"Nah, Tiger. I couldn't get any Kings this year," Nick replied, handing Terence a beer as he took his seat.

"Dig in, everyone," he said with satisfaction.

The table filled with the happy chaos of eating, forks scraping plates, conversation bubbling, laughter carrying over the fence lines. Cassie glanced across at Terence, who was deep in quiet conversation with her dad. The sight caught her off guard, not because it was unusual, but because it felt *right*. The sense of ease, of belonging, washed over her unexpectedly. She smiled.

"So, what's this story your mum says you're working on now?" Bec asked, helping herself to another scoop of Bernadette's famous potato salad.

"Are you still chasing the Allied Patriots?" Nick chimed in.

All eyes turned to Cassie.

"Yeah. Though we've had to pivot a bit since Hayden Foster's murder earlier this week," she said.

"So, it *is* murder, then?" Derek asked, his brow creasing with concern.

Cassie nodded, mouth full of grilled eggplant. "Mm-hmm."

"VicPol won't get too involved," Nick said, shrugging. "We'll just let them kill each other off like they usually do. Saves us the trouble."

Cassie shook her head. "I dunno, Nick. This doesn't feel like it came from inside the Patriots."

"Course it did," Nick said, reaching for a prawn. "They're known for firebombing shit. Foster just pissed off the wrong person, that's all."

"Actually, Dad, I wanted to ask you something." Cassie said.

"Oh yeah?" replied her father, leaning in.

Just then, Olivia's wail cut through the air from inside the house.

"Sorry, everyone. I knew she wouldn't stay down for long," Bec said, already rising from her seat.

"Bring her out here, love. I'll nurse her," Bernadette offered with a warm smile.

"Terence, you want another beer?" Nick asked.

"Yeah, cheers, mate."

Nick disappeared toward the spare fridge in the carport as Bec ducked back inside.

"Go on, Cassie," Derek prompted.

"Your old mate, Graham Golding…"

"*Graham Golding!*" Bernadette shrieked before Cassie could finish. "He's no mate of your father's! We can't *stand* that man!"

"I was being sarcastic, Mum," Cassie deadpanned.

"What's he got to do with anything?" Bernadette demanded.

"Nothing directly to do with this case. His name just came up when I was looking into where Hayden

Foster grew up. I guess I just wanted to know why you two disliked him so much."

"Because the man's a *pig*, that's why!" Bernadette snapped.

Derek sighed. "OK, Bernadette, can I get a word in?"

"You know we went to his wife's funeral last year?" she pushed on, undeterred.

"You *did*?" Cassie asked, genuinely surprised.

"Yes. Anne. Lovely woman. What she ever saw in that man, I'll never understand, he was always so revolting to her, he's one of those men who hates women." Bernadette said with a shake of her head. "I met her quite a few times at different police things your dad would drag me to over the years."

"You never told me you went to her funeral."

"I think you were overseas at the time, working on some story."

Cassie nodded slowly, piecing it together.

"Did you know her parents were famous Dutch academics? *Very* wealthy." Bernadette continued, undeterred. "She was a college principal at one point, too. Their daughter works at Harvard over in America now. Very clever girl. *Hates* her father though. Remember that, Derek?" she said raising her voice.

"I'm not deaf, Berni," he muttered.

"She wouldn't even sit anywhere near him at the funeral!"

"Hmmm," Cassie murmured, chewing on the thought.

"Who are you talking about?" Nick asked as he returned to the table, two bottles of Carlton Draught in hand.

"Graham Golding," Cassie replied.

"You're not still going on about him, are you? Is this because of what he said about you on TV that one time?"

Cassie shot him a glare. "The guy's an arsehole."

Nick bristled. "He just says what everyone else is thinking but don't have the balls to say. That doesn't make him an arsehole. Living in Melbourne's turned you into a woke leftie."

"Woke?" Cassie's voice rose. "Are you fucking serious?"

"Oh, for God's sake, you two," Bernadette snapped, exasperated. "Don't start. You're like children sometimes, the pair of you."

"He started it!" Cassie fired back, then turned on her brother. "And this has nothing to do with being left or right. It's about integrity. People like Graham Golding deliberately set out to create division, and you're proving my point."

Nick just shook his head. "I know you're no fan either, Dad, but everyone at the station wishes he was still in the force. We need someone tough like that again. Now we just pander to criminals. They get more rights than the victims."

"Well… that I agree with you on," Cassie muttered.

"I agree," Derek said, his voice calm but firm. "But we don't need men like Graham Golding back in the force. He was as dirty as they come."

"How so?" Cassie asked, leaning in.

Derek exhaled slowly. "For starters, the only person Graham Golding ever gave a damn about was Graham Golding. Don't be fooled by all that 'tough on crime' bullshit. For him, it was all about power. Divide the public, make them afraid, then position himself as the only one who could fix it.

"That's the real reason why he never became commissioner. Or State Premier. He was too much, even for the conservatives.

"He said whatever needed to be said to make himself look good. He cavorted with crooks. Planted evidence. Manipulated witnesses. He was dangerous. We don't need men like that anywhere near the badge."

He turned to Nick. "You can take that back to the boys at the station, and you'd do well to remember it yourself."

"And girls," Cassie added.

"What's that?" her dad said.

"I said *and girls*. Women. Policewomen. It's not just the boys."

Derek nodded. "Well, I doubt any of them are singing Golding's praises. Your mother's right, he was a very sexist man."

"*Sexist?*" Bernadette cut in. "He was a *misogynist. Homophobe. Racist.* The bloody lot."

"That's my cue," Nick muttered, annoyed, rising from the table and snatching up the empty foil trays. "Thanks for the lunch."

He disappeared into the house without looking back.

Cassie sat largely in silence, as her mother moved the topic onto her roses, before baby Olivia made her reappearance and was passed around to everyone for one last cuddle. Plates scraped clean, the buzz of the day easing into a mellow afternoon hum.

Retreating inside, Cassie reached for her mobile phone, which she had left on one of the living room dressers when she had first arrived. Six missed calls, all from Brian. She sat on one of the armchairs in the corner of the room and dialled.

"Cassie?" he answered straight away.

"Brian, Peter is going to kill you!" she started to laugh, ready to tell him that she had seen him on Channel Seven earlier.

"Cass, they've brought someone in for questioning over Foster's death," he said, dismissing her. Something in his voice, low, tight, serious, cut through her.

She sat up straighter. "Who?"

"His name's Jack Mead."

Cassie blinked. "Wait… Mead? As in…"

"Belinda's son."

Cassie's breath caught.

"Jesus Christ," she muttered.

Cassie ran a hand through her hair, heart thudding.

"Cass… I know you're on leave, but this is going to blow up. The press are already scrambling. Now you've met with Belinda, I thought you'd wanna know asap."

She paused, looking across the room at Terence and her family, all happily chatting with one another as they helped clean up.

"I'm on my way."

ELEVEN

The small rumble came at that moment when every fibre of her body had finally surrendered to the deepest sleep, the kind she'd been desperately craving. For the second time in less than 24 hours, Cassie's slumber was being interrupted by something unfamiliar.

There it was again. And again.

She was so comfortable, so unconscious, her brain fought to convince her that the rumble was part of the dream, that the dream was real, and that she should just stay there. And then, silence. Her body relaxed, sinking deeper into the bed.

But within seconds, it was back, rumbling madly beside her.

This time, Cassie's mind surrendered. The dream fell away, and the vibration persisted, relentless.

As tempting as it had been to stay in Heathton Ridge, Cassie's head was now fully back in the story. And more importantly, back with Belinda Mead. The last thing Belinda needed, or deserved, was another media frenzy dragging her through the mud. Especially after what happened last time.

And Jack? It made sense, on paper, that the son of a woman brutally raped might go after the man responsible. But why now?

Cassie had tried calling Belinda during the four-hour drive back to Melbourne but got nothing. She did manage to speak with Brian again, and one of her VicPol contacts. Though, not much was being said yet.

By the time she returned to her apartment in Elwood, the exhaustion hit hard. The drive, the day, the night before, the emotional whiplash, it all caught up to her. She barely had the energy to make toast for dinner before collapsing into bed, her phone still in hand as she scrolled endlessly for updates on Jack Mead.

But now, something was pulling her back from sleep. Relentless. Unforgiving.

Groaning, Cassie pried her eyes open. A soft glow pulsed from the bedside table, her phone, vibrating. Again.

Without looking at the name, she hit the green button, just to make it stop.

"Cassie!" came the voice on the other end. Brian. His voice was breathless, and there was chaos behind him, sirens, shouting, radios.

"Cassie? Are you there?" he yelled.

She glanced at the screen. 1:33am.

"I'm here," she croaked. "What's going on? Where are you?"

"I can't hear you properly, hang on..." The line crackled. "I'm sorry to wake you, but I thought you'd want to know."

Cassie was already reaching for the lamp, flipping the switch. "Brian. What is it?"

"I'm at the Progress Australia offices in Richmond," he shouted.

"Get back please, sir!" came another voice in the background, firm, authoritative. Police.

"It's totally engulfed. Firebombed."

"What?" Cassie shot upright. "Wait, wait…" She threw off the covers and swung her legs out of bed.

She shuffled through the dark toward the kitchen, flicking on the overhead light. The long fluorescent bulb buzzed to life as she passed into the living room, still a mess of clothes, newspapers and takeout boxes. She dug between the cushions trying to find the TV remote.

Progress Australia.

Cassie had been to their national office in Richmond once before; an old, converted warehouse, now a hub for progressive social policy advocacy. The group had been instrumental in pushing reforms at all levels of government. Naturally, it had made enemies. Especially among the Allied Patriots.

"Cassie, are you still there?" Brian asked.

"Yeah, I'm here. Sorry, go on."

"The fire's massive, I've never seen anything like it." He paused. "But it's not just here, Cass. The new Islamic Centre in Melton's been hit too."

"*What?*" she gasped.

"Cassie?" Brian's voice broke through again.

"I heard you!" she said, louder now, pulse racing.

The newly opened Melbourne Islamic Cultural Centre. It wasn't just a mosque, it housed a museum and art gallery, the first of its kind in the southern hemisphere. The State Premier had committed tens of millions in funding to its construction, touting it as a national symbol of cultural unity. Predictably, it had been a lightning rod for protestors, many of them linked to the Allied Patriots. And now, this?

This had retaliation written all over it.

Cassie shoved aside containers and papers on the couch, finally finding the remote. She flicked on the TV.

Nothing.

The ABC was still running its flagship music video program, *Rage*, as it always had in the dead of night. Tori Amos appeared onscreen, fiery curls flying as she spun in slow motion across a desert playground.

Cassie shook her head.

"Bri, are you doing a piece to camera? There's nothing on the TV yet."

"No, but we've got crews heading to both sites. Progress is just around the corner from Jess's place, we heard the sirens and ran down. It's big, Cass."

"Progress Australia and the Islamic Centre. No prizes for who's behind this," Cassie muttered, rising from the couch and heading into the kitchen, flicking on the kettle.

"Well, that's why I thought you'd want to know!" Brian called down the line, his voice almost lost in the noise behind him. "Cass, they're pushing us back further. I've gotta go. We should have footage up on News24 soon."

"Hey, stay safe, OK? Text me any updates!" she shouted.

"I can't really hear you, Cass!"

"Stay safe!" she repeated, before the call dropped.

As she waited for the kettle to boil, Cassie scrolled through social media. Nothing. No images. No shaky phone footage. No updates. Just the usual noise.

She poured herself a cup of tea, padding back to the couch. For a moment she considered heading to Richmond herself, but the exhaustion won. Instead, she curled up, cup in hand, surrounded by clutter and half-folded laundry.

On screen, Tori Amos was back, this time all in white, seated at a white piano in a stark white room. That fiery orange hair was even more vivid now, the only colour on screen. Cassie blinked, then switched over to News24.

Still nothing.

She sipped the tea, pulled her legs beneath her, and let her body sink into the couch. Just a quick nap, she told herself. She flicked back over to *Rage* and closed her eyes.

* * *

It was the noise that woke her.

Her eyes shot open, heart racing. Despite the kitchen light still buzzing and the low hum of the TV, she'd drifted off again. But outside, it was still night. No morning light. And now, shouting? Sirens?

She muted the TV. Listened. The yelling was closer now. Sirens, louder.

Cassie bolted to the front door and flung it open.

Smoke hit her immediately, hot and acrid, punching the air from her lungs. The sirens were deafening now, approaching fast.

She shoved her feet into sneakers, grabbed her phone and keys, and slammed the door behind her. Bounding down the bricked staircase and out onto the footpath, she arrived just in time to see the flashing lights of a fire truck scream past the intersection at the top of her street, heading straight for Elwood Village.

"Fuck," she breathed, her legs already moving.

She hadn't even thought about where she was running, or what could be burning. A house? A shop? A unit? She wasn't even thinking about Brian's call. She just ran.

The fire truck had stopped on the wrong side of the road, hoses unspooling as firefighters shouted to one another. The street was already filling with people: pyjamas, dressing gowns, tracksuits, blinking and dazed in the flickering light.

Cassie pushed through the crowd, and then…

She saw it.

The shriek tore out of her before she could stop it.

Inside Out was ablaze.

For a split second, her brain tried to convince her it was another dream. All that talk of fire, Tori Amos' flame-red hair dancing across her screen, somehow her subconscious had conjured this.

But dreams didn't *smell* like this. Dreams didn't *sound* like this.

"Get back!" a firefighter barked, herding the crowd onto the footpath across the road.

Even from there, Cassie could feel the heat, *radiant, furious*. She thought of the country bonfires back in the Ridge. Those fires were warm, safe. This one was alive. *Angry*.

The windows crackled and fizzed. Flames hissed from every opening, licking the awnings. Glass popped and exploded. Cassie's skin stung with the heat as smoke swirled upward, lit orange by the blaze, a twisted corkscrew of fire and ash.

And then…

BOOM.

The upstairs windows shattered, sending shards of glass and a burst of flame out into the street. The crowd gasped as one.

"Jason!" Cassie cried, panic rising in her throat. Where was he?

More sirens. More lights. Two additional fire trucks. Police. An ambulance.

Cassie's phone vibrated like it was trying to leap from her pocket. She yanked it out.

"Brian!" she yelled into the phone.

"Cassie?!"

"I'm here, in Elwood! It's the Inside Out. *Fuck!*"

"I know, we just heard. You're actually *there*?"

She didn't answer, nodding instinctively. "Listen, Cass, I'm going to head your way with one of the crew. Can you do a piece to camera?"

SMASH!

Another pane of glass hit the pavement. A deep boom from somewhere inside. Smoke alarms from neighbouring shops screamed as firefighters swarmed.

"Cass?!"

"I'll call you back," she snapped, frantically looking for Jason.

Water burst from one of the hoses, striking the flames through the shattered windows. The fire hissed and fought back, but slowly, smoke began to shift: black to grey, then white. The blaze was retreating.

Cassie spotted a firefighter retrieving an axe from the truck.

"Hey! *HEY!*" she shouted, rushing toward him.

"Get back!" he barked, pointing to the footpath.

"There's a man who lives upstairs, Jason! Did you get him out?"

"*BACK!*" he shouted again, before disappearing into the chaos.

Cassie hesitated, then stepped back.

"Hey!" came a voice behind her, gentle this time. A hand on her shoulder.

She turned to see a young woman, a hoodie thrown over her nightie.

"Jason's OK," the woman smiled. "He got out."

"What?" Cassie shouted.

"*Jason!*" the woman said louder, pointing toward the second-hand bookshop nearby.

Cassie turned and there they were. Ambulance officers, a policewoman, a handful of bystanders. One of them cradled a small dog.

"Moira Rose," Cassie breathed, rushing over.

"I'm sorry, you can't be here," said the young police officer, stepping in her path.

"Jason!" she called out.

There he was, seated inside the doorway to the shop, slumped on a chair, breathing through an oxygen mask. He was covered in black soot, wearing only boxer shorts and a white blanket wrapped around him. He didn't look up.

"I said move on," the officer repeated.

"Alright! *Jesus*." Cassie snapped.

She backed off, still craning for one last glimpse. Above, the heavy drone of the police helicopter closed in, VicPol Air Wing, low and deliberate, hovering like a wasp, trailing a low, creeping dread. Its spotlight beamed down, turning night into day. Further out, another chopper circled, Nine News.

Cassie checked her phone. 2:47am. Five missed calls. All Brian.

The flames were still in retreat. But the smoke, *thick, white, angry,* pulsed into the night sky.

She ducked into a nearby driveway and called him.

"Cass! Are you OK?"

"Yeah, I'm fine. A bit shaken. Where are you?"

"We're almost there. We just hit Elwood. Can we get through?"

"No. The police have blocked both ends. Head down Ormonde Esplanade, then come up my street. Park outside my place, it's only a short walk."

"Got it. We'll see you soon."

Cassie waited at the top of her street as Brian and Gary the cameraman sprinted past. She didn't follow. Instead, she turned and walked back to her apartment, stripping off her smoke-saturated clothes the second she stepped inside.

She showered, filled the kettle, and slumped back onto the couch, but her body still hummed with adrenaline. Every time she blinked, Jason's face came back to her, blackened with soot, eyes glazed with shock, his breath rasping through an oxygen mask. She thought about Inside Out, always a haven of happy faces and noise, now reduced to a smouldering heap. Gone. The thought made her stomach twist.

She reached for her phone, thumb moving automatically. The feeds were now flooded with live footage of the blaze, shaky mobile clips of the crowd, endless chatter dissecting what little anyone knew. Cassie scrolled, numb, until the News24 live update cut away mid-sentence.

A new text flashed on her screen.

Peter Draper.

TWELVE

Cassie glanced at the time. Already after nine. "Shit," she groaned, summoning every ounce of motivation to peel herself off the couch and drag her weary limbs toward the bathroom. She'd showered just a few hours earlier, yet the acrid smell of smoke lingered stubbornly in her nostrils. Hot water cascaded over her aching body, momentarily washing away some of the exhaustion. But the images, the roaring flames, the panicked shouts, remained vivid, replaying on a relentless loop inside her head.

Peter's message had been brief: *Spoke with Brian. Heard you were onsite in Elwood. Hope you're OK! Briefing newsroom at 10am.* It was unusual for her boss to text in the middle of the night, but nothing about the past twenty-four hours, or this entire week, had been normal.

Cassie wasn't up for traffic this morning, but she'd forgotten it was Easter Saturday. The roads were mercifully quiet as she cruised down St Kilda Road, empty roadworks, barely another car in sight.

She hadn't checked the forecast, but Melbourne was pulling its usual autumn trick, lulling everyone into winter mode before throwing a curveball.

Temperatures were tipped to soar back towards thirty over the weekend.

People were starting to linger in parks, takeaway coffees in hand, strolling lazily beneath the mild sun. No urgency. Nowhere important to be. It was as if the day itself had already forgotten the horrors of the night before.

She needed coffee.

Jason.

Cassie flinched as the memory hit, a jolt of guilt and frustration flooding her body.

She parked out front today, the street littered with empty parking bays.

"For fuck's sake," she muttered, patting herself down frantically as she stood on the footpath outside. Her ID pass. Of course. It lay abandoned somewhere in her apartment, overlooked in the sleepy haze that had accompanied her stumble to the car. Peering through the glass doors of the building, Cassie waved impatiently at one of the weekend security guards, who rose from his desk with deliberate slowness and shuffled toward her.

"Good morning," he said formally, oblivious to her simmering impatience.

Thankfully, Brian was waiting in the lobby, leaping to his feet as Cassie entered. He looked every bit as exhausted as she felt. "Have you even been home yet?" she asked, already knowing the answer from the overpowering smell of smoke clinging to his clothes.

Brian shook his head, yawning. "Figured I'd wait until after this briefing. What a night, huh?"

"Is Peter in?" Cassie asked, steering them toward the open staircase and beginning her ascent.

"He's been here for a while already. So has most of the news team. It's running on all the international networks too. The BBC and CNN have already interviewed VicPol command, and the PM is due to speak shortly."

"Jesus," Cassie muttered. "Well, that figures. I expect the PM will call this an act of terrorism."

"That's what we're expecting," Brian replied as they pushed open the doors to the newsroom. "Someone died last night in those fires too."

Cassie's heart skipped a beat. Jason? Had he succumbed to his injuries? Surely not. "Who?" she snapped urgently.

"Cassandra!" Peter Draper's firm voice cut through the room as he stood in his office doorway, motioning her over. Cassie shot Brian a pleading glance as she moved towards Peter. "Who?" she repeated anxiously.

"A cleaner at the Progress Australia offices," Brian shot back.

Cassie nodded slowly, a sense of uncomfortable relief washing through her as she stepped into Peter's office. He closed the door behind her. "Take a seat," he said.

"Firstly, how are you?" he asked, leaning against his desk. "Brian mentioned you know the business owner of the café in Elwood?"

"Yes, Jason Turner, he and his partner Amir, both own it. And I'm fine. Just pissed off with these bastards," she said, scowling.

"They certainly made their mark last night, that's for sure. I spoke with James Lawrence this morning, the Federal Police are stepping in to work alongside VicPol. The word is that the PM has requested US intelligence on the Patriots. We already know funding for these guys is coming from the States, so the orders for last night's attacks may have originated there as well."

"Have they arrested anyone?" Cassie asked sharply.

"Not yet. The arsonists themselves will just be the usual street-level thugs, probably teenagers, either hired cheaply or promised mateship and respect from the Patriots. You know how these groups work."

"*The Lost Boys*," Cassie murmured.

"The what?"

"Nothing," Cassie replied quickly.

"Look, sorry for dragging you in this morning. Truthfully, we've had a rush of new information since I messaged you overnight, but your input in the briefing would still be valuable. Unfortunately, this is likely to put your sex worker contact even more in the spotlight..."

"Belinda. Her name's Belinda," Cassie interrupted. "And she's not a sex worker. She's actually a well-respected lawyer."

"Sorry, Belinda. Well, they've released her son without charge, but the tabloids are already circling. They're suggesting he's Hayden Foster's son. Do you know anything about that?"

"*What?* No. *Really?* They've released him? And no, she never said anything about her son being Hayden's. Is that true?" Cassie fired back.

"No idea. It's what's being reported this morning. Anyway, we should get started. I want everyone ready when the PM speaks, which…" he glanced at his computer screen, "should be in about half an hour. Tracey and a crew are already onsite at VicPol Command where the press conference will take place, but we'll dial her in for this briefing."

"Okay," Cassie nodded. "Whatever I can do to help."

As they filed back into the newsroom, Peter guided his team with the steady professionalism Cassie had come to respect, and expect, from him. No sensationalism, just facts.

Cassie listened carefully as details emerged about the overnight attacks. A fourth assault had failed disastrously: a Molotov cocktail thrown at a Greens MP's office had bounced off the front window and instead hit the masked assailant, engulfing him in flames. CCTV footage showed him desperately stripping off burning clothes before escaping in a stolen car, later found burnt out.

The cleaner who had died at Progress Australia was a Syrian refugee, tragically caught on CCTV trying to fight the blaze before being overwhelmed by smoke.

When her turn came, Cassie felt strangely detached. She kept much of her conversation with Belinda private but shared what Jason had told her about previous threats from the Patriots. As she spoke, a persistent unease gnawed at her, something still didn't fit.

After the briefing, she and Brian stepped out into the corridor, away from the noisy chaos of the newsroom.

"What are you doing now?" Brian asked as they both stood looking out across the city.

"Well, I'm here now, in Melbourne, I mean. No point heading back up to the Ridge. I should get some rest, but I'll hang around until the PM's spoken," she paused.

"Bri, there's something eating at me about all this."

"Me too," Brian said.

"Really?" she asked.

"Yeah, really. It doesn't make sense."

"What doesn't?" she said, turning her back on the city. She leaned against the balustrade, giving Brian her full attention.

Brian stepped in closer. "I was thinking about what James Lawrence said the other day. About Foster being killed by one of the Patriots themselves."

"Go on," Cassie said.

"If that's true, then why retaliate the way they did last night? Why target four completely different places?"

"That's *exactly* what I was thinking!" Cassie said, standing upright now. "They've got no idea who killed him, so they're just lashing out in all directions."

"But then, they brought in Jack Mead..." Brian started.

"...and released him without charge."

"Do you really think he could really be Foster's son?"

They both fell silent, the question hanging in the air as Cassie's thoughts swirled. She had more questions than answers.

"Hey, I almost forgot," she said at last. "I had a call from that football coach, Rodney Lindfield. He gave me some names, Foster's old teammates, the ones he used to hang out with when they were teenagers. We're not likely to get much out of them, but it's something. I want to try reaching Belinda Mead, and I need to find out how Jason's doing, what hospital he's in. I wonder if I should call Amir. He's probably on his way back to Australia as we speak…"

She ran through the list aloud, almost talking to herself.

"Want to give me the names of Foster's old footy mates?" Brian offered. "I can make a start on that if you want to focus on Belinda and Jason."

"That'd be great. But not right now Bri, go home, have a shower, get some rest."

"Hey, if you're not, I'm not. We're a team on this," he said.

That made Cassie smile. "Yeah, we are. Just don't go calling me 'partner' or some shit like that," she grinned.

"Hey, you two, the PM's on," someone from the newsroom called through the door.

Cassie and Brian headed back into the main room, where the Prime Minister had just appeared on the large flatscreen mounted on the wall.

Flanked by officials in dark suits and formal uniforms, Prime Minister Peter Collins stood at the podium, his jaw set, eyes steely beneath the weight of expectation. The Australian, Aboriginal, and Torres Strait Islander flags hung motionless behind him, a silent backdrop to the tension pulsing through the crowd.

"Thank you for being here. I'm joined today by the Premier of Victoria, Ryan Johnston; AFP Commissioner, Mark Howard; ASIO Director-General, Suzanne Cleary; Victorian Police Commissioner, Jacinta Priestly; and Acting Deputy Commissioner of Public Safety and Security, James Lawrence."

"First and foremost, I want to extend my deepest condolences to the family and loved ones of Rami Fadel, who lost his life in last night's attack on the Progress Australia offices. I spoke with Rami's wife, Amina, this morning. She is grieving the loss of a devoted husband and father, a man who fled violence in Syria in search of a better, *safer* life for his young family here in Australia."

"Our thoughts are also with Jason Turner, a former Federal Parliamentary Secretary, who is currently recovering in hospital. Both he and his partner, a former American consulate official and US citizen, lost their home and place of business in Elwood, a site of historical significance for our gay and lesbian community. And finally, our thoughts are also with our Islamic community, Greens Senator Sally McGowan, and others impacted by last night's cowardly and targeted attacks."

Cassie felt her breath hitch as the Prime Minister spoke Jason's name aloud.

"This morning, I convened a meeting of the National Security Committee. The attacks in Melbourne were the sole item on the agenda. I can confirm these incidents are being treated as acts of terrorism. Our law enforcement agencies will have every resource they need to ensure those responsible are swiftly brought to justice."

"I can also announce the establishment of AFP Special Operation Blackthorn; a national taskforce focused on the rise of far-right extremism in Australia, specifically targeting the group calling themselves *the Allied Patriots*. This group has known roots in the United States and is funded, in part, through the proceeds of organised crime. That is why our government, across all jurisdictions, is working closely with international partners, including the FBI."

"Let me be absolutely clear: Australia will not be dragged into the same hatred and division we've seen take hold elsewhere. This is a nation built on diversity, on mateship, and on standing up for one another, no matter our background, our faith, or who we love. Violent extremism, especially when fuelled by bigotry and a twisted ideology peddled by thugs, will not be tolerated under any circumstances."

"I'll now hand over to AFP Commissioner, Mark Howard. Then we'll take questions."

Some in the newsroom didn't wait for the AFP Commissioner. They were already peeling off, hurrying back to their desks or slipping into nearby studios, the buzz of rapid-fire phone calls and the clatter of keyboards filling the space. Others hovered, ears still tuned to the feed, fingers poised above notepads.

Cassie had heard enough. She turned on her heel and slipped back into the corridor, the bright glare from the foyer windows blinding her momentarily. Brian followed close behind, the door swinging shut behind them with a dull thud.

"Well, there you have it. He's not mucking around," Brian said, his voice echoing slightly in the empty hallway. "What now?"

Cassie didn't answer immediately. The adrenaline that had surged through her during the press conference was cooling now, replaced by that familiar, sharp-edged focus.

"It's Saturday Bri. Go home. Get cleaned up and get some rest. I'll see if I can reach Belinda on my way back to mine and then I'll see if I can get in to see Jason."

She started walking again, footsteps soft yet purposeful against the carpet below.

Brian followed closely behind. "Sure. I'll go take a shower. But like I said before, I want to go where you go on this. If you're working today, then so am I."

Cassie was now already halfway down the stairs, her mind ticking over. She didn't have a plan yet, just instincts. But they'd never let her down before.

"Then keep up," she called back, not slowing.

THIRTEEN

Elwood Village was still cordoned off, traffic diverted away from the burnt-out shell of Inside Out. Cassie made her way through the detours toward her apartment, her patience fraying as she inched through the steady traffic of stickybeaks, craning for a glimpse of last night's chaos. The return of the warmer weather and the holiday long weekend had lured everyone out, and beyond the Village, Elwood was its usual lively self. Dog walkers strolled past beach-bound SUVs, mums in Lululemon pushed prams two-abreast along the footpaths, and neighbours could be heard clanging about in their front yards, tending to hedges and lawns. Life went on.

Without wanting to pester, Cassie had only tried once more to contact Belinda Mead on her drive home, leaving a brief voice message offering to help in any way she could. She'd barely been back in her flat half an hour when her phone lit up, Belinda's name on the screen.

"Belinda, hi," Cassie answered quickly.

"Hi, Cassandra." The tone was flat. Measured.

"I… I don't really know what to say," Cassie began. "I just wanted to…"

"It's fine," Belinda cut in, her voice still emotionless. "Thanks for reaching out. Funny, really. I've been dodging media calls all day, yet here I am, calling you."

"I'm so sorry this is happening again. And just so you know, that's not why I was calling."

"No, I get that."

There was a pause. Cassie hesitated, then pushed gently.

"Belinda... off the record, I do need to ask. Hayden Foster. Your son..."

"Off the record," Belinda said with a dry, bitter laugh.

Cassie said nothing. Just waited. Another long silence followed, and then, finally, a sigh.

"I'll talk to you, Cassandra. *On* the record. But only to you. No cameras. No recordings. Just for print."

"Of course. That's not really my patch, but I can bring my colleague, Brian. We could sit with you, help you shape something for the ABC to put out, only if that's what you want."

"That's fine." Her voice softened, just a fraction. "Just... please, Cassandra. Help make this go away."

Cassie knew she couldn't promise that. Not truthfully. But she gave Belinda her word, she'd handle it with care. No feeding frenzies. No clickbait.

Just the truth. Told quietly.

Belinda hadn't been home since her son, Jack, had been taken in for questioning. Instead, she'd given Cassie the address of a friend's townhouse in the inner-city suburb of Carlton North. She was available immediately.

Cassie climbed back into her car and made her way towards Richmond, her phone buzzing in the console beside her, Brian, finally calling back.

"Bri!" she said, snatching it up on Bluetooth.

"Hey, sorry," he said, a little breathless. "I was just getting out of the shower. You ready for me to come over?"

"No, be ready in five. I'm already on Punt Road, heading to yours. Belinda Mead wants to make a statement. She wants us to help."

There was a beat of stunned silence.

"Jesus, Cass. That's huge. Have you told Peter?"

"No. And I won't." Her voice was firm. "I don't want him telling us to stay in our lane. And I sure as hell don't want to lose the chance to do this properly, for Belinda's sake."

Another gap, then Brian's tone softened. "Got it. I'll be out the front."

Cassie hung up and let out a long, slow breath, gripping the wheel tighter as she slipped between lanes. She didn't know exactly what Belinda was going to say. But she had a gut feeling, it was going to matter.

* * *

Cassie and Brian approached the front door of the old two-storey Victorian terrace, currently in a state of renovation. Scaffolding clung to its façade like a second skin. Cassie pushed open the small wrought-iron gate, and together they stepped up onto the tiled front patio, the wooden slats that lay across the scaffolding hung just centimetres above their heads.

Brian leaned in to press the old doorbell, more of a harsh buzzer than a chime. Through the stained-glass window that adorned the upper half of the solid black wooden door, they could just make out a shadow approaching.

"Cassandra."

Belinda stood in the doorway, looking years older than she had only days earlier. Her makeup was gone, smart work clothes traded for a loose sweater and leggings, her hair messily shoved back. Dark circles sat heavy beneath her eyes.

"And you must be Brian. Come in," she said quickly, ushering them inside before closing the door behind them.

"This is my friend Annabelle's place, she's a senior partner at work. Her husband, Paul, started the firm. He's retired now," Belinda explained, her voice trailing down the long hallway as Cassie and Brian kicked off their shoes and tried to keep pace.

"They're in Japan at the moment. As long as I don't bring the vultures to their front door, they've been kind enough to let us stay here for a few days."

She led them through to an open-plan kitchen in a modern extension at the rear of the house. The latest designer furniture and clean, sleek lines. A departure from the ornate historical features in the front end of the house. Large glass bifold doors opened out to a perfectly manicured courtyard garden with a graffiti street-art mural painted in bright colours onto a side brick wall. A narrow plunge pool ran along the courtyard's edge, tucked neatly beneath the mural.

And then she saw him.

The young man sitting on the lounge turned toward them as they entered.

"…and this is Jack. My son."

Jack stood and made his way over, hand outstretched.

He was tall and had clearly inherited his Mum's looks, thick brown hair pushed back from his forehead, bold eyebrows, full lips, and a strong jawline. If this was Hayden Foster's son, it wasn't obvious. There was no fire behind his eyes, no trace of that barely contained rage Foster always carried like a weapon.

"Pleased to meet you," he said, offering a firm handshake.

"Please," Belinda said, gesturing to the round walnut dining table in the centre of the room.

As they each took their seats, she cleared her throat. "Before we begin, I want to make one thing absolutely clear, Hayden Foster is *not* Jack's father."

"OK," Cassie replied, blunt but neutral.

"I don't know where those reports have come from. Typical gutter journalism," Belinda said, the irritation rising in her voice. "Jack's father was someone I had a very brief relationship with, around the same time as that whole incident with Hayden. Jack knows who his father is. But for both their sakes, we won't be naming him. Not now. Not ever."

"That's perfectly OK," Cassie said. "We don't need to know that detail."

Brian remained silent beside her, choosing to watch Cassie in full flight.

"We can make that point very clear in your statement, that Hayden Foster was not Jack's father, while also asking for privacy," Cassie continued. "If you want my opinion, say as little as possible. Make your case, then leave it at that. And Belinda..." she leaned in slightly, her tone firmer, "don't speak to anyone else in the media. I appreciate the trust you've placed in Brian and me, but beyond that..."

"No. I know only too well how these things go. And to be honest, I feel strangely calm about it all." She paused, her expression darkening. "It's not the media that concerns me."

"No?"

"It's the Patriots."

A silence settled over the table, heavy, knowing, and laced with dread.

"There's only so much we can do to shut this down," Cassie eventually said. "I think the news storm that's broken overnight with the attacks will help drown out any side story about Jack, or you. But there's also a risk it could go the other way as well. There are a few things we'll need to address."

"Like why Jack was taken in for questioning," Belinda said flatly.

"Like why Jack was taken in for questioning," Cassie echoed, her gaze shifting to Jack. Brian followed suit.

"Let me," Belinda said quickly, just as her son opened his mouth to speak.

"Jack's always known about my assault. We've never hidden it. We've always been honest about everything." She paused, her eyes dropping for a moment. "There've been times in my life, despite all the good, when things haven't been so great."

Cassie stayed quiet, giving her space.

"I've had issues, with alcohol, on and off, for years. I've had support. I've tried. I've had varying success with sobriety, but there's no denying the impact all of this has had. Hayden, the failed trial, the press. As hard as I've tried to move on, it creeps back in."

She reached across the table and took Jack's hand, offering him a warm, quiet smile.

"Jack's always been my rock. Through it all. And I am so proud of him. Even if he made a poor choice about a year ago."

"What happened a year ago?" Brian asked gently.

Belinda smiled again, this time with a look of calm acceptance.

"Unbeknownst to me, Jack decided to track Hayden down. He'd just finished his Honours in Psychology at Monash, and I think, well, trying to make sense of trauma, the justice system… it all collided. And I think he just needed to *do* something."

Cassie nodded slowly, reading between the lines.

"Jack confronted Hayden one night at his home, the same one that burnt down earlier this week. It didn't go well. They fought. Jack fractured Hayden's jaw."

Cassie glanced at Jack. Her lips twitched, just briefly, and he caught it, returning a faint smile. The tension in the room eased, if only slightly.

"Go on," she said, her voice level.

"A neighbour called the police," Belinda continued. "Jack was arrested. But as soon as both Hayden and the police realised who Jack was, *my* son, all the charges were dropped. It's the only half-decent thing Hayden Foster ever did."

"So, the police brought you in yesterday because of the prior assault?" Cassie asked, turning back to Jack.

"Yes," Belinda answered for him. "But on the night Hayden was killed, Jack was at home. With me. That's what I told the police. And the telecommunications data backed it, his phone never left the house. In my line of work," she added with a slight smile, "that's what we call evidence."

"OK." Cassie opened her laptop. "Then there's really nothing to see here. Let's write your statement together. We don't even need to mention the incident with Foster, and if it leaks, which it probably will, you've given your side, and you don't need to say anything more. No follow-ups, no commentary. You move on. Don't give them anything else to chew on."

"Thank you," Belinda said softly.

It didn't take long for the statement to come together. Cassie and Brian worked methodically, choosing every word with care. Once finalised, they made their way back to the ABC building at Southbank. Cassie felt the familiar pressure tightening around her chest, the weight of responsibility. She needed to get this right. For Belinda. For Jack.

They filed the statement for immediate release, but not before looping in Peter and filling him in on the details. He wasn't thrilled to be informed after the fact, but he also knew damn well the statement wouldn't exist without Cassie. He grumbled, then let it go.

Cassie glanced at the newsroom clock.

"Jesus, Bri. It's five o'clock on Easter Saturday. If I'm looking even half as wrecked as you do right now, I think we need to call it," she said with a tired grin.

Brian rolled his eyes, a lopsided smirk tugging at the corner of his mouth.

"You know what tomorrow is, don't you?" she asked, eyes narrowing, her gaze drifting to something distant and unseen.

Brian blinked. "Yeah. Easter Sunday."

"Yeah, but what's so significant about that?"

He shrugged. "Something to do with Jesus?"

Cassie let out a dry laugh. "It's the anniversary of Joel O'Connor's death. The kid from Carrington."

Brian's smirk faded. He nodded slowly. The room felt colder suddenly, stripped of its usual newsroom buzz.

"You're still thinking about that?" he asked, quieter now.

Cassie just stared into the void, chewing her bottom lip. "I dunno. It's just... if Hayden wasn't killed by the Patriots, or Jack Mead, then who? And why? Something keeps pulling me back to Carrington. Like... I missed something."

She let the thought hang for a beat, then gave a shrug.

"Anyway. Time to call it. I'm sure Jessica's missing you," she teased, nudging him with her elbow. "Did you two get to keep the feather boa?"

Brian's cheeks reddened. "You saw that?!"

"Of course I saw it," Cassie laughed. "Enjoy the day off tomorrow."

With that, she turned and headed for the stairs, already craving the solid night's sleep ahead.

FOURTEEN

Cassie leaned back on the couch, balancing her phone against a half-empty mug of coffee, as the familiar faces of her family filled the screen.

"Happy Easter, Cassie," her mum beamed. "You're missing out on one hell of a lamb roast. I'm just popping it in the oven now." She turned the phone. "Here, I'll put you onto your father."

Cassie smiled, trying to mask the guilt clawing at her. She should've been there. Should've stayed. There weren't many of these gatherings left, not with her dad.

"Hi, Cassie, love." Her dad's face filled the screen like always, just his nose and forehead at first.

She laughed. "Dad, come on. Hold the camera back a bit, you're all nostrils again."

Her guilt gave way to something else. She was glad to see him. Really glad. But the emotion bubbled close to the surface. Her eyes turned glassy, and she blinked fast, forcing a smile as he fumbled with the phone.

"You know, Terence is coming today," her dad said casually. "I reckon you made quite the impression on him on Friday."

Cassie raised a brow. "Doesn't Terence want to spend Easter with his own family?"

144

"His mum's working all weekend. And it's a bit of a drive to Echuca and back just for a quick hello. He's back at work tomorrow afternoon anyway, he tells us. Besides, I've gotten used to having him around. He's practically part of the family now," he said with a wink.

Cassie grinned. "You've been spending too much time with Mum up there."

"Alright, alright," he said, laughing. "So, what about you then Cassie? Any plans today? Are you catching up with friends?"

"Yeah, I'll head out later, see a few people," she lied easily.

The truth was, she didn't really have anyone to call. Not outside work. For years now, the job had been everything. Friendships had never quite made the priority list. There were people she liked, sure, but the effort it took to stay in touch, to reply to a message, to show up, it always slipped through the cracks.

Sometimes, like now, she wondered what it'd be like to have something more than just her work. To say yes when opportunities came knocking. Like Terence. And not just him. Maybe she didn't have to be locked into Melbourne. She could transfer to one of the ABC regional offices. Plenty had done it after the pandemic. Made a life in country towns. It was doable. Wasn't it? Was she ready to go back, after everything?

"You still there, Cass?" her dad said, watching her drift off, as she so often did.

"Yeah. Sorry Dad. Just distracted."

She launched into a recap of the last two days, telling them about the attack on Inside Out, and about

Jason Turner, how she'd been on site, which earned a horrified gasp from her mother.

Cassie had always worn her emotions on her sleeve. It was part of what people respected about her journalism; she was real. Human. But today, that openness felt like a liability. She felt flat, and she knew her parents had seen it too.

Friday felt like a lifetime ago. She missed them. She said her goodbyes and curled up on the couch.

Not long after, a car horn sounded out front. Cassie moved to the window, mug in hand, and peered through the venetian blinds. Outside, her downstairs neighbour stood on the garden path in her Sunday best, waving as a silver sedan pulled away from the curb.

Marcella Lucci, a retired Catholic schoolteacher and widow of more than a decade, mostly kept to herself. But the flowers in her window box were always in perfect bloom, and the smell of her Sunday cooking drifting into Cassie's apartment never failed to make her mouth water. Cassie checked in on her now and then, not out of duty, but instinct. The woman had no children, no visitors, and plenty of opinions.

Cassie stepped outside onto the landing. "Good morning, Mrs Lucci."

The older woman looked up, shielding her eyes. "Good morning, Cassandra. And a very Happy Easter to you."

"You too." Cassie leaned against the brick wall, cradling her coffee mug in both hands.

"You weren't at church this morning?" Mrs Lucci asked, knowing full well the answer.

Cassie hesitated. "Ah, no."

Mrs Lucci clucked her tongue softly. "Today's a very Holy day on the calendar Cassandra. It's the day of our Holy Saviour's Resurrection. He rose from the dead to wash away our sins. It's a day of hope. Of new beginnings."

Cassie offered a tight smile, not trusting herself to respond.

"It's a reminder that even the worst things, death, betrayal, darkness, they can be overcome," Mrs Lucci continued. "We mustn't lose sight of that, especially with all this terrible business in the city."

Cassie's jaw tensed. "You mean the arson attacks?"

Mrs Lucci nodded gravely. "Terrible, just terrible. But even those who act out in darkness, well, forgiveness is always possible. That's the miracle of today."

Cassie blinked. Was she seriously suggesting the people who burned down Inside Out and killed Rami Fadel, the Syrian cleaner deserved *forgiveness* because it was Easter Sunday?

"I don't know," Cassie said, her voice tighter than she meant. "Seems a bit convenient, doesn't it? Wipe the slate clean once a year and pretend none of it matters the other 364 days?"

Mrs Lucci's expression faltered. "We all carry sins Cassandra. Yours. Mine. Even the ones who set fire to that place in the Village. God forgives us if we ask."

A long pause stretched between them. Somewhere nearby, a dog barked.

Cassie's phone buzzed in her pocket, rescuing her from the reply she was about to deliver.

"I'm sorry, I have to take this," she said quickly, lifting the phone and ducking back inside. "Happy Easter."

She closed the door behind her and exhaled. The words hung in her mind: *resurrection, forgiveness, new beginnings*.

But what about the ones who never got theirs?

She glanced at the screen. Peter Draper.

On Easter Sunday?

Her stomach clenched. What now?

"Cassandra," came his voice, low, softened. Not the clipped, calculated tone she was used to. It caught her off guard. He sounded... almost relaxed.

"Listen," he continued, "it's been a hell of a few days. I know you were meant to be in the high country this weekend. With family. This might be a little left field, but if you're not doing anything... Carol and I are having a bit of an Easter lunch. She's done a roast and, as usual, we've over-catered for just the two of us. No pressure at all, just thought I'd extend the invite."

Cassie blinked. "Um..." She wasn't sure what surprised her more, the call, the invitation, or how tempted she was to say yes.

Take the opportunities, Cass, she reminded herself.

"I'd love to."

* * *

The elevator doors opened onto a quiet, softly lit corridor. White ceilings, textured wallpaper in warm cream, and sleek grey-cream tiles underfoot. The kind of upscale interior you'd expect from one of St Kilda Road's glittering towers.

Cassie stepped out, heels echoing lightly as she moved toward the end of the hallway.

806.

The golden numbers were perfectly centred on the dark wooden door, rich timber, polished and expensive looking. She raised her hand to knock, deliberately ignoring the doorbell. Something about using it felt... too polite. Too formal.

The door opened to reveal a woman in her early sixties, shoulder-length silver hair and deep ochre linen.

"Cassandra, welcome," she said warmly. "It's lovely to see you again. Come in, and shoes off if you don't mind. I'm obsessed with these floors."

Cassie looked down at the herringbone-patterned wood stretching across the living area like something out of an interiors blog.

She stepped inside, unzipping her boots and slipping them off. Though she'd always preferred the old-world charm of her art deco flat, there was no denying it, the apartment was breathtaking. Subtle and sophisticated, like stepping into a high-end magazine spread where someone actually lived.

Sculptural ceramics lined a floating shelf above the kitchen, their soft curves catching the light. A huge mixed media canvas, swaths of copper, charcoal, and teal, hung over the dining area, while an abstract bronze sculpture stood in the corner like it had always belonged there.

Through the floor-to-ceiling windows, the Melbourne skyline shimmered in the midday sun. The Arts Centre spire took centre stage from the balcony, where a sculptural chair faced the view like it was meditating.

"Cassandra, come in, come in," Peter called from the kitchen. He was dressed casually in dark jeans and a blue linen shirt rolled at the sleeves, carving into a roast that smelled divine. "Carol has made her famous fennel and citrus salad. I told her she was showing off, but she ignored me, as always."

Carol chuckled from the sink. "He's not wrong. I over-cater like it's a competitive sport. But sit, please. Peter, where's that bottle of wine?"

Cassie was already smiling despite herself.

She took a seat at the sleek black dining table beneath oversized pendant lights that made everything feel a little softer, a little more curated. Then, in an elegant flurry of bowls, platters, and gravy boats, lunch was served.

The conversation flowed easily. Carol asked about Cassie's favourite art exhibitions, Peter shared old newsroom war stories, the kind that still made him puff with pride. It was warm, relaxed, almost familial.

But eventually, the conversation shifted.

Peter set down his fork with a quiet clink, wiping his mouth with a linen napkin. "I wanted to check in on something," he said. His tone was soft but deliberate, the unmistakable voice of an editor easing into the uncomfortable bit.

Cassie knew it well.

"This business with Belinda Mead and her son. I know it's tempting to dig into the *who* behind Hayden's death. But I need you to stick to the story we agreed on. The broader piece, on extremism, radicalisation, how it takes hold."

Cassie nodded slowly, chasing a piece of carrot around her plate. "I get it. And I am. And that's not why I helped her out yesterday."

Peter gave her a look, half gratitude, half concern. "I'm not saying don't explore Foster's past. If there's something there, trauma, ideology, upbringing, it's worth telling. But the murder itself? That's for the police, yeah? We're not in the business of solving active homicide cases. I just want you safe, Cass."

Cass? He'd never called her that before. His tone felt almost fatherly, and his words landed gently, but they still stung. She took a sip of her pinot. "You don't think I know that?"

"I think you forget sometimes," Peter said, smiling faintly. "You lead with your heart. And your gut. And that's what makes your stories brilliant. But it also makes you, at times, a little reckless. It wouldn't be the first time you've gone chasing ghosts that weren't there."

This was about the defamation case again. Cassie shifted uncomfortably in her seat.

Across the table, Carol reached for the salad bowl, steering the mood. "I think we all forget sometimes," she said kindly. "Especially when something matters."

Cassie looked out past the spire, to the skyline beyond. She didn't want to be reckless. But she also couldn't look away. Hayden Foster's murder wasn't some footnote in a broader cultural piece, it was the ignition point. The crack that let all the rot show through.

But she didn't say that. Not here. Not now.

"I hear you," she said instead, offering a small smile that didn't quite reach her eyes.

The pause that followed wasn't long, but it was enough. Just enough to notice the shift. The temperature in the room cooled slightly, and Cassie felt it in the way Carol topped up her wine and launched into a description of an upcoming installation at ACCA, something immersive involving mirrors, light, and submerged audio. It didn't quite stick, but Cassie appreciated the effort.

Peter leaned back, fingers laced across his stomach. "You know, when I was just starting out, I followed a lead on a teacher accused of indoctrinating kids with Marxist theory," he said. "I thought I'd struck gold. My editor, gruff old-school type, told me to park it. Said the real story wasn't the man but the panic taking hold in the education department."

He paused, eyes distant. "I ignored him. Ran it anyway. It blew up. The guy's life was destroyed. Turned out he was clean. My story didn't age well. And neither did my reputation, for a while."

Cassie raised an eyebrow. It wasn't a story Peter told often.

He gave a small shrug. "It taught me something. You can be right about the symptoms, and still wrong about the cause. Timing matters. Perspective matters more."

Cassie nodded, not because it changed her mind, but because she understood. Peter had made his calls. And he'd paid for them.

Later, she helped clear the table, rinsing plates beside Carol at the marble sink while Peter wandered out to the balcony, a whisky cradled in his hand.

"You know he adores you, right?" Carol said gently.

Cassie smirked. "I know."

"He just doesn't want you getting chewed up. This industry already does that in a hundred little ways."

"I'm not afraid of getting chewed up," Cassie said. "I'm afraid of leaving something buried."

Carol handed her a tea towel. "Then keep trusting your gut. Even if Peter gets twitchy about it."

Cassie stayed another half hour, long enough to compliment the roast, make small talk about upcoming art shows, and politely decline dessert. But her thoughts were already somewhere else.

Peter's words had landed, but they hadn't settled. And that conversation with Marcella Lucci kept echoing in her mind. *Resurrection. Forgiveness. Fresh starts.*

What about Joel O'Connor? Where was his fresh start?

It was Easter Sunday. And the anniversary of his death. Maybe there was nothing in it. But that same tug in her chest, that reporter's sixth sense, was pulling her back to Carrington.

She wasn't ready to let go. Not yet.

By the time she reached the lift, her phone was already in her hand.

She typed in the destination:
Banksia Memorial Park Cemetery.

FIFTEEN

Cassie followed the online map as she wound her way through the open gardens of Banksia Memorial Park Cemetery. It wasn't like any cemetery she'd visited growing up. No cracked concrete. No granite slabs leaning sideways under the weight of time. This place was all manicured lawns and ornamental grasses, walking paths threading through native trees and flowering shrubs. The perfume of autumn blooms hung in the air. It felt more like a botanical garden than a graveyard.

Compared to the old Heathton Ridge cemetery, with its crooked wire fences and rows of sun-bleached headstones covered in lichen, this was the Garden of Eden.

She stepped off the bitumen path, climbing a small grassy rise bordered by immaculate garden beds. Brass memorial plaques were nestled beneath grevilleas and banksias, each one modest, almost easy to miss. According to the memorial park website, Joel O'Connor's remains had been scattered somewhere within this very garden bed.

Cassie paused and took a slow breath. Peter's voice echoed in her mind, was this what reckless looked like?

Chasing ghosts in a place built for peace? Maybe. But it was Easter Sunday. And this, this felt right. The anniversary of Joel's death. She wondered if Joel's family ever made the trip down from Queensland. Or if this place, like so many others, had simply become a quiet holding ground for forgotten grief.

She thought of the makeshift memorial out on the road to Heathton Ridge, the weathered wooden cross, the faded plastic flowers, the river gum tree. The ghosts of lives half-remembered. Though there was no letting go of the past. Not for anyone.

Cassie scanned the plaques along the garden bed's edge, her footsteps slow and deliberate on the grass. And that's when she saw her.

A woman stood not far ahead, alone. Shoulder-length dark hair. A flowing black dress that moved gently in the breeze. One hand on her hip, the other hanging by her side. She was speaking aloud, soft, deliberate words, spoken to the person beneath her feet.

Cassie stopped.

She didn't want to intrude. Whoever the woman was talking to, it was a conversation meant for them. Private. Sacred.

Cassie turned and veered toward another part of the garden bed. She crouched beside a plaque she hadn't come to see, pretending to study the name etched in brass. It didn't register. She glanced back.

The woman was still there. Still speaking.

There was something familiar about her.

Cassie waited until she stepped away, her head bowed slightly as she made her way down the small hill toward the main path. She walked slowly, as if reluctant to leave. Her dress caught the light in soft ripples.

As she drew closer, Cassie stood, brushing grass from her hands.

Their eyes met, briefly, but with a quiet charge. Cassie knew that face. It tugged at something just beneath the surface.

Where have I seen her before?

Cassie turned and made her way quickly toward the plaque the woman had just left.

Joel O'Connor.

And then it clicked.

The St Matthews alumni page.

The catering website, the jingle, *"Everything's better with Valetta!"*

Laura. Laura Cassini.

Cassie moved quickly to catch up.

"Excuse me, sorry to disturb you. Are you… Laura Cassini?"

The woman stopped, surprised. Her brow creased for a moment before her expression softened.

"You're Cassandra Murphy," she said slowly. "The journalist. I've seen you on TV."

Cassie nodded. "Guilty."

Laura offered a small, polite smile, but there was caution in her posture.

"I'm sorry, how do you know my name? And it's Laura Rowe now, I only use my maiden name for work."

"Right. I came across your photo," Cassie said gently. "On your business website. That's how I recognised you just now. You were standing at Joel O'Connor's plaque, weren't you?"

Laura's eyes flicked back toward the garden bed, then to Cassie. Her expression shifted. Not closed but guarded.

"Yes," she said quietly. "I was."

A beat passed between them. Not empty, something hung there. Memory. Pain. A shared recognition of something lost.

"I'm not here to make you uncomfortable," Cassie added quickly. "I didn't know Joel was here. Not until today."

Laura's face tightened slightly. "Most people didn't know much about Joel. Not really." She hesitated, then added, "How do you know who he is? …*Was*." The correction landed like a stone.

Cassie opened her mouth, but Laura cut in again, sharper now, suspicious.

"And sorry, did you say *my* website? What is this, exactly?"

"I'm sorry," Cassie said, lifting her hands slightly. "Truly. And I *am* sorry for the loss of your friend. I know this must seem strange. Especially since… you recognised me."

Laura didn't respond, still watching her, still wary.

"I've been working on a story," Cassie continued. "About far-right extremism. One of the men I've been investigating was murdered this past week. He grew up in Carrington. I started looking into his past, trying to understand how he became who he was. And that's when I came across Joel's name."

Laura's expression didn't shift. "I don't understand what that has to do with *me*. Or why you were looking at my website."

Cassie hesitated. "Honestly… I'm not sure. It just resonated. I guess something about Joel stayed with me. And then when I saw your photo…"

She trailed off. There was no version of this that didn't sound intrusive. Not to someone who'd just been standing at her friend's resting place, speaking to the dirt.

Then came the flicker. A small shift in Laura's eyes. A tightening of posture.

This didn't look like coincidence anymore.

It looked like an ambush.

Cassie took a breath.

"The man who was murdered. Hayden Foster. His house was set alight with his body inside. In tracing his background in Carrington, I came across the house fire that claimed Joel. It just… struck a chord. So, I started looking into what happened. And your name came up, mentioned as a close friend on an old Facebook page."

She shook her head slightly. "I can assure you, I'm not investigating you. Honestly, I don't even know why I came here. It just felt right. I just thought I'd pay my respects. I'm sorry if I startled you."

A pause.

"Happy Easter," Cassie said.

Happy Easter?

Cassie winced. For someone who usually had the right words, she felt suddenly foolish.

She turned and made a quick retreat toward her car, shrinking under the weight of her own awkwardness.

"Wait!"

Cassie turned. Laura had taken a few steps forward, slower now, something softer in her face.

"I don't know who this Hayden Foster person is," Laura said, "but I do know your work. If you're here, this isn't nothing. Please. Be honest."

She shifted her weight and studied Cassie's face with eyes that didn't blink.

"You've found something, haven't you? About the fire that killed Joel."

Cassie hesitated. "I'm sorry?"

Laura let out a breath, almost a whisper. "Finally," she said, her voice catching as she looked away. Tears welled in her eyes.

"Why would you say that?" Cassie asked gently.

"Because Joel didn't die in some accident. And he sure as hell didn't kill himself either. I remember the rumours all too well."

Cassie stepped closer. "What are you saying?"

But Laura had gone somewhere else, caught in the pull of memory.

"I always knew…" she murmured.

"Laura, I'd really like to talk more about this. Do you have time to…"

"I can't. I'm sorry." Laura snapped back to the present, glancing over her shoulder. "My husband and the boys are in the car." She motioned toward the only other vehicle parked nearby, an army-green coloured Subaru Outback idling on the narrow road.

"We're on our way to see my mum. She's in a retirement village here in Carrington. I was just passing through."

She hesitated. "But I'll give you my number."

They exchanged details, quick, practical, and then Cassie watched as Laura walked back to the car. The Subaru pulled away, tires crunching softly over the gravel.

As soon as the road was empty, Cassie turned back toward the plaque.

She hadn't expected to feel much, maybe a moment of quiet respect, at most, but now there were only questions, swirling around Cassie's head like a storm.

Cassie knelt on the lawn where Laura had stood moments earlier, her eyes settling on the small brass plaque.

Joel Philip O'Connor

30 November 1980 – 12 April 1998

Beloved son of Glen and Christie, and brother to Amelia.

In our hearts always.

No flowers. No interstate visitors. Maybe his family honoured him in other ways now. Almost thirty years on, grief would have found new forms.

She sat back on her heels and pulled her phone from her jacket, taking a photo of the plaque, before hitting dial.

"Brian."

"Cass! Happy Easter!" Brian's voice was bright on the other end. "What's going on?"

"I'm sorry to call, I hope I'm not interrupting anything."

"Not at all. I went out for Yum Cha with my parents earlier, but I'm home now, just catching up on TV."

"Well, as much as I hate to interrupt *Married at First Sight...*"

"How did you...?"

"Brian. Please." She scoffed. "I don't know how you watch that shit."

"Hey, don't you go knocking MAFS," he said with a grin she could hear through the phone.

"Listen, I'm out in Carrington but heading back soon. Did we ever get the address of Joel O'Connor's family home? The one the burnt down."

"Yeah, we did. I got it from that link to the old news report. I'll text it to you."

"Great. Thanks, Bri."

"What are you doing out in Carrington?"

"Chasing ghosts," she said. "Listen, can I swing by yours on the way back?"

"Yeah, of course."

"I'll be there in about an hour or so. Flick me that address when you can."

"On it now."

Cassie ended the call and headed for her car.

As she turned the ignition, her phone buzzed.

57 Southcote Road, Carrington. See you soon!

Cassie tapped the address into Maps and pulled out through the cemetery's gates, that old familiar twist rising in her gut.

Southcote Road wasn't far. In fact, it was only a few streets away from Hayden Foster's childhood home and from the address of former footy coach Rodney Lindfield where she had been a few days earlier. Carrington wasn't a big suburb. Wedged between the Carrington Highway and three arterial roads, it was a pocket of quiet streets and forgotten corners.

She slowed as she reached the house.

Number 57 stood a little prouder than the homes flanking it, though not as polished as the newer townhouses slowly encroaching on the suburb. Single storey. Mottled peach brick. Its shape was a sharper rectangle, with a steeper pitched roof than the squat, boxy AV Jennings homes either side. A long veranda framed the side facade, its timber posts the deep, dried-blood red of old ironbark. Even the terracotta roof tiles set it apart: flatter, wider than their older cousins.

This was a late 90's rebuild, post-fire. And frustratingly, it told her nothing about Joel.

Cassie flicked through Google Street View on her phone, but it didn't go back far enough through the years to show the original O'Connor home. She switched to Satellite View. That's when she noticed it. The house backed directly onto what appeared to be a park. And just beyond it, a football oval.

She drove to the end of the street and rounded the next corner. On her left, a large sign announced:

OTWAY PARK RECREATION RESERVE

Beneath it, a smaller wooden sign in navy blue and white:

Home of the Carrington Falcons.

Cassie turned in.

A narrow dual-lane driveway led her between two homes which opened into a large bitumen car park beyond. To her right: a tall wire fence, and beyond that lay a squat brick building, and a tiny playground marked "Grove Street Kindergarten." Ahead: a grey

Besser block clubroom, its outer walls marked *Home* and *Visitors*. Beyond that, the footy oval, its four tall goal posts at the closest end to Cassie, towering high above the clubrooms.

But it was the larger playground to her left that caught her eye. New, polished, full of colourful equipment that hadn't yet faded under the sun. Cassie pulled into one of the empty bays in front of it and killed the engine.

She checked the satellite view again. Joel's house sat just beyond the slope behind the playground, on the other side of a rise covered in garden beds and native grasses. She climbed the gentle hill, pushing through low shrubs.

At the top, she could see straight into the backyard of 57 Southcote Road.

The back fence was weathered timber, interrupted by a small wooden gate. There were other gates too, old homes with the same kind of access. Cassie frowned. The gates didn't open onto anything useful, just the landscaped garden she now stood in. Maybe the garden hadn't always been here. Maybe it had once been nothing but scrub and dirt. Maybe it had once been a shortcut. A secret path. A place to run.

From where she stood, the O'Connor's former backyard offered a clear view of the oval, of *their* oval.

Rodney Lindfield's words echoed: *"My lads would've made his life hell."*

Cassie imagined being a seventeen-year-old boy back then, already carrying a secret that made you a target and then living with that oval staring you down every single day. That green field of threat, just beyond the back fence.

She was about to turn back when something made her pause.

A woman was watching her from the house next door, frozen behind a kitchen window, eyes narrowed, mouth pursed. Cassie offered a half-nod, but the woman didn't move.

Cassie retreated, quietly but quickly, back down the hill and toward the playground.

Her footsteps felt loud on the gravel path.

She stopped by the car, turning to face the oval once more. The wind had shifted direction. It brushed against the back of her neck like a breath.

This was it. Here. In this quiet suburban sprawl, Joel had lost his life.

Cassie's pulse quickened as the realisation hit. She was standing only metres from where it had happened. A prickle of unease crawled over her as she noticed the absence of life around her. School holidays. Blue sky. Sunlight spilling across the ground. Yet no kids, no parents, no voices. Only silence.

There was too much silence. Like the place was holding its breath.

She climbed into her car, locked the doors, and pulled away.

As she turned back onto the main road and set a course for the city, Laura's voice echoed in her mind.

"I always knew there was something about that fire."

And now, so did Cassie.

SIXTEEN

Brian's apartment occupied the second floor of a newly converted factory warehouse, tucked into the Collingwood end of Richmond. The split-level space was modest: a small kitchen and living room downstairs, with stairs leading up to a loft bedroom and bathroom. From the living room, glass doors slid open onto a brick-walled balcony, where Brian had set up a lush arrangement of potted plants and hanging baskets. It was here he directed Cassie when she arrived.

Dusk had settled in, and the balcony glowed under a scatter of lanterns and fairy lights strung among the greenery. They sat opposite each other on the outdoor lounge, the sounds of the city folding softly around them.

"Happy Easter," Brian said with a grin, offering her a bowl filled with small chocolate eggs, still wrapped in colourful foil.

"Thanks, you too."

Cassie grabbed one, picking absently at the wrapper with her thumbnail.

"Did you find where the O'Connor house used to be?" he eventually asked.

Cassie nodded, her mouth full. "Humph," she muttered, the chocolate sticking slightly as she swallowed. "That's not all," she added, leaning back into the couch and dropping her scrunched-up foil onto a terrazzo side table beside her.

"No?"

"Remember the Facebook comments about a Laura someone? Joel's friend?"

Brian nodded.

"Guess who I ran into at the cemetery, standing over Joel's memorial plaque?"

"Seriously?" Brian asked, as Cassie unwrapped another egg.

"Laura Cassini. After you left mine the other night, I dug a bit deeper into the two Lauras from Joel's year level. The Cassini's used to own a big Italian restaurant in Carrington back in the 80's and 90's. It's gone now, but Laura runs a catering business under the same name. Valetta's. Anyway, I recognised her straight away from the website."

"Did you talk to her?"

Another "Humph" and a quick nod as Cassie chewed, rushing to swallow. "…and get this, she gave me her number to set up a meeting. But not before telling me the fire that killed Joel wasn't an accident."

Brian just stared at her, silent.

Cassie shifted in her seat, the weight of his stare thickening the air.

Somewhere beyond the balcony, a car horn blared, sharp and jarring against the thickening dusk.

"Now why would she say something like that? The police ruled it an accident. The footy coach hinted it might've been suicide. But something about it still feels off. And here's the kicker. Where the O'Connor's lived? It's only a few streets from where Hayden Foster grew up. And the backyard backs straight onto the football oval where he played as a teenager.

"I know this isn't Heathton Ridge where everyone knows everyone, but Carrington's not exactly a big place. I'd put money on Joel and Hayden knowing each other. And if Hayden hated the gay community back then as much as he did in recent years, which his former footy coach certainly seems to believe..." Cassie trailed off, seeing Brian still struggling to take it all in.

"Okay, so, say Foster did know Joel, and gave him a hard time, that doesn't mean he had anything to do with his death. Not when the police said the fire was an accident. You know what these things are like, Cass. The arson chemists are all over that stuff whenever anyone's found dead."

"In 1998?" Cassie challenged. "And why would Laura say she always thought there was something suspicious about that fire?"

"Well, she would say that, right? Especially if it was suicide. Families and friends, they never want to believe it. It's too painful."

Cassie took a slow breath and let it out, her chest heavy.

"I'm just saying, Cass. It's what? Almost thirty years ago? Even if Foster did have something to do with Joel's death, even if he contributed to it, how do you prove something like that? And how does that even fit the story angle now?"

"Shit, Bri, you're starting to sound like Peter. Thanks heaps," she muttered, deflating.

On the street below, the noise of the holiday crowd rose suddenly, a group of women laughing hysterically as they passed, the roar of a motorbike ricocheting off the balcony walls like a crazed tennis ball.

Cassie stared into space, silent, while Brian sat still, unsure what to say next.

"Where's that list of names? Foster's footy mates?"

"You mean that photo you sent me of your arm?" Brian joked. "They're on my laptop, but you still have them on your phone, right?"

Cassie didn't reply, pulling her phone from her jeans pocket and scrolling with her thumb. Brian took the chance to retreat inside, tugging on a grey Monash University hoodie and pulling his laptop from the leather satchel beside the couch.

"He said one of them was dead," Cassie called.

"Huh?" Brian answered, reappearing and closing the door behind him.

"The football coach, Rodney Lindfield, he told me on the phone that one of these guys was dead. I can't remember who, but let's find out, and how. And see if we can dig anything up on the others while we're at it. Oh…" she added quickly, barely drawing breath, "did you get anything back from the Banksia Historical people before the break? Any class photos?"

She didn't wait for an answer, her focus locked back onto her screen. Brian just smiled. He knew better than to get in the way when Cassie got like this. He was forever amazed at how quickly she could flip from casual to hyper-focused in the blink of an eye. He knew his fate for the rest of the night.

He cocked his head and, with a resigned smile, asked simply: "Thai?"

* * *

By the time they'd finished off the last of the Pad Thai noodles and their second bottle of Asahi each, Cassie had claimed the floor of Brian's living room as her new office.

While Brian had been picking up their takeaway, she'd retrieved a notepad from her car and switched her phone to silent. It was time for work. Now she sat cross-legged on the floor, her back against the couch, scribbling furiously across the blank pages. Brian sat nearby in an armchair, flicking from one website to another on Cassie's command.

"OK, let's just go over all this," she said, ripping out pages from the notepad and spreading them across the floor.

"Right, so Hayden appears in a Year 7 class photo at Carrington High School in 1992, but then in 1994 he's in a Year 8 photo at Egan Park Technical College, which means not only was he kept back a year, but he also changed schools."

Brian nodded obediently.

"And Egan Park Tech was closed in '96, when the State Government shut down the last of the tech schools. Presuming he stayed there, he'd be, what? Year 10, around sixteen years old. And no trace of him in any schools after that."

"That's right."

"OK, so we're assuming he went to Grove Street Primary, it's the only public school in the area. If he was at the public high school, he probably didn't go to... what was the name of the local Catholic primary?"

"Um... Holy Eucharist Primary in Deakin Heights, in the next suburb over," Brian said, glancing back at his screen.

"OK, so Joel O'Connor went to St Matthew's College, so presumably the Catholic primary too, so it's unlikely he and Foster went to school together. But his footy mates..."

She pulled out another sheet. "Scott King, Carrington High. David Grayson, Carrington High. Brice McCrae, Carrington bloody High," she sighed. "OK, but all three of them, like Hayden, were the same age as Joel. I'd bet anything they knew him somehow."

Brian watched as Cassie flicked through her growing pile of notes.

"OK... moving on. We've got an online obituary for a Scott King, aged 24, from 2005. Lines up for age. It says he left behind a son, Eli, but no mention of a partner, wife, or cause of death. One for you," she added, shooting Brian a brief glance.

"There's an ABN listing for a Brice McCrae in Victoria, Rusty Shovel Landscapes, which has a website but no photo or mention of Brice. And nothing online at all for David Grayson, at least, not one the right age or from Melbourne." They both leaned back, surveying the paper-strewn floor like generals planning a siege.

"I need to meet with Laura. And in all fairness to his family, I'll need to reach out to whoever's left of the O'Connors. Rodney Lindfield said Joel's dad was a broken man after the death and they moved to Queensland. The parents mightn't even be alive anymore."

"What were their names?" Brian asked.

"I took a photo of Joel's plaque, hang on," she said, scrolling through her phone. "Here! Glen and Christie O'Connor. And his sister's name is Amelia. I think Facebook had her as 'Millie?' We found her profile page the other night, but it was locked."

Brian's fingers quickly worked his keyboard. "Here," he said as he passed his laptop towards her, an online newspaper article from the Queensland Courier Mail adorned the screen.

Glen and Christie O'Connor: "After the Storm" Meet the Couple Helping Queenslanders Rebuild.

Cassie read aloud: "Glen and Christie O'Connor, pictured, were honoured today for their tireless work as Emergency Recovery volunteers with the Australian Red Cross. The Gold Coast couple, originally from *Victoria*..." She looked up at Brian, her voice rising slightly.

"...have dedicated their retirement years supporting those impacted by natural disasters, most notably last year's devastating Brisbane floods." Cassie scrolled further up. "Bri, this is brilliant. It's from a couple of years ago, but at least we know how to find them." She paused, thinking. "I don't suppose..."

"Leave it with me," he said with a smile.

Cassie exhaled. "I hate doing this, especially when I've got nothing solid. But if Laura always thought something was off, maybe the parents did too. I'll start with Laura, see exactly what she has to say first."

She glanced across the sea of papers, then up at him, poised at his laptop. Her smile softened. "I'm so sorry, Bri. I didn't mean to crash your Easter Sunday. I didn't even ask, where's Jessica tonight?"

"Ah, well, she was going to come over earlier, but I told her not to after you called."

Cassie winced. "Shit, Bri. I'm sorry."

"Don't be." He smiled shyly. "I've enjoyed this. I always do. Watching you work. It's nice to be part of it now. Together." As he said it, his cheeks flushed a deeper red.

Cassie caught it but quickly turned back to her notes, pretending not to notice. She cared about Brian, she truly did, but even the spark of his new relationship hadn't seemed to dull the feelings she knew he still carried for her.

"Beer?" she offered, pushing herself to her feet.

"Um, no thanks. I've got the gym early tomorrow morning. But you go for your life."

Cassie paused at the fridge, leaning her hip against the bench, thinking. "Hey," she said eventually, still lost in thought. "Do you reckon you could see if we can get a copy of the coroner's report? For Joel? Even if it was ruled an accident, there might be something in there. And any report on the fire itself."

"Yeah. OK. It's another public holiday tomorrow, but I'll see what I can dig up."

"Thanks. I want to see if I can get into the hospital tomorrow to visit Jason Turner."

She shook her head softly, the night's weight settling back onto her shoulders.

"Thanks for tonight, Bri."

"You're going?" he asked, rising.

"Yeah." She grinned, sweeping the last two beers from the fridge. "But I'm taking these with me."

* * *

Cassie turned off the main road and wound through the backstreets to her building. She pulled into the rear car park, killed the engine, and glanced at the clock. Eight p.m. Easter Sunday.

Her thoughts were already on bed, the promise of sleep tugging at her. Then, out of nowhere, Joel O'Connor's smiling face flashed in her mind. She shivered, the feeling visceral, as if he were reaching out across the years, acknowledging her visit to his resting place, thanking her. Or maybe trying to tell her something more.

She let the thought linger, then grabbed the beers from the passenger seat and climbed out.

At the front of the building, her steps slowed.

Standing near the letterboxes, hands tucked into his jacket, a familiar face stood. Though here, in Elwood, it all felt out of place. Next to him, a dog sitting dutifully at his side, its tail thumping softly against the pavement as Cassie approached.

"Terence?" Cassie whispered in surprise, her heart skipping a beat. "What are you doing here?"

"Hey," he said with a sheepish grin. "Your Mum gave me your address. I tried to call," he hesitated. "Those attacks yesterday, the news is everywhere. Your parents mentioned at lunch that you were there. That you were friends with one of the guys injured."

"Yeah. Yes. I am."

"I figured you might want company. Or maybe not." He gave a tentative shrug. "Like I said, I tried to call. But if now's not a good time…"

Cassie let out a breathy laugh, the tension slowly easing.

"I'm sorry, my phone's on silent." She said, pulling it out from her pocket. Three missed calls. Two texts. All Terence.

She looked down at Rusty, who was watching her adoringly while drooling onto the footpath.

"Where are you staying?" she asked.

"Well…" he hesitated. "I didn't really think that far ahead. I've got the swag in the back of the Ute. Rusty and I can just sleep down by the water," he nodded towards the other end of her street.

Cassie raised an eyebrow. "It's Melbourne, Terence. You can't just set up camp on Elwood beach."

She sighed and looked again at Rusty, who was now trying to catch his strand of drool with his tongue. "Is he going to do that all night?"

Terence looked down. "No."

"Good. Then both of you are coming upstairs. But keep it quiet, I'm not in the mood for a lecture from my downstairs neighbour."

Walking beside him, Cassie felt the night's chill on her skin and the warmth of not being alone.

SEVENTEEN

They slipped out just before sunrise, the sky still bruised with the last shadows of night. Rusty padded ahead, tail high, his paws kicking up soft sprays of sand as they traced the slow curve of Elwood Beach. The air was sharp, salted, the kind that cleared your head whether you wanted it to or not.

Cassie shoved her hands into her jacket pockets, tugging the sleeves down over her fingers to fend off the cold. Melbourne's brief return to summer had vanished as quickly as it came.

The water stretched out like hammered metal: dull, restless, catching the faintest glimmers of the coming day.

She stole a glance at Terence beside her. His beanie was pulled low, dark tufts of hair poked out from beneath, the smile lines at the corners of his eyes deepening as he watched Rusty race in wide, chaotic circles.

They'd stayed up late. Sharing the two stolen beers slowly as the apartment held its breath around them. Conversation had given way to quiet, not awkward, but thick with things unsaid. There had been a kiss.

Tentative at first, testing boundaries, then something more certain.

When she finally peeled herself away to get ready for bed, Terence had just smiled, squeezed her hand, and claimed the couch, folding himself into the mess of jackets and jeans she'd flung across it earlier. Rusty curled up on the floor beside him. Old-fashioned, maybe. But it made her want him all the more.

Cassie let out a slow breath, watching it ghost into the dawn air. The ache she felt wasn't just desire, it was older than that, heavier. Like recognising a hunger you'd spent years pretending you didn't have.

The beach was empty but for them. The occasional cyclist buzzed past on the path behind, a lone jogger in headphones, but otherwise, the world felt muted. Suspended. As if, for this stolen hour, the storm could wait.

Her phone buzzed in her pocket, shattering the illusion. She fished it out, blinking against the glare of the screen.

A text. Amir.

Hello dear friend. I'm back in Melbourne. Jason's doing OK but he has asked to see you. He's at The Alfred. Do you think you could call in? Amir. x

Cassie stopped walking, thumb hovering.

Terence caught up beside her, one brow lifting. "Everything okay?"

"It's Jason, the one I told you about. He wants me to come by the hospital."

Terence nodded, kicking at a drift of sand with the toe of his boot. "Guess I better head back up to Wang then."

She hesitated, searching his face. "Do you have to?"

His mouth quirked into a half-smile. "Yeah, I probably should. I've got work this arvo. Adulting and all that."

Cassie felt it then, that hollow pang. The end of something fleeting.

"But hey," he added, with a grin she couldn't help but mirror, "you're still taking your leave, yeah? Once this story's done?"

"That's the plan."

"Well, there ya go. We'll see you soon then," he said, flashing her a grin broad and mischievous, like the Cheshire Cat had wandered down from Wangaratta just to rile her up.

Rusty barked, leaping at a seagull that veered too low, feathers scattering in his wake. Cassie laughed, surprised by the sound of it, raw and unguarded. For a moment, it felt like enough.

She drew in a deep breath, the cold air stinging her lungs, and felt something settle inside. Not enough to quiet the restlessness. But enough to steady it.

One step at a time.

* * *

Cassie stepped out of the lift and into the burns unit on the sixth floor of The Alfred Hospital.

"Hi, could you please direct me to Jason Turner's room? I'm a friend, he's expecting me," she said to the nurse at the nearby station.

"Room 617," the nurse replied with a polite nod. "Down the corridor to your left."

"Thanks."

Cassie set off, her sneakers squeaking against the shiny grey linoleum, the overhead lights throwing sharp reflections along the floor. The chemical tang of disinfectant clung to the air, mingling with the soft beeping of monitors behind closed doors. She knew this world too well: the smells, the sounds, the heavy quiet that always sat just beneath it all.

At Room 617, she paused to pump a dollop of hand sanitiser into her palms, rubbing the cool, stinging alcohol between her fingers. A habit learned over too many visits like this one.

She knocked lightly and pushed the door open.

Jason looked up from the hospital bed, a broad smile breaking across his battered face. "Cassie! Come in! Amir!"

From the small ensuite bathroom beside the bed, Amir appeared, ducking his head through the doorway with a sheepish grin. He was tall and lean, with olive skin and a neatly trimmed beard, his dark hair curling slightly at the edges from the humidity of a long-haul flight. There was a weariness clinging to his eyes, the unmistakable glaze of jet lag, but he crossed the room with easy grace, greeting Cassie with a warm kiss on the cheek.

"Cassie. Thanks so much for coming," he said, his accent a gentle blend of American cadence and something softer beneath, a trace of his Iranian roots. He pulled a plastic chair from beside the window, where the view stretched out across the city skyline, and beckoned Cassie to sit.

"How are you both holding up?" she asked, leaning in to kiss Jason's cheek before sinking into the seat.

Jason's arms and legs were heavily wrapped in gauze, a thin blue sheet pulled up to his waist. His torso was bare, covered in bruises and burns, the skin raw in places.

"I'm OK," he said, glancing down at himself. "It looks worse than it is, honestly. I was lucky."

He shifted slightly, wincing. "I went back in to grab Moira Rose. The poor thing was cowering under the bedside table and wouldn't come out. I couldn't just leave her there."

"Of course not. How is she?" Cassie asked gently.

"She's OK," Amir said, sitting down opposite her. "She's at Jason's sister's place. I've checked into a hotel, so she'll stay there until we figure something out."

"You're at a hotel?" Cassie asked, surprised. "When did you get back?"

"About one o'clock this morning," Amir said, pretending to fall asleep against the back of the chair. "I'm just across the road at the Oaks. Jason's sister's family offered, but..." He gave a small, tired smile. "Mordialloc is a bit too far. I'd rather be close to him."

Cassie nodded, her gaze dropping to Jason's hand, bandaged thickly, resting stiff on the blanket. She felt the tightness building in her chest before she could stop it.

"I'm so sorry," she said quietly, looking between them. "I was there, at your place when it happened. Out on the street with the rest of the neighbourhood. I was so scared you'd..."

The lump hit her throat mid-sentence, sharp and sudden. It startled her. It was only ever her dad who could crack her open like that inside a hospital room.

"Sorry," she said quickly, coughing to cover the falter in her voice.

"Don't apologise," Jason said. His voice was steady, but softer now. "It would've been a bloody awful thing to see. Even knowing I made it out. I'm sorry you had to go through that."

He shifted his gaze to Amir, something dark flickering between them.

"I'm sorry we all had to go through that." Jason said quietly. "After all these years, after all this so-called progress, they still come for us."

Cassie sat back slightly, feeling the weight of it settle between them.

"That's actually why we asked you here," Amir said, his voice low as the mood in the room shifted.

"Jason told me you're doing a story on the people who did this?" Amir asked, his face darkening.

"In a way," Cassie said carefully. "I was, but we've shifted gears a bit. We've been digging more into Hayden Foster's life now, but yeah, I'm still looking at the Patriots too. Why?"

Amir and Jason exchanged a look. This time, Jason spoke.

"If you're going to tell Hayden Foster's story," he said, voice low, "just... please don't forget about ours. About the people the Hayden Fosters of the world come after and the lives they destroy."

"Of course not," Cassie said, sitting forward. "That's the whole point of the story. To understand it, maybe even help stop this kind of thing from happening again."

Jason nodded, but there was a sadness in his eyes.

Amir spoke softly at first. "It's just... we've been here before. We thought we'd left the worst of it behind. But now, it feels like the world's shifting again. Like we're sliding backwards. And Cassie, it was bad enough the first time."

He paused, steadying himself.

"We're a proud community. We're resilient. But we've endured a hell of a lot. And we don't want the next generation going through what we did. We've come too far."

Cassie nodded, the weight of his words sinking in.

Amir leaned in now, voice tighter. "And it's not just us, the gays. As a Muslim, living in the States after 9/11 was hell. We were profiled, abused, spat on. My youngest sister, she was walking home from school when a car full of men hurled a McDonald's thick shake at her and screamed slurs. Just because she wore a hijab."

He paused. His hands clenched, jaw tight.

"And now, all these years later, they burn down our house of worship. My place of work. My home. And they do *this*, to my husband."

Cassie said nothing. There was nothing *to* say.

Jason reached out and gently squeezed Amir's hand with his fingertips, then turned back to her.

"I know it's hard to believe, but we're a bit older than you, Cassie," he said with a wink and a crooked grin.

His smile faded. "But it's important you know. It wasn't so long ago that being different was something to be genuinely afraid of."

Cassie hesitated. "Would you tell me about it?"

"Of course," Jason said, his voice softening. "We'll tell you anything you want."

Cassie gave a small nod, settling back in her chair.

Jason looked at Amir again, drew in a slow breath, and began.

"Let's start with the Sydney Mardi Gras. One of the biggest celebrations on the Sydney calendar. But it began in 1978 as a peaceful march for gay rights and an end to discrimination. But it turned ugly very quickly. Many people call it Australia's own Stonewall moment and for good reason."

Cassie nodded. "I know. And I know many of the original marchers were brutally assaulted and arrested by New South Wales Police. Their names and addresses were even published in the newspaper in the days that followed, as some sort of twisted public humiliation meant to 'out' them."

Jason raised his eyebrows. "You know your history."

"From my dad, actually. He never tolerated abuse of power, not from the force, not from anyone. It upset him, knowing how badly the gay community was treated by people wearing the same uniform he wore. My Aunt Valerie in Glasgow is gay, and we were raised to treat everyone equally, and with respect."

Jason nodded, his expression softening. "Your dad's a good man. And one of the rare exceptions back then. Most gay hate crimes went unreported, because the police were part of the problem. Through the 80's and 90's, groups of teenagers would go out hunting for gay men, 'poofter bashing,' they called it."

Cassie shuddered, thinking of Rodney Lindfield's casual laughter over the same thing.

"I'm so sorry," she said quietly.

Jason shifted in bed, wincing as he tried to get comfortable.

"But that was the public sentiment at the time. Especially when the AIDS epidemic hit. In the early-80's, I was just starting high school. We knew about AIDS, but the mainstream media barely talked about it. Gay men were dying, but no one seemed to care. Not until it spread to the general population."

He exhaled slowly.

"Then the Grim Reaper ads hit, those terrifying public service announcements with bowling alleys and crying children. Grim reapers knocking people over like pins. The message was clear: the gays are coming to kill your families with their dirty disease."

Amir gave a sombre nod.

"They only ran for a few weeks," Jason said, "but the damage was enormous. Lasting. If AIDS was the powder keg, those ads felt like the flame. Gay hate crimes spiked. We were already targets, and now we were being blamed for a plague."

Beside him, Amir noticed the strain in his voice and moved to adjust a slipped pillow.

"Thanks, darling," Jason murmured, easing back.

"For some reason, it was particularly bad in Sydney," he continued. "The sea cliffs near Bondi were a known beat. Men would go there at night, for sex, yes, but also to connect. You have to remember this was before the internet. No chat rooms, no apps. Most of us were closeted, terrified of being outed. The beats were one of the only places you could meet people like you, away from the bars and clubs."

He paused, eyes distant.

"There are still dozens of unsolved murders. Gay men bashed and thrown off those cliffs, mostly by groups of teenagers. Many were written off as suicides. The police never investigated them properly. No one cared enough to."

The room fell quiet. Cassie could feel the air change, heavier now, grief thick as dust.

Jason turned back to her, his voice lower.

"I'll never forget something I heard as a kid. I was only twelve or thirteen, at a mate's place for a barbecue. His dad was standing at the grill with a bunch of other suburban blokes, beers in hand, laughing."

He took a breath.

"And then he said it, like it was nothing. Just another punchline: *'The only good poofter is a dead poofter.'*"

The silence that followed was deeper. More final. Cassie sat frozen, the words hanging in the air like smoke.

"I was still in the closet when I first started sneaking into the clubs. But it felt like I'd stumbled into Narnia. This whole other world where people embraced you for who you were. There was colour and music and joy. But we always had to watch over our shoulder. We'd walk to and from the clubs in groups, just to stay safe."

He looked at her, voice soft now.

"We're grateful we can walk down the street as husbands today. That this country, mostly, accepts us. But when people see a Rainbow Flag and call it overkill… when they see Drag Queens and claim we're trying to convert their children… they don't understand. They don't know we celebrate pride because it was hard fought. And we know how quickly things can be taken away."

Amir nodded. "And we celebrate not just for ourselves, but for those who can't. If my parents hadn't left Iran for the United States, I might not be alive. Being gay there is still a death sentence. Australia isn't perfect, but it's paradise by comparison."

Jason reached for Cassie's hand.

"Whatever you show in your story… just make sure it helps swing the pendulum back. It feels like everyone is so angry all the time now, and hate crimes are on the rise again, not just against gay people, but against anyone who's seen as different.

And you, this is why we love you; you've always made sure the voices most impacted by your stories are the ones front and centre.

I still believe most people are inherently good. I think they just need reminding. That it's our differences that connect us, not divide us. That the world isn't as bleak as it's made out to be. We need to hear that now more than ever."

He paused, then said with quiet conviction:

"Because, Cassie, we know what it is to live in fear. We can't go back to that. We won't go back."

* * *

Cassie left the hospital with the morning sun warming her back, Jason's words still echoing in her mind. As the city stirred to life around her, trams rattling past, office towers casting long, sharp shadows, she felt the familiar pull of responsibility tighten around her ribs. But this time, it wasn't just about the story. It was about the people. The history. The fight still unfinished.

She opened up her contacts, scrolling until she found the number she'd saved only yesterday. Her reflection caught in the glass, tired eyes, windblown hair, but sharp beneath it all.

It was time to chase ghosts.

EIGHTEEN

Eltham sat within Melbourne's 'green wedge' in the northeast, a pocket of preserved bushland homes exempt from urban sprawl. Unlike the flat, patchy grassed properties of Carrington and its rapid development, Eltham's steep blocks were a tangle of native shrubs and wildflowers, towering gums lining the nature strips. Many homes were barely visible from the road, swallowed by dense foliage, their driveways the only sign of habitation.

Cassie parked on the quiet street and made her way up the steep bluestone-paved drive. Built into the hillside, the two-story house was a mottled mix of cream and brown brick, an olive-green wooden veranda running the full length of the upstairs level.

The attached garage had been repurposed into a commercial kitchen, its roller door replaced with sleek, black-tinted glass, the only part of the house visible from the street. Near the front door, a small patch of reclaimed garden had been flattened into a gravel parking space. A single white transit van sat there, VALETTA'S CATERING scrawled across its side in bold lettering. Above it, a cartoon bowl of spaghetti and meatballs tilted mid-air, as if flung from the van in transit.

From the trees above, a kookaburra let out a cackling call, heralding Cassie's arrival.

The glass sliding door of the garage squeaked open. "Cassandra, hi."

Laura Cassini stood at the entrance, smiling. "Thank you so much for coming. Please, come in." Her sweet-smelling perfume lingered in the air as Cassie followed her inside.

"Can I make you a coffee?" Laura asked, already moving towards a gleaming industrial espresso machine.

"I'd love one, thanks."

"Latte? Espresso?" She switched on a noisy grinder.

"Flat white. Strong. Thank you."

Laura was dressed casually, but Cassie couldn't help noticing how effortlessly glamorous she looked. Dark blue denim, matte-black ankle boots, a cropped black jumper over a crisp white button-down. Her makeup was flawless, subtle yet polished, her dark chestnut waves with blonde highlights falling just past her shoulders. Large silver-and-glass earrings dangled as she moved, posture perfect, gliding rather than walking. She had the presence of the on-air presenters Cassie worked with, women who radiated both class and confidence.

The converted garage was pristine. A double-door fridge gleamed against the back wall, flanked by sleek, uniform white cabinetry. To the right, a broad stainless-steel island faced a row of modern ovens and gas stovetops. To her left, a high timber table sat beneath a window, four stools perched neatly around it on a marble-patterned rug. Cassie slid onto a stool.

"*Mum!*"

A door in the far-left corner suddenly opened, revealing the rest of the house. A teenage boy, maybe thirteen or fourteen, stepped into the room. Black tracksuit pants and hoodie, spinning a soccer ball between his hands.

"Max wants to go to the park. Can we go up for a bit?"

"Liam," Laura said pointedly, nodding toward Cassie.

The boy turned, flushing. "Oh, sorry, hi. Nice to meet you." He extended a hand, shaking Cassie's firmly.

She smiled, amused and a little impressed by his good manners. "Nice to meet you too."

"Max wants to go, or *you* want to go?" Laura asked.

"I want to go!" came another voice, higher pitched. A younger boy, around ten, entered the room. Cassie recognized the features of Down syndrome immediately.

"Hello, I'm Max!" He beamed, sticking out his hand. "You're the lady from TV!"

Cassie grinned, his joy infectious. "That's me. Nice to meet you, Max."

"Yes, you can go. Anything to get you away from your screens for five minutes."

"Thanks, Mum!" Both boys bolted back through the house. Moments later, the front door slammed.

Cassie turned, catching a glimpse of them sprinting down the driveway, their voices fading into the distance.

Laura shook her head. "School holidays." She returned, a coffee in each hand, sliding a white porcelain cup toward Cassie. "Are you married Cassandra? Kids?"

Cassie wrapped her hands around the warmth of her cup. "No, neither. Maybe one day. And it's only Cassandra for the cameras. Call me Cassie, or Cass, whichever you prefer."

Laura smiled, acknowledging the invitation. She plucked a few almond crescent biscuits from a glass jar in the centre of the table, placing them on a small plate.

"I have to admit, I was rather startled yesterday at the cemetery," Laura said, studying her over the rim of her cup. "My husband and I mostly watch the ABC, so I knew who you were straight away. I am a big admirer of your work. But then to hear you say my name, and Joel's, I apologise if I came across as rude, it was just a bit unexpected."

"Please, there's no need to apologise. I get it. I'm sorry to have startled you, especially given the time and place."

"Well, after the initial shock wore off, I must say I was, and am now even, a little star struck to be honest."

"There's no need to be, I can assure you. I can be pretty boring really," she grinned.

"I don't believe that for a second," Laura's tone softened, but her gaze stayed sharp. "The stories you've done? The bastards who've been put away as a result? That's not boring. I've watched you for years, Cassie. I can tell you're a strong woman."

Cassie felt heat rise to her cheeks. She wasn't sure if it was the compliment, or the conviction in Laura's voice, that unsettled her more.

Cassie smiled. "Well, thank you for saying that. My dad was in the police force, the senior sergeant in the country town where I grew up. I like to think I'm following in his footsteps, just in a very public way."

Laura's expression softened. "Is your dad no longer around?"

"No, no, he's still with us. Well, for now." Cassie hesitated. "He has stage three bowel cancer. They're still treating it, but..." She trailed off, breaking eye contact.

"I'm so sorry to hear that," Laura said gently. "I lost my own dad a few years back. Heart attack. You grow up knowing that one day you'll lose your parents, but it doesn't make it any easier when it happens." She smiled sympathetically. A brief silence followed before she met Cassie's gaze again, her expression shifting. "So, Joel."

Cassie straightened, slipping her phone from her bag. "Right, of course." She tapped through her apps. "Do you mind if I record our conversation?"

"I'm not sure I feel comfortable with that, if that's OK. Especially since I still don't know what this extremist person has to do with me, or Joel."

"Of course," Cassie said, setting her phone down. "Like I mentioned yesterday, I've been building a profile on Hayden Foster, the man who was killed last week. I was looking into his involvement with the

Allied Patriots, but it's turning into something bigger. A piece on extremism more broadly, how people get pulled in, what's driving it. I'm still trying to connect the dots."

Laura's gaze didn't waver. Cassie hesitated. There was something about Laura that unsettled her. She was used to leading interviews, controlling the flow, but something about Laura's presence shifted the dynamic. Cassie had only been here minutes, yet she already respected her and wanted to make the right impression.

"Look, I was honest with you yesterday when I said I was just paying my respects. But I have to ask. What did you mean when you said you had your suspicions about the fire that claimed Joel's life? I know the police ruled it as an accident, but, if there's something you want to tell me, maybe there's something I can look into? I don't know how helpful it will be almost thirty years on, but I'm certainly willing to try."

Laura leant back now, shifting her gaze and staring back through the front windows, eyes distant. "It's a lifetime ago, you know? But when I think about him, it feels like yesterday." She took a steadying breath. "Where do you want me to start?"

"Wherever you want."

Laura poured water from a blue glass bottle into two empty glasses and slid one across the table. "As close as Joel and I were, we barely knew each other in the first couple of years of school. I mean, I *knew of* him, but we weren't friends. That changed in Year 9. When we connected, we *really* connected. We were both outsiders, I guess. After we found each other, everyone else just melted away."

Laura glanced out the window again before continuing.

"I could be myself around Joel. Or at least, the self I thought I was back then. I hated school. I was always in my older siblings' shadows, straight-A students, good at sport, church every Sunday. I was the youngest by eight years. I barely knew them. And my parents? Always busy with the restaurant. I felt... forgotten. So, I acted out. By 15, I'd already been suspended twice, run away from home, hung out with older kids. I thought I was having a great time."

Her smile faltered.

"And then I met Joel."

Cassie leaned in slightly. "What was he like?"

"Different from me. I was loud, rebellious. Joel was quiet, polite, especially around adults. My parents adored him."

"Sounds like a good kid."

"He was. Gentle. Kind. But in those last couple of years, he changed. He started standing up for himself against some of the boys at school who gave him a hard time. He was finding his voice." Laura gave a soft laugh. "I probably had something to do with that. But he was also a dreamer. Always talking about getting out of Carrington, out of Australia."

She finished her espresso, setting the cup down carefully.

"Our houses backed onto a big reserve. We'd sneak out late at night and meet up at the playground, me chain-smoking cigarettes, him talking about moving away to London, New York... places where he thought he could just be himself."

"And what about you?" Cassie asked.

Laura smiled faintly. "Oh, I couldn't wait to leave either. This was the 90s. Nirvana, teenage angst. None of us wanted the lives our parents had." She glanced around the sleek kitchen. "Funny, isn't it? I spent years rebelling against my parents... and here I am now, keeping good old Nonna Valetta alive."

She shook her head, half amused, half wistful.

"Is it true that Joel may have been gay?" Cassie asked.

Laura smirked. "Not *may have been*. Joel *was* gay. I think that's why I felt so safe around him."

"Was he out?"

Laura scoffed. "At a Catholic high school? In the 1990s? God, no. He wasn't even fully out to himself. I still remember the night he tried to tell me. We were at the playground in the reserve. He looked like he was in agony. I just said, 'Joel, you do know that I know you're gay, right?'"

She sighed. "The horror on his face... Back then, you didn't even *say* those words out loud. And the shit he copped at school, especially from the footy boys, it was awful."

"Did his family know he was gay?"

"Possibly. But Joel certainly didn't tell them. He barely admitted it to me at first." She shook her head, the sadness clear. "That's why I took him under my wing. Brought him into my world."

"What do you mean?"

"I was already sneaking into nightclubs by the time we became friends. One of them was a gay club, 3 Faces, on Commercial Road in Prahran. Drag queens, hot guys dancing with their shirts off, and no one trying to crack onto me. Perfect."

She smiled. "I took Joel there in '97. We were both sixteen. I thought maybe if he saw other gay people living their lives, he'd feel less... terrified."

"Did he?"

"At first? He was like a deer in headlights. But after a few weeks, he wanted to go back. And then he *loved* it. The dance floor, the music, the freedom. He even joined a support group for gay teens. They met at some café in Elwood..."

"Inside Out?" Cassie interrupted, surprised.

Laura's eyes widened. "Yeah! You know it?"

Cassie nodded. "I live around the corner. It was one of the places firebombed over the weekend."

Laura's face paled. "I had no idea. I heard one of the places targeted was in Elwood, but between the school holidays and the kids... I wasn't really paying attention."

She sat back heavily, exhaling.

"God. I didn't even know that place still existed."

Cassie considered mentioning Jason Turner but decided to push forward.

"You said Joel made you feel safe," Cassie said gently. "I'm sure he felt the same about you. Especially when you introduced him to a world where he didn't have to hide."

Laura smiled, touched. "Thank you. That means a lot."

Cassie hesitated for a moment, then asked, "Laura, I'm sorry to bring this up, but the night of the fire, why do you think it wasn't an accident?"

Laura drew in a steady breath.

"Alright. Well, I saw Joel on Good Friday, a few days before. His family had gone to Phillip Island for the weekend, but Joel stayed home, he told them he needed to study. Truth was, we had plans to go out Sunday night. To 3 Faces." She smiled faintly.

"Unbeknownst to Joel, my sister had scored us tickets to *Resurrection*, a big gay dance party at Dome nightclub. Alexandra really liked Joel. She had heaps of gay friends at Uni, so she got it. Anyway, Joel had heard a rumour that Dannii Minogue was going to perform at *Resurrection*. He was obsessed with the Minogue sisters, but especially Dannii. There was this one song, *Remembrance*, I think it was called, something like that anyway. He played it over and over. Drove me insane."

Cassie laughed quietly, shifting in her seat. "You weren't a fan?"

"God, no." Laura grinned. "I was into hip-hop, R&B, a bit of rock and grunge. But Joel? He was all about pop. Madonna, Savage Garden, and after those nights at 3 Faces, it became all about Eurodance. But Kylie and Dannii?" She laughed. "*Obsessed*."

She poured herself another glass of water. Cassie, eyeing the plate of biscuits, gave in and grabbed one. Laura caught her and grinned.

"Go on, they're homemade."

Cassie took a bite, brushing powdered sugar off her jeans.

"So, Joel didn't know about the *Resurrection* tickets?"

"Not at first. I went over to surprise him on Good Friday. We were both working Saturday, me at the restaurant, Joel at the Carrington cinemas. We weren't going to see each other again until Sunday night."

She smiled at the memory, then her face fell.

"Two hours. That's how long I stood outside that bloody nightclub, waiting for him. Two hours. Neither of us had a mobile phone back then, but I didn't need to call him to know something was wrong."

Cassie watched Laura's hands as she brushed biscuit crumbs into a tidy pile.

"Cassie... there's no way he would have missed that, no way." Laura's voice cracked. "The idea of seeing Dannii Minogue singing his favourite song? And instead, he just 'goes to bed early,' 'leaves the gas on'? Please."

She exhaled sharply.

"And before you ask, yes, there were rumours he killed himself. No. Not a chance. He was *finally* finding his voice. Finding himself."

Cassie nodded slowly.

"When did you first hear about the fire?"

"Not until the next day. I'd stayed over at my sister's flat in Abbotsford. Mum called me..." Laura's voice wavered. "He was my best friend. Losing him..." She trailed off, the weight of it still raw.

Cassie reached across the table, resting her hand over Laura's. "I'm so sorry." But even as she spoke, her mind flashed to Kimberley Taylor. To the others. The car wreck. The wooden cross by the roadside. She blinked, the thought disappearing.

Laura smiled faintly, her eyes glazed with tears. "It's good to talk about him. To remember who he really was. Actually..." She stood, crossing to a nearby shelf. "Would you like to see a photo?"

She returned with a wooden frame cradled in her hands.

"This is us."

Cassie studied it: two teenagers, arms slung around each other, grinning against a backdrop of a huge outdoor stage, hordes of people everywhere. Joel wore the same cheeky grin she'd seen in his school photo. Laura, however, was almost unrecognisable: dark eye makeup, orange lipstick, short bleached-blonde hair slicked back into cornrows.

"Is that really you?" Cassie asked, grinning.

Laura laughed. "Yep. That was at the Big Day Out music festival. We went to see The Prodigy. Joel bleached my hair for me. Mum nearly killed me." she laughed.

Cassie handed the photo back.

"Was Joel seeing anyone?" she asked.

"As in dating? No, not at all. Though in those last few months…" Laura paused.

"Something in him shifted. He hinted he'd met someone, but I think it was just physical."

"Did he say who it was?"

"No. I assumed he'd met someone from that support group, but I don't know. He was really cagey about it. Looking back, I don't know if he was ashamed of it or proud of it. Either way, he was a bit cocky, like it was this big secret that he wouldn't tell me about."

"Did Joel ever mention Hayden Foster?"

Laura frowned, thinking hard. "No. I don't remember that name at all. Sorry."

Cassie picked up her phone and flicked through her notes. "I've got a list of guys who played footy with Hayden in Carrington. Maybe you'll remember a name... or Joel might have mentioned one." She hesitated. "What about David Grayson?"

Laura shook her head. "No."

"Scott King?"

Another shake. "No, sorry."

"Brice McCrae?"

That name landed differently. Cassie caught it, the slightest flicker, a shift in Laura's posture.

Laura hesitated, then shrugged lightly. "Hmm. No, I don't think so."

She's lying, Cassie thought. It was subtle, but unmistakable. Almost as if sensing Cassie's doubt, Laura shifted again, clearing her throat.

"No, wait. Brice... yeah. I knew Brice. Well, *knew of* him. He went to St Matthew's originally but moved to Carrington High when his parents split up. I dunno... maybe Year 10? Year 11? He lived on the same street as me, but like I say..." she shrugged.

Cassie nodded but made a mental note of Laura's hesitation.

"When it came to the boys who gave Joel a hard time, there wasn't one who stood out," Laura said. "It was the footy boys, full stop. That's just what it was like back then, toxic as hell. I know things have changed, but not enough.

"I'm just glad our boys' soccer club is the polar opposite of how things used to be. Inclusive, accepting. Just... so different."

She paused, picking at a crumb on the table.

"I do remember there was a bit of drama once with the local footy club back then, actually. Their coach got into trouble for hiring strippers for the boys after they won the premiership one year."

"Rodney Lindfield?" Cassie asked, raising an eyebrow.

"Yeah, that's right! God, I haven't heard that name in years. It was a whole scandal, for all of five minutes, until everyone laughed it off because half the dads were there egging it on. *Boys being boys*, that kind of thing."

Cassie sat forward.

"Laura... what do you really think happened to Joel?"

Laura hesitated, staring into her empty coffee mug.

"I don't know," she said finally. "It just never made sense. And it still doesn't." Laura's voice cracked. "Losing someone like Joel at that age... You have no idea what that kind of trauma, losing your best friend, and the guilt that comes with it, can do to a person."

Cassie didn't speak.

Because she did know.

She remembered kneeling by the makeshift cross at the bend outside Heathton Ridge. The way the wind howled through the gums that day, like the whole world was wailing with her.

She scraped through uni. Barely. Grief clung like wet clothes, heavy and inescapable.

It was Auntie Val, no-nonsense, chain-smoking, sharp-eyed Valerie, who got her the job at BBC Scotland as an escape from Heathton Ridge. She had to run as far away as she could.

That's where she met Simon Davies. The golden boy of the newsroom. Cambridge-educated, camera-ready, utterly magnetic.

Still broken, she thought maybe he was what she needed. Maybe he could rescue her.

He took her under his wing. Then dragged her under with him.

Alcohol. Cocaine. Nights that ended in tears. Mornings she couldn't remember. Simon was brilliant, and cruel. The kind of man who could charm an audience and eviscerate a partner. Always just enough affection to keep her tethered. Always just enough cruelty to keep her small.

She'd carried the shame of that for years. Not the relationship, *him*. The fact that she'd let someone like that get so close. Trusted him. Thought she'd be smart enough to spot a man like that from a mile away.

She wasn't.

So yes. Cassie knew exactly what trauma could do. It could bury you if you let it.

Cassie blinked as she found her breath.

"One more question. Did you ever take it to the police?"

Laura's face twisted with disdain.

"Police? Yeah. I tried. I was told I was just a 'silly little girl.' That they'd done their job. That there was nothing more to it."

Cassie's jaw tightened, she'd heard that before. "Who told you that?"

Laura's voice was low and bitter.

"That former big-wig cop who became a politician." She paused, eyes narrowing. "Graham. Graham Golding."

NINETEEN

Cassie's mind was already racing by the time she reached her apartment. She barely remembered the drive home, no clue if she'd run a stop sign or drifted through a red light, so tangled were the questions and scenarios looping through her head.

Graham Golding.

It wasn't hard to imagine him brushing off a grieving teenager, especially if the boy she was mourning didn't fit the narrative he wanted to protect. That sounded exactly like him. But the knot in Cassie's gut was tightening now, and she couldn't ignore it. She knew the risks of confirmation bias. Her personal dislike of Golding could easily cloud her judgment. Even so, this was a thread worth pulling.

She sat at her kitchen table, laptop open, as flecks of dust floated through the afternoon light like specks of gold. She sighed when the first search result popped up: Wikipedia.

She scrolled past the grinning photo, at least a decade old, concealing the receding hairline and sunspots. It was all curated. Glossy. Like a press release dressed up as a legacy.

Graham Golding. Born 1956. Spouse: Ana 'Anne' Golding (née Rumann), deceased. Children: Kathryn Golding, Evan Golding, Justin Golding.

More glossy photos followed: national awards, red carpets, radio studios. Page after page of glowing biographies listing his achievements, volunteer work, community contributions.

She skimmed down to the early career section. That's what she wanted. District Commander, Outer Eastern Melbourne, Victoria Police. Based at Banksia Police Station. Cassie opened a new tab and pulled up Google Maps.

Banksia Police Station.

This wasn't some sleepy suburban outpost. It loomed, a hulking two-storey box of dark mirrored windows and bureaucratic bulk. Across the road, the Banksia City Council building looked positively modest by comparison.

Banksia. *Carrington.*

Cassie ran quick searches on each of the three children.

An old Harvard article popped up first, welcoming Kathryn Golding from Australia to their Boston campus. A little digging on the Harvard website revealed a more recent photo, and a name change: Dr Kathryn Whitmarsh, School of Education and Early Childhood Development.

Evan Golding had also followed their mother into education, but his photo on the Ferndale Secondary College website was striking, not just because of the resemblance to Graham, but because, in his principal's portrait, he wore a football jersey instead of the usual suit and tie. Even with a smile, he looked cold. Guarded.

Justin Golding proved trickier. No photos, no social media, no news stories. Just a dry business listing: an ABN for Justin Johann Golding, locksmith, Banksia. No website, just a name in the online yellow pages. Strange, Cassie thought. That's him, no doubt, the European middle name, the location. If the family lived near Carrington, he hadn't moved far.

That gave her another idea.

She trawled the old school photos she and Brian had used to track down Hayden Foster and his mates, but came up empty for Justin, no class shots at Carrington High, no records from Egan Park Tech. Nothing.

She sighed, pushing back from the table and wandered into the kitchen, flicking on the kettle. Leaning against the sink, she stared out the window to the apartment block next door, another two-storey Art Deco, not too dissimilar to her own. From where she stood, she could just make out one of the old plane trees out front, its golden leaves now sparse, clinging on.

As the kettle rumbled toward its finale, Cassie turned, her mind ticking over. She walked back into the lounge, sat down, and opened Facebook. A few clicks took her to the St Matthew's alumni page, and soon she was scrolling through the old Class of 1998 photo, the first one where she'd spotted Joel.

About a hundred students in total, girls-only seated in front, hands clasped together on their laps, with several rows of boys and girls standing behind, a sea of red, black, white, and gold.

Cassie's eyes sharpened as she studied the names beneath the photo, fingertip tracing each one down from the top row. There it was, second row from the top, halfway along: Justin Golding.

She counted across the faces to match the name. There he was. Average height, hair parted in the middle, flopping into his eyes. He and two other boys stood side by side, arms crossed, none of them smiling like the others.

"Hmm," Cassie murmured.

Same age. Same school. Same year as Joel and Laura. Laura had mentioned Graham Golding, but not a word about going to school with his son.

Cassie grabbed her phone and dialled.

"Cassie, hi. I wasn't expecting to hear from you so soon," came Laura's voice on the other end. "Is everything OK?"

"Yeah, fine thanks. I just wanted to ask… you mentioned Graham Golding earlier. Did you go to school with any of his kids?"

There was a pause. Then, "Yes. Justin. He was in the same year as Joel and I."

"You didn't mention that before."

"I didn't think it was important. *Is* it important?"

"No, maybe. I don't know. Can I ask… what was he like?"

A groan down the line, then a sigh. "Well, he certainly wasn't a friend of mine. To be honest, I can't remember him having many friends at all. He was an angry kid. Always looking for fights, got into trouble for graffiti, that sort of thing."

"Was he mates with any of the footy boys?"

"No. He hung around a couple of other troublemakers, the guys who'd deal weed, neither of them played footy though. Honestly, he was mostly a loner. Always angry. And… he had a darkness about him, if I'm honest. His older brother was the footballer. He played for the Falcons."

"Evan?"

"Evan, yeah. Two years above us, I think. Now *he* was an arsehole."

"In what way?"

"Look, I didn't know him well, but the school held him up to be a hero, the next AFL superstar, and he loved it. He was a lot like his dad. Super arrogant, looking down on everyone else. I don't think he and Justin were close. Justin wasn't into sport at all, from memory."

"How was Justin toward Joel?"

"Joel?" Laura echoed. "Oh, the same as the rest of the guys he was desperate to impress. He treated him like shit, that I do remember. But I think that was more about Justin trying to get in with the others. Wanting to be accepted. Can I ask why you're asking about Justin?"

"No reason," Cassie said lightly. "Just… looking at who was who back then."

"Well, as I said, I didn't like him at all, and not many others did either."

Cassie ended the call, setting the phone down as her fingers drummed absently on the table, the long-forgotten cup of tea still waiting in the kitchen.

A sour taste crept into her mouth. Graham Golding had been in charge of the local force when Hayden Foster was a teenager. He would've known every family in the area, especially the ones causing trouble. Not only that, but with Graham's football-star son, Evan, there was now a direct connection with Hayden through the Carrington Falcons Football Club.

What if Hayden Foster hadn't just been another one of Golding's problem kids? What if he'd been one of his assets? The kind of 'lost boy' a senior cop might quietly flip into a snitch.

And if that was true, how long had it gone on?

A troubled boy with no father, a mother who was described as 'odd'. Golding could have been the steady male figure Hayden craved. What was it that Belinda Mead said to her? He acted with the confidence of someone who knew he could get away with whatever he wanted.

She thought about her dad's words too, how Golding had used thugs and underworld figures to do his dirty work. Was that what James Lawrence knew?

Then again, Foster had always claimed to hate the police. Or at least, that was the image he projected. And Golding hadn't worn a badge in years.

Cassie shook her head, unsettled.

She didn't have a shred of proof.

But it was enough to warrant a closer look. She needed more before she took anything to James Lawrence.

And then there was Justin Golding. A loner desperate for approval, a temper, a streak of cruelty, and not only did he know Joel, but he'd been one of his tormentors. Cassie tucked the thought away, a mental pin for later, and turned her attention to another name on the list of Hayden's old footy mates.

Brice McCrae.

She remembered the flicker across Laura's face when she'd mentioned that name. Subtle, but telling. Cassie was certain of it.

A quick Google search brought up the website for *Rusty Shovel Landscapes*. The homepage banner linked to active Facebook and Instagram profiles, so Cassie followed the trail, scrolling through pages of before-and-after garden makeovers. Lush, polished, magazine-worthy transformations. The business looked substantial. Fleets of smiling young men in branded polos working jobs across the city.

But no photo of Brice.

She dug deeper. An ABN lookup revealed the business was co-owned by Brice McCrae and someone named Elliot Petrovic. Cassie ran a search on the second name. Nothing of substance. Just a locked Instagram account belonging to what looked like a teenager, the profile picture showing him cuddled up to a girl. Cassie dismissed it.

Out of curiosity, she flicked back to the St Matthew's alumni page. No Elliot Petrovic in the 1998 class photo. Then she pulled up the Carrington Falcons' Under-17 premiership team photo from 1997. Again, no sign of him.

She sent the name to Brian in a quick text: *One for later*.

Cassie thought back to what Laura had said, how she and Brice had lived on the same street. It gave her an idea.

Diving into old phone records, she cross-referenced the surnames of Hayden's old footy mates, along with Laura Cassini and Justin Golding. It took longer than she liked, but eventually she pieced together the childhood home addresses of Hayden Foster, David Grayson, Joel O'Connor, Laura Cassini, and Brice McCrae, no Scott King, though. The Goldings, of course, didn't appear in the records. Cassie wasn't surprised. Given Graham's senior position in the police at the time, their listing was likely suppressed.

Next, she matched those names to current Carrington listings. Only one hit: *S. Grayson, 5 Meyrick Court*, the same address as in '98. Everyone else had moved on, but not this one.

She opened Google Maps and looked up all the 1998 addresses. As expected, Hayden, David, Joel, Laura, and Brice had all lived within a few minutes' walk of one another. A tight little bubble of suburban streets, side by side. In fact, Laura and Brice hadn't just lived in the same street, they'd been mere houses apart.

She stood, stretched, and wandered into the kitchen. Outside, the plane trees were now no more than shadows against the night sky. Not that she noticed. Or cared.

Her mind was still ticking. Still restless.

She returned to her computer, but the screen blurred before her eyes. Focus shot. She checked the time.

7:30pm.

She didn't have nearly enough to justify the next call. It went against her own code of ethics. But she couldn't shake the thought of Joel's family hearing about her investigation second-hand, blindsided, with no warning. Better they hear it from her.

Cassie opened Brian's email, took a breath, and dialled the number.

It barely rang twice.

"Hello, Glen O'Connor speaking."

"Mr O'Connor, hi. My name's Cassandra Murphy. I'm a journalist with the ABC in Melbourne. I'm sorry to call you so late."

"No, that's alright. We've just finished dinner, actually. From the ABC, did you say?"

"Yes, that's right."

"Well, that's a turn up for the books. What can I do for you, Cassandra Murphy from the ABC?" His voice lifted, projecting, announcing it to whoever else was in the room.

"Is now a good time to talk? I may need a few minutes."

"Sure, hang on a second, just let me sit down. Here we go. Right. I've got my wife Christie here with me, Cassandra. Do you mind if I pop you on speaker?"

Cassie smiled faintly at the click. "Not at all. Hi Mrs O'Connor, it's Cassandra Murphy."

"Hello," came the soft, clipped reply.

"So, what is this all in aid of then, Cassandra?" Glen asked, direct now.

Cassie swallowed. "Mr and Mrs O'Connor, I've been working on a story about the terror attacks in Melbourne over the weekend."

"Oh yes, we saw that on the news. Terrible business."

"We believe the attacks were in retaliation for the murder of a member of a group called the Allied Patriots last week. A man named Hayden Foster."

A silence.

"Right. Go on," Glen said.

"Well, I've been looking into his past. He grew up in Carrington in the 80s and 90s, the same time your family lived there."

"Yes, that's right, we were in Carrington then. You're after information about him, are you? I'm afraid I don't know the name. Christie?" His voice softened. "No, sorry, neither of us knows him."

"Thanks, but that's not the main reason for my call."

Cassie couldn't see them, but she felt it, the shift. A tightening of the air.

"I'm sorry, Cassandra, what is this about?" Glen's tone cooled.

"I spoke with an old school friend of your late son's earlier today. First, I want to say how deeply sorry I am for your loss."

Silence.

"In speaking with this friend, she told me she had raised doubts about the fire that claimed Joel's life. And I was wondering if…"

"Now listen here, Cassandra. If this friend..." his voice curled with disdain, "...is that Laura Cassini, then you can forget about any conspiracy theories she's thrown your way. That girl was endless bloody trouble. Always putting ideas into our Joel's head. She won't let the boy rest. I mean, it was almost thirty years ago for God's sake. We went through all this with her back then!"

"I..."

"Did you know it was the anniversary of Joel's death yesterday?" he cut in, sharp now.

"Yes, I did, and..."

"...and you thought it fit to call us today, to ask about nonsense theories regarding our son's passing? What's the matter with you people? Do you have no common decency?"

In the background, Cassie heard it, a soft, heart-wrenching sob. Mrs O'Connor.

"Look, I'm really very..."

"Do not call this number again, do you understand? I don't even know how you came to have it in the first place. Please, just leave us, and our Joel, in peace."

The line went dead.

Cassie sat frozen, phone still to her ear, as silence settled thick around her. Then the heat hit, sharp, rising fast. "Shit," she muttered, flinging the phone onto the coffee table. It skidded, clattering to the floor with a dull, unsatisfying thud. "*Shit!*"

She pressed her palms to her face, exhaling slowly. The weight of the call sat heavy on her chest, but beneath it, anger still sparked, low and persistent.

She'd tried to do the right thing. To give the O'Connors the courtesy of a heads-up.

And she'd fucked it.

But no more tap-dancing around people's feelings. She was too far down this rabbit hole to turn back now.

Cassie dropped her hands, eyes narrowing on the darkened screen across the floor. If answers wouldn't come to her, she'd go after them. Door by door. Wall by wall. Starting tomorrow with Brice McCrae and David Grayson.

Time to knock louder.

TWENTY

Cassie woke with that brittle, stubborn kind of determination that usually came after a night of fragmented sleep and unresolved questions. She didn't know how the pieces fit, or if they fit at all, but she needed control over something. Anything.

She'd stopped briefly on her walk, as usual, to take in the ocean. But it seemed just as restless as her this morning. The weather, too, couldn't make up its mind. The sky was sullen, the kind of overcast that felt personal. A strange breeze teased at change, like Melbourne itself couldn't decide what to become next.

Typical Melbourne, Cassie thought, as she trudged back to her flat, second-guessing what the hell to wear.

Brian was already waiting outside his apartment when she pulled up, two takeaway coffees in hand.

"I fucking love you," Cassie said, clutching the coffee like it might save her life.

"You say that now," Brian deadpanned. "Let's see how you feel when I start quoting police reports."

Brian just grinned as Cassie pulled away from the curb, weaving through the city streets towards the freeway entrance.

"Are we even sure he's going to be there?" Brian asked as Cassie merged lanes a little more aggressively than necessary.

"I have no idea. But the long weekend's over, so I'm certainly hoping so. We'll go to Brice first in Deakin Heights then head back to Carrington. Both suburbs are in Banksia, so they're not far away from one another. I've got a current street address for an *S. Grayson*, I'm assuming David's parents are still there, even if he's not. It's a start."

Cassie flicked the indicator and changed lanes, a little too fast for Brian's liking, but he'd long since accepted her particular brand of defensive driving.

They sipped their coffees in silence as the Melbourne traffic pulsed around them, the city slowly waking from its Easter slumber. The Dandenong Ranges loomed ahead as Cassie took the Carrington Highway exit, bound for Deakin Heights.

The signage looked brand new: *Rusty Shovel Landscapes*, bold and proud across the chain-link fencing that boxed in the car park. The gates stood open, a procession of dual-cab Utes all branded with the same rusted shovel logo lined up neatly inside.

Another sign crowned the factory building at the rear of the block. There weren't many other complexes with such a fortified presence in the small industrial estate, but then, not many had such flash-looking equipment on display either.

Cassie and Brian parked on the street out front and made their way through the open gates, spotting a man dressed in black cargo shorts, a black, white and red long-sleeved flannelette shirt, and a grey beanie, hosing down one of the Utes, a soapy bucket sitting nearby on the ground.

"Excuse me? Hi," Brian called out.

"Yeah?" came the reply.

"We're looking for Brice McCrae," Brian said, while Cassie studied the man closely.

"Well, you're in luck, mate, 'coz you just found him. Just gimme a sec," he said, walking over to the wall and turning off the tap, cutting the water to the hose.

"What can I do for ya?" he asked, wiping his hands dry on his shorts.

"My name's Brian Cheng, and this is Cassandra Murphy. We're from the ABC. We were hoping we could have a word?"

"ABC, huh? Well, g'day!" Brice said, surprised, reaching out to shake their hands. "Sure, come inside."

He greeted them with the cheerful energy of someone running late for three other things, wiping his boots on the mat as he stepped in.

"You've caught me at the right time. The crew's not back till tomorrow. I told 'em to take an extra day with their families, so it's just me flying solo today," he chuckled.

He gestured to two well-worn bucket seats across from a desk buried under paperwork, then dropped into a swivel-style captain's chair behind it.

Cassie clocked him as mid-forties, but the pallor and deep-set lines across his face added a few extra years. He wasn't tall, and he was a lot leaner than she'd expected. His movements carried a wiry restlessness, though with a fragility too, as if the strength didn't run as deep as it once had. Something about the picture tugged at her, familiar somehow, though she couldn't place why. Still, she figured he spent more time behind a desk these days than lugging bags of cement.

"How about you?" Brian asked, taking his seat. "You didn't want an extra day with your own family?"

Brice shook his head, smiling. "Me? Nah, no kids. Just me."

He clapped his hands together lightly. "So, what brings the ABC to my door?"

Cassie leaned forward, steady and direct. "Mr McCrae…"

"Mr McCrae?" he interrupted, screwing up his face. "It's just Brice," he said with a grin.

Cassie smiled back, his goofy charm disarming. "Brice."

He nodded, pleased.

"I'm sure you're across what happened in Melbourne over the weekend?"

"The Collingwood win? What a cracker of a game!"

Cassie let out a small laugh at Brice's enthusiasm.

"I was actually referring to the firebombing attacks."

"Oh, yeah, I saw that." His face darkened. "Don't tell me one of my guys is mixed up in that?"

"No, nothing like that," Cassie assured him. "We'd been looking into one of the members of the Allied Patriots before the attacks, Hayden Foster, who was murdered at his home last week."

Brice's face fell as the penny dropped. "Ah, yeah. Nugget. I saw that too. You're here because I used to know him, right?"

Brian glanced at Cassie. "Yes, actually. We understand you were one of his old footy mates?"

"I think 'mates' is a bit of a stretch. We knocked about a bit as kids, played footy together, but geez, that was donkey's years ago. I haven't seen or heard from him since high school, I reckon."

"So, nothing in recent years?" Brian asked.

"Nah, mate. Bugger all. I don't really see many of the guys from back then, to be honest."

"Your business is here in Deakin Heights. Banksia. You don't ever come across old school friends or footy teammates, given you're still so close to where you grew up?" Cassie pressed.

Brice shifted uncomfortably. "Nup," he said flatly, his cheerful tone dimming.

Cassie eased back. "I'd appreciate anything you could tell us about Hayden from back then. We've heard he used to get into a lot of fights. Do you know why he'd get so angry?"

Brice scoffed. "Now that's an understatement. Nugget was a loose cannon. A few sheep short of the top paddock, ya know? You had to watch what you said around him. Even if you were his mate. There was no *why*."

"Did he ever talk to you about his home life, about losing his dad maybe?" Brian asked.

Brice shrugged. "Yeah, nah… we didn't really talk about that kinda stuff back then. But I know he treated his mum like shit. I wouldn't be surprised if he hit her too, you know?" he added, frowning. "It was messed up."

Brian wrote a note whilst Cassie pressed on. "So, you weren't good mates?"

Brice sighed. "Alright, I guess you could say we were sorta mates there for a while. We'd hang out after footy training, just for something to do, ya know?"

"Was there anyone else who hung around with you two?" Cassie asked.

"Yeah, a couple of the boys," Brice said.

"Could you give us their names? Maybe they'd have more to tell us," Cassie pushed.

Brice screwed up his face. "Geez, it was so bloody long ago. He did hang out with Dave a fair bit. David Grayson. They were pretty tight actually. He was another strange unit."

"In what way?" Brian asked.

"He'd also kick off for no reason. But he was as thick as shit too. He didn't hang around long, though. His mum got sick of having the cops turn up all the time. She sent him to live with his dad up in New South Wales. Newcastle, I think. His mum and dad were separated, his old man worked in the mines."

"Do you remember when this was?"

"Yeah, actually. Year 11. 1997. I remember because he left the day after my 17th birthday party gathering. October."

Cassie and Brian looked at one another.

"Any idea how we might contact him now?" Brian asked.

"Nah, mate. Like I said, I haven't seen or heard from any of those blokes in years. Life moves on and all that."

Cassie took a breath, studying Brice's face. "Do you remember a girl named Laura Cassini? She lived on your street back in Carrington."

Brice smiled, but a sigh followed. "Yeah, I remember Laura."

"It sounds like there's a story there," Cassie grinned tactically. "Is that a *good* remember or a *bad* remember?" Cassie asked, keeping her focus sharp.

Brice glanced at Brian, then back at Cassie. "Neither really. What's Laura got to do with Nugget?"

"We're just looking at all the people who were around back then, who Hayden may have come into contact with, that sort of thing."

Cassie didn't push further, but she clocked the hesitation. Just like when she'd asked Laura about Brice. There was more there.

"I've got another name to throw at you," she said, shifting gears. "Joel O'Connor."

"Didn't know him," Brice said quickly. Too quickly.

"Are you sure?" Brian cut in. "You both went to St Matthew's until you left for Carrington High in... was it Year 10?" He said, referring to his notebook, which in itself seemed to make Brice uncomfortable. "You just said you remembered Laura Cassini, and she and Joel were apparently very close. It'd be strange if you didn't know him."

"Oh yeah, nah, I knew who he was, but we weren't mates or anything. I remember him with Laura, yeah, but honestly, I don't even remember her that well either." Brice smiled again, but this time it felt off. Forced.

Cassie watched his face carefully, let the silence hang for a moment, then tossed out the final card.

"One more, and then I promise we'll let you get back to it," Cassie smiled. "How about Scott King?"

The mood changed entirely.

"Yeah, Scotty. He was my best mate. And he had nothing to do with Nugget. Scotty was one of the best people you could ever meet. Nugget wasn't. If Scott's name has come up, it was only 'coz he hung around me."

"I'm so sorry for your loss, I know he passed away quite some time ago." Brian said. "Do you mind if I ask you how he passed?"

"I do as a matter-of-fact mate. But since you already have, Scotty took his own life. But I'm pretty keen not to talk about it if that's OK?"

"Of course, again, I'm really very sorry," Brian said, looking across to Cassie.

"Well, that's all from us, Brice. Thank you very much for your time," Cassie said, rising. Brian followed, reluctant.

"Yeah, no worries. Sorry I couldn't give you more on Nugget. Like I said, donkey's years ago," he smiled.

Cassie and Brian made their way through the main glass door, stepping into the fenced car park beyond. Brice followed closely behind.

"Oh, sorry Brice," Cassie said, turning back. "One more name. Do you remember Justin Golding?"

"Justin Golding!" Brice repeated, suddenly animated. "There's a name I haven't heard in yonks. Yeah, I remember him."

"Would he and Hayden Foster ever have been mates?" Cassie asked.

"Nugget? And Justin Golding?" Brice let out a laugh. "Buckley's. No chance. Justin was a try-hard. He thought he was some kind of gangster, selling dope and tagging trains, but it was all an act. Nugget saw straight through him. We all did."

Cassie smiled. "OK. Thanks again, Brice."

Brice closed the door behind him, still chuckling at the suggestion of Hayden Foster and Justin Golding.

Brian glanced at Cassie as they made their way through the yard.

"Wait till we get back to the car," she said quietly.

Cassie slid into the driver's seat and started the engine. She pointed the car back towards Carrington, eventually pulling into a small group of shops along the highway.

An abandoned milk bar. An IGA supermarket. A bottle shop. A doctor's surgery. A takeaway pizza shop. A newsagency. And on the corner, a hairdresser still advertising perms in the window.

The pair sat in the car in silence for a moment, eyeing each other.

"What did you think?" Brian finally asked.

"He seems pretty genuine," Cassie said. "But there's definitely something more between him and Laura Cassini."

"I picked up on that too."

"When I mentioned Brice's name to Laura, it was the same thing. A shift."

"What do you think that's all about?" Brian asked.

"Not sure. And did you see his reaction when we mentioned Joel? Not once did he mention the fire. That would've been huge news in Carrington at the time. And yet, he reckons he didn't know him. For anyone else, I'm sure that's the first thing they'd mention."

"I felt awful asking about his mate, Scott." Brian said.

"No, don't feel awful. We had to ask. And you know what, you were actually really great in there. Some of those questions…"

"You think?"

"Yeah, I do." she said, impressed.

Brian smiled. "So, what are you thinking?"

Cassie shook her head. "I don't know yet. But there's something here Bri, I can feel it. Let's head to the Grayson house. Brice said David moved north in '97, before Joel died, but I bet he can give us a hell of a lot more on Foster. I don't expect he'll want to speak with us, but maybe even his Mum might know something. C'mon." Cassie said, already pulling out of the car park.

"Is it far?" Brian asked, wrestling his seatbelt back into place.

"This is Carrington. Nothing's far from anything," Cassie muttered, eyes flicking to the GPS as she navigated out onto the road. One street to the left, two to the right, and there it was: Meyrick Court.

Cassie's sigh was loud and sharp as she pulled up outside Number 5.

A temporary wire fence lined the front of the property. Behind it, the house stood hollowed out, doors and terracotta roof tiles already stripped, a skeleton waiting for the excavator. The garden beds, once someone's pride, had surrendered to nature, weeds snaking through the brittle remains of azaleas and creeping over lava rocks.

"Shit," Cassie said, leaning back in her seat. "Is anything left of this bloody suburb?"

Brian gave a sympathetic wince. "Do you want to get out? Have a look around?"

Cassie's hands tightened on the wheel.

"No. There's no point. Come on, let's head to where the O'Connors used to live. We'll start door knocking from there. We need more on Hayden Foster, more on the fire that killed Joel O'Connor, and if we're lucky, something on Graham fucking Golding. The pieces are there, Bri. We just need to make them fit."

She dropped the car into gear and peeled away from the curb.

Outside, Carrington watched in silence.

Its old ghosts beginning to stir.

TWENTY-ONE

Cassie cut the engine and sat for a moment, eyeing the house through the windscreen.

"This is it. Or at least, where it was. The O'Connor place, before the fire," she nodded towards the single-storey late-90s-built peach-coloured brick imposter now standing in its place.

"I couldn't find any photos of the original," Brian said. "I spoke with someone at Banksia Council, it was a double-storey place, but they didn't have any images on file."

Cassie nodded.

They stepped out onto the nature strip, the mid-autumn grass brittle beneath their boots. Around them, Carrington wore its age differently. The post-war brick veneers were faded but defiant. Above, the overcast sky pressed down, draping the street in shadow and making it feel even older. Though development had crept into the suburb, demolishing and replacing, it hadn't here. Southcote Road had been left behind.

Cassie hoped the memories had, too.

She and Brian split the street. He crossed to the far side, while Cassie turned to the house directly in front of her. The O'Connors were long gone, the house rebuilt, but as she stood at the end of the driveway, she felt it, that catch in her breath. Joel.

She made her way up the concrete driveway, admiring the brightly coloured toran strung above the wooden front door. She knocked.

At first, nothing. She was about to give up when faint footsteps reached her ears. The door creaked open a fraction.

"Hello?" A tentative voice. A young woman stood peering through the narrow gap.

Cassie offered her best professional smile. "Hi, my name's Cassandra Murphy. I'm with the ABC. I was wondering if you've lived here in Carrington for long? Perhaps I could have a quick chat?"

The woman shook her head politely. "Oh, no. Sorry." And with that, the door eased shut.

"Right," Cassie muttered, turning on her heel. "Off to a great start."

The next half hour was more of the same. Despite school holidays, most doors stayed shut. The few that opened led to dead ends, renters who hadn't heard of the O'Connors, blank stares at the mention of Joel, or 1998. Some didn't even know their own next-door neighbours, let alone a family from nearly thirty years ago.

At the end of the road, she waited as Brian crossed back.

"Anything?" she asked.

He shook his head.

Cassie sighed. "Patience, Bri. Ninety percent rejection, ten percent foot in the door."

"Yeah, but that ten percent's starting to feel like a myth." He grinned. "Which way now?"

Cassie scanned the T-intersection. "This is Grove Street. That reserve I mentioned is just over there," she said, nodding left. "Let's stay on this side for now. You head right, I'll take left. Cross over at the end, work our way back and we'll meet back here."

Brian gave a mock salute and peeled off.

Cassie turned to her side of the street. More doors. More polite rejections. Until three houses in, she struck a flicker of luck.

Cassie could tell by the shape of the house that it was one of the originals, but it had been dressed up to look new. Rendered grey façade, terracotta roof sprayed charcoal. A merbau deck wrapped around the front, hiding what was once a concrete porch. The bones were still there, if you looked.

Cassie had barely reached the top step when the front door rattled open. Dogs barked furiously. Somewhere inside, a baby wailed.

"Sorry! Just a sec!" a woman called, wrestling with the security screen. "Would you get out of the bloody house!" she shouted, hopefully at the dogs, though Cassie wasn't entirely sure. The barking faded, a door slammed inside.

"I'm so sorry about that," the woman said breathlessly, opening the door fully. She was dressed in sweatpants and an oversized jumper, juggling a baby on her hip, while a toddler peered shyly from behind her legs.

"No, *I'm* sorry. I can see you've got your hands full. I promise I'm not selling anything. I'll be quick."

The woman squinted at her. "Do I know you?"

"My name's Cassandra Murphy. I'm with the ABC."

"That's it!" she said, beaming. "Oh my God, what are you doing at my front door? Sorry, I look a right mess!" She laughed, cheeks flushing.

"You look like a mum. And by the looks of things, one who's doing a bloody good job."

"Oh, thank you. But I don't know about that!" the woman laughed again, adjusting the baby.

Cassie smiled, crouching slightly. "Hello there!" she said to the toddler, who ducked back behind his mother's legs.

"I won't keep you. I'm looking into a house fire from the late 90's, just around the corner on Southcote Road. I'm trying to find someone who lived in the area back then."

"Oh, right! Well, you're in luck. I grew up here. This was my family home. My parents retired and downsized and handed it over to us."

Cassie's heart lifted.

"I vaguely remember something about a fire, but I was pretty young. Sorry, I don't think I can help much."

Cassie's hope deflated.

"But I can tell you who would know," the woman added. "Reita Wallace. She knows everyone. She used to be the local Avon lady, you know, selling women's cosmetics door-to-door. My mum could never get rid of her, always hanging around to gossip."

Cassie smiled. "Does she still live locally?"

"Oh yeah. Same house. Over on Windham Road, a few doors down from the old milk bar, which is one of those dodgy massage places now." She gave a conspiratorial grin. "You won't miss Reita's place though. Just look for the gnomes."

Cassie jotted it down. "Thanks. You've been a huge help. I'll let you get back to it. And goodbye to you too," she added, smiling at the toddler, who peeked out again before hiding once more.

"You're welcome! And good luck with your story!" the woman called after her.

Cassie waited until she reached the footpath before pulling out her phone, thumb hovering as she tapped Brian's contact.

"Meet me back at the car," she said, heading back in the direction of where the O'Connor's house once stood.

"Got something?" Brian asked, breath puffing visibly in the crisp autumn air as he approached.

"The suburb gossip."

"Bingo!" Brian grinned.

"C'mon, let's go."

When they reached Windham Road, Reita Wallace's house was exactly where the woman said it would be. And it wasn't hard to pick out.

Lemon-cream bricks, dulled by time. A sun-bleached terracotta roof sagged slightly under years of neglect. Aluminium window frames, their once-sharp edges softened by dust and rust, crouched beneath blue-and-white striped awnings rolled up like tired, forgotten flags. The front porch was a stub of concrete, flanked by white metal railings that had long since lost their shine. The front yard was mostly lawn, but nature was slowly reclaiming its ground. A sprawling maple leaned over the footpath like a nosy old neighbour, and a wild, variegated bush had annexed the front corner with quiet defiance.

But it was the driveway that sealed it.

A long strip of white pebbles lined one side, glinting like bone under the muted daylight. Nestled among them was an army of garden gnomes. AFL scarves wrapped around their fat little necks. Some pushing wheelbarrows. One leaned against a ceramic toadstool, smoking a pipe with the satisfaction of a pensioner at happy hour.

Cassie stared. The place felt like a relic. Like it had outlasted half a dozen developers by sheer force of personality.

"I guess this is the place."

Brian followed her gaze, smirking. "Subtle, isn't it?"

Cassie shook her head, stepping out. "If those little bastards start moving, you're first in line, Bri."

He laughed, falling in beside her as they made their way up the path, crunching over loose pebbles as they passed. The gnomes watched, unblinking.

Cassie reached out and pressed the doorbell. A tinny chime echoed within, followed by the slow creak of a wooden door settling into its hinges.

"Yes, can I help you?" came the greeting, voice warm but measured.

Reita Wallace stood framed behind the flyscreen, hands planted on hips. She was immaculate in a way that felt like defiance. Tailored blue slacks, a crisp white blouse scattered with cornflower-blue blooms, and a long string of faux pearls that swayed gently as she moved. Her hair was coiffed into a silver bouffant, not a strand out of place. Mauve lipstick, precise. She was in her seventies, Cassie guessed, though her posture suggested she hadn't ceded an inch to the years.

"Reita Wallace?" Cassie asked.

"In the flesh, love. And you are?"

"My name's Cassandra Murphy. This is my colleague, Brian Cheng. We're with the ABC. We're hoping you might spare us a few minutes."

"The ABC? Well, this is a pleasant surprise. You'd better come in." Reita's brows lifted, but her smile held steady. "Wipe your feet," she added as she pushed open the flyscreen door.

The hallway was steeped in lavender furniture polish and something sweeter beneath, orange slice biscuits, maybe. The kind of smell that wrapped around you like a memory. Family photos lined the walls, a gallery of suburban life: Reita at footy fundraisers, draped in Christmas tinsel, reigning supreme at Tupperware parties. She wasn't just a resident here. She *was* Carrington.

"Make yourselves comfortable," Reita said, gesturing to a well-worn lounge suite. "I'll pop the kettle on. I've got some instant somewhere, but I prefer the Jarrah if you don't mind. A little luxury never hurt anyone."

"Jarrah sounds perfect, thanks," Brian said, easing into the couch.

"And for you, love?" Reita turned to Cassie.

"I'm good, thanks."

"Suit yourself."

From the kitchen, Reita's voice floated back as the kettle roared to life.

"Lloyd? *Lloyd*!" she bellowed, projecting through the open kitchen window, its lace curtains fluttering in the breeze.

"It's the ABC!"

A scoff followed. "He's out the back, pottering around with some junk he's dragged home from hard rubbish. He thinks he's a bloody restoration expert now. But you can't tell him otherwise. It's all a complete waste of time, of course."

Cassie exchanged a smile with Brian. This woman was gold.

Moments later, Reita returned with two mugs. She moved with the sure-footed grace of someone who didn't care if you thought she was slowing down.

"There we go. Those mugs are Robert Gordon, you know. Proper *Australian* pottery." She said, aiming a pointed glance at Brian. "It cost me an arm and a leg, so mind you don't drop it."

He lifted his hands in mock surrender before accepting the mug. "Huh!" he said, lifting it high enough to read the print underneath. "Made in China! Just like me!" he grinned.

Reita gave him a look that could sandpaper varnish. "Yes, well. Just don't drop it."

"So," she said, settling into her chair, smoothing her slacks. "What brings the ABC to my doorstep? Don't tell me it's my gnomes! You're not from *Gardening Australia*, are you?"

Cassie smiled. "I'm afraid not. We're actually looking into a house fire from 1998. Over on Southcote Road."

The shift was subtle, but Cassie caught it, the slight dip of Reita's shoulders, the softening of her mouth.

"Ah. The O'Connor boy. Very sad."

"That's right, Joel O'Connor. We were hoping you might be able to tell us a little about the people who lived in Carrington back then," Cassie said, settling into the couch's sagging embrace. "We've got some names, if you wouldn't mind us running through them?"

"Go right ahead. I can't promise I'll know all of them, but I did know most of the women over the years. Who would you like to start with?"

Cassie nodded to Brian, who flipped open his notebook with the kind of reverence usually reserved for sacred texts.

"Well, how about we start with the O'Connors?" Brian asked.

Reita's face softened. "Yes, well, I knew Christie quite well. Lovely woman. She was a teacher at the primary school. Not Grove Street Primary, where my two went, but the Catholic one over in Deakin Heights. Holy Eucharist." She suddenly stood. "Oh, biscuits!"

She disappeared into the kitchen and returned moments later, offering an assortment of Arnott's favourites stacked neatly on another glazed piece of pottery. Cassie and Brian politely declined as Reita placed the plate on a pouf in the middle of the room.

"Joel always seemed like such a sweet boy," she continued. "He used to be fascinated by all my makeup samples when he was little. Very polite. They were a nice family."

"Were there ever any... concerns?" Brian asked gently.

Reita pursed her lips, considering. "Concerns? No, not that I recall. I know her husband was a Vietnam vet. I'd heard he liked a drink, but plenty did back then. Still, you never really know what goes on behind closed doors, do you?"

Cassie nodded, making a note. "What about a boy named Hayden Foster?"

Reita's brow furrowed. "Sara Foster's son?"

"That's right," Cassie said.

"I knew of Sara. Bit of a strange one, bless her. I think she had a few issues, mentally, I mean. And I'd heard rumours that her husband used to rough her up before he died, but I never met him. She never wanted me calling around, either. Mostly kept to herself. As for the boy, I only knew him by reputation, and it wasn't a good one. Though with a father like that, it's any wonder."

Brian looked over at Cassie and then wrote in his notebook.

"We know Hayden had a mate, David Grayson, I think his mother may have still lived on Meyrick Court until very recently."

"Yes, right, well that would be Sandra Grayson."

S Grayson. Cassie smiled.

"Again, another one I didn't know too well, she never bought much from me. The occasional lipstick and eyeliner but I don't think she had a lot of money to spend. Single Mum. I think she used to work shift work at one of the factories in Deakin Heights. I don't think her son's name was David though. That doesn't ring any bells. I thought it was Harry or Henry or something. It was something like that, but it definitely wasn't David. I wouldn't be able to tell you anything more there though I'm sorry."

Cassie shifted forward, as though suddenly getting her bearings. "Reita, does this street back onto the reserve? The one where the Carrington Football Club is?"

"The Falcons! It sure does! Otway Park. The houses on the other side of the street back straight onto the football oval."

"Did you happen to know the McCrae family? Or the Cassinis?"

"Oh, very well indeed." Reita sat up straighter, like a curtain rising. "The Cassinis lived right across the road, number 23. They were wonderful neighbours. Rosa was a good friend of mine. And then Rochelle, or 'Shelly' rather, and Allister McCrae lived a few doors up from them to the right. You might know Allister, he worked as a cameraman for Channel Ten, I think." She peered at Brian, expectant.

Both he and Cassie shook their heads.

"So, you'd know their children too?" Brian prompted.

"Oh yes. I remember Leo Cassini mowing our lawns for a while there when Lloyd had his hernia operation. Lovely boy."

"And Laura?" Cassie asked, leaning in.

Reita's lips twitched. "The youngest. Always in strife, that one. Nothing like her brother or sister. She's half the reason poor Raymond had heart troubles, if you ask me. Especially after…" She trailed off, eyes darting sideways.

Cassie's tone softened. "That sounds interesting."

Reita leaned closer, voice dropping theatrically. "Towards the end of high school, Laura fell pregnant. Quietly, of course. She had a… *termination*." She whispered the last word, as if the walls might be listening.

The words hung heavy in the air. Cassie felt Brian's glance but kept her eyes on Reita.

"And funny you should ask about Shelly McCrae at the same time," Reita added, rising to gather the untouched biscuits. "Because it was *her* son who got Laura pregnant. Young Brice." She clucked her tongue, a sound halfway between gossip and pity.

Cassie's pulse kicked. *Bingo.*

As if on cue, the sharp crack of ceramic smashing against the tiled floor echoed from the kitchen.

"Oh, *bugger*!" Reita exclaimed. "My Robert Gordon plate!" She crouched to collect the broken biscuits and shards of porcelain, muttering about the price of 'bloody Australian pottery' as Brian stepped in to help.

"Oh, you're a good man, isn't he?" she said, winking at Cassie.

Cassie returned the smile, though her mind was already elsewhere.

"Brice McCrae and Laura Cassini," she said, more statement than question.

"Oh yes," the woman replied. "They were an item for quite some time. Shelly worked in social services,

238

and although she and Allister had separated, they both stepped in at that point to support both Brice and Laura. They firmly believed that Brice needed to take responsibility for his actions. I think they even considered keeping it at one point."

She paused, leaning forward slightly.

"But the Cassinis wouldn't have it, devout Catholics. I remember Rosa wanted Laura to have the baby and give it up through the Church's adoption program. But as always, Laura made her own choices."

A small, tight smile.

"I suppose these things all work out for the best in the end, don't they?"

Cassie didn't answer. She and Brian exchanged a look, the kind that didn't need words.

Eager to debrief and be anywhere else, Cassie stood.

"You're off already?" Reita complained.

"I'm afraid so but thank you, you've been very helpful."

Brian sculled the rest of his coffee, gently handing the mug across to Reita.

As they reached the front door, a photo caught Cassie's eye. Framed on the wall was a football fundraiser: a younger Reita in a navy-and-white striped jersey, front and centre at a cake stall, laughing as a man slung an arm around her shoulders, grinning wide. Graham Golding.

"Sorry, Reita, is this you and Graham Golding?" Cassie asked.

Reita stepped up beside her, cheeks flushing. "Oh yes. How lucky we were to have him in the neighbourhood. A real man's man. And always the charmer with the ladies." She said with a grin, blushing. "He would've made a fine Premier of this State too, if they'd given him the chance."

Cassie fought to keep her expression neutral.

"Do you know where they lived?"

"I sure do! They lived on the corner of Grove Street and Carrington Highway, on the highway side. It's all gone now, of course. The house, along with the two next to it, were bulldozed a few years back to make way for a new childcare centre. But the Goldings had moved out long before that. 1998, it was."

"1998?" Cassie's voice snapped sharp.

Yes, that's right. They moved the same week as my mother's funeral. I remember that well. Anne brought over a casserole and told me to keep the dish since they were already packed up and ready to go. That was July. Why anyone would move house in the middle of a Melbourne winter is beyond me. But they moved to Balwyn, so I assume they wanted to be closer to the city, with Graham heading into politics. Anne gave me their new address at the time, though I couldn't tell you where it is now."

"You've been more than helpful, Mrs Wallace. Thank you so much," Cassie said, glancing at Brian. They were thinking the same thing.

"Oh, you're more than welcome. Sorry you didn't get to meet Lloyd," she added, shooting a glare toward the back door.

"Maybe next time," Brian smiled.

They said their goodbyes, stepping out into the brittle autumn air. The gnomes lined the driveway, silent sentries. Neither of them looked back.

Inside the car, doors slammed. Cassie exhaled a laugh that tasted like disbelief.

"What the actual fuck?" she said, shaking her head. "Are you *serious*?"

"About which bit?" Brian deadpanned.

"I told you there was more to this, Bri. Who moves house when their kid's halfway through Year 12? Winter of '98? That's only a few months after Joel's death. This stinks."

"And Laura and Brice. That's a whole new thread."

Cassie raked a hand through her hair, eyes wide. "We need to meet with Peter. There's too much here now for this to be a coincidence."

Brian nodded slowly. The weight of it all hung between them.

Cassie started the car, shooting him a sideways glance. "And you… 'Made in China'?" She smirked. "I thought you were from Geelong."

"I am," he said, grinning wildly.

Cassie burst out laughing.

The clouds had broken, and the late sun spilled low across the sky, stretching long shadows over the cracked bitumen. As they drove away, Cassie's voice softened.

"Sometimes," she said quietly, "the ghosts aren't lost to the past. They're just waiting for you to come looking."

TWENTY-TWO

They returned to the ABC in silence, neither of them reaching to fill it.

The newsroom was a ghost of its usual self. School holidays had stripped the place bare, half the team off, the rest running on caffeine and fumes. Cassie's boots echoed off the polished foyer tiles as they headed for the stairs.

"I'll check if the boardroom's free," Brian offered. "Want me to grab Peter?"

"Yeah. I'll dump my stuff first," she muttered, already heading for the next flight.

Brian returned a few minutes later, laptop under one arm, coat half-off. "The boardroom's booked, and Peter's tied up in a meeting. I'll check back in a bit."

Cassie barely acknowledged him. She sat motionless at her desk, save for one hand flipping a Post-it note between her fingers like a nervous tic. Her eyes were distant, locked somewhere her mind hadn't quite caught up to.

"You know, something's off," she said finally.

Brian leaned against the desk. "Which part?"

"Laura and Brice," she said, voice quiet. "It's not just the pregnancy. I get why they kept that hidden. It's something else."

She shifted in her seat. "Back in high school, I dated one of the Mudlarks, Heathton Ridge's footy team. Joshua Browne. He dragged me to every bloody game. Rain, hail, or forty-degree heat. The girlfriends always sat together, the same spot every week cheering them on from the sidelines. We went to the awards nights, the afterparties. I knew every boy on that team. We all did. Even the boys from out of town. You knew who was who."

She looked up at Brian. "So, when Laura tells me she didn't know Hayden Foster or David Grayson? And what about Scott King? He was Brice's best mate! Nah. Not buying it. Not with how intimate she and Brice were."

Brian raised an eyebrow. "You think she's lying?"

Cassie hesitated. "I think she's hiding something. I just don't know what."

She stood, restless. "I want to meet her again. But this time not at her house. Somewhere neutral. Somewhere she can't curate the narrative. Let's see if she'll meet us in Carrington. People behave differently when they're back on old ground."

Brian nodded slowly. "Okay."

"I do believe what she said about Joel though. That part feels real. There's something about that night, where Joel was meant to be, what actually happened, it doesn't add up."

Cassie's voice dropped. "And then there's the Goldings. Moving house in the middle of 1998, right after the fire the killed Joel. Reita Wallace reckons it was because of Graham's political career, but I looked into that last night. He was District Commander of Outer Eastern Melbourne until 2001. Then Deputy Commissioner in charge of Regional Victoria. He didn't enter politics until just before the 2006 election. The timing doesn't stack up."

She began pacing now. Her thoughts were no longer quiet theories, they were jostling for space, colliding and accelerating.

"And then there's Hayden. Dying in a house fire. We've ruled out the Patriots. Saturday's retaliation attacks proved that, yeah?"

"Yeah."

"So, who then? That wasn't some drive-by Molotov cocktail job. He was attacked first. That's deliberate. That's up close. That's personal. Whoever did it knew exactly what they were doing and wanted him to know why too. Hayden was no giant, but he was built like a tank. Whoever did it had to be bloody strong."

"Or they caught him off guard," Brian said, thinking aloud.

Cassie pondered the idea. "Maybe. A mate? Someone he let in. Someone he trusted. And then there's James Lawrence." She slowed. "Asking us about Hayden's past… I've got a theory."

Brian sat. "Let's hear it."

"All those times Hayden got off. Charges dropped. Cases folded. These weren't minor offences. Multiple assaults, drug offences, incitement, firearms, the rape allegation. Any other guy would've been locked up for a long time."

"I checked on his lawyers like you asked," Brian said. "No single firm stuck with him for long. No consistent representation. No standout names."

Cassie looked up, sharp. "Which means someone else was looking out for him."

Brian stilled. "Someone with pull."

"Someone inside VicPol. Or with serious political clout. Someone who could move between systems, law enforcement and the underworld, manipulating evidence, witnesses... Maybe even the person who brought Hayden into that world to begin with."

Brian's expression darkened. "Graham Golding."

Cassie nodded slowly. "My dad said Golding had people. Thugs. Underworld fixers. He never got his hands dirty, but he knew exactly how to make things happen.

"Think about it. Hayden's father was violent. He dies while Hayden's still a kid, leaving him with a mother struggling with mental illness, isolated, paranoid, closed off from the world. And Hayden grows up angry. Resentful. Even his own mates were scared of him."

Brian shifted, listening carefully.

"I keep thinking about what Doctor Taylor said to me. About the 'lost boys.' Maybe Graham Golding saw that. Saw Hayden's rage and used it. Gave him what he craved most. Purpose. Protection. Power."

"But Hayden hated the cops," Brian said. "Look at the protests during the lockdowns."

"And there's the kicker," Cassie said. "What if that whole 'fuck the cops' persona… was just that. A persona. What if Foster was…"

"…a fucking police informant?" Brian finished, low and stunned.

Cassie blinked, then laughed, short and sharp. "Jesus Bri. A *fucking* police informant?"

"You're rubbing off on me," he shrugged.

Cassie smiled, but it faded just as quickly. "It'd explain the whole up-close-and-personal attack. If someone found out that he had informed on *them*…"

"They'd want him gone. And they'd want to do it themselves. Look him in the eye."

"Exactly."

She paced again. "Let's look at anyone recently released from prison with direct connections to Foster. Golding has been gone from the force for years, so it might be someone who has been locked up for quite some time."

Brian nodded obediently.

Cassie continued. "Which, if we're right about this, means that this absolutely circles back to Carrington. We need to find David Grayson."

"How does Joel O'Connor fit in all of this though?" Brian asked.

"I'm still working on that, but I have a theory there too."

"Go on."

"Not yet. But you can help me. I need to see his coroner's report."

"I'll chase it. I've got someone who owes me," Brian said, already walking.

Cassie opened her laptop. "I'll track down Grayson."

Brian paused in the doorway. "Race you. Loser buys the beers."

Cassie smirked. "Get your wallet ready."

She slipped into one of the edit suites and shut the door behind her. The room was cold and airless, the flickering monitors casting a ghostly light across the walls. It felt like a bunker, like she'd sealed herself off from everything except the task at hand.

Outside, the city buzzed on, but in here, time stilled.

She stared at her laptop screen and then typed: David Grayson. Newcastle. Mining.

The search crawled. Then, results.

There were multiple court listings for a David Hugh Grayson: Newcastle District and Cessnock Local. Offences dated back to 2011, 2012... but the files were sealed. She couldn't access the records without formal application. Still, she took screenshots. Then fired off a Signal message to one of her more reliable police contacts. She didn't have time for formal process.

Back on Google, another result caught her eye.

Vale: Mark Grayson (1955–2010)

A corporate obituary. Plain text on the Eureka Basin Operations website. Clean. Sanitised. The kind of write-up companies used to honour someone without actually saying anything.

Cassie scanned it.

Originally from Melbourne, Mark joined Eureka Basin during the establishment of our exploratory operations near Cessnock in 1993 and remained a dedicated member of our underground team for seventeen years. Known for his grit, loyalty, and straight-talking manner, Mark exemplified the values of our company. He is survived by his sons, David and Harley.

Harry or Henry, Reita had said.

Cassie narrowed her eyes. *Harley.* A brother.

Cassie leaned back in her chair, lips pursed. She stared at the blank Google homepage for a moment before her fingers moved again, this time, typing Harley Grayson.

It took mere seconds.

Harley Grayson: proprietor of Evergrow Supply Co., a wholesale nursery supplier based in Deakin Heights.

Cassie stilled. *Deakin Heights.*

Her eyes tracked down the Evergrow homepage, clean design, sharp branding. Corporate. Anonymous.

A tab caught her eye: Proud Suppliers For.

She clicked.

The logos loaded slowly. University partnerships, horticulture research centres, a tissue culture facility in Canberra.

Then, down the bottom, near the edge of the screen, a familiar logo: Rusty Shovel Landscapes.

Cassie froze. Her heart gave a slow, heavy thump.

Brice McCrae.

The circle was closing. And fast.

A knock broke her trance. Brian stepped in, grinning.

"You're shout."

"Already?" she smirked. "God, you're good."

"That said…" he added, stepping beside her. "What've you got?"

She spun her laptop around and walked him through the breadcrumb trail, the court listings, Evergrow, Harley Grayson, Rusty Shovel.

Brian's brow furrowed. "But Brice told us he hadn't seen or heard much from David since he moved to New South Wales in '97."

Cassie nodded, slowly. "Exactly. And if Harley Grayson is his brother, and Harley supplies Brice's company… come on. You'd know. You'd definitely know."

"So, another lie?"

Cassie tapped a pen absently against her thigh. "That's what I don't get. I understand Laura and Brice not wanting to talk about their relationship. The trauma and shame, all that. But this? This feels deliberate."

Brian sat beside her, nodding slowly. "He's hiding something."

"Yep. And now I want to know what. Let's pay him another visit too."

Brian checked his screen. "I'm still waiting on the coroner's report. Should be any second."

Cassie grinned. "So, you don't have it. Does that mean you're buying those beers?"

Brian raised an eyebrow. "Have you got David's home address and phone number?"

"Touché."

A soft chime sounded from his laptop. Brian grinned.

"And that's your shout."

He dropped into the seat beside her and clicked open the PDF attached to an otherwise blank email. Cassie leaned in. He scrolled and then turned the screen toward her.

Cause of Death
1(a) Smoke inhalation and thermal injuries
1(b) Residential house fire
Manner of Death
Accidental

Cassie exhaled slowly. "This tells us nothing," she said annoyed.

She scanned the document again, jaw tightening. "Anyone could have made it look like an accident."

"You want me to chase the CFA report?" Brian offered.

"No," she said quietly, looking defeated. "If it had been something suspicious, it would have said."

She let the sentence collapse under its own weight.

Brian didn't move.

Cassie dragged a hand down her face. "Thanks anyway, Bri."

"Want me to grab Peter now?" he offered.

She glanced at the clock. After five.

"No. Peter can wait. I've just thought of something else." she said, looking back at him.

"Do you remember what Belinda Mead told us? About why she dropped the case against Hayden?"

"She said it was the media circus. And that it got too hard, especially after becoming a new mum."

"Right, but she also mentioned VicPol. She told me that it was the police who discouraged her from going through with it."

Brian tilted his head, the thought catching up to both of them at once. "You're thinking…" he said.

"I am," Cassie replied, already reaching for her coat. "Feel like making a house call on the way to those beers?"

* * *

The wrought iron gate let out a weary squeal as Cassie pushed it open. The scent of sawdust still lingered in the air, sharp and dry, but the tools had fallen silent. The scaffold out front stood empty now, the workday done.

Brian trailed a step behind her, hands tucked into his jacket pockets, eyes scanning the house.

"They've made some progress."

Cassie gave a faint nod. She stepped up carefully, the tessellated tiles still slick from the late afternoon rain. She rang the doorbell.

After a few moments, it opened.

"Cassie!" Belinda Mead said, a flicker of surprise on her face. "Oh, and Brian, right?"

He gave a polite smile. "Evening."

Belinda wore a navy wool jumper over jeans, her hair bundled loosely at the nape of her neck. She looked like someone at the end of a long day.

"Is this a bad time?" Cassie asked.

"No," Belinda said, stepping back. "Come in."

They crossed the threshold into the quiet hallway. Cassie folded her coat over one arm as they followed Belinda through to the rear living area. The hum of the fridge was the only sound.

The renovations were clearly ongoing, drop sheets folded in a corner, a smell of paint still clinging to the air, but the space was warm.

Cassie took a seat at the walnut dining table near the tall windows, the light outside fading to blue-grey. Brian slid into the chair beside her.

"Can I get you something?" Belinda asked, one hand on the fridge door. "Tea? Coffee?"

"We're fine, thank you," Cassie said.

Belinda gave a small nod. The fridge door stayed closed. She moved to join them, smoothing her jumper as she sat. Her expression was cautious. Curious but closed.

Cassie let a beat pass. Just long enough to let the tension stretch.

"I need to ask you a few more questions," she said. "From back then."

Belinda's face didn't change. Just a faint narrowing of her eyes. "I've already told you everything I can remember."

"This isn't about Hayden. This is about the trial," Cassie said. "Or rather, the trial that never happened."

Belinda looked away. "Right."

"When we spoke, you said you dropped it because of the media pressure. You'd just become a mum, that it was all too much."

"That's true," she said. "I didn't want to be front-page news. Especially not for that."

She paused. The house creaked quietly in the silence. A pipe clicked somewhere in the wall.

"And yet there I was," she added, with a bitter smile, "talkback fodder. Strangers calling in to debate whether I was credible. Whether a sex worker could be raped at all."

A silence fell.

Cassie shifted forward slightly. "You told me that it was the police who actively discouraged you from pursuing the trial. That's why I'm here."

Belinda exhaled slowly. "Yeah, well. They were careful about how they said it, but the message was obvious. The media circus. My background. Hayden's young age. It was made very clear to me that I'd be the one on trial."

She looked toward the back courtyard, where the garden caught the last of the light.

"You know how it was back then," she said. "This was long before all the supposed reforms. And it's still shit."

She turned back to them, her voice tight. "Try being a sex worker in the 90's. My job was enough to discredit me before I even opened my mouth. Honestly? Maybe they were right. Maybe they did me a favour."

"Do you really believe that?" Brian asked, gently.

Belinda gave a hollow laugh. "No! Of course not! I wanted my day in court. I wanted that bastard locked up. I wanted to feel… like someone believed me. But I couldn't do it. I wasn't strong enough. Not with a baby. The thought of being torn apart on the stand…"

She trailed off. Silence thickened around the table.

Cassie leaned in, her voice low. "Belinda, do you remember who exactly it was who encouraged you to drop the trial? Was it a caseworker, a senior investigator maybe?"

Belinda's eyes darkened. "Yeah. That's the strange part. I remember it clearly. He wasn't part of my case. He just showed up one day at my flat. He said he was there to help."

Cassie exchanged a glance with Brian.

"He was polite," Belinda continued. "Smiling, well-spoken. He said he'd seen cases like mine destroy women. He told me I deserved to heal. To move on. It sounded like kindness."

She looked down at her hands, then up again, with a flicker of anger.

"If I'd known then what I know now about his politics, I'd have kicked him off my porch."

Cassie's pulse thudded. "Belinda, I need to know who. What was his name?"

Belinda took a moment, her brow furrowed in thought. Then she said it, flatly. With a twist of disdain.

"Graham Golding."

TWENTY-THREE

Climbing out of her car, she made her way up to street level from her usual spot in the underground car park. She paused on the footpath, staring into the foyer of the ABC building through the same big glass windows she usually looked *out* from.

Everything felt in reverse now. Like she could see what was in front of her, but it didn't quite make sense.

She and Brian had gone their separate ways the night before, a raincheck on the beers. After their meeting with Belinda, Cassie had reached out to James Lawrence instead. She needed something more concrete. No more theories.

She pressed the silver button on the traffic light pole and waited. As the familiar clicking signalled it was safe to cross, she dropped her head and stepped onto Southbank Boulevard.

She took the back way in, slipping through the Arts Centre's underground carpark and into the shadowed corridors of the lower levels. As she ascended the escalator, golden ceilings shimmered overhead, and the lights above glittered like chandeliers. The red carpet of the main foyer stretched before her like the promise of a Hollywood premiere.

But not this morning.

Cassie turned and made her way to the Arts Centre café and bar, tucked discreetly to one side. Usually buzzing with the pre-show crowd, sipping wine and nibbling canapés, today it was quiet. Empty. A sanctuary.

Just what she and Acting Deputy Commissioner James Lawrence needed.

"Cassandra," came the warm, velvety greeting as she reached the table tucked by the tinted windows. Outside, the small dining courtyard sat empty, fairy lights twinkling through the gloom, potted greenery drooping in the drizzle.

Not even the most devoted brunch crowd would brave this morning.

"James, thanks for meeting me." Cassie pulled out the black-cushioned chair and sat opposite him.

"Coffee?" he asked, gesturing to the cappuccino in front of him.

"That'd be great." She nodded.

James signalled to the waiter, who arrived promptly, took Cassie's order, and vanished again leaving the two alone.

"I'm sorry I couldn't see you last night," James said. "I'm sure you can appreciate how hectic things are at the moment."

"Of course. No worries at all." Cassie nodded. "How's everything going?"

"Well, these things take time. Even longer when you've got multiple agencies squabbling over jurisdiction. But there's pressure to get some arrests on the board. I don't think we'll be waiting much longer."

Cassie nodded again, politely this time. She hadn't come for updates.

"But that's not what you wanted to talk about, is it?" he said, locking eyes with her.

"No. It's not."

Before she could speak, a porcelain cup landed gently in front of her. The waiter disappeared again without a word.

"Last week, after Foster's death, you asked me about his personal life. His past," Cassie said. "Even though you claimed it was a Patriot-related murder. So why the questions?"

James gave a slow nod, as if he'd expected this.

"As I said at the time, I know how good you are at your job. It would've been remiss of me not to ask. You never know what detail might become important."

Cassie studied him, just as he now studied her.

"*Do* you have something for me?" he asked.

Cassie leaned back, a sly grin forming. "I think you might have something for *me*. Something you were hoping I already knew, maybe even more than you do."

James grinned.

"Go on," he said.

"Off the record, for now, can you tell me if Hayden Foster was working as a police informant?"

"I'm going to assume that question comes with some kind of evidence," he asked, without even so much as a flicker of surprise at Cassie's question. "Or at least an educated theory?"

"I wouldn't have come to you if it didn't."

"I can tell you this, Hayden Foster was never listed as a registered informant with Victoria Police. At no time was he ever on our books."

There were holes in that answer big enough to drive a convoy through. He knew it. She knew it.

"How about off the books?"

James drew a long breath and let it out slowly. He reached for his cappuccino, took a measured sip, and set the cup back in its saucer with a soft clink.

"Hayden Foster was a thug. And I've no doubt he was a rapist. If things had progressed further for him inside the Patriots, he was a potential terrorist too. He's not the sort of person you traditionally recruit as an informant, on or off the books."

Cassie said nothing. Silence was always her best move.

James considered her for a long moment. Then he nodded.

"There were rumours," he added. "Not recent, years old. That he had a friend in the force. Someone with enough weight to keep him out of trouble."

"Someone with power," Cassie said.

James turned, stared out the rain-slicked window as if searching for something long gone. A moment passed.

"Something like that would be... incredibly hard to prove." He glanced back at her. A smile tugged at the edge of his mouth. "Unless, of course, you really are that good at your job."

"Let's say I am," she replied. "And let's say I've got more than just an educated guess about who Foster was connected to. How *do* I prove it?"

James shrugged lightly. "You'd need a trail. But if you're chasing someone smart, someone protected, there won't be one. No bank records. No legitimate calls. Any communication would've been face-to-face or through burners. Our forensics team has already been through Foster's digital footprint. There's nothing. Nothing helpful for what your chasing, anyway."

"So that's it?" Her tone tightened. "You're saying we can't prove it?"

"I didn't say it's impossible." James leaned back, arms crossed. Calm. Guarded.

"I've already had one defamation case brought against me in the past year," Cassie muttered. "I can't run with a story built on smoke and suspicion. You know how this works. Powerful people have powerful lawyers."

James raised an eyebrow. "Are you willing to share just who it is you're thinking of? Off the record of course."

"I think it's someone who once held significant rank," she said.

His eyes sharpened.

She hesitated. Then gave him just enough. "In the force... and in politics."

James held her gaze for a long moment. No shift in posture. No flicker of emotion. Just stillness.

Then, finally, he nodded. "You've got your father's good instincts," he said quietly. "Trust them."

That was all. No name. No confirmation. But it was all she needed.

"But tread carefully. And don't trust anyone inside the force, even your contacts. If you do find anything, come directly to me." James reached into his jacket, pulled out his wallet. "I'll get these," he said, nodding at the coffees. He stood, pausing before walking away.

"Whatever you're chasing, don't wait too long. Some truths don't stay buried forever."

He turned, took a few steps, then stopped.

"And some? Some get buried deeper."

And then he was gone.

* * *

Peter Draper stood as they entered, the skyline behind him dull and slate-grey. He closed his laptop and gestured to the couch.

"Cassandra. Brian. Come in."

They sat, side-by-side, across from him. Peter eased back into his chair, leaning forward.

"I'm sorry I couldn't see you both yesterday. I take it that things have moved quickly since Saturday?"

"They have," Cassie said.

Peter gave a small, expectant smile. "Good. I've heard Nine might be prepping something for *Sixty Minutes*, with a similar angle, so it'd be good to get this wrapped up soon. Where are you at?"

Cassie didn't flinch. "We think Hayden Foster may have once worked as a police informant. Off the books."

Peter blinked once. "An informant? That's... not what I expected to hear. But that's a hell of a lead, if it holds. Have you got proof?"

260

She held his gaze. "Let's just say the source is credible, even if the details are still fuzzy."

"Credible how?"

"I spoke to someone this morning who'd know. He didn't confirm it, but he didn't deny it either."

Peter sat back slightly, arms folded, eyes fixed. "Go on."

"We're trying to confirm who Foster was working for. And if we're right... this is a much bigger story than we planned."

Something flickered behind Peter's eyes. "Name?"

Cassie glanced across to Brian, and then back to Peter. "Graham Golding."

He paused, lips pressed thin. "That's a serious accusation."

"It's a working theory," Cassie said. "But the connection may go back to the late 90's in Carrington."

Peter leaned forward. "Out in Banksia?"

Cassie nodded. "Foster and Golding lived there, just streets apart. We think there's a link through the local footy club. But there's more."

She flicked another glance at Brian. He gave a subtle nod.

"There was a boy," she continued. "Joel O'Connor. He died in a house fire in '98. The official ruling was accidental, but... I think there may be more to it."

Peter's brow furrowed. "Why do you think that?"

Cassie laid it out. Laura Cassini, the missed dance party, Hayden's violent history, the interference in Belinda Mead's case. She spoke clearly, methodically, but her heart was hammering.

Peter rubbed his jaw. "Are you saying that Hayden Foster was somehow involved in the fire that killed this boy?"

"I'm certain someone was. Who, we're still working on. I visited Jason Turner in hospital on Monday. From the Inside Out café in Elwood."

Peter's face softened. "How is he?"

Cassie hesitated. "As you'd expect. He'll recover physically, but he and Amir are traumatised."

"I can imagine."

Cassie leaned forward. "While I was there, they spoke about the gay hate crimes of the 80's and 90's, how groups of teenage boys would roam the streets at night, hunting for gay men to bash. He also said community attitudes, particularly from police, were just as brutal."

Peter's face darkened. "Yeah. I'm familiar. And he's right, it was brutal. I was still reporting when the Tasty Raids happened in '94. Victoria Police stormed the gay nightclub with a trumped-up warrant on the pretext of drug possession, but that was never what it was really about.

They strip-searched patrons, right there on the dancefloor. Humiliated them in front of the entire club. Pure intimidation.

It took two decades for the force to apologise. And when they finally did, it came with one of the biggest legal settlements in the state's history."

He exhaled hard. "What are you saying then? That Foster killed this O'Connor boy in some kind of gay hate crime attack, and Golding, what, protected him? Recruited him?"

Cassie didn't answer.

Peter shook his head. "Think what you like about Golding, but you're jumping the gun. Do you have *anything* linking Foster to O'Connor? Or Foster to Golding?"

"Not directly," she said softly.

The pause was heavy.

Peter leaned back, pinched the bridge of his nose. "You need to be careful, Cassandra. You've already dodged one defamation bullet. I don't need us being slapped with another. And you *know* who Golding is. What he's capable of."

She nodded. "That's why we've come to you."

"The O'Connor boy. What do you have beyond the memory of a grieving friend?"

"Nothing concrete."

Peter sighed. "I'm not saying she's lying. But grief does strange things. It reshapes the truth. If the coroner called it accidental…"

"What if they got it wrong?" Cassie cut in. "You know how easy it would've been to cover it up back then. Golding was the District Commander. He was on scene the morning after."

Peter's tone sharpened. "Focus on Foster and Golding. *That's* the story. If Foster was an informant and Golding was his handler, or protector, that's what matters. Not a 28-year-old fire with no shred of proof."

Cassie sat silent.

Peter stood and walked to the window. He stared out for a long moment, then turned back, the cityscape glowing cold behind him.

"You're on dangerous ground. If what you're saying is true, if Golding's tied up with criminal figures, this is more than a story. It's a threat. Think about what that might do for every case he was ever a part of."

His gaze cut through her. "Don't make it personal. Don't be reckless."

Cassie nodded. "I won't."

"Then do it by the book. And keep me updated. Regularly."

She hesitated. "What about Joel O'Connor?"

Peter shook his head. "Until you've got more than hunches and heartbreak, leave it for now. Focus on the Foster–Golding connection. Get that story. Once it's solid, you can hand the rest over to James Lawrence. If VicPol thinks it's worth looking into, they will."

Peter took one look at the expression on Cassie's face and groaned.

"OK, do it," he said, his voice tightening. "But for God's sake, stay away from Golding himself, and members of his family."

He didn't finish.

His voice dropped, roughened by something heavier than caution.

"You're poking a bear, you two. And one that will bite back. *Hard*. So, poke it carefully... or not at all."

Cassie held his gaze. "We'll be careful."

Peter looked between them one final time. "Don't make me regret this."

* * *

Cassie and Brian collapsed into the chairs at her desk, exhaustion giving way to that strange, weightless relief that comes when chaos finally begins to make sense.

"Jesus, Cass," Brian muttered. "You could have told me about James Lawrence."

She managed a tired smile. "I'm sorry. Everything moved so fast, I just needed to get it in front of Peter while we had the chance."

He shook his head. "So, you were right all along."

"We don't know that for sure. Not yet. But I can feel it, we're close."

Brian nodded. "What now?"

"We need David Grayson. If he was Foster's best mate back then, he has to know something. I mean, if he's anything like Foster, he'll probably tell us to fuck off, but it's still a lead. I tried one of my VicPol contacts yesterday, but I haven't had a response yet. I'll try again now."

Brian stood. "Can I do anything?"

"Yeah. Call Laura Cassini. See how she responds to you, not me. Try to get her to agree to meet. Both of us, ideally."

Cassie glanced at her phone.

"It's still early, she might even see us today. Find somewhere neutral. Public. Actually... she said Joel used to work at the cinemas at Banksia Plaza. See if they're still there, and if so, check if there's a café nearby."

Brian gave a mock salute. "Got it."

"Oh, and Brice McCrae. See if you can get a hold of him too. If we can see them both today, lock it in."

Brian nodded and peeled off toward one of the spare desks, phone and laptop in hand.

Cassie flicked through her contacts again.

"Come on, Brent," she murmured. "Pick up."

TWENTY-FOUR

Laura Cassini had welcomed the call. Welcomed the chance to meet Cassie again, and even with Brian. The location had surprised her, but she hadn't hesitated.

They found the café easily enough on the second floor of Banksia Plaza, choosing a booth tucked close to the internal walkway.

Despite the school holidays, the place was quiet. Too quiet. A few kids milled around outside the cinema, clutching popcorn tubs and oversized drinks, grandparents trailing behind with weary eyes, but even that felt more like an echo than a buzz.

Maybe people had gone away for Easter.

Maybe the cost-of-living crisis had kept them home.

Or maybe places like Banksia Plaza, once the pulsing heart of the suburbs, were simply fading, eclipsed by the ever-growing juggernaut of online retail convenience and curated lifestyle precincts.

Whatever the reason, the centre felt like a ghost of its former self. And maybe that was the point.

"She's here," Cassie said, nodding toward the ticket booth across the hall.

Laura made her way across, smartly dressed, unhurried. She leaned in to kiss Cassie lightly on the cheek.

"Hi, Cassie. Nice to see you again."

Cassie wasn't used to that kind of familiarity, but Laura had that unshakable confidence, like she'd been taught from birth how to steer a room. Cassie found it oddly comforting.

"This is my colleague, Brian."

"Hi Brian, lovely to meet you," Laura said, extending a perfectly manicured hand. No kiss for him.

"Thanks for coming out, I know it's a bit of a drive," Brian offered as she slid into the booth opposite.

"It's fine. I've just got the boys settled into their seats. They'll be good through the previews, but I'd like to duck back before it starts." She said, nodding back towards the cinema.

"Have you been back here in recent years?" Cassie asked.

"I've driven past, but I haven't been inside." Laura gave a small laugh. "It's strange. I don't think they've touched it since the 90s."

Cassie followed her eyes as they drifted past tables and sugar caddies.

"This used to be a Sanity music store," she said softly. "God, I loved that place."

Her gaze swept the walls, taking in the framed stock images of Italian vistas and coffee plungers where glossy posters of silverchair, TLC and Alanis Morissette once lived.

"If you came in from the front," Laura added, "where the Maccas and KFC are now, that's where Valetta's used to be. Our old restaurant. They bulldozed it years ago though of course."

"Is it hard to see it gone?" Cassie asked gently.

Laura paused. "Not really. I'd seen it from the road before, so it wasn't a shock. But sitting in here... This is where we used to hang out after school. Sneaking ciggies out front behind the bus stop. And Joel worked here, at the cinema. This place was our little world."

She gave a slow, wistful look around.

Cassie nodded, then glanced at Brian. Meeting here had been the right call.

"Laura, there are a few things we need to ask you," she began. "Some of it might be difficult. If you'd rather not talk about anything, I completely understand. But there are things that don't quite line up with what you told me last time."

"Oh?" Laura tilted her head slightly. "Such as?"

"Such as Brice McCrae."

A flicker passed through Laura's expression, so quick it might've gone unnoticed. She nodded once. "Okay."

"When we first met, you said you didn't really know Brice. That you didn't remember him well, even though you grew up only a few houses apart."

Cassie paused, watching her carefully.

"We've since spoken with him."

That did it. A soft exhale. A shift in her shoulders. The performance dropped. She nodded.

"How is he?" she asked, voice quieter now.

"He seemed well," Cassie replied. "He's a bit of a character."

Laura gave a dry, fond laugh. "Yeah. He always was."

They let the silence sit.

"I did know Brice," she said at last. "We were together in high school."

She met their eyes now. No more veils.

"I didn't mention it before because... it felt irrelevant to Joel. And because it was tied to a part of my life I've worked hard to forget."

"The pregnancy?" Brian asked.

Cassie shot him a sharp look. He winced.

Laura blinked. "Did he tell you about that?" Then, more softly, "Of course he did."

"We were seventeen," she continued. "Stupid and scared and with no plan. Well, that was until Brice got it into his head that we could keep it and start a life together. I mean, we couldn't even hold down part-time jobs or pass maths for God's sake."

She looked away for a moment, then back.

"He had a big heart. But he was chaos, always on the go. The teachers could barely keep a straight face whenever they had to tell him off for something, because he was such a bloody clown."

A small smile played at the corner of her mouth.

"I know the other girls hated me for dating him. He was that guy: funny, good looking, magnetic. And I loved him. I did. But not enough to stay tied to Carrington. Or to being a Mum at seventeen. Or to Brice, who couldn't stay tied to anything."

Her voice softened.

"He didn't take the termination well at all. After that, something in him just… shifted. He stopped being that happy-go-lucky footy kid. He started hanging with the wrong crowd. Drugs. Fights."

She swallowed.

"And then, after Scott died..."

She didn't finish. She didn't have to. The silence did the rest.

"I've always wondered if I was somehow to blame," she said, almost to herself. "Maybe unfairly. But still."

"I think maybe it is unfair, to you," Cassie said gently. "We all make choices. He made his. That's not on you."

Laura half-shrugged, eyes drifting again.

"I hate to ask," Cassie said, her voice low, "but when did all this take place?"

"I can give you the exact date. The second of March 1998. A Monday." Her voice was clear, steady. "Joel came with me to the clinic. We were both still in school uniform. We wagged school to go. I remember everything. As much as I try to block it out, I never can. The world changed that day."

Cassie felt her chest tighten.

"I'm so sorry," she said, leaning in. "Laura. March of 1998? That's only a few weeks before…"

"Yes." Laura cut her off. "Joel."

She took a breath.

"I tried to keep it together after the termination. Because in doing so, I'd also lost Brice. Joel was all I had left. That's the real reason he didn't go away with his family that weekend. He stayed for me. That dance party, *Resurrection*, it was meant to bring me back from the dead too."

Her voice trembled just slightly.

"Joel was desperate to go. I mean, the very thought that Dannii Minogue might show up was enough for him, but I'd been a mess. And he stayed. Because that's who he was."

She looked up, eyes glassy now. Her voice cracked, just slightly.

"Something happened that night. Someone *did* that to him. I know it. I lost everything that year. It changed me. It changed everything."

Cassie leaned in, her voice soft but steady. "Laura... I know I've already asked you about Hayden Foster, but I need you to think again. Do you remember *either* him or a mate of his named David Grayson? It's important."

Laura sighed, long and hard.

"They were arseholes," she said at last, her lip curling. "I'm sorry I wasn't honest with you last time. Again, it was all tied to that time with Brice. I just...'"

Cassie shot a look at Brian.

"What can you tell us about them?" she asked.

"Like I said, arseholes. I only really knew them through Brice's footy team. He hung out with them for a while, God knows why. But I put a stop to it. I mean, yeah, I was hanging out with some of the older kids and getting up to no good myself, but this was different. There was something about those two. Nugget was a psycho, and David..."

She hesitated.

"David was a creep."

"What do you mean, creep?" Brian asked.

"He was always perving on the girls. Saying all types of gross stuff. There was just something off about him. You could *feel* it."

Cassie nodded slowly, absorbing the details.

"Laura," she said gently, "when we last spoke, I asked you about Justin Golding. Graham Golding's son."

Laura's face dropped the moment the name left Cassie's lips.

Cassie noticed. So did Brian. But she pressed on.

"Do you remember ever seeing Hayden Foster or David Grayson with Justin Golding? Or his older brother, Evan? Or even their father, Graham?"

Laura didn't speak at first. She just sat there, as if she hadn't heard. But something had shifted behind her eyes, like an old slide carousel clicking into place.

"No," she said eventually. "I don't."

But her voice had changed.

There was something dark sitting just behind her words now, an old memory, raw and jagged. One that had surfaced without warning. Her eyes flicked away, landing on the café wall as though seeing the ghosts of CD shelves long gone.

Whatever she was remembering, it wasn't nothing.

It was something.

And it hurt.

There was a pause. Then Laura glanced at her watch, the memory folding itself away as the present crept back in.

"Another name," Brian said quickly, sensing time was slipping. "You mentioned Scott King, Brice's best mate. Can you tell us anything about him?"

Laura nodded, her voice regaining some of its earlier steadiness.

"Sure. Scott was a good guy. Quiet, mostly. But funny in this dry, unexpected way, one of those people you'd forget was there until he dropped a one-liner that left everyone in stitches."

She smiled, a real one this time, warm and fleeting.

"Scott and his mum lived in government housing. She worked at the servo near the Banksia police station, but they never had much. They struggled."

Her voice darkened slightly.

"She had this boyfriend. One of those blokes who'd get completely drunk, off his face, at the Under-18s footy and scream abuse at the umpire like it was the AFL Grand Final. Scott hated him. Honestly, I don't even think Scott liked footy that much, he just followed Brice. Wherever Brice went, Scott was right behind."

She paused.

"He was more into music. He played guitar, even mucked around with a band for a while. He was also a massive stoner. I'd see him some nights, late, out on his back deck, smoking a bong, while I waited for Joel near his back gate."

"Scott's house backed onto the reserve too?" Cassie asked.

"Yeah. Just a few houses up from Joel's. He saw me a few times, just smiled and gave me a nod. We both knew we were up to shit we shouldn't have been at that hour."

A faint, sad smile tugged at her lips.

"He was quiet. But decent."

She hesitated.

"I didn't hear what happened until a few days after the funeral. I was in my mid-twenties by then. I hadn't spoken to anyone from school, or from Carrington, in years."

Cassie hesitated, then leaned in again, softer now, but firmer in intent.

"Last time we spoke, you said Joel had been seeing someone. That he hinted at something physical. A secret. You said he got cocky about it, like he was hiding something."

Laura stilled.

"Yes," she said slowly, guarded now.

"I need to ask," Cassie continued, her voice gentler. "Was it *something* he was hiding, or *someone*?"

Laura looked down at her hands, as though they held the answer. When she looked up again, the mask had cracked, not broken, just enough to let something else through.

"I've thought about that a lot," she said, measured. "The way he acted. The way he wouldn't tell me. I think... yeah. He was hiding s*omeone*. Not just for the sake of privacy. But to protect it. Or maybe to protect himself."

"And you don't have any idea who it was?" Cassie asked quietly.

Laura's pause was just a second too long.

"No," she said. "But I think whoever it was... it mattered."

She swallowed, eyes darting momentarily to the walkway behind Cassie, then back.

"I think he was proud of it. And ashamed. All at once. Like it was something beautiful and awful at the same time. And I think he knew, if it ever came out, he'd be destroyed for it."

Cassie sat with that for a moment. It ached.

"And what about the people around him?" she asked. "People who might've wanted to hurt him because of it?"

Laura nodded once.

"There were people like that. Nugget. David. They were cruel, because cruelty gave them power. And Joel? Joel never fought back, at least, not against them. He just... endured."

"And Brice?"

Laura met her eyes.

"Brice wasn't perfect. But he loved Joel. Not like that, not romantically. But as a person. I think when Joel died, it shattered something in him too."

Cassie studied her for a beat. There was something else there, buried deep beneath the surface. Not quite guilt. Not quite fear. But weight.

"The truth is never simple," she said, almost a whisper.

Then Laura blinked, as though coming back to herself.

She looked at her watch again, throwing a glance toward the cinema foyer.

"Right. Well, thanks for clearing some things up for us," Cassie said gently. "If anything else comes to mind, you've got my number."

They all stood.

"Enjoy the movie," Brian added.

Laura returned his smile. "Thanks. It was nice to meet you."

She turned to Cassie one last time. "Thank you for taking this seriously. It's nice to finally be heard."

Cassie and Brian watched in silence as she crossed the walkway and disappeared into the dark corridor of the cinema, swallowed up by shadows and sound.

Only when she was gone did either of them speak.

"Are you thinking what I'm thinking?" Brian asked.

"Are you thinking she's steering us?" Cassie asked quietly.

Brian nodded. "She's not lying. Not entirely. But she knows more than she's letting on. That bit about Brice?"

"That wasn't deflection," Cassie said. "It was protection."

"And what did she mean by *the truth is never simple*?"

Cassie shook her head slowly as she bit at her cheek, lost in thought.

"Do you want me to try calling Brice again? He might answer this time."

Cassie stood, slinging her bag over her shoulder. "No. Let's just pay Brice another surprise visit."

She headed for the escalator, then glanced back.

"But first, I spied the food court downstairs. Lunch?"

TWENTY-FIVE

"I shouldn't have had that third samosa," Cassie groaned as she turned off the highway and into the grid of industrial streets.

Brian snorted. "Mate, you said that after the second one."

"I meant it then. I mean it now. I feel like I've swallowed a grease trap."

He smirked. "You could've gone with the açai bowl."

"Say *açai* one more time and I'll make you walk the last two blocks."

Brian chuckled under his breath.

They turned into the cul-de-sac where Rusty Shovels was based. Cassie's light mood faded as her eyes landed on the white Crime Scene Services van parked inside the gates.

"Is that the police?" Brian asked, shifting forward in his seat.

Cassie pulled up at the curb, killed the engine, and instinctively reached for her phone, not to check anything, just to have something in her hand.

"Should we wait here?"

Cassie threw him a look. "You're an investigative journalist now, Brian," she said with a grin. "Let's go investigate."

They walked straight past one of the officers, who was packing equipment into the side compartment of the van. He didn't even glance at them.

"Right, well, thanks again, Mr McCrae. We'll be in touch. And get those cameras charged up," called another officer as she stepped out from the main office alongside Brice. She didn't acknowledge Cassie or Brian either.

Brice lit up when he saw them. "The ABC? Again?" he beamed. "Geez, it must be a slow news day."

Cassie didn't smile. "What happened?"

"C'mon, I'll show ya."

Inside, the office looked like it had been picked up and shaken. Papers were scattered across the floor and desk. Filing cabinet drawers had been yanked off their runners and lay awkwardly beside their carcasses.

"A break-in?" Brian asked.

"Well, I ain't redecorating, mate," Brice quipped.

Brian grimaced, realising how dumb the question sounded.

"What did they take?" Cassie asked, already scanning the space with a forensic eye.

"That's the weird part. They didn't take anything." Brice rubbed the back of his neck. "There's equipment in here worth a fortune. The Ute keys sit right there..." he pointed behind the front desk "...and not one of them was touched."

"Point of entry?" Cassie asked, her gaze flicking to the doorframe, the windows, scanning for damage like the seasoned cops she grew up around.

"Well, they used bolt cutters on the gate. But in here? The cops reckon they picked the locks. And here's the kicker, everything was locked again this morning when the crew showed up. No fingerprints either. Like it was a bloody ghost or something."

Cassie walked slowly through the room, stepping around paper trails.

"What do you reckon they were after? Banking details? Client accounts?"

"Maybe. They went through all the staff files, so could've been looking for bank info, but nothing's missing. Not even the spare change on the desk."

"No CCTV?" she asked.

Brice sighed. "Nah. We swapped to these new fancy battery-powered one's last year. Better image quality and I can stream it on my phone, but the bastards are always going flat. I haven't been up the ladder to charge them for weeks."

"So, nothing was recorded," Brian said, jotting it down.

"Nah. We'll get the sparky back tomorrow and chuck the hardwire ones back up again. It's a pain in the arse, really."

Cassie stood in the middle of the mess, frowning. It didn't feel random. It felt precise, like someone searching for something they didn't find.

Brice watched her silently. "But you two didn't come here for this, did you?"

"No. We didn't," Cassie said. "But if this is a bad time…"

"Nah, she's right. Let's sit in the factory. I'll leave this crap for later."

He turned toward the side door, a cough catching hard in his throat. He pressed a fist to his chest, cleared it with effort.

"You alright?" Brian asked.

"Fine," Brice muttered, waving it off as he pushed open the door. "Bloody weather's all over the place. Everyone's crook with something."

They followed him into the larger space beyond, where the ceiling rose high and the cool echo of clanging tools and a forklift trolley bounced off concrete. The smell of mulch, petrol and damp wood sat heavy in the air.

"Oi, Dylan!" Brice called out, voice still rough. "Move that ride-on back in, will ya? I don't know why it's still sittin' out the front."

A young worker gave a quick nod and disappeared out the roller door.

Brice gestured to a little table near the kitchenette, surrounded by a hodgepodge of mismatched chairs. A folded newspaper and a chipped coffee mug sat on one end.

"Grab a seat," he said, sprawling comfortably. "What can I do for ya's today?"

"I've just got a few more questions about Hayden; *Nugget*," Cassie said.

"Fire away."

Brian took the lead. "You laughed when we mentioned Justin Golding last time, that Nugget and he would never have been mates."

Brice scoffed. "Yeah, you got that right."

"What about you? Were you ever mates with Justin?"

"Me? God no." He barked a laugh. "As I told ya's, Golding was a dick. His older brother was alright, though, Evan. Great footy player. But Justin? Nah."

Brian glanced at his notes. "Well, what about Evan Golding, then? Did you ever see Nugget with him? Could they have been mates?"

Brice shrugged. "Dunno. I guess. Maybe."

"What about their father, Graham Golding? Did you see him around the club?"

"Oh yeah, Graham was always there. The Goldings were like royalty at the club. Big financial donors, that sort of thing. They even had their name on a plaque down in the rooms. But I don't remember ever seeing Graham with Nugget. He could've I guess, but not that I remember."

Brian paused. Cassie stepped in.

"Brice," she started carefully. "Last time we were here, we asked you about Joel O'Connor."

Brice shifted in his seat but said nothing.

"You told us then that you didn't remember him," she continued. "And you also said you didn't really remember Laura Cassini either. But she remembers you. Very well, actually."

Cassie let the statement hang. No follow-up. Just a slow, intentional silence.

She and Brian leaned back, waiting.

Brice scratched his cheek. "Yeah, well... it's a long time ago now, you know?"

"So, you don't remember being in a relationship with her, then?" Brian asked, calm.

Brice let out a short laugh, too loud, too forced. "Geez, you guys are like the cops!"

Neither of them flinched.

Let them fill the silence with what they fear you already know, her dad always said.

Brice squirmed.

"Yeah, alright. So what? We hooked up for a while back in high school." He shrugged, but the tension in his shoulders said otherwise. "And as for Joel... mate, that's all in the past, you know? It was a pretty shitty year, to be honest. But I don't wanna talk about any of that."

Cassie let the silence settle for a beat, then pressed on.

"Brice," she said, shifting slightly in her seat, "Nugget and David Grayson. They were pretty tight right? That's what you told us last time, that they were good mates."

"Yeah, they knocked about a fair bit."

"But you also told us you didn't know where either of them ended up after your days in the footy club. That's right too, isn't it?"

"Yeah, nah. Not for twenty-plus years at least. I told ya's Dave moved up to New South, but I wouldn't know where he is now."

Cassie nodded, offered a small "hmm," and let the quiet stretch between them.

Her eyes drifted around the factory, pallets of soil bags, trays of plants, the forklift now parked neatly to the side.

"It's a great setup you've got here," she said casually. "Those trees over there look good."

Brice followed her gaze. "Teddy Bear Magnolias. They're going out to a display home site in Clyde tomorrow. It's a big job. We've got contracts with some of the volume builders, so it's going gangbusters at the moment."

"Can I?" Cassie stood, wandering toward the crates. Both Brice and Brian rose to follow.

"I live in an apartment," she said lightly. "I don't have much space, but I wouldn't mind something for the front balcony. These are beautiful."

"You could definitely get away with a Magnolia in a pot," Brice added, crouching beside one of the crates. "Does your balcony get much sun?"

"A bit, yeah. I do like these. Maybe I can pick one up

whilst we're down here. Who's your plant supplier?"

She watched the shift hit him like a change in air pressure. Not his words, his posture. The recalibration. The pause before he responded.

"Ah, we get 'em from a few different places. Depends on what we need."

Cassie didn't answer. She flipped a leaf, inspecting it without looking at him.

"How about Evergrow Supply? Do you use them at all?"

This time, she met his eyes.

Brice hesitated. Swallowed. "Yeah. Evergrow. Yeah, we use them."

Cassie held his gaze a second longer than was polite, then turned back to the crate.

That was all she needed.

He was unsettled.

And he knew she knew it.

"Maybe not a Magnolia," she said lightly. "Looks too nice for my balcony. Knowing me, I'd probably kill it anyway."

Brice gave a vague smile, but the spark was gone.

"Thanks again, Brice. All the best with the clean-up. I hope they catch whoever's responsible."

Cassie nodded to Brian.

"Yeah. No worries," Brice muttered, but the easy charm had vanished.

As they made their way back toward the roller doors, Brian glanced around the factory floor.

"Does your business partner work onsite as well?" he asked casually.

"I noticed there's only one desk in the office. What did he have to say about the break-in?"

Brice blinked. "Business partner? Nah mate, it's just me."

"Oh, sorry," Brian replied, stopping to flick through his notebook. "I thought you co-owned the business with... sorry, here it is. Elliot Petrovic?"

Brice's face drained of colour. Like the bottom had dropped out of him.

"Ah... nah. Silent partner," he muttered, nodding a little too quickly.

Cassie clocked everything, the flicker in his voice, the way his hands shifted toward his pockets, the hollowness in his eyes.

She considered pushing. Just one more question.

But it was too late. He'd shut down.

"Thanks again, Brice," she said instead. "You've been very helpful."

"Yeah. See ya's." He managed a weak smile, but this time it was forced.

They stepped back into the light.

"That's it?" Brian asked as they walked down the driveway.

"It's all we need," Cassie said.

"He's not going to tell us anything else about Hayden or David. Even if he does know more, which he does."

Cassie opened the car door and climbed into the driver's seat, pulling it shut with a thud.

She waited until Brian had done the same before speaking again.

"Okay, so the footy club is definitely the link between Foster and Golding. It has to be."

"He couldn't say either way though if he'd ever seen the two together."

"No. But there might be someone else who can." She groaned, already regretting the words as they left her mouth.

Brian raised an eyebrow. "Do I want to ask?"

Cassie started the engine. "Let's just say... bring your patience."

Brian grinned, eyes lighting up. "Lead the way."

* * *

"G'day there, love!" came the familiar voice. "And g'day, who's this then?"

Rodney Lindfield appeared in the doorway, wearing the same oversized windcheater from last time, now with a smear of something unidentifiable across the sleeve. A mug of tea steamed in one hand, the other resting casually on the door.

Cassie gave a small wave. "Rodney, this is Brian. He's with me."

"Are you the cameraman coming to film my interview?" Rodney chuckled.

"Something like that," Cassie said, managing a smile while giving a slight shake of her head to Brian, as if to say *just go with it.* "Got time for a couple of quick questions?"

"For you, love? Always." He stepped aside with a theatrical sweep of his arm. "Come in, come in. Just don't mind the dog, he's had a rough day."

"I didn't even know you had a dog," Cassie said. "Was it outside last time?"

"Yeah. He had crook guts then. He always gets the shits after I give him a bone."

Brian glanced down at the ancient Labrador sprawled across the tiles. "He looks dead."

Rodney snorted. "It wouldn't be the first time someone thought that. Follow me!"

Cassie threw Brian a look, he was now holding back laughter.

"Do you want a cuppa? The kettle's still hot!" Rodney called as he made his way into the kitchen.

"No thanks, Rodney, we're both good. We really won't be long," Cassie said with a smile.

"Alright, well take a seat," he offered, quickly shoving a pile of papers and clothes to the other end of the living room table.

Cassie hesitated, but Brian made the decision for her, pulling out a chair and sitting, a big dopey grin spread across his face.

She gave in and sat, dragging out the wooden chair beside him.

"Rodney, I want to ask you a few more questions about the time Hayden Foster, *Nugget*, was at the club."

"You're still on about him?" Rodney raised a brow but nodded. "Okay. Fire away."

"Do you ever remember him spending any time with the Golding family?"

"You mean Graham's boys?" he asked.

Cassie nodded. "Or maybe even Graham himself?"

Rodney leaned back in his chair, brow furrowed as he thought.

"No. Not that I remember. Graham was always down at the club of course, Evan was a champion player. But Nugget?" He shook his head. "I mean, it's possible, but I can't say I ever remember seeing them together."

Cassie felt her hope dip as she glanced at Brian.

"I mean, there was Justin, of course," Rodney added.

"Justin Golding?" Cassie asked, sitting up straighter.

"Yeah. Graham tried to get him into footy, but he was hopeless. Afraid of the ball. I let him play one year just to keep Graham happy, but he didn't last the distance. He quit just before the finals, from memory."

"Do you remember when this was?"

"Yeah, around the time Nugget played in his first premiership. You remember, it was that team photo you showed me last time."

"Were Justin Golding and Hayden Foster in the same team?"

"Oh yeah. I don't think there was ever any love lost between those two," Rodney chuckled. "Nugget didn't have a lot of time for anyone who didn't know their way around the ball."

Cassie's eyes widened. She looked to Brian, who took the opportunity to step in as she mentally rearranged the puzzle pieces.

"What about the other boys you mentioned to Cassie? Hayden's footy mates. Were any of them close with Justin Golding?"

"Nah. Justin copped it from all of them, really. I mean, I can't say he didn't deserve it, but... nah, he kept to himself and spent most of game time on the bench. It didn't make Graham happy, that's for sure."

"Rodney," Cassie started gently, "just how close were those other boys with Nugget? The names you gave me, David Grayson, Brice McCrae, and Scott King."

"Thick as thieves," he said without hesitation.

"You're sure about that?"

"Oh yeah. I used to see the four of them hanging out at the club rooms long after practice. I'd sometimes wander down to check on things on non-game days, and I'd find the four of them just sitting around, like they had no other home to go to."

"Do you remember anything about David Grayson? He left for New South Wales in 1997. The same year we're talking about now."

"Yeah, of course. Now he and Nugget were *very* close. Wherever Nugget went, Dave was always two steps behind."

"Do you ever keep in touch with any of the boys?"

"Only the ones still around Carrington. I'll run into 'em sometimes at the IGA, or down the pub. They'll stop and say a quick g'day, but most've moved on with their lives." He paused, and for a moment, the sparkle in his eyes dimmed.

"Have you ever seen David Grayson?"

"Dave? Nah. Though I wouldn't know him if I fell over him these days. I saw him a few times after he moved up to live with his old man. He'd come back for school holidays, visit his mum and his little brother and watch the boy's play. His little brother played in the Juniors for a bit, but not for long. I couldn't even tell you his name."

Cassie glanced at Brian. Something was forming. Another thread.

"Rodney, thanks so much for your time."

"Oh, no worries, love." He paused, shifting in his seat. "But listen, you still haven't asked me about my Hall of Fame yet. Just all these questions about Nugget. You *do* want to do that interview with me, don't you?"

There was something smaller about him now. The bravado that had coloured their last visit, the pride, the old coach glow, had faded. In its place sat something quieter. Frailer. Lonely.

"We'll be in touch," Cassie said, her voice softer than before.

She meant it.

And she found herself, quite unexpectedly, feeling sorry for him.

TWENTY-SIX

Cassie pulled onto the freeway, merging into the flow of late afternoon traffic, city-bound, but her mind was already miles ahead.

"What do you think?" Brian asked, craning his neck to double-check she wasn't about to sideswipe a Kenworth.

Cassie's eyes flicked to the rearview. "I know what *I* think. What do *you* think?" she said, easing her foot off the accelerator as they hit a hundred.

Brian exhaled. "Honestly? I don't know."

Cassie's phone buzzed.

"Finally," she said, eyes flicking to the screen. "Hang on Bri, this might be our lead on David Grayson."

She tapped to answer through the car's speakers and looked across at Brian, putting a finger up to her lips. He nodded.

"Brent. *Finally*."

"Hey Cassie, sorry I didn't get back sooner. I've been flat out since Saturday. It's been fucking chaos."

"All good. I'll be quick. I need your take on those screenshots I sent, the guy in them. David Grayson. I just want to confirm if the guy from those New South Wales court files is the same one I'm chasing."

Brian looked at her, eyebrows raised.

"I'm guessing your guy's from Melbourne. Mid-forties?"

"That's him. Grew up in Carrington. He might have a juvenile record too."

"Oh, he does. And more. It's not great."

"No?"

"No, not at all. You want the New South stuff?"

Cassie gave a look like: obviously.

"Uh, yes please."

"There's only a couple from Cessnock: assault, disorderly conduct. But the serious stuff's out of Newcastle: child abuse, soliciting a minor online, grooming, possession of child sexual abuse material. He did time for those."

Cassie froze. The words hit like a punch to the lungs.

"Shit," she breathed. "Is he still inside?"

"No. He got out a few years ago and then changed his name. That's probably why you can't find anything on him."

She straightened in her seat. "Wait, what?"

"Yeah. He kept the 'David,' and changed the surname to 'Smith.' Real needle-in-a-haystack stuff. I guess after what he did, he didn't want to be found. He moved further south and was living in a caravan park just outside Goulburn until recently."

"Until recently? Where is he now?"

"About six feet under. He's dead."

Cassie jerked the wheel, cutting across three lanes toward the Forster Road off-ramp. Brian clutched the door like a man about to meet God.

She pulled up onto the grass verge, indicator ticking like a metronome.

"What happened? When?"

"Three months ago. Caravan fire. Official report says he left the gas stove on. He was a heavy drinker, so… it tracks."

Cassie wasn't listening. Her thoughts were spiralling.

Another fire.

Another death.

Another ghost.

"You still there?"

She blinked. "What?"

"I said, ruling was accidental. No sign of foul play."

Cassie stared at the large road sign directly in front of her, her mind racing.

"Send me everything you've got," she said, her voice low.

* * *

Cassie's apartment was dim, lit only by the glow of a light in the hallway, the laptop and the muted flicker of the TV, which had been on for hours without sound. A half-eaten noodle box balanced precariously on a pile of notes. Brian leaned back on the couch, nursing a beer and eyeing the wall like it might answer all their questions.

Cassie sat opposite him, barefoot, legs tucked under herself, her fingers smudged with pen and satay sauce. The whiteboard she sometimes used for interview prep was propped up behind her, now littered with arrows, question marks, and underlined names. At the centre, circled twice: JOEL O'CONNOR.

She took a sip of beer and exhaled.

"Nothing about any of this is accidental," Cassie finally said. "They were both there that night. Hayden and David."

Brian nodded slowly.

"Something happened to Joel O'Connor. Something violent. And now the two men who might've held the answers are dead," she continued.

Cassie reached for the noodle box, poked at it, then abandoned the idea. She grabbed her phone, checking the time for the hundredth time.

Brian leaned forward, elbows on his knees. "You sure this is a good idea?"

Cassie didn't answer. Just gave him a look.

She'd already rung the main Harvard switchboard earlier, only to be told that Dr Kathryn Whitmarsh wouldn't be in her office until nine a.m.

It was now 10:59 p.m. Melbourne time.

She was back on the phone. Ready.

Bingo.

"Oh yes, hello again. Dr Whitmarsh is in now, I'm happy to see if she can take your call. May I ask who's calling?" "Yes, it's Cassandra Murphy from the Australian Broadcasting Corporation."

"One moment, please."

Cassie drummed her fingers restlessly on the coffee table. The hold music kicked in, a nauseatingly upbeat voice extolling the virtues of Harvard's postgraduate programs, followed by an equally chipper man spruiking the bloody rowing club. She rolled her eyes.

Across the room, Brian sat quietly in the armchair, scribbling something on a torn scrap of notepad paper.

Then...

"Hello Cassandra? This is Kathryn Whitmarsh. How can I help you?"

Straight to the point.

"Hi Kathryn, thanks for taking my call."

"Not at all. You're up late, it's what, eleven p.m. over there?"

"On the dot."

"Well. I wish I could say that it was the first time I've taken a call from an Australian journalist, but let me guess, this is about my father, isn't it?"

"Actually, yes. That is why I'm calling."

"Great," she said, dry. "What's he said this time? Actually, don't tell me over the phone. I'm in front of my computer. Do you have Zoom?"

"I do, yeah. I've got my laptop right here."

"Great. And it's Cassandra Murphy?"

"That's right."

They exchanged email addresses and ended the call. Cassie refreshed her inbox obsessively until, finally, the invite came through. She clicked the link and waited for it to connect.

"Hi, Cassandra. This is better," Kathryn said as her image filled the screen. Her hair was pulled back in a loose ponytail, dark circles under her eyes betraying either a late night or a heavy week.

"Sorry that took a while. I Googled you before calling back. I was ready to hang up if you didn't match your photo. You wouldn't be the first to reach out digging for dirt, and not all of them are who they claim to be."

"That's fair," Cassie said. She appreciated the bluntness.

Brian slipped her the note. One word, underlined: *recording?* Cassie gave a subtle shake of her head, tucking the paper under her laptop.

"So, what is it this time?"

"There's not a lot of detail I can go into about my investigation…"

"Well, if you can't give me that, I'm afraid I can't give you anything."

Cassie nodded. "Fair enough. But I need you to know that this is incredibly sensitive…"

"…and *you* need to be sure I'm not going to hang up and call my father?"

"Yes."

Kathryn leaned back. "I haven't spoken to that man in a very long time. The last time I saw him was at my mother's funeral in Australia, a year ago. Before that, it'd been nearly a decade. I can guarantee you, whatever this is, I won't be reaching out to him."

Cassie nodded, scribbling a note in the corner of her pad as Brian leaned forward, alert.

"I'm actually looking into something that happened back in Carrington in the late 1990s."

"Carrington?" Kathryn's brow lifted. "Wow. That's going back. That's where I grew up. I don't know how much help I'll be, I moved out when I was nineteen. What was that, 1995 maybe? Mum and Dad sold the house not long after. It's been years."

"That's fair. I'm trying to get a clearer picture of your father's connections back then, specifically, whether he had any criminal figures acting as off-the-books police informants."

"From Carrington?" she repeated. "No, I don't think I can help there. Look, we had some pretty shady people come around the house, sure. Everyone knew they were crooks. He didn't even try to hide it. And yeah, there's always been talk about him being mixed up with underworld types, especially from you lot in the media. But nothing's ever stuck. Not yet anyway."

Cassie shifted slightly forward. Brian mimed drinking, then pointed at the whiteboard. She ignored him.

"Do you remember someone named Hayden Foster, or *Nugget*? He was the same age as your brother, Justin. In fact, they played football together."

Kathryn frowned, shaking her head. "Hayden Foster... no, I don't think so. I don't remember Justin ever mentioning anyone by that name. I don't even remember Justin ever playing football either to be honest. That was more Evan's thing."

Her face faltered, just slightly.

"Justin didn't really have many friends," she said. "He didn't bring people over. That said, I moved out not long after he started high school. I wouldn't have known who he was hanging around with. Is this about Justin? Is he in some kind of trouble?"

"No. At least… aside from the Falcons, there's nothing linking him directly to Hayden. Not yet."

Cassie caught Brian's raised eyebrows. She gave the smallest nod.

"Do you have any reason to think he might be in trouble?"

Kathryn hesitated. "No, not trouble. Admittedly we don't talk all that often, but I know he's struggled since Mum died. They were close. He was the only one who could calm her down when Dad was being a bastard. I've always worried about him being stuck over there with the other two. At least he had Mum."

"The other two?"

"Dad and Evan."

Cassie didn't miss the chill in her voice.

"Justin didn't get along with them?"

Kathryn laughed bitterly. "Dad and Evan are two peas in a pod, both controlling narcissists, both obsessed only with themselves. Evan was the golden boy. He could do no wrong. The two of them would gang up on the rest of us. Mum, me… but Justin? He copped it the worst. They belittled him. Undermined him. Made him feel like nothing."

Her tone cracked, just a little.

"I tried. God knows I wanted to stay and protect him, and Mum, but I couldn't. I was nineteen. I had to get out. Justin never really recovered from their torment. I think that's why his marriage broke down, to be honest. And I'm convinced all the stress is what led to Mum's health issues. The crap Dad said at her funeral? It was all performance. But that's him to a T."

Cassie leaned forward. "Sorry, did you say Justin's marriage broke down?"

Brian sat up straighter.

"Last year, around the same time Mum died," Kathryn said. "I never understood what he saw in her. *Melanie.* She was obsessed with our father. That's how she and Justin met, actually, she was an intern who worked on Dad's political campaigns. It was Dad who introduced the two of them. God knows why. That's around the same time Justin joined the force. I think Dad had a moment of redemption when it came to Justin at that point. It didn't last long."

She looked down for a moment, voice softening.

"I think Melanie was more in love with Dad than she ever was with Justin," Kathryn said. "She treated him the same as they did. Cruel. Calculated. And after the divorce? Dad took her side. Supported her. He never spoke a word to Justin. His own son."

Cassie's eyebrows lifted slightly.

"Dad's set her and the girls up in some townhouse in Hawthorn," Kathryn went on, her voice like glass about to shatter. "Pays for the whole lot. That's your model father, bankrolling his pet intern while kicking his own son to the curb. In politics, he paraded around on a ticket of 'traditional family values,' but no one ever dare talk about how he treated his own. And don't even get me started on the string of affairs he had while married to our mum. If there's one thing I can't stomach, it's a hypocrite. And make no mistake, whatever polished image he peddles to the Australian public, behind closed doors he's something else entirely."

She paused, then exhaled and shook her head, as if catching herself slipping too far into old wounds.

"Anyway, you said this was about a Hayden somebody?" she said, shifting the conversation back into neutral.

"Hayden Foster," Cassie said. Then, after a beat: "Sorry again, but did you mention that Justin was on the force? You mean... as in, a police officer?"

Kathryn gave a sad, almost amused huff. "Yes. Well. For about five minutes, anyway. I think he was desperate for some kind of approval from Dad. Some kind of recognition. He made it through training, but the damage was already done. He had no confidence left."

Cassie felt movement beside her. Brian shifted on the couch and silently pushed a notepad across the table. In scrawled block letters: *WHAT YEAR DID JUSTIN JOIN?*

Cassie gave the slightest nod but didn't break stride.

"As a kid, you'd have thought he was full of it, confidence, I mean," Kathryn continued. "He got into a bit of trouble, acting out. But slowly... the light just went out of him."

"What happened?" Cassie asked.

"He quit after a year. Worked security for a while over at Banksia Plaza. Night shifts. Then the incident happened, and that was the end of that."

Cassie leaned forward slightly. "Incident?"

"He was working late. Some kids, teenagers, were loitering in the public toilets in the back car park. He confronted them, and they beat him to a pulp. I mean, they nearly killed him. I still can't believe he survived. No cameras, no witnesses. Just him, left bleeding in the gutter. He didn't want to pursue it, which I never understood."

Kathryn swallowed hard.

"He had a breakdown after that. He couldn't leave the house for months. Eventually, he started his own locksmith business, got back on his feet. But honestly?" She looked straight at Cassie. "I still worry about him. I always have."

"Do you think he ever... stayed in touch with your father?" she asked gently.

Kathryn gave a bitter laugh. "You don't come back from what he and Evan did to him. No. The only thing keeping him tethered to the other two was Mum, and now she's gone. As for his girls... he tried to be a good dad, he really did. He loves them unconditionally. But of course, Melanie went for sole custody and got it. He couldn't put up the fight. At least not anymore."

Kathryn let out another long sigh. "But that was always Justin. Always chasing something that wouldn't love him back. And when things went wrong... he'd lash out. Misdirected anger, mostly. At the world. At himself."

Cassie felt Brian sit forward slightly, but he said nothing. Just watched.

In the background, they both heard the faint knock of a door. Kathryn's eyes flicked upward.

"She's here? OK, just one minute," she called offscreen.

Then, back to Cassie: "Cassandra, I'm afraid I have to go. And I'm sorry, I know I gave you absolutely nothing about this Hayden person. I hope something I said helped, but honestly, I can't offer anything about Dad's contacts. Especially not from back then."

"No, really, thank you. I appreciate your time."

Kathryn gave a small, tired smile.

Then the screen went dark. Cassie sat motionless, staring at the black rectangle, her own reflection faint in the glass. She closed the laptop slowly. Across the coffee table, Brian met her gaze.

Neither of them said a word.

TWENTY-SEVEN

The heavy grey skies that had been brooding over Melbourne for days finally gave way overnight, soaking the city in steady, relentless rain. Cassie had stirred around one a.m., just long enough to toss an extra blanket over Brian, still curled on the couch. The sound had always soothed her, like the ocean at the end of her street. In Heathton Ridge, rain drumming on a tin roof was almost meditative; here, the terracotta tiles dulled it. But still, it was something.

After settling Brian, she'd stayed up for a while, not chasing leads or digging through files, just watching water thread down the windows. Letting the noise fill her ears so her mind didn't have to. Any moment of stillness was a small mercy.

She must've drifted off, because when she stirred again, the rain had eased to a drizzle and the hum of morning traffic rose from the street below.

She padded barefoot past the kitchen into the lounge. The couch was empty, a fold in the blanket marked where Brian had been. Then the front door clicked open.

Brian stepped inside, shaking off the umbrella he'd found in the entryway. Two coffees and a brown paper bag in his free hand.

"I didn't mean to wake you," he said quietly.

"You didn't," she smiled.

He passed her a coffee and pulled out the breakfast bagels. Not the familiar white packaging with the black Inside Out logo she knew so well. A quiet tug in her chest. The thought of Jason and Amir not being around the corner anymore filled her with a dull sadness. She wondered how they were faring. Safe at least, that was all that mattered.

Brian handed her a napkin and sat at the bench, peeling the lid off his coffee.

"You hungry?"

"Starving."

They ate in silence for a few minutes, the rustle of paper, rain ticking faintly on the windows. When Cassie finally spoke, her voice was low.

"We need to see Justin Golding."

"Is that a good idea? Peter was pretty clear…"

Cassie shrugged. "We've already spoken to Kathryn."

"Yeah, but that's because you were sure she wouldn't speak to her father."

"Do you think Justin would either, after what Kathryn told us last night? Not likely."

Brian went to speak but returned to his bagel.

"I need to see him, Bri," Cassie said. "I was sure this all centred around Hayden." She stared out the window. "And now…"

Brian looked over. "Now?"

She turned back to the couch. "I can't stop thinking about what Jason and Amir told me. About how gangs of teenage boys would go out hunting to bash gay men. What if that's what happened to Joel? What if Hayden and David made their way into Joel's house that night to beat him up? Maybe they meant to kill him. Maybe they didn't. But then they panicked. Burned the place down to destroy evidence. The O'Connor house backed onto the footy oval. It would've been easy to get in and out unnoticed."

Brian put his bagel down and nodded.

"I agree. There's no way Hayden and David dying in house fires, months apart, is a coincidence. If David had been living in New South Wales since the late 90s, the only common link is Carrington. Rodney Lindfield said David came back to Melbourne on school holidays. Joel died at Easter. It fits. So, who killed them then? And why now? Why wait almost thirty years?"

"Exactly. Why?" she echoed, prompting him.

Brian exhaled and leaned back.

"Because you feel like that moment put you on the path you've been on ever since. And after losing your mum, your wife, custody of your kids… you've got nothing left to lose."

Cassie gave a small, knowing nod.

"Laura said Joel had been seeing someone. Not dating, but intimate all the same. What if that someone was Justin Golding? Closeted or not, he wouldn't be the first straight bloke to seek out men for sex. But think about it. He grows up in a house where he's belittled by an angry, homophobic father and bullied

306

by his older brother, the family's golden boy. If Justin was attracted to men, imagine the self-hatred he'd have carried. A lot of gay hate crimes are committed by men struggling to come to terms with themselves."

"True?" Brian asked.

"True. They take out their self-hatred on the people who reflect what they can't accept in themselves. Remember that mass shooting in Florida in 2016? The gunman pledged allegiance to ISIS, then walked into a gay nightclub and killed forty-nine people, injuring dozens more. Afterwards, men came forward saying he'd been a regular there, active on the apps, hooking up with other men. If that's true, he was living a brutal internal battle, wanting what he'd been taught to despise, while clinging to an ideology that would kill him for it. That's not just internalised homophobia, Bri. That's an internal war."

She leaned forward. "And what about the guys who don't fit the stereotype? Blokes working on oil rigs. Running out onto AFL grounds. They're not the ones marching at Pride or posting glitter selfies, so they don't see themselves reflected anywhere. Half the time they're stuck in places where casual homophobia is just the air they breathe. Then you've got hate groups like the Patriots pumping poison into everyone's feeds, and men in power, like Graham Golding, propping up the same old prejudice, giving those groups permission to go harder. Imagine what that does to someone's head. That kind of isolation eats at you. No wonder the suicide rate in the gay community is still through the roof." Her voice cracked with frustration.

"So, they explode... or implode?" Brian said.

"For some, yeah. God, we're deep into the twenty-first century and those shitty old rules still haunt us. Men are supposed to be *this*, women are expected to be *that*. If people were just left alone to be themselves, we wouldn't be in this fucking mess."

Brian sat in silence, absorbing it.

Cassie took a breath and steadied herself. "I can't help but wonder about that other thing Kathryn told us," Cassie went on. "About those teenagers who bashed Justin while he was working security. She said it was in the line of duty. But a public toilet block? In the back car park of a shopping centre? In the middle of the night? Why would a security guard be patrolling a toilet block alone at night? I mean, it's plausible, but…"

"…but what if he was in there for other reasons?" Brian said.

"Exactly. What if Justin had been cruising for sex, only to be set upon by a group of teens out for a bashing?"

"That would certainly explain why he didn't want to pursue it further with the authorities. The fear of being outed. But what you're saying, Cass… wouldn't that mean it was Justin who killed Joel?"

Cassie didn't answer. She just stared at him. Waiting.

Brian's eyes widened. "Justin was the one who told them about Joel."

"Now you're there." Her voice was quieter. Sad.

"I think Justin and Joel were having a sexual relationship. But Justin couldn't handle it. He couldn't handle the self-hatred. Desperate to fit in with Hayden

Foster, to be more like the kind of man his dad admired, he saw an opportunity."

She leaned forward, sipping her coffee.

"I think Justin told Hayden and David he knew a way to get to Joel. And I think all three of them went there to bash him that night. And I think Justin's lived with the guilt ever since.

"And then all these years later, like you said, he loses everything. The only things tethering him to a world where he didn't have to think about what he'd done. I mean, what was it you said about the person who killed Hayden? You said they'd either have to be strong, or..."

"...or have taken him by surprise."

Cassie nodded.

"We thought that meant maybe it was someone he knew. Someone he trusted. Someone he let in. But what if it was someone who knew how to break in without making a sound? Someone who could come and go like a ghost."

She met his eyes.

"Like a locksmith."

Cassie whispered it.

"Fuck."

They stared at each other.

"The break-in at Rusty Shovel," Cassie said, eyes widening.

"But why would Justin break in there?" Brian asked.

"He was looking through personnel files. He was looking for Brice's address."

"Why?"

"Shit, Brian." More pieces fell into place. "Laura said Brice was furious about the abortion. That he cut her loose and started hanging around with some bad people. Who was it that went with Laura to the clinic for the termination?"

Brian froze. "Oh shit. Joel."

"That's why he's been so cagey. He was there too that night. And if he was there, I'd bet anything Scott King was too. Maybe that's the real reason he took his own life: the guilt."

Cassie turned to him, the last of the pieces now locking into place.

"It wasn't just Hayden or David. It was all of them. The bloody five of them."

* * *

"Come on, Bri..." she muttered, leaning forward to look up at Brian's apartment building through the windscreen. "Five minutes my arse."

The rain had picked up again, light but steady, turning everything outside into a watercolour. She sighed and checked the time. 10:11 a.m.

Just as she reached for her coffee, the building's side door opened. Brian stepped out, hair still damp, shirt half-buttoned, shoulder bag slung across his chest. He jogged past her window with a nod, clicking open the gate to the car park. Moments later, his silver Honda Civic pulled out behind her, headlights flashing. She took off, Brian slotting in behind.

She was still mulling over ways to engage Justin Golding, but one thing was clear: they'd both need their own cars for this.

The Monash was slick with rain and already clogging. Cassie stayed in the middle lane, wipers working overtime, Brian's headlights steady in her rear-view. The closer they got to Carrington, the heavier the clouds seemed to press down.

She tapped the screen to redial Rusty Shovel Landscapes.

Still no answer. Straight to voicemail. Again.

She tried once more, then gave up.

Thirty-five minutes later, they rolled through Carrington's outskirts, every front yard slick with rain. They turned into Deakin Heights, toward the small industrial estate. The gate to Rusty Shovel Landscapes was open. Cassie parked beside a shiny work Ute, Brian pulling in behind her. The gravel was sodden, puddles stretching like lazy mirrors across the lot.

"Shouldn't we just go to the police now?" Brian asked.

"If Brice was there that night, he's likely now the next target. One conversation, then we go to James Lawrence, I promise."

A young worker in high-vis stepped out of the warehouse, clipboard under one arm. "Can I help you?"

Cassie recognised him from the day before. "Hi, it's Dylan, right?"

"Yeah, that's me."

"We're looking for Brice," Cassie said.

"He's not here. Back Monday."

"Is he working from home?"

"Nah, he and Elliot took the dirt bikes up to Eildon for a few days."

Cassie flicked a glance at Brian.

"His business partner?" Brian asked.

Dylan frowned. "Elliot works here, but he's not Brice's business partner. Elliot's Brice's son."

For a moment they stood in the drizzle, rain ticking on car roofs, a magpie warbling somewhere in the grey.

"Want me to leave him a message?" Dylan asked, shielding his face.

"No, that's fine. We'll call past next week," Cassie said. Then, quickly: "Sorry, Elliot's surname threw us. Petrovic."

Dylan shrugged. "I think that was his mum's last name."

"Right. Thanks." Cassie managed a smile.

He nodded politely and ducked back inside.

"I thought he said he didn't have any kids?" Brian said.

Cassie looked across the road. A white van rolled by slowly, tyres hissing through water.

She chewed the inside of her cheek, eyes narrowing.

"Well?" Brian said.

Cassie stayed still at the car door, rain light but steady.

"Cassie?"

"You can bet Brice has gone off the grid because he's figured all this out as well. It means he's safe for now, but who knows for how long. We'll look into Elliot later."

She turned to him, her look enough.

"Justin?" Brian sighed.

She nodded. "I want to see him face to face, Bri. But we can't just rock up as reporters. We need a plan."

Brian raised an eyebrow. "What kind of plan?"

Cassie's mouth curled into something that wasn't quite a smile.

"I'm working on it."

TWENTY-EIGHT

Otway Park Reserve lay quiet, the rain-soaked playground keeping the kids away this time. Across the oval, two teenagers kicked a footy between them, but as the drizzle began needling Cassie's windscreen, they bolted for the nearest path back into the suburban maze.

Brian's headlights cut through the sideways rain as he pulled in beside her. Cassie groaned. She hated getting wet. But in the line of duty...

They stepped out, jackets pulled tight, meeting in the middle of the empty car park.

"You're absolutely sure about this?" Brian asked, glancing around as rain sheeted across the asphalt.

"You have got to stop asking me that. I'm sure. And I need you to be too if this is going to work."

Brian nodded.

"Stick to the plan. If he doesn't show, we both leave. If he does, I need you out of sight. Park out on Grove Street and wait."

"Cass, I really don't like this. What if he recognises you?"

"So what? He wouldn't have a clue why I'm here."

"Really? Standing metres from where Joel died?"

Cassie met his eyes. "That's exactly why it has to be here, Bri. This is what we do. Keep your phone on." She pulled hers out. "Time to make the call."

She dialled.

"Hello? Rapid Lock Services?" She pitched her voice high, frantic. "Oh, thank God, you're the first number that came up on Google. I've locked myself out of my car and it's pouring... No, I'm not with the RACV," she added, shooting Brian a look.

"I'm at Otway Park Reserve in Carrington, near the playground. I'm the only car here, you can't miss me. Blue Volkswagen Golf. Older model. No, older than that... I don't know the year." She rolled her eyes at Brian.

"Please, I really don't want to be stuck out here in the rain, and it'll be getting dark soon... Oh, you can come? Brilliant. I'll wait over at the footy clubrooms. I'm not going anywhere." A fake laugh. "Yep, this number's fine. See you soon."

She stuffed the phone into her jacket.

"Let's do this." She locked her keys in the car and slammed the door. "There. Done."

"Cass..." Brian gave her a final uneasy look. "Be careful."

"I will. And don't park out the front. Go further down the street."

Brian gave a reluctant nod, then reversed and disappeared.

Cassie waited until he was gone, then jogged across to the footy clubrooms. The car park side offered no shelter, but the oval side had old wooden benches beneath rusted eaves. She sat on the edge beside a door marked HOME TEAM, pulling her sleeves down over her hands.

Orange lights buzzed above, locked behind metal cages. On the concrete in front of her, someone had graffitied a crude penis in white spray paint.

She could picture it, Hayden Foster waiting here to run onto the oval, Rodney Lindfield barking slurs from the sidelines. Maybe this was where the infamous celebration with the strippers had taken place.

She rubbed her hands together, heart ticking faster than she wanted to admit. What the hell was she doing? She was about to meet the very person she now suspected had orchestrated Joel O'Connor's death and was possibly out there dealing in some twisted form of reckoning, leaving two more bodies in his wake. The air felt heavy, unsettled, as if something more foreboding lay beyond the rain clouds.

She checked her phone. No messages, no missed calls. Just her own reflection in the black screen, pale and drawn. *Come on. Come on.*

The minutes dragged, each one making her second-guess. She tried to steady her breathing, tried not to imagine shadows shifting at the edges of the oval.

"Come on," she muttered.

Right on cue, her phone buzzed.

"You're here? OK, I'm just coming around now."

Cassie stepped out into the open, walking slowly toward the car park.

A battered, old people-mover sat idling just off-centre. Its sliding side door was already open, revealing a ramshackle workshop crammed into the gutted back: keys, rods, tools, and rust.

A man crouched low beside her car, already at work.

"Hi!" Cassie called out, forcing a bright tone as she approached. Her heart thumped hard and erratic in her chest. "Thanks so much for coming. I thought I was going to be stuck here all night."

"No worries," said Justin Golding quietly.

It was the first time she'd seen him in person. Until now, he'd been little more than a fading face in the Class of '98 yearbook photo. And even that memory felt vague.

He looked like anyone you'd pass on the street. Average height. Average build. But there was something off. Something small. The way he hunched into his jacket. The way his eyes flicked past her, never quite landing. Meek. Quiet. Sad, even.

Gone was the brooding, angry teen Laura had spoken of, the one who'd do whatever it took to get in with the 'cool' kids. This was the man Kathryn had described. A shell. Shrunken. Hollowed out by whatever life had done to him, or whatever he'd done to it.

No fight left.

Was this really the guy who killed Hayden Foster and David Grayson? Cassie felt a flicker of doubt ripple through her chest.

She forced a grin, pushing the nerves down. "Still get many damsels in distress locking themselves out these days?"

He gave the barest of smiles. "Not these days," he said flatly, voice distant.

He wasn't interested in small talk. He wasn't interested in her.

Cassie's gaze drifted beyond him, toward the fence line behind the playground. Toward the ghost of Joel O'Connor. Her mind was already scrambling. She'd focused so much on luring him here, she hadn't properly planned what to say once she was standing face-to-face with him.

He was nearly done.

Shit.

She tried again. "You must live nearby if you got here that fast. You're in Carrington, yeah?"

A nod. No words.

He moved back to the van.

Think, Cass.

"This'll do the trick," he muttered, sliding a long, flat rod between the window and the frame. There was a soft click. The lock popped. He reached in and retrieved her keys, handing them to her without meeting her eye.

"Thanks so much," Cassie said, trailing him back toward the van. She needed to buy more time. Find a hook.

She kept her tone casual, light. "I'm not from around here, actually. I've just moved down from Queensland. The Gold Coast," she lied. "My cousin moved up there from Melbourne when she was a kid. She said I should visit where she grew up. Carrington."

He said nothing. Just slid the van's side door shut with a dull thud.

"She lived just over there," Cassie added, gesturing vaguely toward the fence line. "Her name's Amelia.

Millie, they used to call her. You might know the family? The O'Connors? She had a brother, Joel, but he…"

She trailed off. Too late.

He stopped. Slowly turned.

His eyes locked on hers now, not flicking away, not darting. Still. And something else: the meekness was gone.

A chill prickled at the back of Cassie's neck. The air shifted.

He didn't speak right away. Just stared. Long enough for her to feel it tighten in her chest. Her fingers curled tighter around the keys.

Then he stepped forward. Not fast. Just deliberate.

His voice came low and calm.

"What the fuck is this?"

Cassie blinked. Her mouth went dry.

"I'm sorry?" she offered, half a beat too late.

Another step.

Cassie clocked the object in his hand, a screwdriver. Held low, half-hidden, like it was second nature. Like he didn't even realise he was gripping it.

Or like he absolutely did.

She took a careful step back, voice steady. "I need you to take a step back, please."

"No," he said, still advancing. "Not until you tell me what this is really about."

He was close now. Too close. She could see the twitch in his jaw, the stubble along his chin. The heat in his eyes.

"Tell me what the fuck is going on," he spat. His voice was no longer calm, it was sharp, cracked, rising from somewhere deep.

Cassie held his stare, refusing to back down. Her thumb pressed hard against the sharp edge of the car key in her palm. If she had to use it, she would.

Then…

"Hello! Hello there!" came a sing-song voice from behind the trees.

Brian.

He emerged from the shadows, hands out in an exaggerated shrug, a big goofy grin. "Sorry to bother you both, but could you help with directions? I seem to be incredibly lost."

Justin's head snapped around. His face twisted.

"Fuck off."

Brian didn't flinch. He took a step forward, his grin vanishing.

"No. *You* fuck off."

Justin froze.

Brian stepped in again, voice flat and hard now. "We know who you are, Justin. And I've already called the cops."

Cassie moved sideways, careful and fast, her shoes crunching softly over the gravel as she edged toward her car. Justin's focus was fixed on Brian now.

Justin's eyes darted between them, the fury bubbling to the surface. "Who the fuck are you?" he barked. "What is this?"

"We're leaving," Brian said, calm and cold. "And you're staying put until we're gone. Clear?"

Cassie yanked the door open and jumped in. She threw the car into reverse, headlights slashing across the car park as she swung around.

"Get in!" she shouted.

Brian backed toward the passenger side, never taking his eyes off Justin until the door slammed shut beside him.

"Forget my car," he said, breath tight. "We'll come back for it. Just drive."

Cassie didn't hesitate. She gunned it, tyres spitting gravel as they tore out of the car park and onto Grove Street, then down toward Carrington Highway, without so much as a glance in the rear-view mirror.

A few blocks later, Cassie swung into a McDonald's car park and cut the engine. The headlights died. Darkness swallowed the cabin, save for the distant, jaundiced glow of the golden arches bleeding through the windscreen.

Neither of them spoke.

They sat in silence, breathing hard, the shock of it all catching up to them.

Cassie's hands were still clamped to the steering wheel, knuckles white. Her fingers tingled with pins and needles, her body only now realising it could start to crash.

Brian spoke first, quietly. "Are you OK?"

Cassie didn't answer straight away. She stared ahead, eyes glazed, watching the rain snake down the glass.

Then she exhaled, a ragged breath that seemed to hollow her out. "I'm fine," she said, too quickly. Then softer: "I was ready to deck the guy."

Brian let out a breath, half-laugh, half-shudder. "I know. That's the part that had me worried."

She gave a weak laugh, but it cracked halfway out of her throat. Her hands were shaking now. She rubbed her face, dragging her fingers down hard like she could press the fear back into place.

"Jesus, Bri."

He looked at her, voice gentler now. "You were brilliant, you know that?"

She didn't reply.

"I didn't even mention Foster," she said finally. "One second, he was this sad middle-aged bloke, and the next... I saw it in his eyes. Like something just snapped." She looked over at Brian. "He knew. He knew exactly who I was. Exactly what I was doing."

Her voice thickened. "If you hadn't been there..." She stopped herself. Swallowed hard.

Brian didn't push her.

She shook her head. "I walked in without a bloody strategy. I wasn't thinking. I just wanted answers."

Brian stayed silent, letting her spiral out the last of it.

She looked down at her hands again, flexed them like she was checking they still worked.

"He's our guy, Bri. And I think he could've killed me."

The words landed hard between them.

"What do we do?" he asked.

Cassie stared out at the dark horizon. When she spoke, her voice was steady again, cold, clear.

"Now I'm sure that it's Justin, we need to speak to Brice McCrae. If he really was there that night, that's who Justin will go after next. You can bet Brice knows it too, that's why he's gone bush."

Brian frowned. "How do we find him in Eildon?"

"We start with his home address just to make sure he's not still there. And if he isn't, we take this to James. We'll talk to Peter first, then hand it all over to VicPol. We don't have the smoking gun on Graham Golding yet, but if they arrest Justin... maybe something will shake loose."

She paused, jaw tight.

"I don't want to take any more chances. He's seen us both now."

She turned to him, something flinty in her eyes.

"Let's go get your car. You can follow me there."

* * *

Back to the highway and then down a kilometre or two, a turn off led to the far end of Deakin Heights. Here the streets grew steeper. The gardens became more tangled and overgrown, as the houses edged deeper into the foothills of the Dandenong Ranges.

Lansdowne Road sat just a block from the edge of the national park, where the towering gums pressed close, their canopy thick. The rain had stopped, though the heavy dark clouds above still hung low, even lower still here. The road narrowed as it climbed, the homes more scattered now, tucked behind wild gardens and veiled by dense bushland.

Cassie didn't need GPS.

Brice's place announced itself.

Two houses ahead to her right, a dual cab Ute sat parked against the gutter, a trailer attached with two dirt bikes loaded on the back. But it was something else that grabbed Cassie's attention. A familiar white transit van squatted in the drive, its cartoon logo of a spaghetti bowl spilling down the side. Valetta's Catering. *Laura.*

Cassie slammed the brakes just as Brian pulled in behind her.

She checked her mirror, then signalled for him to back up. Reversing carefully, she slipped into the shadow behind a parked car across the road. Brian rolled to a stop two houses behind.

She grabbed her phone and dialled.

"Bri, do you see what I see?"

"Is that..?"

"Yep. It is. What the bloody hell is she doing here?"

"I thought she told us they hadn't seen each other in years."

"She did."

Movement caught Cassie's eye.

A young couple appeared at the base of the driveway, wrapped around each other in that dramatic, overly tactile way people were when they thought the world was watching. Early twenties, she guessed. The boy, tattoos snaking down his hands and up his neck, pulled the girl against him. They kissed like they were the last two people on earth.

Cassie cracked her window, straining to catch a word.

"Message me when you get there," the girl said at last, peeling away. "And watch out for kangaroos!"

The boy just smiled, stuffed his hands in his pockets, and ducked behind the side fence toward the house.

As if on cue, the parked car that Cassie was hiding behind blinked to life.

Cassie saw her chance. "Brian, stay where you are," she said, hanging up as she stepped from the car.

She intercepted the young woman mid-crossing.

"Hi," Cassie said brightly, disarming. "Sorry, I'm a bit lost. I'm looking for Brice McCrae's place?"

"That's OK, these streets are tricky. It's across the road," she said pointing. "I've just come from there."

She was warm, open, with a soft Filipino-American lilt. Cassie smiled back, reading her quickly.

"Perfect. Thanks so much."

"You're lucky to catch him," the girl said. "They were supposed to leave hours ago."

"Oh, that's right, I forgot he told me that. They're heading up to Eildon, right?" Cassie said convincingly.

"Last minute boys' weekend," the girl smiled.

Cassie glanced toward the transit van and gave a vague nod. "Has he got company?"

The girl tilted her head. "I think Brice said it was an old school friend. I haven't really been inside the house. Elliot and I spend most of our time in his bungalow out the back."

Cassie remained motionless, eyes fixed on the house.

"I'm Angel. Elliot's girlfriend," she added, breaking the pause.

Cassie's gut tightened. She kept her tone light. "Brice's son, right?"

Angel beamed. "That's right. And sorry, you are?"

"Amelia," Cassie said smoothly, slipping Joel's sister's name into play for a second time. "Brice has been doing our garden. I just wanted to pick his brains about some changes my husband's after."

Angel accepted the lie with an easy nod. "Nice to meet you."

"Lovely to meet you too. I might come back another time. I don't want to disturb him if he's busy. They're back Monday, right?" she asked, fumbling with her keys.

"That's the plan. It just depends. Brice's new medication is really helping, but they'll play it by ear." Angel's smile held, but there was sadness behind it. "Still, it's nice they can have some time together."

"It is." Cassie nodded softly, but her pulse raced. *What exactly did she mean by that?*

Angel waved and climbed into her car. Cassie lingered a moment as she watched the taillights disappear into the distance, then climbed back into her own, the picture shifting again in her head.

She grabbed her phone and opened up Instagram. Elliot Petrovic. Her hunch was right. That locked profile from a few days earlier. The profile photo matched. Elliot and Angel. Despite not being able to see Elliot's full profile, there was link to a website in the bio that she had dismissed earlier. She clicked and waited as a website for a rock band named *The Strays* loaded on her phone. She scrolled.

Elliot Petrovic, drummer.

Still holding her phone, she dialled.

"Hey, what's going on? Who was that?" Brian asked.

"She said her name's Angel. She's Elliot's girlfriend. Hey, listen, he's also in a band called *The Stays*. Can you dig further? I…"

Cassie stopped mid-sentence as the front door swung open, flooding the porch with light.

Brice. And Laura.

"Shit," Cassie hissed. "Get down. I don't want them to see us." She shoved her seat back.

Through the narrow slit of her window she watched the transit van ease down the drive, reverse lights glowing as it rolled past and away.

"Alright, mate, let's do this!" Brice's raspy voice called out as the front door slammed shut.

The two men appeared at the bottom of the drive, tossing rucksacks into the back of the Ute before climbing in. The engine fired, loud in the still street, and moments later the dirt bikes rattled off behind them.

Cassie pressed flat as the Ute growled past. Her heart hammered against her ribs. She didn't move until the sound of the engine had bled completely into the night.

"Cass?" she heard Brian's voice on the other end of the phone. She lifted it up to her ear as she sat up, shifting her chair back into place.

She was too wired to think. Too raw to keep talking.

"What the fuck is going on," she finally said.

"What do we do? Did you want to take this to James? Peter?"

Cassie didn't answer straight away.

"Not tonight. At least we know Brice's safe. For now." She sighed. Exhausted.

"Get some sleep, Cass. We'll pull it apart tomorrow."

She looked in her rearview mirror and gave him tight nod.

"Lead the way."

TWENTY-NINE

The sky over Melbourne had finally cleared after two days of gloom. Patches of blue broke through ragged cloud, the Yarra catching stray shafts of light, rippling like fractured glass. The forecast warned of high winds by afternoon, but for now the city was holding its breath.

Inside, the newsroom pulsed with its usual rhythm. Fluorescents buzzed overhead, keyboards clattered in uneven bursts, phones rang, chairs rolled, the espresso machine hissed like a pressure valve about to blow.

It was the sound of routine.

Except it wasn't.

Cassie sat cross-legged on the carpet in front of her desk, ringed by documents, clippings, photos, scribbled notes. Shoes off, her toes pressed into the coarse weave of the carpet. Hair pulled back messily, she scrawled arrows and circles in biro.

Brian crouched a few feet away, sleeves rolled, marker in hand, working on a whiteboard they'd stolen from an empty studio. His boxes were neat, his handwriting disciplined. He was building a timeline: names, dates, phone calls, meetings. His voice stayed silent, but the squeak of the marker was steady, methodical, almost hypnotic.

The two of them had barely spoken. They worked in parallel, their silence companionable, their focus sharp.

Cassie shuffled through another stack of printouts, the smell of old toner and cold coffee clinging to the pages. In the corner of her vision, the office carried on: Tracey snapping at a producer over a missed segment, someone trundling past with a camera tripod, an intern balancing three lattes like her life depended on it.

By mid-morning, the floor around them looked like a paper graveyard sprawled in overlapping layers. A few colleagues slowed as they passed, curious, then quickened their pace again.

Cassie paused, rubbed her eyes, and sat back on her heels. And then she felt it, that rare, elusive moment when the fog lifted and the mess began to align. The connections were there, faint but undeniable, like stars emerging in a night sky.

Her pulse lifted. She pushed herself upright, spine cracking as she stretched.

"Ready?" she asked, brushing her palms against her jeans.

Brian capped the marker and stepped back from the whiteboard. The wall of names and arrows loomed like some ominous mural. He exhaled, nodded slowly. "Yeah. Let's give it to Peter."

They'd barely made it halfway across the corridor when a voice sliced the air.

"Guys!"

Tracey Longthwaite stood by the glass doors, one hand pressed to her headset, the other clutching her phone like a weapon. Her foundation couldn't mask the sudden pallor in her cheeks.

"Have you heard?" she asked, voice thin.

"Heard what? What's happened?" Cassie asked, already moving toward her.

Tracey just shook her head, throat working. "You'd better come to the newsroom."

Cassie and Brian shared a look. Something in Tracey's eyes told them this wasn't a routine wire drop.

"What is it?" Cassie pressed.

For the second time in a week, staff spilled from edit bays and meeting rooms, drawn like filings to a magnet. They gathered in clumps around the big flat screens on the far wall. A hush fell as someone nudged the volume higher.

The press pack appeared first, a thicket of boom mics and lenses. Then he stepped forward.

Graham Golding AO.

The former Victoria Police Deputy Commissioner. Former Member of Parliament. A man who had built a career on command, still carrying himself as though the air bent to his presence. His usual suit and tie were replaced by a royal-blue zip-up cardigan, a checked shirt poking out at the collar. His face was drained, hollowed by something deeper than fatigue.

Cassie's mouth fell open, stomach tightening. The sound of his voice pulled her back to other press conferences - fires, disasters, inquiries - moments when he had wielded language like a shield. She shot a glance at Brian. *What the hell?*

"It is with profound sadness that I confirm my son, Justin, was the victim of a cowardly and senseless hit and run overnight in Carrington."

Cassie gasped, sharp, involuntary, drawing the eyes of half the newsroom.

"Emergency services responded quickly, and I personally wish to acknowledge the tireless efforts of the ambulance crews and the exceptional medical staff here at Banksia Hospital. They fought for many hours but, tragically, despite all their efforts, and mine to be here at his side, his injuries were simply too great. He passed away a short time ago.

Justin was my youngest son. He worked hard as a small business owner, and he was the father of my two granddaughters, Ruby and Matilda. Like many men, he wasn't without his demons - none of us are - but he faced them in his own way and did the best he could.

I want to thank the many members of the public who have already reached out with messages of condolence. Your loyalty and friendship have always meant a great deal to me, and in this difficult time I draw comfort from knowing I continue to have the community's respect and support, just as I had throughout my long career in public service.

I ask now for privacy to allow myself, my family, and those closest to us the space to grieve. I trust members of the news media will honour this, and I expect nothing less.

Finally, I have every confidence that Victoria Police will use every resource, every power, every discretion available to them to find whoever is responsible for this cowardly act. I know they will not rest until justice is done.

That's all I will be saying on the matter. Thank you."

As the cameras dropped and the live feed cut back to the studio, silence held in the air.

Cassie didn't move. Just stared at the screen, frozen.

Beside her, Brian was equally still, eyes wide, lips parted, the colour drained from his face.

They looked at each other.

No words. Just the kind of glance that said everything.

The newsroom buzzed faintly around them, muffled. Distant. Like sound underwater.

"Cassandra! Brian! Conference room. Now!"

Peter Draper didn't break stride as he stormed from the studio gallery, slicing through the newsroom like a blade. Cassie and Brian exchanged a look and followed him down the corridor in silence.

Peter didn't sit. He stood at the head of the table, gripping the back of a chair like it was the only thing holding him steady.

"Can you please explain to me why I've just had Kathryn Golding..."

"It's Whitmarsh," Cassie interrupted, slumping into her seat.

"Excuse me?"

"Whitmarsh. Kathryn Whitmarsh. Her married name."

Peter's eyes bulged.

"Whitmarsh, Golding, I don't give a damn what her married name is. What I care about is that she's Graham Golding's daughter. And that she just called to tell me you rang her two nights ago, asking all sorts of probing questions about her brother, who, twenty-four hours later, ends up dead in a hit and run."

Peter never got angry. The fact that he was now had Cassie's skin prickling.

"I thought I made myself very clear to both of you. Stay the hell away from Graham Golding and his family. And what do you do? You walk out of here and go straight to his daughter."

"Peter, I needed to..."

"Cassie." His voice dropped, ice threading through it. "What you needed to do was follow instructions. If Graham Golding is connected to what happened to that poor boy whose ghost you've been so hellbent on chasing, then contacting Kathryn may have tipped him off that you were closing in. Did you think of that?"

"She hates him," Cassie shot back. "I knew she wouldn't speak to him."

Peter stared at her, jaw clenched.

Cassie hesitated, then: "It wasn't just Kathryn."

Brian turned sharply toward her, eyes wide.

"Excuse me?" Peter hissed.

"I mean... I didn't just speak with Kathryn."

Peter stood there, waiting. Daring her to keep digging.

"I needed to see him, Peter. I believe he was responsible for Hayden Foster. For David Grayson. And I believe he was going after..." she trailed off.

Peter gripped the chair so tightly Cassie thought it might splinter.

"Tell me you're not talking about Justin Golding. Cassandra, please tell me you didn't go and see Justin Golding."

"He didn't know who I was…"

"For fuck's sake, Cassandra!" Peter roared.

"Peter…" Brian started, but Peter rounded on him.

"And you? Did she drag you into this mess too? Go on. Tell me. What happened?"

Moments later, even the visitors in the foyer felt the boom of Peter's "YOU WHAT?" shaking the conference room walls upstairs.

"Peter, if you'd just listen!" Cassie snapped, steel in her voice.

"I'm done listening," Peter spat, slamming the table with the flat of his hand. "You've kicked off a shitstorm of monumental proportions. You know what's going to happen next? VicPol will knock on my door, asking why one of my journalists shows up on Justin Golding's call records as one of the last people to see him alive."

He shook his head in disbelief.

"And when they realise you tried to entrap him, without evidence, without clearance, it'll be me they hold responsible. My newsroom. My leadership. My fucking arse on the line."

"That isn't what we were doing!" Cassie fired back.

Peter didn't blink.

"Go home. Both of you. I need to call legal and get them up to speed on this bloody mess. And if you've got your own lawyer, Cassandra? I'd suggest you call them too."

He paused. And just for a second, the fire in him dulled. Enough to let something personal slip through.

"Cassandra… you know I've always had your back. I've gone to bat for you. I've believed in you. But this?" His voice cracked. "This isn't good. You've crossed a line."

He raked a hand through his hair, jaw still tight, trying to pull himself back from the brink. "Just… go home. Let's see how we can sort this."

He didn't look up. Just hung his head, gaze fixed on the table like they weren't even there.

Cassie didn't say a word. But the silence clung to her like ash.

She and Brian stepped into the corridor. The quiet between them thick as smoke. A Triple J presenter hurried past, eyes down, slipping into a studio. The door snapped shut behind her.

Cassie could' feel the hives on her neck start to settle as they climbed the stairs. It took a lot to trigger that old stress response now, something she thought she'd grown out of years ago.

But this was different.

It wasn't the dressing down. She could handle verbal cage matches in her sleep.

It was Peter.

Someone she trusted. Respected. Admired.

And the part that stung the most? The part that made her want to crawl out of her own skin?

Deep down, she knew he was right.

She'd crossed a line. Betrayed his trust. Screwed the whole thing.

And that made her furious.

At herself.

At Cassie Murphy. Because Cassandra Murphy wouldn't have let this happen. Cassandra Murphy had instincts. Boundaries. Control.

She'd done the one thing she swore she wouldn't.

She'd been reckless.

Maybe she was losing her edge.

Maybe she didn't even want to do this anymore.

Maybe it was Terence, and the pull toward someplace, *someone*, other than here.

Maybe it was the slow, unbearable grief for her dad, still here but fading, that she'd been trying so hard to ignore.

They reached her desk. Cassie stood frozen, exhaling hard, trying to catch up with her own thoughts.

"You okay?" Brian finally asked, awkward but sincere.

Cassie turned, her breath hitching.

"I'm so sorry," she said quietly.

"For what?" he asked.

"For *what*?" she scoffed, bitter. "For dragging you into this shit. This isn't how I work. I thought we had it. I really thought we were close."

She let out a breath, shaky.

"What if Peter's right? What if we've fucked the whole thing up? What if Justin had nothing to do with Hayden and David? What if we're the reason he's dead?"

She rubbed her face with both hands, dragging them down like she was trying to scrape the guilt off her skin.

"And what if you were right?" Brian started. "That he did have something to do with it. What if he was the next target all along? What if it had nothing to do with us turning up at all? And what the hell was that press conference all about? *I* this, *me* that. Not once did Golding say that he loved his son."

"Fuck," Cassie muttered.

"And speaking of sons, are we going to discuss Elliot? There's still more to this, Cass. We're not done yet."

Brian shifted his weight, watching her unravel. It didn't matter what he said now, she had tuned him out. He hated seeing her like this, so raw, so off-centre. This wasn't the Cassie he knew. But what could he say that wouldn't sound hollow?

"I need air," she said, grabbing her bag from the desk and throwing her jacket over her arm.

"Want me to come with you?"

"No. Go home, Bri. Do as Peter says. Don't worry about me."

She walked out before he could answer, bag tight in her grip like it was the only thing holding her together.

* * *

Cassie sat in her car for what felt like forever before she moved. After leaving work, she'd just driven, no destination, no plan. It could have been minutes or hours. She had initially headed north up the Hume. But what would she say when she pulled into Heathton Ridge? There were no answers there. She turned back but had no idea where she'd gone after that, or how long she'd been on the road.

But somehow, she'd ended up back here. Elwood.

She was lost in her head, the weight of everything pressing in, until the irritating scrape of a broom broke through. Behind her, under the buzzing streetlights and the last of the fading light, Marcella Lucci was out again, fighting a losing battle with the gale as she swept furiously at the autumn leaves skittering across the rear car park and side path, as if they were plotting her downfall.

Doesn't she have something better to do? Cassie thought, the bristles rasping against the concrete like nails on a chalkboard.

She grabbed her bag and slammed the car door harder than she needed to. It wasn't just noise, it was punctuation. Her way of saying: *Not tonight, Marcella. Let me be in my own fucking head.*

Inside the apartment, she dumped her bag and threw her jacket back on. She shoved her phone and keys into her pocket, heading back out and closing the door behind her.

She wasn't going to find peace in there.

She didn't want quiet. She needed the wind. Waves. Salt. Fury.

She needed the cleansing chaos of Port Phillip Bay.

Hands shoved deep in her jacket pockets, Cassie walked the short stretch through her neighbourhood. The air was thick with the smell of home-cooked dinners and early-week relief, people shutting the world out, tucking themselves in.

At Ormond Esplanade, she didn't bother with the pedestrian button. She waited for a break in traffic and crossed, head low, the wind clawing at her hair.

Down the narrow path, over the footpath, and then, there it was.

The wind hit like a wall, and she inhaled sharply, filling her lungs with salt and cold.

Behind her, the city noise dulled. In front, the sea churned and crashed, waves hammering the shoreline like they wanted to tear it away.

A lone Norfolk Island pine loomed above her, its branches thrashing in the wind.

Cassie sank onto a bench beneath it, the wooden slats damp with salt spray. She didn't care.

She stared into the dark water, letting the fury of it all rush through her. The wind, the waves, the mess she'd made, the grief she hadn't faced, the doubt that wouldn't let her go.

The city behind her kept moving. But for now, she didn't have to.

Here, in the biting wind, with the sea raging and the bench trembling beneath her, Cassie finally let herself go quiet.

Fifteen minutes passed. Maybe more. That strange place between solitude and fury.

Then her phone began to vibrate in her pocket. She cursed herself for not switching it off.

She cursed harder when she saw who it was.

Laura.

Cassie answered, voice flat. "Laura, I'm sorry but…"

"Cassie!" Laura's voice was frantic. Jagged. "I don't know what else to do! I think he's in serious trouble. This wasn't supposed to happen, I swear to you. We had no idea he'd go after Justin. It wasn't supposed to go like this!"

Cassie clutched the phone tighter, the wind screaming around her. She stood, turning her body, trying to shield the receiver from the chaos.

"It wasn't supposed to go like what? Who's in trouble?"

She stumbled across the beach path, searching for shelter, anything to cut through the storm of sound.

"I'm sorry I didn't tell you sooner," Laura said. The desperation was still there, but it had sunk into something heavier. Defeated.

Cassie dropped into a crouch beside the wire fence that lined the foreshore garden beds, gripping a timber post, anchoring herself as the wind howled.

"Laura," she said, steadying her voice, "if you need my help, then you need to start by telling me what the *fuck* is going on."

THIRTY

1998

The caravan groaned and jolted forward as Glen O'Connor gently pressed the accelerator of his late-1980s Mitsubishi Pajero 4x4. Chains clanged somewhere behind him.

"All good?" he called out from the open driver's side window, glancing back at Joel. His son gave a half-hearted thumbs-up, looking as unimpressed as when Glen had dragged him out of bed minutes earlier. Barefoot in blue-checked flannel pyjama pants and a faded grey *X-Files* t-shirt, Joel yawned, blinking at the overcast sky beginning to glow with the first hints of dawn. He went through the motions, indulging his dad's request for help, knowing that in a few minutes, the house, and the weekend, would be his alone.

Glen put the Pajero in park, yanked the handbrake, and climbed out to inspect his handiwork. The second-hand 1978 Franklin Truline, cream with a yellow stripe slicing through the middle, had been a long time coming. After years of sweating it out in a canvas tent on family trips to Phillip Island, he'd spent countless

Sundays scouring *The Trading Post* before finally getting his hands on the old relic.

"Perfect," he declared, ruffling his son's messy brown hair. As expected, Joel grimaced and recoiled from the unwanted touch.

"C'mon, mate. We're gonna miss you this weekend. It won't be the same without you annoying your sister and giving me grief." Glen shot him a wry smile.

Before Joel could respond, the front wire security door crashed open, slamming against the brick wall.

"Jesus Christ, Amelia!" Christie O'Connor's voice rang out from inside the house, breathless with frustration. She emerged, juggling the last of the bags, thrusting them at Glen, who had already played Tetris with the crowded boot.

"I'm *so* sorry," Amelia retorted, her voice dripping with sarcasm, pitched for the entire neighbourhood to hear.

"Would you please keep your voice down?" Christie hissed through gritted teeth, ironically just as loud.

"This is so unfair," Amelia huffed, slumping into the back seat, arms crossed, her pout exaggerated for dramatic effect.

"We've been over this," Christie sighed, turning to Joel. "Your brother's staying home to study. It's his big VCE year, isn't that right, darling?" She leaned in to kiss his cheek.

"Bye, Mum." Joel smirked, winking at Amelia. She bristled.

"He's not gonna study! He's gonna…"

Her protest was cut off as Christie slammed the car door, muffling her voice. She turned back to Joel, her expression softening. "You will do your homework, won't you darling? I want you to make the most of the peace and quiet."

"He'll be right, stop fussing," Glen cut in, shutting the boot with a grunt. "C'mon, let's get going. I wanna beat the traffic."

She sighed, climbing into the front seat. "Alright. Now remember, Auntie Linda's picking you up Sunday at noon for Easter lunch with your nanna. The telephone number for the caravan park is on the fridge next to your father's mobile number, just in case you need anything."

Joel leaned against the window, a mischievous grin spreading across his face. "You know… you could just get me a mobile phone of my own."

Christie scoffed. "We've been over this. When you finish school, with good grades, then absolutely."

"Everyone else is getting one," he complained.

"We're not everyone else!" she snapped back.

Glen slid into the driver's seat. "Alright, mate! We're off. Get that homework done." The Pajero grunted forward, the Franklin lurching behind, leaving a patch of yellowed grass in its place.

"Oh, and don't forget to tape *Hey, Hey, It's Saturday* for me!" Christie called as they pulled onto the road. "Wendy Matthews is on this week, and I've just bought her new CD! The video's already in the thingy ready to go, goodbye, darling! Love you!"

Joel waved, then flashed a quick middle finger at his sister. She shrieked, "Muuuum!" as the Pajero

344

disappeared down the quiet street, and he chuckled to himself, the weekend stretching before him like a blank slate.

Joel crashed straight back onto his bed and looked blankly up to the ceiling. Over Christmas, his parents had let him convert the disused downstairs rumpus room into a bedroom. He no longer had to share bedroom walls, his parents on one side, his little sister on the other. His obsession with music made the arrangement ideal, his parents appreciated the newfound peace, and Joel relished the privacy. The room's sliding glass door led directly to the backyard, and the wooden gate in the back fence led onto the reserve beyond.

Joel let out a slow breath and rolled onto his side, his gaze drifting over the patchwork of posters that had been with him for years. Björk in all her eccentric glory, The Prodigy mid-snarl, an anonymous DJ lost under green laser lights. *Doctor Who* stood beside *Buffy the Vampire Slayer*, Leonardo DiCaprio smouldered from *Romeo + Juliet*, a shirtless Mark Wahlberg kept watch above a faded map of London, and Toni Collette beamed from a *Muriel's Wedding* poster tacked proudly by the door. The real prizes were two giant movie posters, *Scream 2* and *Mortal Kombat*, liberated from the walls of his casual job at the cinema, edges still curled from the pins. Surrounded by them, he closed his eyes, the comfort of familiar faces and stories easing him back into sleep.

By noon, he had showered and demolished two bowls of Nutri-Grain and three slices of vegemite toast, before sitting at the dining room table with his Year 12

Biology textbook. As desperate as he was for his own independence, a sadness crept in as he glanced across at the empty living room. There were so many happy childhood memories wrapped up in this place and he loved his family, even Millie. The ever-troubling thought that his own truth may one day destroy that happiness, for him and his family, was an anxiety he tried so hard to push down. But lately, for some reason, it was all he could think about. One day soon, he'd have to tell them. And that upset him deeply.

A sudden loud bang against the front window made him jump.

"Ahhhhhhh!!!" Laura Cassini squealed, dancing in the front garden, waving a champagne bottle over her head. Dressed in blue jeans, a black T-shirt, and a purple jacket with faux-fur trim, she froze mid-dance, staring at Joel through the glass.

"Let me in, ya dickhead!"

"You scared the shit outta me! Get off the garden, Mum will kill you!" Joel laughed, rushing to open the door.

Laura barrelled inside, hugging him tight before setting the bottle down on the side table.

"Champagne?" Joel asked, looking confused.

"I swiped it from the restaurant. We're celebrating." Her eyes sparkled.

"Oh my *God*!" She grabbed his hands, bouncing up and down, before pulling out two small yellow squares of cardboard paper from her jeans pocket. "Guess who just got us tickets to *Resurrection* at Dome on Sunday night?"

"No way!" Joel gasped, his excitement sending shivers down his spine.

"No *way!*" he repeated, his voice an octave higher.

"Yes way!" she laughed.

Joel's breath hitched. "Oh my God, that's where…"

…where Dannii Minogue might make an appearance? It sure is!" Laura squealed again, clapping.

"But it's over-18s." Joel's excitement wavered as he inspected the tickets.

"It's. A. Gay. Dance. Party." Laura enunciated each word dramatically. "No one checks ID because no one cares. Just like when we sneak into 3 Faces."

"Are you sure?"

"Yes, I'm sure! And you're welcome."

"Oh my God, I love you! *Ahhh!*" They both shrieked, jumping up and down on the spot.

* * *

By the time Laura left that evening, the sky had darkened. Joel threw the tuna casserole his mum had left for him into the microwave, before eating a few quick mouthfuls. "You have to eat fish on Good Friday, Joel!" she had insisted. He scoffed it down, checked the clock, and jumped in the shower.

Still towelling off, he heard the back gate click. He unlocked the sliding door to the backyard, glancing at the bedside clock as it ticked over to 8:00 PM. Right on time. His hair still damp, he pulled on a pair of satin boxer shorts, the sting of Lynx Africa biting at his armpits.

Moments later, a shadowed figure appeared in the doorway.

"Hey," Joel said, nodding, trying to sound more 'manly' than he had with Laura a few hours earlier.

"Hey." The visitor's baseball cap was pulled low, hiding his eyes. "I can't stay long."

"All good. What do you wanna do then?" Joel asked, grinning.

The visitor smiled awkwardly and stepped further inside.

"No one's home, right?" His voice wavered.

"I told you, they're gone all weekend. Relax."

The boy just nodded.

This wasn't the kind of connection Joel truly craved, but it scratched an ache he didn't know how else to soothe.

He'd been terrified the first time. He'd always imagined his first encounter would be like the movies, a slow, nervous kiss with a high school crush at a party. Something tender. Something real. Not an anonymous hookup in a grimy public toilet at Otway Park Reserve late at night.

But six months ago, after years of pushing it all down, something inside him had broken. He couldn't keep waiting. He needed to feel the kind of touch and affection he watched his straight classmates share so freely, with confidence, without shame.

He'd sat in that cubicle, heart in his throat, half-expecting no one to show, half-certain he was about to get bashed. But someone had come. And it hadn't been anonymous at all.

He'd recognised the voice instantly. His whole body had shaken, terrified, as the door clicked open. But the visitor had been gentle, even kind. Unexpectedly so. From that first encounter, a ritual had formed.

Now, most nights, his visitor slipped into the house under the cover of darkness. Ten minutes of stolen intimacy. No words. No tenderness. Just skin and need and silence.

He'd once mumbled an apology for how he'd treated Joel at school, *"That's just how it is, you understand that right?"* and warned him never to speak to him in public.

"Thanks. See ya," the boy muttered, yanking up his pants before vanishing back into the backyard, Joel closing the sliding door behind him.

He was good looking, sure. And Joel enjoyed the brief moments they shared. But he wasn't what Joel had imagined or hoped it would be like.

He ignored the voice screaming inside him, the part that wanted more, the part that knew this wasn't love, and let it go. It was what it was.

Joel locked the door, pulled on some clothes, and wandered into the lounge to finish his bowl of tuna and rice in front of the TV.

* * *

Saturday passed in a blur.

Joel worked the busy day shift at the cinema, choosing to walk instead of riding his mountain bike beneath the dry, overcast sky.

By 7:30 PM, he was back home and crashed out on the couch, right as *Hey, Hey It's Saturday* hit its stride. Plucka Duck was in full flight, Red Faces brought its usual mix of the ridiculous and the inspired, and Dickie Knee popped up with his trademark one-liners. He waited eagerly for Molly Meldrum's *Melodrama* segment, only to be met with disappointment. No Molly tonight.

Then finally, from host Daryl Somers: "Ladies and gentlemen, Wendy Matthews!" Joel hit record on the VCR remote, grinning. His mum would be happy.

A knock at the front door broke the moment.

A takeaway pizza from Valetta's. The box was covered in hand-drawn dicks. Laura's handiwork, of course. The delivery guy went bright red, practically tripped over himself as he backed away, but Joel just laughed, shaking his head.

Classic Laura.

He closed the door behind him, still smiling, the house warm and still and perfectly his.

* * *

Sunday morning, the house phone rang violently. Joel ignored it at first, but it rang again seconds later.

"Happy Easter, darling!" His mum's voice was bright. "I hope you're not missing us too much! The Easter Bunny may have left you a little something in the wardrobe of your old bedroom!"

She reminded him about lunch with his Nanna and Auntie Linda before his dad's voice cut in from the background. "Hurry up, Christie! That call's costing a fortune!"

"Be quiet, Glen, I'm getting off!" she snapped, then softened. "I love you, darling. Miss you."

"I love you too, Mum," he said, but the line had already gone dead.

At four p.m., after Auntie Linda dropped him home, he spotted a note wedged in his bedroom's sliding door. Barely legible scrawl: *Tonight. 8.*

His visitor had never come during daylight before. That was a surprise. And a problem. Mr. Emerson next door might be deaf as a post, but he never missed a beat. Joel made a mental note to tell his visitor not to do that again.

He glanced at the clock. It would cut things close to get into the city to meet Laura. Still, a rush of adrenaline surged through him. *Screw it. It'll be quick anyway.* It always was. Then straight to the train station.

He slid a CD into the stereo and cranked the volume. As *Sash!* blasted through the house, he grinned and headed for the shower.

* * *

The four teenage boys sat on the wooden benches outside the football clubrooms, the lone streetlight above buzzing against the black sky. A waning gibbous moon slipped between low cloud cover, casting long shadows over the oval and parklands. The usually busy

Carrington Highway lay still. Most people were either away for the long weekend or recovering from Easter Sunday feasts. Tonight, it was just the boys. And they were ready.

"C'mon!" Hayden Foster bounced on the balls of his feet. "Where is this cunt?"

"He'll be here, Nugget. Take a chill pill," David Grayson muttered, pulling a Winfield Blue cigarette from his pack, lighting it, and leaning back against the cold brick wall.

Dressed in black jeans, a long-sleeved Korn tour t-shirt, and a red-and-black flannel tied at his waist, Nugget kept twitching as he shadowboxed the air. His voice went high and manic. "I'm just pumped for some faggot bashing, boys!"

The crack of a can snapped the air.

"Pass us another one, Scotty," Brice McCrae said, kicking his empty VB into the shadows.

Scott King handed him a fresh can without a word.

"You good, mate?" Brice asked, voice low.

Scott nodded, hair spilling from beneath his hoodie. Brice cracked the beer and took a long swig.

"So, is it true about you and Rachel Kennedy?" Nugget asked, tossing David a smirking glance.

"What about Rachel Kennedy?" Brice straightened, suddenly interested.

"Old Gracie-boy here hooked up with her at Tommo's party Friday night!"

"You!?" Brice barked. "And Rachel Kennedy?! Get fucked! As if!"

"Fuck off, Brice, ya cunt," David muttered.

"Well?" Nugget pushed.

"She let me touch her tits, but that's it. She's frigid as."

"Rachel Kennedy let *you* touch her tits!?" Brice exploded, laughing. "She wouldn't piss on you if you were on fire, you fat fuck!"

Scott looked on, chuckling quietly.

"Go fuck yourself, McCrae. You too, Scott." David barked.

Brice kept laughing to himself, taking another drink. "Rachel Kennedy... Jesus."

"Anyway," David said, leaning forward, flicking ash from the end of his cigarette, "her sisters hotter. And *she's* not frigid."

"Her sister? Isn't she, like, twelve, ya pedo?" Brice said.

"She's in Year 8!" came the reply, grinning.

"You sick fuck," Brice muttered, shaking his head.

"Oi. He's here." Scott's voice was low, nodding toward the road.

They all looked up to see a shadow peel off the footpath and cross the oval toward them.

"Fuck, I hate this cunt," David said.

"We all do," Nugget replied, his voice dark now.

"Do we even know how he set this up?" David flicked his cigarette into the gutter, eyes scanning the group.

Scott threw a quick look at Brice and then looked away, into the dark.

Hayden spat. "Who gives a fuck? He's delivered us a gift tonight, boys."

He stood taller, that twisted grin spreading wide as the figure stepped into the glow of the streetlight.

"Justin, my boy!" Nugget beamed, clapping the new arrival hard on the back. "Right on fucking time."

THIRTY-ONE

Cassie pulled into East Cliff Road, easing off the accelerator as her phone's map glowed beside her on the passenger seat. Number 24, down the end, on the left, just one house back from the beach.

Though bougie Brighton was barely a stone's throw from Elwood, it felt like another world. The street was lined with the same giant London plane trees, but their branches were stripped bare, twisted webs of shadow against the night sky.

Every mansion loomed behind towering brick walls, only their upper floors catching the spill of streetlights. Some were grand, gothic estates from a century ago, whilst others had been razed and replaced with French-provincial replicas or sharp-edged cubes of glass and steel. Tennis courts rose behind the fences like private kingdoms, just visible above the walls as Cassie crept past.

But unlike Elwood's lively streets, Brighton was deserted. Not a person in sight. Only the cold, unblinking eyes of CCTV watched her approach.

At the dead end, Cassie pulled in behind wooden bollards where bitumen gave way to grass, sand, and the dark hush of the sea beyond. She killed the engine, climbed out, and walked back toward the home of Graham Golding.

The house sat behind a high, white-rendered brick fence, veiled in manicured ivy. Two black steel gates, etched with mid-century geometric squares, formed the last line of defence.

It was modern, though modest by Brighton's standards, a white box of clean lines and glass balustrades. Lacking the pretension of its neighbours, it had a quiet, coastal elegance, like something perched above the Great Ocean Road. Still, it reeked of money. And like everything here, it was a fortress.

Cassie's pulse quickened as her eyes landed on the white Ute in the driveway: *Rusty Shovel Landscapes*, parked bumper-to-bumper with a sleek black Jaguar, the front gates closed. Locked.

Her gaze darted down the length of the fence. To the right, the brick gave way to a narrow, hedged pathway that snaked toward the beach. She moved quickly, ducking into the shadows, breath misting in the cold air.

At the rear of the property, low scrub and coastal grass backed directly onto the sand. A weathered timber fence divided the manicured yard from the dunes. Cassie scanned for cameras, nothing obvious, and, heart pounding, grabbed a crossbeam, hauling herself up and over.

She landed low in a crouch.

From here, the house loomed above her, a quiet sanctuary against the wind. The rear kitchen was lit like a stage. Floor-to-ceiling glass framed the scene inside with cruel clarity.

A dull thud reverberated from inside. Voices. Heated.

Cassie slipped closer, keeping her footsteps light, heart hammering. She got as close as she could to a side window, which lay slightly ajar.

Brice stood near the island bench, shoulders rigid, fists clenched. Graham Golding faced him from across the counter, arms folded, composed, cold, coiled. Between them sat a glass of scotch, its amber contents trembling in the vibrations of their raised voices.

Cassie ducked lower behind a cluster of potted agave, slipping her phone from her jacket. Her thumb hovered over the screen.

Get this right, Cass.

She hit record. The tremor in her hands steadied. That cold, familiar rush took over.

"Grow up." Graham's voice was a low snarl. "I knew Justin wasn't capable of this. He was weak. Just like his mother. No, I knew it was you. The second you called me, going on about how Justin had broken into your business, you thought you were being clever. Don't take me for a damn fool."

"If you knew I'd staged it," Brice shot back, breathless, "why did you have him killed?"

"Because I had to be sure." Graham's voice chilled further. "Besides, even that idiot would've figured it out eventually. I couldn't risk him getting sentimental and running his mouth."

He gave a short, bitter laugh. "And let's be honest, that's what you wanted, isn't it? You'd already taken care of David and Hayden. Justin was next, right? I did you a favour. You should be thanking me."

"Thanking you?!" Brice's voice ricocheted off the glass.

A silence followed, stretched so tight it felt like the air itself might snap. Cassie's fingers clenched tighter around her phone.

"Oh, come on. Don't be like that," Graham said. "You're not like the others. You've got more balls that's for sure. I'm impressed. Maybe I should've invested in you rather than Foster, the bloody idiot. He was too hot-headed. Though he did prove useful. For a while."

Brice exhaled, backing away from the bench, shoulders collapsing like a marionette cut loose.

"I know it was you who started the fire," he said. "Before he died, Scott told me. He said he saw you go into the house. He was in his backyard, smoking, trying to calm down after what we'd done. That's when he saw you. With Justin. But only you went through the gate.

"We may be the ones who killed Joel that night. But you…" his voice cracked "…you could've told the truth. You could have saved his family some of the pain. You should have held us all accountable! That was your fucking job!"

Graham chuckled, a slow, sinister thing.

"What?" Brice rasped. "What's so fucking funny?"

"Killed him?" Graham gave a snort. "You lot couldn't kill a bloody fly."

Brice froze.

Graham leaned in, resting his palms on the counter. His eyes glinted under the kitchen lights. "You didn't kill him, you useless little cunt. Sure, you boys gave him a decent belting, you may have even knocked him out. But killed him? No. He was very much alive when I got there. Sitting up on the floor against the bed, bloodied and bruised. Begging me to call an ambulance."

Cassie's breath caught. Brice's eyes flared wide in shock.

"He made threats. Against Justin. Against me. *Me*! I was on track to be Commissioner for fuck's sake. I wasn't about to let my life go to shit because of some little *faggot*."

The word cracked through the room like a slap. Brice gasped - a raw, broken sound - and Cassie felt her stomach twist, bile rising at the venom in Graham's voice.

"He was seventeen!" Brice's voice cracked, breaking on the words. "He was just a kid. We all were."

"Oh, don't go getting all sanctimonious now," Graham said, calmly. "Yes, I finished what you couldn't. And yes, I started the fire. But it was *you* who killed that boy, you and the others, the moment you decided to walk through that gate. And you know it. I was simply cleaning up your fucking mess."

He paused.

"And I'm pretty sure it wasn't your old mate Scott who called the firies. Even he knew I was doing the right thing."

Brice's entire body shook. "Scott killed himself thinking *we* killed someone that night. It broke him. It broke me. It broke all of us. And it was *you*? You evil *fuck*!"

Cassie's heart pounded in her ears. Her knuckles ached from how tightly she gripped the phone.

Graham's hand slid slowly toward a drawer beneath the bench.

Cassie saw it.

Brice didn't.

He was caught in the tide of grief, of betrayal, of a new truth detonating in his chest.

"Did you know Scott had a son?" Brice said, voice trembling. "His name's Elliott. His Mum fell into drugs after Scott died and gave him up. Do you have any idea what happened to him then? The endless foster homes? The resi units and all the shit that happened to him?"

He shook his head, choking back tears. "It took me years to adopt him. To bring him back from the brink. He lost more than his dad that night, and it's because of *you!*"

Graham growled. "Oh, calm down."

Brice's eyes widened. His chest heaved, struggling to stay upright beneath the weight of it all.

"Don't tell me to calm down!" Brice roared.

He paused.

"I've got cancer," he finally said, steadying his breath. "They don't reckon I've got long."

He looked down, voice thick.

"But it's not the illness that's killing me. It's the guilt. That's what's been eating me all these years. Spreading like fucking rust, eating away bit by bit. The cancer's a fucking blessing by comparison."

He swallowed hard.

"I used to lie awake at night, terrified that one day we'd be caught. But then, it changed. I started fearing something worse. That we'd gotten away with it. That we'd never be held to account for what we did."

His face crumpled.

"You could've saved him. You *should* have."

"...and I should've been fucking Prime Minister," Graham muttered. "Life's a bitch."

Brice let out a bitter laugh and glanced around the polished kitchen.

"You know... Scott told me something else before he died," he said, steadier now. Something steel creeped back into his voice.

"He said that night wasn't the first time he saw Justin at Joel's back fence."

Cassie's lungs locked.

She hunched lower in the dirt, wind slicing at her cheeks.

She'd been right.

But it didn't make the truth hurt any less.

Graham flinched. Barely. But it was enough.

Brice went on.

"Scott said he followed him one night. Watched him go into Joel's bedroom."

He paused.

"He said that when he got to the window, he saw..."

"Enough!" Graham roared, his voice splitting the air like thunder.

Cassie slapped a hand over her mouth to silence the cry rising in her throat. Her heart thundered. Her stomach lurched. The sour rush of bile burned up her throat and she doubled over, trembling, the phone still recording in her hand.

Silence fell, vast, suffocating.

"You want me to justify my actions to you?" Graham growled. "I did you a favour. I gave you a second chance. If I hadn't..."

"What? If you hadn't murdered Joel and buried our secret? Joel would be alive! So would Scott! So would your own son! You didn't do this for us. You did it for *you*!"

Brice twitched, a man being torn from the inside out.

"Fuck!" he shouted, hunched over, fists tight at his sides.

Graham stood motionless, watching.

"So, what now?" he asked at last. "You're here to end me too? Go on then. Get on with it."

Brice drew in a shaky breath. Lifted his chin. His tears had dried into raw, pink streaks.

"I'm not here to kill you," he said quietly. "You don't get off that easy."

Graham tilted his head, one brow arched, eyes gleaming like a wolf's.

Brice squared his shoulders. His voice sharpened, stripped of doubt now, only fury remained.

"You're going to turn yourself in."

Graham laughed. "And if I don't?"

"If you don't..." he took a step closer "...I go to the media with everything. Cassandra Murphy has already been sniffing around. It won't take her long. Imagine what she'll do with this."

Cassie's heart jolted at the sound of her name. A chill rushed through her blood. She pressed herself lower into the dirt, the phone still rolling. Every nerve was on fire.

For a moment, Graham didn't move. Perfectly still.

Then slowly, a smile ghosted across his lips.

"Well," he murmured, "aren't you full of surprises. Alright. I'll go. I'm tired anyway. Tired of carrying all this."

He took a slow step forward.

"Come on," he said, voice almost gentle now. "I'm ready."

Brice hesitated.

And that was all it took.

Graham lunged. Metal flashed, a glint of silver under the lights, and then the knife was buried in Brice's stomach.

Brice let out a strangled gasp, his eyes wide with animal shock. He stumbled back, clutching at the blood blooming across his shirt.

Cassie's mouth opened in a silent scream as she watched him crumple, knees buckling, body folding like a rag doll. The sound of him hitting tile rang out, wet and final.

She slapped a hand to her mouth as her stomach heaved, almost dropping the phone.

Inside, Graham moved calmly. Almost methodically.

He knelt beside the body, pulled a phone from his pocket, and tapped in a number.

"Yeah," Cassie heard him say, his voice low, measured. "We've got another situation. I need you to come and take care of it. I'm at home." A pause. "A clean up. And hurry up."

Cassie let out a small, involuntary noise, a whimper, a gasp, something from the pit of her soul. Whatever it was, it was louder than she had expected.

Graham's head snapped up.

He froze.

Eyes narrowed.

Like a predator catching scent.

Cassie's heart slammed against her ribs.

Move.

She scrambled back, thorns raking her arms, breath tearing in and out as she fumbled for the fence.

Now, Cass. Move.

Her hands scrabbled at the timber slats, splinters tearing into her palms. She hauled herself up, feet slipping. A jagged edge tore her skin, she barely felt it, and then she was over, landing hard in the sand with a grunt that knocked the air from her lungs.

She ran.

Heart pounding. Legs flying. Air burning in her throat.

Get to the car. Get to the car. Get to the car.

Behind her, the wind howled, charged, electric.

She tore across the sand, shoes heavy as she ran, until her car appeared through the scrub like a lifeline. She yanked the door open, dove inside, and slammed it shut. Her hands shook so badly it took three tries to jam the key into the ignition.

The engine roared to life as she pressed hard on the accelerator.

She threw it into reverse, spun around, and tore down East Cliff Road, heart battering her ribs like it wanted out. She didn't look back.

Her fingers fumbled over her phone's screen as she swerved onto the Nepean Highway and floored it.

"Cass?" Brian's voice was groggy. "What..?"

"I'm coming to yours," she choked out. "Brian, I... I need..." She drew a jagged breath, swallowing the sob clawing its way up.

"Jesus Cass, are you OK? What's going on?" he said, panic rising in his voice.

"I need to be somewhere safe."

"Yeah. Of course, Cass. I'm here. Just drive safe, okay? I'll wait out front."

She nodded, tears turning the streetlights into blurred halos.

At the next red light, she jammed the phone on her knee, fingers flying. She attached the video file. Her thumb hovered.

Then she hit send.

To: James Lawrence

CC: Peter Draper

Subject: *Graham Golding. Confession. Murder.*

File uploading. Sent.

Cassie exhaled a ragged breath. Opened his contact. Hit call.

"James," she said as soon as he answered, voice barely above a whisper, "you need to meet me at Brian Cheng's. I'll text you the address."

There was a beat of silence. Then simply: "Are you safe?"

"I will be," she said, pressing harder on the accelerator. "Check your inbox. Then meet me there."

She hung up, gripping the wheel until her knuckles went white.

Melbourne flew past her window, the wind now starting to calm. An empty tram, quiet streets, the restless shimmer of the bay.

Cassie stared ahead, swallowing hard against the sob rising in her chest.

The city was waiting.

The story was coming.

And Cassandra Murphy, bloodied, breathless, still standing, was in the fight.

She picked up her phone. Dialled one last number, as the sobs finally broke through.

Three rings. Then a familiar voice.

"Cass? Cassie? Is that you?" came Derek Murphy.

THIRTY-TWO

Commercial Road in Prahran had once been the beating heart of Melbourne's gay "village." From the 1980s into the early 2000s, its stretch of no more than a kilometre was crammed with queer-friendly bars, nightclubs, cafés, bookstores, and health centres. Every Saturday night, thousands would flock here, dressed to the nines, driven by a simple mission: to party.

But time had a way of shifting landscapes, both physical and cultural. Nearly two decades on, that vibrant strip was now a ghost of itself. The community had dispersed, scattering to every corner of Melbourne. Technology did the rest, chat rooms, social media, dating apps, reshaping how people connected. The once-crucial need for a dedicated "gay village" had somewhat faded. Clubs stopped advertising themselves as 'gay' or 'straight'; they were just clubs, all welcomed. Even that had waned in the aftermath of lockdowns. The new generation craved different things on a Saturday evening: festivals, house parties, life drawing classes with cheese and wine, Netflix marathons on the couch. The once-deafening roar of nightclub culture had softened to a distant buzz.

But there were exceptions to this. And tonight was one of them.

Tonight was a gentle reclamation. A nod to what once was. A tribute to a young man whose hopes, whose dreams, whose entire life had been stolen.

Cassie eased her car into a spot on the rooftop carpark of the old supermarket. The slam of her car door echoed against the concrete, followed by the metallic clink of her keys locking it. Below, Commercial Road stirred. Music pulsed from a recently closed nightclub, hijacked for one night only, transformed into a dance floor of epic proportions.

Cassie walked to the carpark's edge and leaned against the barrier, looking down. The line snaked along the street, revellers dressed in everything from sequins to feather boas, their laughter carrying up to where she stood. Their joy was infectious, but tonight it carried weight. Tonight, it wasn't just about a party.

Lifting her gaze, Cassie took in the city skyline, its glittering lights softened by the aftermath of a late spring storm. The rain had moved east, leaving behind a night thick with the perfume of jasmine and wet bitumen. There was a promise in the air, of summer, of renewal, of things finally beginning to heal.

She caught her reflection in the car window and smirked. The smoky eye makeup was a bit much for her taste, but it wasn't about her tonight. Not really. Though she knew the moment she stepped inside that club, eyes would turn her way. People would make it about her. The "journalist who'd cracked the case." The one who'd finally pulled back the curtain on a secret buried so long, it had rotted the very foundations of the institutions meant to protect those who needed them most.

In the months since that night at Graham Golding's house, Melbourne, hell, all of Australia, had been shaken. Another towering figure exposed. Another man who had built an empire of trust and authority, only to abuse it for power, ego, and the sheer intoxication of control and self-interest. The headlines had been relentless. The commentary, deafening. And through it all, Cassandra Murphy had stood at the centre. Unflinching. Unwavering.

In the end, Golding chose not to face any of it.

Men like him could survive losing the trappings: the mansions, the Jaguars, the aged Scotch. But what they couldn't survive was the fall itself. The obliteration of reputation. The knowledge that their legacy would be nothing but ash and rot. Hours after Cassie had fled his property, police found his body alongside Brice McCrae's.

Cassie knew he would have seen her face on the CCTV. Knew she'd been there, crouched in the shadows of his empire. And in the end, Graham Golding did the only thing he knew how: he controlled the terms of his exit. One last act of defiance.

You're not going to catch me.

By mid-year, the Prime Minister had fronted the cameras, announcing that the Allied Patriots were now officially designated as a terrorist organisation. Predictably, the United States hadn't followed suit, but in Australia, their networks lay in ruins. Arrests made. Cells dismantled. For the first time in a long time, it felt like the country could breathe again.

But Cassie knew better. She always did.

Beneath the surface, that old unease still simmered. The undercurrents of anger, fear, and hatred never truly disappeared. They just changed shape. Found new platforms. For weeks after his suicide, social media feeds were still choked with tributes to Graham Golding. Despite the evidence, despite his own confession, there were still those crying 'fake news,' still baying for Cassie's blood online. A man-hater, they called her. A liar. The architect of his downfall.

Still, for now, a kind of normalcy had returned. Or something close to it.

But tonight wasn't about politics. It wasn't about Golding, Brice McCrae, Hayden Foster, or the lost boys. It wasn't about the echo chambers of social media, or the endless, grinding fight for truth.

Tonight was Joel's night.

Cassie straightened her shoulders, drew in a breath, and headed for the stairs.

Before she'd even finished crossing the road, a voice rang out, bright and unmistakable: "Here she is!"

Jason Turner emerged from behind a makeshift ticket booth at the club's entrance, grinning like a kid on Christmas morning. Before she could react, he swept her into a hug, squeezing her tight.

The line of partygoers turned, recognition spreading like a ripple. A smattering of applause broke out. A few whistles. Cassie winced, flashing a small, awkward smile, raising a hand in a half-hearted wave. She'd never liked this part, the attention, the hero label.

But she'd learned to take it for what it was. Gratitude. Respect. Maybe even love.

Jason was beaming as he looped an arm through hers. "Come on! No queue for you tonight." And just like that, she was ushered inside.

Inside, the music exploded.

Every colour of the rainbow shimmered beneath the sweep of strobe lights and a slowly turning disco ball. A thumping remix of Zoe Badwi's *Freefallin'* rattled the walls, bass vibrating through the soles of Cassie's boots. She stood still, blinking against the assault of light and sound, like a deer in headlights.

For a moment, she imagined Joel. That first time, all those years ago, stepping into a space like this, nervous, excited, out of his depth but desperate to belong. The thought made her smile.

After the dust had settled on Golding's demise, Cassie kept her promise to Jason and Amir. Despite the fresh grief of learning the truth about their son's death, Joel's family gave Cassie their blessing to produce a one-off documentary tracing the history of Australia's queer community, its violence and joy, its long fight for justice, and the hard-won celebrations of pride, with Joel's story at its heart. His story, his stolen life, became the thread that tied it all together.

The hashtag had trended within hours: #HisNameWasJoel. It hadn't stopped there. Vigils lit up cities across the country. Communities demanded answers to the gay-hate crimes still languishing in unsolved case files. What started as an uncovered cold case ignited a social movement, even garnering international attention. For once, people had listened.

And tonight? Tonight was another reclamation. A lost brother welcomed home. A community taking its power back, turning grief into celebration. This wasn't a wake. It was a party. For Joel. For all the Joels.

"Cassie!"

She turned to see Brian approaching, wearing less clothing than she'd ever thought possible. His usual modesty abandoned in favour of body glitter, tiny shorts, and that bloody canary-yellow feather boa swiped from the Good Friday Appeal. Beside him, Jessica Brady matched his sparkle, her grin as bright as the sequins clinging to her skin.

"Brian, oh my God," Cassie laughed, eyes wide as she took in the sheer amount of exposed flesh, not quite knowing where to look.

"Hi Cassie," Jessica said, leaning in to kiss her cheek, leaving behind a dusting of glitter.

Cassie grinned, shaking her head in disbelief as the trio headed towards the bar.

"Drink?" Brian offered, already flagging down the bartender.

"Always."

As a new track kicked in, something distinctly Sophie Ellis-Bextor, though the name escaped her, Brian leaned closer. "Where's Terence?"

Cassie's smile softened. "He couldn't make it," she shouted over the music. Both Brian and Jessica's faces fell, the disappointment clear.

"He wanted to," Cassie added, "but you know, it's a busy week for us."

The thought of Terence, knee-deep in moving boxes, brought a quiet warmth to her chest. Things between them had moved faster than she'd expected, yet somehow it felt right. They'd just signed a lease on a house along the Murray River. It was close enough to Wangaratta for Terence's work, within easy reach of the ABC's regional office in Albury for Cassie and, most importantly, only a stone's throw to the high country and to Heathton Ridge, so she could spend more time with her family.

They weren't giving up their old lives entirely. Terence would rent out his place in Wang for a year. Cassie would hold on to her Elwood flat as her Melbourne base. But there was no denying that it felt like the start of a new chapter.

Her father's cancer had been held at bay these past few months. The treatments had bought them time. Borrowed, maybe, but precious all the same. The Murphys, Derek included, had reached a quiet acceptance. There was no outrunning the inevitable. But there was still living to be done.

And standing here, surrounded by a sea of beaming faces, bodies swaying to the beat, Cassie knew she was exactly where she was meant to be.

For Joel.

For herself.

For now.

The lights dimmed, and the music faded into a soft pulse, as a figure emerged onto the stage. A hush rippled through the club.

She was a vision, towering in six-inch heels, her hair teased into a platinum halo, with what appeared to be a stuffed seagull attached to the side, and dressed in a bleached denim catsuit with shoulder pads so sharp they could cut glass. Her makeup was art: sharp cheekbones, exaggerated lashes, a glittering slash of lipstick that dared you to look away.

The crowd erupted as she struck a pose, milking the applause for just a moment longer before lifting the mic.

"Good evening, my darlings!" she purred, voice rich with theatre and warmth. "For those of you who don't know, and shame on you if you don't, I am the one, the only, *Trish 'n Chips*!"

A fresh cheer went up.

"Now, tonight is special. Tonight is not just another party. Tonight, we gather to remember a beautiful soul, a fierce little fighter, and a bloody icon in the making who was taken from us far too soon, our Joel."

A ripple of whoops and applause swept through the crowd, raw and heartfelt.

"Joel loved this community with his whole heart. And let's be honest, it wasn't always an easy love, was it?" Trish continued, her tone softening. "But he believed in us. In what we could be, in what we could fight for. And thanks to a certain stubborn little journalist..." she gestured dramatically towards Cassie, "...the world now knows Joel's name. His story. His truth."

The spotlight found Cassie where she stood with Brian and Jessica. She gave a small wave, cheeks flushing as the applause found her again. This time, she let it wash over her.

"Thank you, Cassandra Murphy," Trish said, voice rich with genuine emotion. "For giving our brother the justice he deserved. For listening. For standing beside us."

There was no need for more words. Trish let the moment breathe, before snapping back into show mode.

"And now, my darlings, it is my absolute pleasure to introduce Joel's favourite song, a 90s banger from the one, the only, Miss Dannii Minogue!"

The crowd roared as the opening strings and synths of *Disremembrance* blasted through the speakers. Out of the haze from the smoke machines, another queen, Coral Bleach, slunk onto the stage, dripping in holographic pink. When the chorus hit, a line of backup dancers in pastel leotards burst forward, high-kicking and spinning as confetti rained down in a glittering storm.

The club came alive.

Hands in the air, bodies moving as one, the dance floor became a kaleidoscope of joy.

Tonight was for Joel.

But it was also for every battle fought. Every victory, no matter how small. Every life that had been pushed to the margins but refused to stay there.

In that moment, surrounded by glitter and sweat and unfiltered joy, Cassie realised something simple and profound.

They hadn't just reclaimed Joel's story tonight. They'd reclaimed theirs.

"C'mon, Cass!" said Brian, as he and Jessica sculled the rest of their drinks and headed towards the dancefloor.

"Just a minute," Cassie said, reaching for her phone that was buzzing in her handbag.

The light of her screen blinked to life. One unread message.

Laura Cassini.

Cassie's breath caught. That familiar weight settled low in her stomach, the same one she'd carried since that night.

Laura had been a complication Cassie hadn't seen coming. On paper, she should've been part of the reckoning. She'd known what Brice McCrae had done. He'd come to her, not long after killing Hayden, and confessed to his part in Joel's death. She'd sat with the knowledge. Protected herself.

And yet, in the end, it was Laura who convinced Brice to turn his crosshairs onto Graham Golding, by using Cassie instead. A quieter vengeance. One that would burn longer.

In the black-and-white world Cassie had built her career upon, that should have made Laura complicit.

But her father's words still echoed, long after their call on that fateful night six months earlier:

Doing the right thing doesn't always mean following the law, Cass.

Coming from a man who'd lived his life by the badge, the weight of that admission had rattled her. But it had also given her permission to see the grey.

That night, Cassie had made a choice, to acknowledge that truth often came wrapped in messy, human complexity. The impossible balance between justice and mercy.

She opened the text.

Thank you.

Two words. Simple. Heavy.

She slipped the phone back into her bag and looked up. On the dancefloor, Brian and Jessica waved her over, their faces flushed with laughter, sparkling under the wash of pastel lights.

Cassie took a breath.

It wasn't about the next story. Not tonight.

It was about this moment.

The music. The joy. The people who refused to be forgotten.

As *Disremembrance* soared through its final verse, Cassie stepped onto the dancefloor.

And as the crowd erupted into cheers, Cassie closed her eyes.

Not to block it out, but to feel it. All of it.

The weight. The lightness. The bittersweet pulse of memory and hope.

For once, she wasn't chasing the truth.

She was living in it.

And as the lights spun above her, scattering fragments of rainbow across every face, Cassie smiled.

Because this, this was the story.

And tonight, it belonged to all of them.

SUPPORT

If you are impacted by any of the themes or content within this book, support is available (Australia):

Lifeline: 13 11 14
Beyond Blue: 1300 22 4636
1800RESPECT: 1800 737 732
QLIFE (LGBTIQ+ support): 1800 184 527

If you are reading from outside Australia, please consider reaching out to a trusted local support service or crisis helpline in your country. Help is available, and you deserve to be heard.

You are not alone.

THE SOUNDTRACK TO RESURRECTION

We all know how important music is, how our favourite artists and tracks become the soundtrack to our lives. When creating the characters in *Resurrection*, one of the very first things I did was build a playlist for each of them. It helped me climb inside their heads, especially on the days when writer's block hit hard. Their songs became my compass, guiding me toward what they might say, do, or feel in any given moment.

Like Joel, Laura, Brice, and the others, I was a teenager in the 1990s. So, curating this soundtrack was not only easy, it was also cathartic. And just like the characters themselves, the playlists are a mix of grit, grief, rebellion, identity, and love.

Here are some of the tracks drawn from the playlists of Cassie, Brian, Joel, Laura, Brice, Hayden (Nugget), David, Scott, Justin, and some honourable mentions from me: J.T! I hope they help you step into their world, and into the mood of *Resurrection*.

Cassandra "Cassie" Murphy

Resilient, principled, and quietly heartbroken, Cassie's playlist is equal parts power and vulnerability. These are the songs she runs to when she's chasing the truth, and the ones she plays when she's not sure she wants to catch it.

"Jolene" – Dolly Parton

"Edge of Seventeen" – Stevie Nicks

"Sober" – P!nk

"Old Country Soul" – Christie Lamb

"So Caught Up" – The Teskey Brothers

"Jungle" – Tash Sultana

"Better in Blak" – Thelma Plum

"Resolution" – Matt Corby

"Real Men" – Tori Amos

"Unstoppable" – Sia

Brian Cheng:

Thoughtful, indie, tinged with melancholy. Beneath the cool exterior is a current of loneliness and yearning, the kind he never puts into words. His songs aren't about anthems or rebellion, they're about connection, loss, and the spaces in between.

"Motion Sickness" – Phoebe Bridgers

"A Sky Full of Stars" – Coldplay

"Somebody That I Used to Know" – Gotye, Kimbra

"The Less I Know the Better" – Tame Impala

"Slow Dancing in the Dark" – Joji

"Take Me Where Your Heart Is" – Q

"Still Feel" – Half Alive

"Talk Is Cheap" – Chet Faker

"Innerbloom" – Rufus Du Sol

"Coffee" – Beabadoobee

Hayden, David, Brice, Scott, Justin – "The Group" (1998):

Raw, aggressive, and soaked in 90s male bravado, the boys' soundtrack is all distortion and defiance: grunge riffs, hip-hop swagger, and stoner anthems. Beneath the noise, though, are songs of alienation and despair, the cracks showing in the armour they wore too young.

"Smells Like Teen Spirit" – Nirvana

"Longview" – Green Day

"Jeremy" – Pearl Jam

"Hits from the Bong" – Cypress Hill

"Hit 'Em Up" (Single Version) – 2Pac, Outlawz

"A.D.I.D.A.S." – Korn

"Killing In the Name" – Rage Against the Machine

"Black Hole Sun" – Soundgarden

"Creep" – Radiohead

"Under the Bridge" – Red Hot Chili Peppers

Laura (1998):

Fierce, restless, and unapologetic, Laura's soundtrack brims with rebellion and attitude. Behind the grit and swagger, though, are songs that reveal her fragility; a fight to define herself in a world intent on boxing her in.

"When I Grow Up" – Garbage

"Just A Girl" – No Doubt

"You Oughta Know" – Alanis Morissette

"Whatta Man" – Salt-N-Pepa, En Vogue

"Pony" – Ginuwine

"No Diggity" – Blackstreet, Dr. Dre, Queen Pen

"Regulate" – Warren G, Nate Dogg

"Ready or Not" – Fugees, Ms. Lauryn Hill, Wyclef Jean, Pras

"Gangsta's Paradise" – Coolio, L.V.

"Waterfalls" – TLC

Joel (1998):

Longing, defiant, and full of hidden ache, Joel's music is the sound of a teenager searching for freedom and love in a world that never gave him space. Euphoric on the surface, yet aching underneath, his songs are escape and confession all at once.

"Army of Me" – Björk

"Confide in Me" – Kylie Minogue

"Frozen" – Madonna

"I Want You" – Savage Garden

"What Is Love?" (7" Mix) – Haddaway

"In the Evening" (Full on Radio Edit 1996) – Sheryl Lee Ralph

"Stay" – Sash!, La Trec

"Set You Free" – N-Trance

"Disremembrance" (Flexifinger's Radio Edit) – Dannii Minogue

"Viva Forever" – Spice Girls

Honourable Mentions – J.T.

Finally, these tracks round it out. My own signature at the end of the mixtape. They acknowledge much of the music woven through the book, along with some personal favourites from the 90s and beyond that helped shape the world of *Resurrection*. Emotional resonance, defiance, and a pulse of hope.

"Firestarter" – The Prodigy

"Abuse Me" - silverchair

"Cry" – The Mavis's

"Beloved" – Wendy Matthews

"To Her Door" – Paul Kelly, The Messengers

"Outside" – George Michael

"Little Bird" – Annie Lennox

"If You Could Read My Mind" – Ultra Nate, Amber, Jocelyn Enriquez

"Freefallin'" – Zoe Badwi

"Not Giving Up on Love" – Armin van Buuren, Sophie Ellis Bextor

"Pride" – Johnna

ACKNOWLEDGEMENTS

RESURRECTION was a deeply personal project for me. Not only was it my first foray into writing fiction, but it also came from a world of lived experience. I want to thank those from the LGBTQIA+ communities who shared their real-life stories with me, and to those who cast their eyes over the first draft and provided important feedback.

My sincere and heartfelt gratitude goes to Johnny Whitehead, Diane Minnis, Gerard O'Connor, Jessenia Marquez, JoJo Zaho, Paul Scott-Williams, and Mitch Brown. I am humbled by your strength, resilience and advocacy.

A huge word of thanks goes out to members of my "dream cast" of incredible Australian talent from stage and screen, who I pictured bringing my characters to life if RESURRECTION were ever adapted to screen. To Nathan Phillips (my Brice McCrae), and Dennis Coard (my Derek Murphy), thank you for sharing your kind words of support and inspiring my characters! A special word of thanks also goes to Tania Doko, Victoria Madden and Roz Hammond, amazing artists and storytellers in their own right, for your generous support.

To my good mate, Nelson Aldridge, a proud Taungarung man, who helped me bring Terence Young to life with authenticity and respect, thank you for this and for your ongoing friendship.

Thanks to Ash Hart, my editor and writing mentor; Nick Castle for a stunning cover design; and to Sarah Kennedy for bringing Resurrection to life so powerfully for the audiobook!

To the communities of Port Phillip, Melbourne, Knox, and Alpine Shire; thank you for the inspiration. Whether through formal research or simply walking your streets or sitting in your cafes and pubs, your people and places breathed life into this story's settings, both real and fictional.

To the other many individuals and organisations who shared their time, expertise, and lived experience during my research, there are far too many of you to list, but know this: every fact, insight, and side anecdote you gave me added depth and authenticity. I am sincerely grateful.

And finally, to my family. Thank you for letting me disappear down yet another rabbit hole, chasing every obsessive detail. Thank you for your patience on all those nights and weekends when I was hunched over the keyboard, or away scouting for inspiration, instead of being present with you. You've been endlessly supportive, and I love you for it.

The next Cassandra Murphy thriller, coming soon...

BROKEN

Some wounds never heal.

Some minds never rest.

Across the border country of Victoria and New South Wales, terror spreads after two separate shootings leave four people dead hundreds of kilometres apart. Different weapons. Different methods. Same chilling precision.

As the body count rises in the bush and talk of *two snipers* working in tandem grips the nation, fear becomes its own contagion.

In the sleepy Murray River town of Burnanga, investigative journalist Cassandra Murphy is meant to be taking time off with her partner, Terence Young. But when a desperate call from controversial influencer Annika Bloom pulls her back to Melbourne, Cassie is drawn into a tangle of paranoia, deception, and revenge that stretches far beyond the city.

As Cassie digs deeper, the violence creeps closer to home until past and present collide, shattering everything.

Because in a country haunted by trauma, not everything that breaks can be seen.

And not everyone who goes missing wants to be found.

www.ingramcontent.com/pod-product-compliance
Lightning Source LLC
Chambersburg PA
CBHW020508260626
47156CB00006B/1912